LAST HURRAH

*A compelling tale of greed,
control, self-preservation...and vindication.*

A NOVEL

ROBIN DAWSON

ISBN 978-1-7772278-1-4 (Hardcover edition)

First Edition. Printed in Canada 2020 by Robin Dawson
Cover Design and Typesetting by Monique Taylor, ccdesign.ca

This is a work of fiction. Names, characters, places, and incidents either are the product of the author's imagination or are used in a fictitious context and any resemblance to actual persons living or dead is entirely coincidental.

Published by Robin Dawson
www.robindawson.com

For Pauline.

You were always by my side.

CHAPTER 1

Was it a nightmare? Or was Algy's pill a lot more powerful than billed?

As Tom Fraser struggled to make sense of his immediate surroundings, amidst a deep grogginess, all he could remember was his mother's voice calling him from across a river. 'Don't let us down Pippin…you are all that's left.'

She'd been gone for over eight years. But he had never forgotten her beauty and the ever-present warm and infectious smile. Now here she was. Why, after all this time? Only she called him Pip. Those little rosy cheeks, under a mop of tousled golden hair. 'You're my little Pippin,' she'd fondly tease him, 'the apple of my eye.' It had to be her. But how had she entered his crazy, mixed up head at this moment?

His body ached, his head was heavy, and the light was far too bright. And now the airline stewardess wanted him to return his seat to the upright position and fasten his seat belt. 'We shall be landing at New York, JFK, shortly,' it was announced.

What lay ahead was daunting. Only yesterday, he was on top of the world, cruising to the last at Cheltenham, with a double handful. He'd dreamt about such a moment a thousand times. It was the horse, he'd always believed; any old fool looks good if they've got the horse. But young Mr. T. Fraser, claiming the seven pounds allowance, was all of that, and his unchecked bravado had launched his charge too soon, reaching for a long one, clipping the top of the gorse hurdle. And that was about all he could remember, prior to waking up in the field ambulance.

'Just lie still, sir. Here, drink a bit of water. You've had a bump on the head. But, considering the tumble you've taken, you're a lucky fella,' so the cheery paramedic had told him.

After a cup of restorative tea and assurances from Dr. Bailey, in the weighing room, that no bones appeared broken and 'you should rest for a few days, Mr. Fraser, per our concussion guidelines,' a chastened and thoroughly shaken Tom had been driven home.

That they'd stopped off for a few pints, to ease the pain, couldn't have helped, what with the medication that Doc Bailey had loaded him up with. But nothing could have prepared him for the shock this morning.

Lying still, during restless moments and the sweats of the witching hour, brought on by the potent cocktail of drugs and alcohol, and not wishing to move his aching frame, he'd been conscious of the vibrations coming from his phone. Who would be messaging him at this hour? He just wasn't up to checking and had drifted off, dreaming of riding a winner at the Mecca of steeplechase racing: 'I was going to be upsides the champion jockey, with a ton in hand and smiling, I was even going to look stylish, as I swept away up the hill to the cheers of punters. Yes, those mugs had even bet on me!'

That dream would have gone on and on, but for the Honourable Algenon Sinclair chauffeur of the night before and now, it appeared, nurse and tea-maker. 'Christians awake, salute the happy morn'! Come along, Tommy boy, you are on the front page of the *Racing Post*, turning arse over teakettle. Famous!'

'Fuck you! Oh, Jesus, that hurt!' Tom picked up the phone. Very little charge, but two text messages.

The first, timed at 4:55 a.m. from Dad, in Lexington, Kentucky: 'You'll know him when you see him. Just like his mom!' What on earth did that mean? The second, that he had heard buzz just before the tea eruption burst into his room, timed at 6:45 a.m., from Billy Beagle. 'Call me as soon as you get this message. Urgent!!!' and he'd left a Lexington number. Up at that hour, 1:45 a.m. Kentucky time. Strange!

What was urgent was why Tom now found himself about to land in New York. As he tried to make sense of the conversation with Billy Beagle, through the haze of the 'wee sleeping draft' that Algy had given him, to 'help you through the flight,' plus, of course, more wine that he hadn't needed at lunch, he wondered, What now?

CHAPTER 2

William Firestone Beagle III was a pillar of Kentucky Bluegrass bloodstock. Generations of Beagles had held court at Hickory Hall in Bourbon County, just outside Lexington, pioneered by Nathaniel Beagle whose mother, Missie Courtwright-Harris, a daughter of the Mayflower settlers, had arrived in the Midwest, in the wake of the Civil War.

An ex-Marine, with a stint in Vietnam, Billy, or 'Dawg' as his close friends called him, stirred the mint juleps in these parts and if, as Tom Fraser's father Robert had been, you were a friend of the folks at Hickory, you were definitely in good standing.

So, the call had been as shattering as it had been surprising when he learnt the reason.

Bob Fraser and Billy Beagle had hunted with the Iroquois hounds. They'd played on the same University of Kentucky (UK) football teams. Bourbon County boys, they'd grown up and fallen in love with the thoroughbred. Kentucky and the bluegrass was home.

As Tom drove up the tree-lined drive, with mares and their newly arrived foals grazing idly in the paddocks each side, he wondered why Mr. Beagle had insisted that he come directly to see him before speaking to anyone?

A handsome man, approaching his mid-seventies, yet still standing well over six feet, his dad had said Billy Beagle was the finest quarterback the University of Kentucky had ever had, and could have easily played in the NFL. There was a way he spoke, in that charming drawl of the region, his impeccable manners and presence that conveyed the trust and belief that had enabled him to sell thousands of yearlings over the years through the local Keeneland sales, to receivers as grateful as all those he had found with his passes on the football field.

Tom couldn't imagine Mr. Beagle without a tie and, as he welcomed him into his beautiful oak-panelled study that looked out across immaculate lawns to more paddocks and tobacco barns stretching off into the distance, down towards the Paris turnpike, he noticed that today was no exception. The ubiquitous khakis, topped by a pale blue cotton shirt and yellow polka dot tie: yellow and black being Hickory Hall's famous racing colours. Billy Beagle had the permanent tan of someone who has lived well and in the sunshine.

'Dear Tom, what a terrible business. Please come in.' The handshake was firm, but there was no hug as he gestured Tom to a sofa in the bay window. 'I'm so glad that you have got here so soon. Here, do sit down. I'll just shut the door.'

Beagle perched at the other end of the sofa. 'Now, since our conversation - which I would appreciate you keeping to a minimum when the police speak to you and ask you how you found out about your daddy - there have been some developments that I'm afraid are very worrying. They will have many questions for you, Tom. But let me just fill you in on what I know.'

Beagle stood up and walked to the window, gazing out at his mares. Without turning, he continued. 'Your father and I have known each other for a very long time. We went to UK together, hunted together. If he hadn't had that fall and broken his leg so badly, we'd have served together in the Marines. I'm really proud of the job he did over at Caledonia.' He paused briefly before continuing. 'So much history, so many champions have stood there, over the years. But, recently, it had lost its soul. Lost the magic. You know how tough times have been for local breeders since the boom of the '80s? And, I don't know why, but the sport just isn't what it used to be, despite John Gaines, the Breeders' Cup, and all the NHRA stuff. There just aren't the investors out there anymore. And...' he sighed and scratched the back of his balding head, stretching as two black and white Springer spaniels who were lying on sheepskin rugs in front of his desk looked on from their perches of comfort. 'This became a big, big problem,' he continued, 'Tom, do you know how many farms the banks now own?'

'No, sir,' Tom mumbled.

'Well, it's downright unhealthy for the business. And what has happened is that the vultures have moved in. I don't know just how much you know about what has been going on at Caledonia since your mom's death. When was that?

Six, seven years ago?'

'Sir? 2009, sir. Eight years.'

'How time flies. Well, the fact is that those people that your dad got involved with, Dr. Delmontez and his associates, were too good to be true. I should have known.' Beagle paused. 'Your father was desperate, he was going to lose the farm. When he came to me and asked what I thought about taking on a partner, I was in two minds; it's always good for horse racing to bring in new blood, but I wasn't sure about these people.' He paused again, looking out the window. 'This is really bad, Tom. I'm not sure quite what happened two nights ago. But I have a feeling that it's to do with drugs and killing horses to collect insurance. The reason I wanted to talk to you before you speak to the police is to mark your card, because, as bad as this is, and believe me Mary-Lou and I will do anything we can for you; we cannot have this scandal damaging the reputation of Kentucky bloodstock, down here, during these already tough times.'

Tom sat, wondering just how bad things were, and whether his father's death or the fate of Keeneland and the perceived integrity of horse racing was of more concern to his host. The silence was heavy.

'At the beginning,' Beagle continued, 'it was new money, lots of it, and, when you are struggling, you don't tend to worry about where it's coming from. This guy Delmontez shows up at the sales and the word gets out that he wants to buy a farm. He's brought up some interesting horses from Brazil and Chile. They win a few races and he sells them. Now he's got some more, better horses, and buyers are after him. But, like too many stories that are too good to be true, there are problems. One horse gets sick and dies before his first race at Del Mar. Another has an accident in a paddock, breaks a leg, and is put down. Nobody thinks much about this, as both horses were insured. So, Dr. Delmontez sure wasn't out of pocket. Now I feel very guilty about this, Tom, but we at Keeneland need to look after people like this and, realizing your dad's worries at the farm – did you know that the bank was threatening to call his loan, back in 2008? – well, it was a tough time and I introduced Hector Delmontez to him. I thought I was doing him a favour.' He paused again, almost looking, Tom thought, for his approval. 'Well, they moved in, and you remember the doctor's manager? I think protector is a better description. Ramon something, I think his name was?'

'No, sir,' blurted Tom.

Beagle rambled on. 'Well, to cut a long story short, Hector's a salesman. And, at some sort of convention of American racetracks that he put on in South America and invited, it seems, all the key players and shooters in the racing world to, your dad found out that his new partner was up to no good. He was bringing in mediocre horses from South America, along with drugs, cocaine, and other stuff, selling the horses for inflated prices and legitimizing, in the process, his drug sales; effectively laundering his own dirty drug money, and more recently, I hear, some of his dubious new clients' and associates' illegal money into clean. Anything not sold was heavily insured and then became the victim of unforeseen circumstances: a colic, a road accident, you name it. And, it didn't take Hector Delmontez and his people long to figure out that your dad needed cash, so they sucked him in, I'm afraid! This Ramon guy is a brute. Was, I guess. And I hate to say this, but I have always wondered just what happened to your mom. They said it was a plane that crashed into the foothills of the Andes, when your parents were down at the convention, but I've always wondered about that...' he trailed off.

This was truly disturbing to Tom. 'Mr. Beagle, sir, did these guys kill my father?'

'Now, that I don't know. I do think, though, that he found out about the killing for insurance and wasn't at all happy about it.' He paused, not sure for a moment how to continue. 'Not too long ago, he mentioned to me that Ramon had suggested that some of the Caledonia stock would be worth more dead than alive. I never trusted that guy. Y'all heard what happened?'

'Well, only what I have read online and from stuff in the *Lexington Examiner* that I picked up at the airport this morning.'

'There was a fire in the Maple barn. You know, the old broodmare barn, down on the pike. It was Saturday night and there were very few people around. Bobby Mattock, you know Bobby, your dad's foreman, saw the flames. By the time he'd called the fire department out of Paris and got on down there, the whole barn was going up. It's been dry and that old tobacco shed next door acted like kindling. The heat was so intense it singed all the paint right off your dad's truck, and it was parked over a hundred yards away. Phew! They had no chance, your dad and Ramon Diaz. They want to know what they were doing, down there at that time of night, both burnt unrecognizably. You know that Magnolia's gone, too?'

At a time like this, Tom hadn't even thought about which horses may have perished. But this was awful. The one bright spark, the one reason that got his dad out of bed so many mornings, when all he had to look forward to was the bank on the phone: 'Mr. Fraser, is that old mare of yours in foal? She's getting on Mr. Fraser, has she another champion in her? Do you really feel it was a smart move to send her to Galactic Star, at her age, for that type of money?'

It had driven Tom's father to cut back and do many things he would not ordinarily have done. And now it was obvious that the most dire consequence of his association with Hector Delmontez and his henchmen had cost him and his prized mare their lives.

'She was in foal, wasn't she?'

'Yes, and due. What a tragedy!'

Magnolia, the big mare with the lop ears, devouring stride, and regal pedigree. The best filly to come out of Kentucky since Ruffian, so they said. If she'd been a champion on the track, she was a goddess in the breeding shed, foaling four champions and, in total, winners of fifteen Grade 1 races on both dirt and turf. Still only sixteen, she had to have another champion. She was priceless and nothing would have persuaded her proud owner to part with her.

As the two men gazed into space and considered the sheer enormity of this loss, there was a knock at the door and Mary-Lou Beagle entered to enquire if Tom would stay for some lunch. 'You must be hungry, Tom, after all the travelling you've done. Please come and tell me what you have been up to? I have some homemade soup and Billy's favourite, meatloaf with lotsa gravy.' Her timing was impeccable and her hug most welcome.

Laura Fraser, Tom's mom, had been a golf and bridge friend of Mrs. Beagle's, and over the years had enjoyed many games at the Idle Hour Club, as they'd discussed their families and the local horse gossip. Similar in age, that made her at least twenty years Billy's junior. Like him, she'd maintained herself in considerable style: trim, fit, tanned, still a definite head-turner.

Over lunch, the Beagles wanted to know all about Tom's time working for leading steeplechase trainer, Bill Bass, near Lambourn, on the Berkshire downs of England. And Tom told them about his unfortunate and very painful last flight crash, the previous Saturday at Cheltenham.

'What are you going to do now, Tom?' Mary-Lou asked.

'Mrs. Beagle, to tell you the truth, I'm not at all sure about anything. It's only just dawning upon me just how serious this all is.'

'Do you have somewhere to stay? Y'all welcome here, if it's too hard to return home. And you let me know if you need any help with the funeral arrangements.'

'Well, that's so kind of you. But, right now, I need to figure out where I stand, meet the police who want to see me, and check in on a few friends. So, if you don't mind, considering home at Caledonia isn't where I really want to return to, I'm going to turn down your kind offer for the time being and go see my buddy Mark O'Malley, who has a place in town, on Transylvania. He's an agent and maybe I can get busy doing some local work with him. I'm afraid I've lost my cell phone, but you'll be able to get me at Mark's,' he said and gave her the number.

As Billy Beagle escorted Tom to his rental car after a tasty but rather awkward lunch, the mares were coming in, whinnying for their feed. This was a magical time in Kentucky: so much hope in the air, as tomorrow's champions danced and played. 'If you need anything, Tom, please don't hesitate to call. This is a rough go. Maybe you should take a break from Lexington and the proximity of all this sadness? Go visit your Aunt Vera, down by the Shenandoah, perhaps? In the meantime, though, consider what we have discussed today to be between us. The police may well rumble Delmontez's game, but you want them to believe that it was his and nothing to do with your dad. Ok? And,' he added, 'I hope you meant it when you said you'd lost your phone. Don't find it. You hear me!'

'Yes, sir,' Tom replied, without telling him that he'd left it behind in England in the rush to catch his plane.

CHAPTER 3

The drive back into Lexington usually took about half an hour. But Tom was in no hurry. So that, combined with what rush hour traffic there was on Circle 4, the town's ring road, it was dusk by the time he arrived at 246 Transylvania Avenue.

Mark was playing the piano and Tom waited in the looming darkness for a few moments until the tears abated. So much had happened so quickly that he hadn't had time to cry.

Back a few years, when Tom was a freshman at UK, he'd been hanging out at Dooley's, a bar that many students frequented, and this bald guy had started chatting up his date. And the trouble had been that she had enjoyed it! Their subsequent friendship could easily have never blossomed, but there was something about this guy and, after a couple of pints of Guinness, they were the best of friends. That's just the way Mark was: a smiling, moon-like face set below a shining dome that often belied the substance and charm within that the young ladies of Lexington found irresistible and his numerous clients found so trustworthy and endearing. A friendly hug was never so welcome.

The local papers and social media were feasting on the fire at Caledonia Farms. Two suspicious deaths. A champion broodmare incinerated. Rumours of drug dealing and insurance fraud. In Lexington only three things made news: University of Kentucky basketball and football, and matters involving racehorses. So a bit of scandal, involving the latter, had tongues wagging.

Mark had studied music at Trinity College in Dublin, but like so many of his fellow countrymen had succumbed to the horses and wanderlust. Led on by great optimism and the extraordinary excesses of the '80s, he ended up in Lexington, looking after the incoming waves of foreign purchasers of bloodstock. There wasn't a bar or golf course within fifty miles that he hadn't frequented and, in entertaining his wide network of clients and friends, he'd developed many invaluable contacts along the way.

As a refuge for Tom, this place of music and gourmet food was a welcome port in a very troubling storm.

In the immediate future he appreciated that the police had to be dealt with and he needed to meet with his father's lawyer and accountant to pick up the pieces and see what was left. But at that moment a pint of Guinness and good old Irish hospitality was what he needed more than anything, and it wasn't long before he was away with the fairies.

◆ ◆ ◆

The next morning, down at the police station, Detective Dave Watson was a typical ex-serviceman, quite possibly one of Billy Beagle's ex-marines, with a shiny bullet-shaped head, square shoulders, and burgeoning gut that accentuated a prematurely hunched posture, brought on by years of wearing cumbersome belts full of weapons, handcuffs, and truncheons around his fulsome waist.

It was only 10:00 a.m. that mid-March morning, but Watson was already sweating through his dark green Kentucky police shirt; with badges and medals, and numerous pens both filling and adorning its breast pocket. Watson liked uniforms, orderliness, and, by the looks of things, starch.

The institutional room was small, windowless and fuggy, with a metal desk and three battered chairs. Watson sat across from Tom, and another detective, whom he'd introduced as Dewey, stood in the corner.

Watson turned on a tape recorder and went through the routine of explaining the situation, circumstances, who was present. Then, after perfunctory condolences, he hit him with a question that he wasn't expecting. 'Mr. Fraser, do you think that your father killed Ramon Diaz this past Saturday night?' It came out of nowhere and left him speechless. 'Well?'

Before Tom could answer, Watson continued. 'Things were not, apparently, going well at Caledonia Farms.' He checked his notes. 'Was the victim blackmailing your father? And he killed him because he resented his boss, Dr. Delmontez, taking over control of the farm?'

This broadside clearly needed to be dealt with by a lawyer. Tom replied that he had no idea what Watson was talking about. Besides, his dad was dead, too. So what was Watson saying? Tom had been away in England and, beyond confirming who he was and his relationship to Caledonia and Robert Fraser, his father, the deceased, he could not discuss anything further. At that the meeting ended, with Watson requesting his reappearance, plus lawyer, the following morning.

The trouble was that this incident turned out to be just the first of several debilitating frustrations, because Tom next went to the ATM machine and found his account had been frozen. Then the same with his credit card when, ignominiously, it was turned down after filling his rental car up with $50 worth of gas. It seemed that because Dad had been subsidizing his meagre pay in England, with various guarantees on credit cards, all these privileges had been summarily withdrawn, upon his death.

Mark thought this was very amusing when Tom had called him, from an old payphone, to come and rescue him and the car and return the latter before a search warrant was put out for its recovery.

Now, bereft of funds and needing a lawyer, Mark came to Tom's rescue. 'You will stay with me and you can use one of my vehicles to get around in,' he added jovially, 'until the storm abates. Then, maybe, we can work the upcoming yearling sales together?'

With no immediate family left, there really wasn't much alternative at that moment. So, although embarrassingly indebted to his dear friend, this appeared to be the only solution.

'We need to get you down to your dad's lawyer's office, pronto, as he may be able to put you back in business, cashwise?', Mark suggested.

Sure enough, Bernie Schaefer of Schaefer, Greenberg & Gold did offer some hope. 'No retainer required,' he had said, which was good news off the bat, 'because your father was such a respected member of the local equine community in Lexington. But all monies are temporarily tied up while the estate is being probated and the criminal investigation is ongoing.' Schaefer was at least upbeat about the situation. It was also agreed that he would accompany Tom to the police station the following morning.

'You're slightly bollocksed,' was Mark's assessment. But his upbeat mood did, at least, give Tom solace and a place to hang his hat. With this comfort in mind, they repaired to Dooley's for several pints of Guinness and Mark mentioned that Algy Sinclair would be coming over for the sales in July, joking about the Brits and asking him what he'd made of them while Tom was in Europe? And they had a good laugh about John Ward-Clarke of Classic

Bloodstock Services (CBS), who had sent a message that 'if he couldn't find anywhere better, perhaps Mark could put him up?'

A rather pompous young bloodstock agent who, most annoyingly as far as his rivals were concerned, was doing far too well. Jah-nny, as his American clients called him, used to have himself paged frequently at sales so that everyone would know that he was on the grounds and doing business.

Those who knew John laughed. But, as he said, those who didn't got to hear about him and presumed that he was busy. Indeed, presumably so busy that his cell phone had to be constantly engaged and therefore obviously knew what he was doing. And it had worked because, like a lone lamp in the dark drawing moths, such tactics never ceased to attract new and often gullible victims.

W-C, or Bog as his mates had nicknamed John, was just plain irritating. Nobody knew quite where he'd sprung from, and he was altogether far too smooth. But in the game that goes on at every sale, he was doing a good job keeping his head above water by looking out for number one.

The boys laughed a lot that night, which was a good thing, as there really hadn't been much reason for humour of late.

CHAPTER 4

Bernie Schaefer obviously knew Detective Watson, so preliminaries were short and to the point. Twenty minutes after explaining that his client was not in the country at the time of the fire and had no connection or knowledge of ongoing business at Caledonia Farms or between his late father, Ramon Diaz, and Dr. Hector Delmontez, Tom was back out on the street.

No enquiry was made as to how he had learned of the fire and deaths of his father and Diaz. Tom was just requested to advise the police station of any travel plans and be available, if and when they had questions in the future.

Once this was over and they were back in his office, Schaefer explained the dire circumstances at the farm and Tom's late father's beleaguered finances. Caledonia Farms had been bankrupt. Considering the value of farms had plummeted during the past ten years or so, its sale in the prevailing market wouldn't have come close to covering debts. But as this was the sorry state in which many other horsemen in the Lexington area found themselves, there was not much the bank could do. So, with no other options, Bob Fraser had been forced by circumstance to sign over the property to Hector Delmontez in a deal that allowed him to continue running the farm.

The bottom line was that Tom was impecunious, family-less, and in need of a serious reality check. An only child, who had grown up on a famous Kentucky farm and been thoroughly spoiled by adoring parents, it had seemed preordained that one day he would take over from his father. After graduating from college, it just seemed natural to travel the world and gain experience in the fields of thoroughbred racing and breeding. And this had taken him to Europe where, after a stint at a stud farm in county Tipperary, Ireland, he had fallen in love with fox hunting and steeplechasing, ending up as junior assistant to prominent trainer, William Bass, at his stables perched high upon the Berkshire Downs between West Ilsley and Blewbury, in England, where the turf on the gallops had not been disturbed by a plough for centuries and the larks soared across endless skies.

Until the previous Sunday morning, not even a week ago, he hadn't a care in the world and becoming a successful amateur rider had been his main ambition. Trips to obscure country racecourses at places like Fakenham, Uttoxeter, Ludlow, and Wincanton were like playing an exciting new golf course every day. Some clockwise, some counterclockwise, up and down, roundabout, they took some getting to know and, when it came to Cheltenham, you needed a GPS to stay on the right track.

National Hunt racing was the embodiment of horsemanship. Originating from the days when intrepid riders challenged each other to race across open country to a church steeple on the horizon (steeplechase) or from point-to-point, which is where Tom had started out, booting along a well over-the-hill, but comfortable, conveyance in the Heythrop Hunt members' race, even though he wasn't a member.

That day Algy Sinclair had been, though. And it was walking back through a ploughed field, after being ignomiously unseated at the farthest point from home, that the two had met during a long and silent trudge, each rueing their incompetence in the saddle, but far too proud to admit it.

The racing of horses has been embedded into the fabric of British and Irish country life for centuries. Even today, as the sport struggles to maintain the interest of contemporary audiences, horse racing is still a big deal that is avidly covered by all forms of media, with a newspaper presence that makes sure that every punter can see when their favourite horses, jockeys, and trainers are participating.

Indeed, it appeared to Tom that the leading riders had the same appeal to their fans as NASCAR drivers back in the United States. But this was better because a car is a car and, when it crashes and burns, the next one looks exactly the same. Whereas the character and longevity of hurdlers and steeplechasers, that sometimes had careers lasting up to ten years, made for ongoing love affairs. So much so, that the Barbour-cum-welly-cum-trilby clad aficionado bellowing his lungs out, as the field jumps the last at Cheltenham, is probably the most noble and caring fan in all of sport.

His boss, Bill Bass, was a brusque character who had little time for people, preferring the company of his horses and dogs. For him, Tom was cheap labour, related to one of his most loyal owners who might just introduce him to a new American owner, with deep pockets.

Compared to some flat yards, the sixty horses and twenty staff at Downs House was a small operation. But, as the governor would say, 'It's all about percentages, knowing your horses and their limitations and running them where they belong. A beaten horse is a sad horse. So don't run 'em before they're ready or where they can't put up a good performance.' And results spoke for themselves, as the Bass stable trundled along at around a 23% strike record. If they're no good, there is no point paying training bills, was his mantra.

For Tom, this had been a completely novel experience, as was the whole European routine, style of training, riding, feeding, even shoeing. Everything was so different.

Back home, in the USA, horses had been housed in large barns on the racetracks where they competed. And, because they spent their whole time travelling on forgiving dirt or turf, they were shod with the same aluminum shoes in which they ran. Whereas in Europe, trainers were based in isolated training centres and much preliminary fitness was achieved trotting for miles uphill on paved country lanes: so these horses would wear heftier steel shoes to train in and were then fitted with racing shoes (plates) for each race. This, of course, meant removing them after a race, and consequently the whole structure of the European-based racehorse's foot is different to their North American counterpart. North American horses tend to have shorter toes and be shod more upright to get traction on dirt based racetracks, whereas the Europeans, because their shoes are changed more frequently, have to have longer toes, otherwise there would be nowhere to hammer in the nails, and consequently their feet tend to be broader and more shallow: better suited to turf racing and softer going.

As each racecourse was different, compared to the standard counter-clockwise ovals of the United States and Canada, so too were the gallops: long, flat, and straight at Newmarket; mostly uphill and undulating at Lambourn; and down across the chalk downs to the famous stables at Manton and Beckhampton, near Marlborough, where legendry trainers like Fred Darling and George Todd would lock up their stable lads at night so they could not communicate information to professional gamblers!

Tom had just revelled in the lore.

Prize money, excepting at the highest level, hardly enabled an owner to cover his expenses, so National Hunt racing was largely considered to be the pastime of country folk, who in days gone by would have owned a horse or two, hunted them, and then raced them if they were competitive.

As Bill Bass would lecture new owners: 'The valleys of despair and disappointment are far deeper and longer than the mountain peaks of victory and joy are short and high. Yachts and fast cars don't pay dividends,' he'd say. 'But, if you own a promising young horse, the sky is the limit and the pleasure and craic, unequalled.' After a few too many gin and tonics at one of his frequent Sunday lunches, he would also go on to pronounce that 'the road to ruin was paved with slow horses and fast women,' so that's why he was single and kept his stable competitive.

Bill had given Tom a chance, and taught him a great deal in his own gruff way. Riders, he said, were accessories. A good horse was like a loaded gun in Bill's opinion: it could go off in anyone's hands. This was partly how Tom had ended up at Downs House in the first place. His mother's older sister, Vera Montagu, had a farm in Virginia and had bred a few nice horses over the years, racing the fillies and selling the colts. Her little operation on the banks of the Shenandoah carried the name of that famously romantic river, and there was not a more stylish or daring woman riding to hounds in Jefferson County.

Four years previously, Vera, who had introduced one of her better mares to the hunting field, when she had proven to be barren at stud, found her charge completely too strong and unmanageable at the sight of hounds and the call of the horn, and had ended up in Middleburg hospital with a broken back when she'd bolted after taking on a five-bar gate. So, the mare had been shipped over to Bill Bass, in England, where she had proved to be a very smart two-mile chaser. That family connection was why Tom had been there and, once he'd shown her trainer that he was not a complete liability, he'd put him up on her for Tom's first ride under official rules, in a two-mile handicap chase at Sandown Park for amateur riders.

It had been daunting to debut on such a fabled racecourse for such an exacting taskmaster. Tom could not recall any of Bill's instructions beyond 'Don't let her piss off with you, on the way to the start!'

At least they'd got there in one piece. And the rest had been a cakewalk, as the bold mare, now eleven, had taken charge, carrying her intrepid rider straight to the lead, jumping like a stag. Tom had been just a passenger.

Afterwards, on the drive back to Berkshire, Bill had had little praise for his protegé, muttering instead to himself about headstrong women and loaded guns!

Tom knew that he would never forget her name, though: Fusillade!

CHAPTER 5

April in Kentucky meant Keeneland races: a short three-week meeting at the charming little racetrack just outside Lexington that, in the racing calendar, directly precedes the Kentucky Derby on the first Saturday of each May.

Keeneland encompasses the complete thoroughbred experience: hosting bloodstock sales throughout the year and featuring two short, three-week-long race meetings, one in the spring and the other in fall. While the state might be more famous for its Derby, held seventy-five miles down Route 64 in Louisville, at Churchill Downs, for the purists Keeneland consistently represents some of the finest thoroughbred horse racing held anywhere in North America, and nobody was more proud of it than its CEO, William Beagle III.

Tom's family, going back for generations, had all been members of Keeneland, which in racing circles was a bit like being a member of Augusta National for golfers. Keeneland and being part of Kentucky blue blood, as much as the bluegrass itself, was crucial. If you were in with the right boys, the hardboots as outsiders would often refer to them, your path was infinitely improved, with special privileges that extended across the international world of the Turf.

As he lay in bed that first morning at Mark's, he thought about the tumult of the previous week and wondered just what lay ahead. What had really happened to Dad? What will happen to the farm? What am I going to do now? Something was nagging him, something he'd not, so far, mentioned to anyone. What, exactly, did that last text from his dad mean? 'You'll know him when you see him. Just like his mom.'

He knew that he needed to get out to the farm.

First, though, there was a funeral or, more accurately, a memorial service. Both bodies had been cremated on the spot so that eliminated any visitations: not that his dad would have wanted one anyway. But, with the police not holding onto the bodies, the matter had to be attended to. And at breakfast, Mark mentioned that Mrs. Beagle had called.

'I'll say one thing for you, Tommy boy, you may not have any family left, but you're sure well in with the right folks, round here.'

Tom muched on his toast. 'I guess I'll need to get some money from Shaefer to cover all of this. It'll be a big affair, you know, with all the publicity and all.'

'The good news is, you don't need a coffin!' Mark was his usual cheery self. 'I think a service, at that church near the farm. You know, the little stone chapel on the corner of Woodford and Glen? It's small, so you won't get too much of a crowd. Then repair to the Keeneland Club for a few tales and one or two cocktails.'

'And who's gonna pay for all that?'

'Come on, Tom! It's not that bad. Schaefer must have something up his sleeve and the Beagles'll help you with the old Butler Cabin.' Mark always called the Keeneland Club that because the green colours matched those of Augusta, the good ol' southern manners of the members, and his likelihood of ever being asked to be a member of either institution being about as likely to happen as his winning The Masters.

In due course, as always seems to happen at such times, the gears ground forward and, with much helpful input from Mary-Lou Beagle, a date was set.

'That's just so perfect, dear,' she'd said. 'Well, no. Nothing about this is perfect. But it will give your dad's friends time to make travel arrangements. You know that Clayton Bagwell will want to come from NYRA (the New York Racing Association) and the folks in Maryland and Virginia, your Aunt Vera, they'll all want to be there.'

The announcements were clear. A private service for family only. However, that didn't seem to put off some who had read the glowing obituaries in the *Daily Racing Form* and other racing papers around the globe. The world of international bloodstock may well be, at the core, as competitive and incestuous as any business. But, on the surface, those involved at least professed the sharing of common interests and goals. So, when a pillar at the epicentre died in such circumstances, curiosity, if not respect, easily overcame mutual rivalry.

The Episcopalian service was short, but the singing robust. The urn was adorned with the red and white colours of Caledonia. Tom knew that his father had loved hymns and the small organ was put through its paces by a confused looking lady in a shawl, who had protested that this was an occasion for prayer, not celebration, cranking out 'Praise, My Soul, the King of Heaven,' as the hundred or so apparent family members filed out into the spring sunshine.

The daffodils were in full bloom and Tom reflected upon his father's love of nature and how he'd often name his foals after flowers. An early foal, in late January, would perhaps be called Snowdrop. Then onto Tulip, Hyacinth, and his favourite, Primrose; of which there were plenty in the banks and hedgerows alongside the road back into town.

Mark was officially family. 'I'll call myself the worst man,' he'd said. 'And you know that Billy Beagle and his friends will wonder what the hell's he doing here.'

A friend in need is a friend indeed and, at this time, the humour was a welcome currency. 'That and a few drinks and you'll see this through,' he'd said. But the latter, much as they might have been welcome, were the last thing he needed when it came time to being civil to some of the mourners in attendance.

Senor Delmontez oozed, 'Dear Tom, how nice to meet you. Your father spoke so highly of you. You have my sincerest sympathies. He was my friend, a great man.' Col. Butcher, from the Jockey Club in Canada, attended along with Woodbine executive, Calvin Weiner. 'I know, Tom, what great respect E.P. (E.P. Taylor the Canadian breeder of the great Northern Dancer and long-time leading consignor at Keeneland) had for Caledonia and your dad.' All the way from England, Jos Danvers of Classic Bloodstock Services, said 'Too bad about that little tumble at Cheltenham last week, Tom. Ha! Ha! Just want to say that when,' - if, more likely, he thought - 'you ever make it to Newmarket, you will be our most welcome guest. The High Flyer Sales have been good to your father over the years.' Blah! Blah! Blah!

Mark was enjoying every moment of it: the loyal and generous friend, but artful schmoozer, flirting with the young ladies who were serving the delicious canapes and chatting up the very delightful Missie Van der Meer, wife of T.J., Billy Beagle's director of breeding and racing operations.

As some had come so far, they fortunately had planes to catch and, mercifully, things petered out relatively quickly, leaving Tom to usher the last few well-wishers out, while Mark hoovered up what was left of the sumptuous fare and made sure that as many shakers and manoeverers on hand as he could introduce himself to had his card and particulars. 'Boy, you could live your whole life down here and not even know these people existed,' he exhorted.

'Man, that was something, getting 'em all in the same room: captive and conducive.'

'Yea, and it sure looked like you and Ms. Van der Meer hit it off pretty well!'

'One sexy beast. Oh my!'

'Well, one word of advice, matey. Don't mess with the number two man's wife, if you know what's good for you in good 'ol hardboot country.'

'You weren't doing so bad, yourself! Who was that fancy dame in the wheelchair, with the black fedora, that I saw you chatting with?'

'That,' said Tom, 'was my Aunt Vera. My mom's sister. She has a farm down in Virginia. She's invited me to go and stay. Thinks it would be good to get away from Lexington and all the stuff that's going on. I rode my first winner, under rules, for her at Sandown, on the very horse who sadly put her in that chair. A lovely lady. That was so sad.'

'Who was the guy, in the suit?'

'Which guy?'

'The guy with your Aunt Vera.'

'Oh, him? That's Basil. Long story. I'll tell you all about him another time.'

Mark geared down his Porsche, appreciating the throaty roar and, probably, all the nice things he'd like to do to Missie Van der Meer. Maybe, in this backwater of culture, she'd like him to play her a tune on his piano? She'd be someone he'd definitely get the main vehicle out for. 'You know what I think?' he shouted over the car's roar.

'What?'

'Go down to stay with your auntie. You've got nothing to lose. They have steeplechasing there in the spring and fall. Great fox hunting country.' The roof was down, and the wind carried away his voice as they sped along. 'As for Miss Missie, if you don't knock, nobody is going to open the door. And, in this business, you know as well as anyone, it's who you know, not what you know. It's contacts. The right contacts.'

'Sure do. I sure do,' sighed Tom, and long before Mark rolled up to 246 Transylvannia, he was asleep.

CHAPTER 6

Mark's fleet of vehicles filled the driveway and his garage. Top of the list was his Porsche 911, sleek and black, always parked inside when not ferrying those that its owner wished to impress to golf outings, the races, and fine-dining experiences. Number two, the runaround, a Jeep Cherokee: functional but inconspicuous. And number three, a beat-up old Dodge Ram pickup for country cruisin': ubiquitous, off the beaten track, in these parts. 'You don't want the locals figuring you're a big shot, doing too well at their expense, if you're gonna get their confidence and do any good in this business, round here,' Mark believed.

So it was, in the Jeep, that Tom headed out to Caledonia Farms. Set in six hundrend acres of prime Bourbon County pastures, just off the Versailles Pike, it was an iconic Kentucky farm, with imposing, pewter-coloured wrought iron gates between classic local stone pillars; set back from the road with neatly mown lawns flanked by overflowing beds of spring flowers. The black, creosoted paddock railings, for almost half a mile either side, exuded neatness and quality. There was no doubting that whoever owned this property was a heavyweight in the local bloodstock community, however bad business might be.

Visitation was by appointment only and all trades were directed to the side entrance, for horse vans, off Montgomery side road. Tom pressed the intercom and waited. A pair of cardinals hopped about on the lawn beside the gates; the male scarlet, resplendent with his gold plume, rooting a worm out of the ground for his lifetime mate, so much more demur in her light brown and flecked orange trim. Tom buzzed again and again. No answer. He could have called up to the office on the new phone that he'd picked up that very morning. But, bearing in mind what had transpired, maybe Margaret was preoccupied? So he drove on around to the rear entrance, passing the charred remains of what was left of the main broodmare barn.

At the back gate there seemed to be a tangle of yellow plastic tape blocking off access, and a man in the generic grey uniform of a security guard emerged from the lodge gatehouse.

'No admittance at this time, sir. I'm sorry, but Senor Delmontez's orders.'

'Excuse me, but I'm Bob Fraser's son, Tom. We own this place.' Or we did, thought Tom, until what Shaefer had told him the previous day about the situation with the bank and Delmontez occurred to him.

'Well, sir, I'm sorry, but I have my orders. Nobody to be allowed in.'

'This is ridiculous. I was born here, this is my home, my dad owns this place. I gotta get in. I need to speak to someone. Who is your supervisor?'

'You wait here, sir.' The guard turned and walked a few paces back towards the gates, pulling a radio from his pocket and speaking to someone. While he did this, Tom dialed the main office, but to no avail. The phone rang and went to voicemail.

After about five minutes of to-ing and fro-ing, the guard returned. 'They're coming down to see you, sir. You just wait here, please.'

And in due course a black Ford pickup truck came down the drive and stopped on the other side of the closed gates. In it there were two men that Tom had never seen before and behind them, in the twin-cab, Chuck, the stallion man. The two men got out and Tom could hear them speaking rapidly in Spanish. The taller of the two, dressed in jeans, cowboy boots, a black shirt, and baseball hat with El Gruppo on it ignored the guard and walked up to the other side of the gate.

'Hola! You! This is private property of Condor Corporation. Senor Delmontez is boss.' His English was broken and deeply accented. 'You-a speak to meester Chuck.'

At this point, Chuck, who had by this time exited the truck and come up alongside the much taller Latino, nervously reinforced the message. 'Good to see ya, Master Tom. I don't know just what's goin' on. But, since your daddy's death and all that stuff, these people have taken over. I don't rightly know what to say, but we have our orders from Dr. Delmontez. He's the boss now, I guess?'

While the security guard didn't appear to be armed, Tom had no doubt that the tall Latino and his burly sidekick, who had a distinctive and angry-looking scar running diagonally from his left eye to the point of his jaw, meant business and needed little provocation to escalate this standoff.

'That's all right, Chuck. Let me get to the bottom of this. I'll be back.' Turning to the three men who stood in his path, he asked, 'And who have I had the pleasure of meeting? Just so I know who to complain about?'

Before either Latino could respond, the security guard stepped forward and presented him with a card. 'Call this number, sir.'

As Tom backed out and drove off down the dusty side road, he wondered what was going on. This was not what he had expected. He thought about what Billy Beagle had said about counterfeit horses and drugs. Pulling into a gas station, just outside Nicholasville, he ordered a late breakfast and called Shaefer.

Bernie Shaefer was in court, but his secretary said she'd make sure he'd call Tom as soon as he returned to the office. So Tom drove back to Lexington and took exit 5 off Circle 4 and headed over to Bluegrass Transport (BGT).

◆ ◆ ◆

BGT was owned by Dick McClure, a dour Scot who had left Dundee on the east coast of Scotland as a young man, some forty years previous, with fierce determination and a hammer of a fist that, during his travels throughout the United States, had landed him, after many heroic defences of Scottish pride and above all the merits of malt whiskey over bourbon and rugby being so much tougher than the sissy NFL, in more small-town jails across the Midwest than he cared to remember, before finally touching down in rural Kentucky.

The '80s were a time when international bloodstock had caught fire on the back of the great Northern Dancer. As horsemen from around the globe descended upon Kentucky to partake of this feast of equine blue blood, Dick had spotted an opportunity. He had bought his own horse van and put together charter flights between Cincinnati, just up the road across the Ohio river, and airports like Orly and Beauvais (just outside Paris, in France), Stanstead in England, and Shannon in Ireland.

At the outset, these Flying Tiger charters were precarious ventures, with rickety kit-like stalls and, until the organizer knew that he had the critical number to cover costs, were very risky undertakings.

It was money up front to book the plane, so Dick drove a hard but fair bargain. This is what it costs from A to B, which includes all services from the moment the hammer drops in the sales arena to delivery: board, insurance, and transportation. No exceptions. Only discounts for ten horses or more.

Each flight accommodated close to sixty horses, with the break-even point being 25. Dick had done his sums correctly and been uncompromising about extending credit on the turf, which he knew, as many a bookmaker can attest, is really only recoverable through blunt intimidation.

'Let the Paddys and Brits, with their rich Arab clients, get on with it', was McClure's MO. As a true Scot, with short arms and deep pockets, he was leery about investing in anything that ate and could die. So, you play with the horses and we'll chauffeur you around.

Martin O'Sullivan was director of shipping, and while Tom had never met him, he knew that his father had used the company on many occasions. So, wishing to learn more about the new boss of Caledonia and his central and South American dealings, he felt this would be a good place to start.

O'Sullivan was a Dublin man. A bit of an unmade bed to look at, with crumpled khakis and a golf shirt with a prominent stain on the front of his ample girth; earned, as his boss knew only too well, from the many expense receipts he'd written cheques for, from bars around town.

There wasn't a farm in Kentucky that didn't have some sort of Irish connection and most of BGT's employees originated from the Emerald Isle. Indeed, Dick McClure knew only too well that the Irish Mafia, as he referred to them, had their fingers in most pies flavoured in any way by horses.

'You know, that's the question everyone is asking,' said O'Sullivan, as he welcomed Tom into his chaotic office, festooned with piles of sales' catalogues and Coggins health certificates; the walls covered from floor to ceiling with sporting prints and winner's circle photos from Beulah to Belmont. There was Martin, in tweeds, with Fergus Mahoney at Churchill Downs; with Tommy McGovern in Chicago, at Arlington; and at Belmont, sporting a natty trilby, with Marcus Townsend and a bunch of serious looking bearded men, after the Man o' War Stakes. It was easy to see that our man Martin got about and kept himself in elite company on the turf.

After introducing himself and receiving the standard, warm Irish welcome and over-the-top flattery of Caledonia and his father's and Dick McClure's mutual Scottish heritage, Tom asked Martin what he knew about Hector Delmontez.

'He showed up about ten years ago, in California. Brought up a couple of fillies from Chile or Peru, I can't remember exactly when. You know, they do all their own shipping? Well, into the US, anyway. We have moved on some of their stock to Europe. But most of it comes via Condor Air, one of his many companies. He also owns a ranch down in Argentina, Haras de Maya, and a bunch of operations throughout Colombia and Venezuela. Condor Aviation is registered in Caracas. They move just about anything. Very private, though. And they won't share space with anyone from up here. We had a client wanting to move some Polo ponies up for the season in Wellington, Florida, just a few months ago. Good money, but they had no interest. You see that pile of Coggins over there?' He motioned to a stack of government-stamped health papers that looked like it was about to slide off his desk into a large dog basket, whose occupant had made his own mess below, but seemed absent. 'Those are South American–bound shippers going outta Cincinnati tomorrow night. We'd like to do more business with them because their money is good. The boss likes that.'

Tom had been taking all of this in, thinking about the two Spanish-speaking hombres at the farm, wondering about who their boss, who was currently keeping him off the property, was and what had Dad known about his operation? What had happened to him and Ramon Diaz? Why were they at the broodmare barn late at night? How had a fire started? What had happened to the farm's star mare?

'You any idea how many horses these guys have?'

'Here, in Kentucky? The US?'

'Yep, roughly? Do you get to do the local vanning? I mean, if Condor comes into Cincinnati, do you guys van their horses to Lexington or wherever?'

'Sometimes, yes. Good payers. No nonsense. Always on time. As I say, they are good customers. I just wish that we could work with them a bit more on imports. I guess that now that they have Caledonia,' he hesitated awkwardly, not sure if his guest wanted to hear this. 'I suppose they must be closing in on around a hundred head, what with mares and foals, etcetera'

'Well, thank you Martin. You have been most helpful.'

'Oh, one thing. You know I said that they were good payers, good people to do business with?'

'Yes?'

'Well, they…how should I put it? They tend to be accident prone. They don't have much luck.'

'What do you mean?'

'Well, for such a well-run operation, accidents. Last month they had a horse fall off the ramp in Cincinnati. Broke his neck. Just like that. It was awful. Our guys were doing the vanning that day, and you know that these things happen. But, we were just talking about it the other day, they don't seem to have had much luck recently. That horse in Cincinnati was apparently worth over a million dollars!'

As Martin walked Tom out to his car, he exclaimed, 'Well! If I'm not mistaken, that's Mark O'Malley's Jeep you have there. Holy smoke. If you're a friend of Mark's, we must have a pint down at Dooley's.'

Indeed, many, thought Tom as he drove off, with a truck-full on his mind.

CHAPTER 7

Detective Watson might well have not had concerns about foul play or skullduggery, so far. But the tone of the message left on Tom's phone by Brad Kirchner of the FBI suggested that other law enforcement were treating the fire at Caledonia a lot more seriously. The Feds had been called in, as Ramon Diaz's name had surfaced on a list at Interpol and, by the sounds of things, he had some particularly bad form that Kirchner needed to discuss, pronto.

At the FBI local field office, Special Agent Kirchner was quickly down to business. 'Mr. Fraser, are you aware that your father was a drug dealer?'

'No, sir,' said Tom respectfully, but nonetheless shaken.

At this point Bernie Schaefer interrupted. 'This is outrageous! My client is not, and was not, involved in this matter. This is sheer speculation!'

'We've been talking to the banks. I repeat, banks,' putting exaggerated emphasis on the plural, 'and we don't like what we've seen. You did know that Robert Fraser filed for bankruptcy in 2008, didn't you?'

'Excuse me, but this is none of my client's business,' Schaefer interrupted sharply.

'Well, I would only have been thirteen at that time. So, I had no idea, then, what was going on.' Tom volunteered

'That's enough, Tom,' Schaefer cut him off.

'How long have you been away in Europe, sir?

'Just over a year, until…'

'And why did your parents, Mr. and Mrs. Fraser, go down to Caracas,

Venezuela, in 2009? Did they know Senor Delmontez at that time? Do you know what happened to your mother? Let me see. Yes. She was killed in a plane crash, in one of Senor Delmontez's planes, owned by Condor Aviation - when your parents were down there. What was the relationship between your parents and Senor Delmontez?'

The room had no windows, and for the first time Tom felt the stuffy air. Indeed, the whole experience was beginning to feel very claustrophobic and threatening. 'Sir,' he said, defensively, after absorbing this rapid-fire assault. 'I wasn't there, I was at high school, so I don't have any idea.'

At this point Schaefer addressed Kirchner. 'Agent, my client has nothing more to say. He is staying in Lexington. He has a lot on his plate at this time. You know how to contact him, or me, and we will do everything we can to assist you with your enquiries, as I can assure you that this whole experience has been most troubling for Mr. Fraser. He wants to find out why his father died more than anyone. That's all for now, Tom.'

Back at Schaefer's offices, Tom raised the issue of his fees, now that the seriousness of the case had escalated. But he was brushed off with assurances that all matters were being taken care of and warned not to discuss Kirchner's concerns with anyone, or text, e-mail, or engage in any communications regarding the matter. Tom wondered whether to tell him about his father's text, but then thought about what Billy Beagle had said and left it at that.

As he drove back to Mark's he realized that he should keep his head down and nose out of this. But he had to find out what had happened that night. Had to get in touch with someone working at the farm or who was there, before Delmontez and his crew took over.

◆　◆　◆

Mark was playing the piano and, as Tom poured himself a beer in the kitchen, the melodic sound of Schubert cooled his troubled mind as much as the air conditioning.

Upon his entrance, Mark broke into a Bluegrass-cum-Gospel melody of his own composition. 'Oh, Keeneland, Keeneland...Oh. Kee-ee-ene...land,' he sang. Oh, Shenandoah, perhaps, thought Tom, thinking of his Aunt Vera's open invitation.

'Looks like you've got a fancy invitation from the hardboots.' Mark smiled, bunging him an expensively embossed envelope.

Indeed, for the following Saturday, April 23: 'The Fellows of the Bluegrass request the pleasure of your company at the Iroquois Hunt Club, for cocktails and canapés after racing.' It was addressed to Mr. Thomas Fraser and guest.

'Well, you know who that guest is, don't you Tommy boy?' Mark chortled. 'Just can't wait to check out a few more of them southern society dames. Know what I mean, jellybean?'

For Tom this was good news, that he had powerful friends. But bad news, because they and all their guests would only have, apart from the Kentucky Derby in two weeks time, one topic of conversation on their minds: the deadly fire at the farm; and, as his diligent lawyer and Billy Beagle had warned him, the less said about that the better.

An invitation to such an A-list event of local luminaries and their guests was just a small, but subtly essential, date on the turf's perennial social calendar that kicked off in Dubai with the World Cup at the end of March; flowed onto Kentucky for Keeneland, the Kentucky Derby, and thence Triple Crown, and would then move on to the lawns of Royal Ascot in June, before Saratoga, Deauville, and Del Mar in August. From there, back to Keeneland in September, the Arc in Paris, and onto to wherever the Breeders' Cup was being held that year. All the bloodstock heavyweights and their deep-pocketed clients would be there.

Mark took the 911 in for a deluxe car wash and had his and Tom's dark blue blazers dry cleaned. 'We need to look the part. This business is all about impressions. Loads of bullshit. And boy, I'll tell you, you're sure going to see a pile of that that evening.'

Two weeks before the first Classic of the year, the last prep of any consequence for the famous Run for the Roses, was the Lexington Stakes that Saturday afternoon. Keeneland, with the dogwood and azaleas in full bloom, looked its best, with a capacity crowd enjoying itself in the spring Kentucky sunshine. In many respects, it is the Augusta National of racetracks in the United States: no concrete, no industrial surroundings, just beautifully crafted dry stone walls, immaculately mown lawns, flowers, singing birds, and a vista of paddocks, full of mares nursing their newly arrived foals, stretching off into the distance.

◆　◆　◆

Once upon a time, not too long ago, the members at Keeneland thought that the jarring sound of a commentary of races would spoil the tranquility of their delightful little haven. So races were run in silence, enabling fans, who were expected to be so knowledgeable that they didn't need anyone to call the positions of the horses during each race, to hear thundering hooves race past the stands, out into the country and back home again, to polite cheers of encouragement.

Amongst this perfect setting, like a passing circus that only lasts for a few fleeting weeks each spring and fall, the athletes and their handlers exuded the quality that comes with exclusivity. 'Too much of any good thing is never a good idea,' Billy Beagle preached: professing that, if he had his way, he'd shut down seventy-five percent of racetracks in North America. 'It's why the sport elsewhere, in Europe and Australia, is still popular, maintaining its charm. It's the old Sinatra phenomenon. When Frank comes to town, he sells out. But, you put Frank out there a hundred days in a row, nobody will buy tickets, in the end.'

Billy Beagle was king at Keeneland, hosting European and Middle Eastern royalty. Arab Sheikhs' planes parked at Lexington's Bluegrass airport, just across the Versailles Pike, were evidence of this and, in the past, HRH the Queen of England had stayed chez Beagle. Today, in the paddock to inspect the runners for the Lexington Stakes, he was resplendent in a khaki-coloured linen suit, light pink socks that peeked out from his highly polished tan loafers, some sort of noteworthy club tie, and a broad-brimmed panama with the familiar black and yellow band of Hickory Hall. At his side was Sheikh Ali Al-Bhakandar, a bearded gentleman in an immaculately tailored white tropical suit; and his senior bloodstock adviser from England, Jos Danvers, attired in the typically understated but classic Brit-style that suggested Jermyn Street and one of Locks' finest panamas, adorned by the band of some exclusive cricket club. At a discreet distance, Mary-Lou Beagle, Missie Van der Meer, and a tall and distinguished-looking lady, whom Mark figured must be Mrs. Danvers, stood back in the shade, out of the way of business. Their pastel-coloured dresses and wispy hats blending nicely with the colourful myriad of jockeys' silks.

This ritual annoyed Danvers, as he felt that in such a confined space, with so many fractious and highly strung beasts, only those directly involved in the business should be allowed. But here he was, on someone else's turf, holding his most important client's hand. So, whether he liked it or not, he'd suck it up and cash the cheque.

Sheikh Ali had a stud farm outside Newmarket, a London residence in Belgravia, and a formidable estate in Ashdown Forest, less than an hour south of the city, besides extensive holdings throughout the Emirates. The oldest son of Sheikh Mohammed Al-Bhakandar, from the small Emirate Island of

Ras-al-Bhandit that had once controlled the very strategic Straits of Hormuz, who had emerged as a primary player in the burgeoning oil fields of the then Crucial States back in the mid 1950s, Sheikh Ali had been educated at Harrow and passed briefly through the officer training program at Sandhurst. Now, just as his father had sought the guidance of British-based expertise in developing his oil fields, he was getting the same sophisticated massaging of his UK-based real estate and bloodstock interests. For the latter, the close-knit connection between Newmarket in England and Lexington in Kentucky put him centre-stage.

The Hickory Hill box was, of course, right on the wire. From there Billy Beagle and his illustrious guest watched a lightly raced but regally bred chestnut colt, from the local Green Sleeves Farms, run on nicely to take the main prize. The crowd applauded politely. Mark advised his new friends that, in his humble opinion, the winner's trainer, Sonny Hayes, whom he knew was a patient horseman, would be unlikely to rush his charge into the Derby.

It had been classic Mark. He and Tom had ascended to the second floor of the clubhouse, and were on their way out to watch the race, when there appeared to be a slight commotion and a white parasol tumbled from a box above, down onto the seats in front of them. Retrieving it, Mark had returned it to its blushing owner, Deidre Danvers. And, before he knew it, he was sitting in a box surrounded by three lovely ladies.

As they left the racetrack, Tom couldn't believe it. 'You are crazy, man!'

Mark was laughing, the roof was down, Van Morrison was playing. He hummed along. 'I'm just your ball and chain.'

CHAPTER 8

The cocktail party was like something out of *Gone with the Wind*, with a regiment of handsome young men in neat Iroquois Hunt Club uniforms opening car doors: Bentleys, sleek Cadillacs, a Ferrari or two. Mark's 911 looked everyday. And he and Tom were swept into a reception area and fueled with champagne before being led out onto a terrace, looking southwest upon the setting sun. Below, perhaps a hundred people were engaged in murmured conversations on lawns that bordered nearby paddocks, while between them white-jacketed waiters flitted with trays of oysters and delicious-looking canapés, as the fireflies sparked and crickets buzzed in the gloaming.

'Oh, Mark! There you are! Please, I want to introduce you to my friends, Mary-Lou Beagle and Missie Van der Meer.' It was Ms. Parasol, Diedre Danvers.

Mark went into his full-blown charm routine. 'Three roses! I, alone, am not worthy of such company. This is my friend, Tom Fraser, an altogether much more charming man than I.'

'Oh, Tommy!' cried Mary-Lou Beagle. 'We know Tommy. I'm just so glad you boys could come! Let me introduce you. Missie, Dee, this is young Tom Fraser. You heard the terrible news about his dear daddy? You know, the fire? A terrible, terrible thing.' The ladies looked awkward, as you do when you are supposed to show sympathy, but don't know those you are supposed to direct it towards or exactly why.

'You know,' said Deidre, turning to Mark, 'this gentleman rescued me at the races, when I stupidly dropped my parasol.'

'We wouldn't want the fierce old Kentucky sun to blemish your fair English skin, would we now?' gushed Mark.

Deidre tittered. 'Do I detect Irish mockery there?'

'You can take the man out of the bog, but you can't take the bog out of the man.' Mark laughed. He had used this line so often, but it always worked. What a smoothy, thought Tom. They'd only been five minutes at an event which he had positively dreaded coming to, and here they were schmoozing with three Kentucky belles. Well, two and an English rose, to be precise.

'Mark plays the piano,' said Missie Van der Meer. 'I'm gonna git heeem to give me lessons,' she added with a smile, her southern accent drawing out the proposition. I'll bet you are, thought Tom. And Teddy over there is going to be real happy about that, I'm sure.

Where Billy Beagle went, T.J. - his P.A., or sidekick or shadow; some folks weren't so kind - as he was universally known in these parts, was never too far away, especially when it came to business related to Keeneland and Kentucky bloodstock affairs. Now he was engaged in a conversation with a portly man, in an ill-fitting, shiny black suit and silver bolo tie, and three other men who could have been triplets, dressed by their mother in standard Kentucky socializing gear: khaki pants, loafers, blue Brooks Brothers button-down shirts, and dark blue blazers. Tom felt almost part of a uniformed local bluegrass fraternity.

'Let me introduce you boys to my husband, T.J., and Sherriff Bickley,' said Missie.

Gerry Bickley, had the round and ruddy face of someone who liked his Jim Beam, and by the looks of things had had an overdose of sun that afternoon at the races, putting his complexion into overdrive. 'Sure good to meet you boys,' he began. 'This here is Bob Walcott of the NHRA and Terrence Reilly and Bobby Ferguson. They're doing a wonderful job running our game,' the sheriff gushed, as he engulfed Tom's hand in his sweaty grasp.

'You heard about the terrible barn fire at Caledonia Farms last week?' continued Missie, 'this is Bob Fraser's son, Tom. He's an amateur steeplechase rider. And Mark here, well…'

'Sure did,' chimed in Bickley, as he took over the conversation, while Mark and Missie drifted off to discuss Andrew Lloyd Webber, Mark's music, and interest in racing and breeding. 'A tragic loss for Lexington and the bloodstock world. And a great mare, too. What was her name?' Bickley drawled on.

'Magnolia,' interrupted Walcott, 'an Oaks winner and Eclipse champion. She was one running fool and never missed a beat in the breeding shed. A great loss. She was in foal to Galactic Star. That foal would have been worth a pretty penny. I must go over and commiserate with Dr. Delmontez. I see he's talking to Mr. Beagle and his friends from Canada.'

At the mention of Delmontez, the hairs on the back of Tom's neck rose and his gaze followed Walcott's passage across the lawn to where Billy Beagle was holding court.

Sheriff Bickley was now engaged in an animated discussion on casino gambling, river boats, and their threat to horse racing, with the remaining two NHRA boys riveted to every word. So, Tom wasn't noticed as he excused himself from the rant and joined the Beagle crowd. This was an opportunity to politely confront the man who had unceremoniously taken over his birthright. After his recent experience at the farm, he needed an explanation.

As a waiter arrived with a platter laden with sweetbread stuffed vol-au-vents, the conversation abated momentarily and Tom was able to catch Billy Beagle's eye. 'Oh, Tom, so good of you to come. I hope you have found some people you know. I'd like to introduce you to Senator Travis Wardle; he's our man in Frankfort.'

'And Washington!' boomed the Senator, to peals of laughter.

'Did you meet Cal Weiner, from Canada, at your daddy's funeral,' Beagle continued and Tom shook Weiner's hand, acknowledging the brief words they had exchanged at the funeral. 'And, I'm not sure whether you two know one another.' He turned to Hector Delmontez. 'Tom, this is Hector Delmontez, whose Condor Corp were involved with your dear father and, I believe, are now going to be working with you on continuing the great work at Caledonia?'

This was news to Tom. Delmontez's outstretched hand grasped his like a vice and his intense stare from dark eyes, set deeply into a broad and ridged forehead, took Tom temporarily by surprise. 'It is a pleasure, Tom. You must come out to the farm, as we have much to talk about.'

It was hardly an occasion for a confrontation. So, as much as Tom wanted to ask the shifty-looking Venezuelan what his game was and why his thugs had treated him in such an unfriendly manner, when he'd attempted to do just that the day before, he held his fire.

Billy Beagle looked on, his mood-metre finely tuned. 'If you gentlemen will just excuse me, I need to have a word with our guests from the UK.' The consummate diplomat, in an incestuous world of egos and conflicting standards, his position was to uphold the notion of Kentucky as the centre of the bloodstock world, while all the time defending its shaky image as the worst state in North America when it came to race-day medication and the use of anabolic steroids; with many of his good friends in the Lexington area, some of the guests that very evening, the worst culprits when it came to preparing young stock for the sales' ring.

Now, having exited from the obvious awkwardness between Tom and Hector, he was smiling congenially with Jos Danvers of Classic Bloodstock Services and Henri de Banguet of France's Société d'Encouragement, two blue chip promoters and regulators of international horse racing.

In the '80s, buyers from Saudi Arabia and the Emirates had come to Kentucky with a mission. And, combined with the Northern Dancer phenomenon and emergence of major players from Ireland, France, and Japan, the bloodstock industry in Kentucky had prospered greatly. But, over the past thirty years or so, these deep-pocketed buyers had exported most of their purchases to bolster their own breeding programs, to such an extent that now more and more mares were travelling in the reverse direction: to be bred to the best stallions in Europe.

Indeed, it was becoming apparent that this was not just for pedigree and precociousness on the racetrack, but soundness and longevity. The lack of those two key elements in the elusive equation that confronted breeders, when they sought to make a perfect match to produce the perfect racehorse, being attributed to the commercialism of American breeders who favoured speed and a quick return on their investments, over the patience, stamina, and old-fashioned horsemanship required for classical performance.

It was an unfortunate fact, that the indiscriminate and unfettered use of drugs in the breeding and racing of horses in North America produced an unsound and increasingly unsaleable product.

Billy Beagle was acutely aware of this, and that PETA and other animal rights' agencies were focusing unfavourably upon his sport. But he was stuck between a rock and a hard place: the foal crop was down 30% and falling like a stone, and revenue from betting was plummeting. There were just too many horses as a result of the insane '80s and, come the millennium, the bottom had fallen out of the market, with dozens of breeders walking away from farms.

Now, those struggling to survive expected to be kept in business. But four and five horse fields that were the result of an attempt to drastically reduce the use of anti-inflamatory, and often pain-killing drugs, on race days were not the answer, either, because the odds and pools in such races did not represent any value for the punters from whom revenue was the sport's lifeblood.

In Europe there was a predominance of turf racing and now North American players could bet on races around the globe, with big fields and attractive odds, twenty-four-hours a day, at exciting tracks like Shatin in Hong Kong and

Meydan in Dubai. There was variety and quality. It was real entertainment. The competition worried Beagle immensely.

'Mr. Weiner and I are partnering in an exciting horse that we have arriving this week from Argentina,' Delmontez addressed Tom. 'A beautiful pedigree that traces back to Nearco, with a bottom line of Marcel Boussac's classic French stamina. El Cordobes is a truly exciting prospect. He won his first two races by over 20 lengths, then was sadly injured, preparing for El Classico, our top two-year-old race down there. But now he's back, winning again, and we hope to run him a few times here in the United States, to show you what a good horse he is before he retires to stud.'

'Yes. Hector and I are expecting great things, and we will be sending him mares from Canada,' Weiner chimed in, clearly having drunk the good doctor's Kool-Aid. 'My bloodstock partner, Mike Rogers, thinks they will be great matches for this outcross of blood. It's something that Federico Tesio did in Italy, between the wars, and E.P. Taylor made a cornerstone of his success at Windfields, up where I'm from in Canada. Never stop pruning, eh! Weed out the weak, non-productive stock and bring in fresh blood.'

Weiner, a tall, thin man with an unfortunately pronounced squint, had had a few drinks and, when this happened, he tended to peer almost leeringly at those he was addressing. Tom found this rather unnerving and wondered if he was just another snake-oil salesman, the like of which his father had warned him about. These people, he had said, use their position and coveted lifestyle to grossly oversell. They have the platform and all the connections to persuade new investors to back their schemes, based upon the supposed successful involvement of people (themselves) who are already doing well in the business.

Weiner looked slick and altogether untrustworthy, and Tom already knew that Delmontez was up to no good. So, after arranging for a visit to the farm the following Monday at 11 a.m., he bid them adios.

The schmooze-fest was winding down. Tom went to find Mark, which did not turn out to be too hard, as he homed in on the loudest laughter, finding his good friend the centre of a lively conversation. 'Tom, we're off to the Derby, thanks to these lovely ladies. To a box, no less! Friends,' he said, turning to the gathering, 'this is my good friend Tom Fraser, budding amateur jockey,' emphasizing am-ma-teur, to giggles 'Gentleman par extraordinaire,' he added making a sweeping bow. 'Unfortunately though, it looks like we are leaving, ladies. Alas, far too soon. But we will see you on the first Saturday of May.'

As they thanked their hosts profusely, on the way out, Tom marvelled at his friend's infectious charm that enabled him to fit in, no matter the circumstances.

Driving home, the man beside him was calm. 'A word of advice, my friend,' he imparted, 'this business involves a great deal of partying and drinking. But do not make the mistake of getting pissed on a night like tonight, as there will be those there that will not let you forget, despite their own excesses. Make no mistake, there will be many dull spots at sales, or between races, when your clients will get loaded at the bar, and its very tempting to join them. Just a word of caution. After my first glass of champagne, I have been been drinking Perrier, all evening, so you have a sober chauffeur to drive you home. You know that the local constabulary just love nailing foreign guys in Porsches for DUIs.'

Tom laughed.

CHAPTER 9

It was Derby week. No need in these parts to qualify the famous Run for the Roses with a state demarcation. And, as Tom drove out to Caledonia, the pundits on the radio were discussing the merits of various leading contenders and their most recent prep races. May blossoms lined the hedges, and as farm after farm passed by, in a blur of green paddocks enclosed by grey stone walls and neat fencing, it seemed like Bluegrass country knew that its signal event was nigh.

This time the main gates were open, and even though there was a pickup parked behind the lodge nobody challenged him. He knew this territory so well: carpets of bluebells and an avenue of maple and beech trees which, once in full bloom, would cover the drive and provide welcome shade during the hot and humid Kentucky summers.

On the surface, it was as though nothing had changed. As Tom parked outside the main office, he wondered whether Rupert, his dad's much loved but rather old and smelly, by his last recollections, Springer would come bounding out to greet him. But no. Although the place was the same, there was now a quietness about it.

Margaret Winters was not in her usual spot at the desk in the reception area, from whence she would always greet visitors with her local Kentucky charm and ply young Tom with homemade brownies. However, the door to his father's office was open and he could hear someone on a phone. Entering, Hector Delmontez motioned Tom to sit down in a chair in the big bay window that looked out over immaculately mown lawns. Hector was speaking animatedly in Spanish and Tom wondered whether that language ever lent itself to a slower drawl.

Looking around, the paintings and win pictures were still there, and the table in front of him was covered, as usual, with *Blood-Horse* magazines and sales catalogues.

Gazing out the window, deep in thought, he was momentarily startled by the arrival of Delmontez at his side. 'Tom, so glad you could come out this morning. Please forgive me, these days telephones control our lives, no?'

A clearly most refined Hispanic gentleman, he spoke beautifully correct English, with just a tiny tinge of Latino charm, as he extended his manicured and well-tanned hand. The firm hand, and Tom was ready.

Slight of figure, Hector's angularity and refined features were accentuated by his tan which, this morning, was offset by pale blue chinos and a white polo shirt. A very fit man, Tom figured him to be probably a bit older than the fifty-ish that he looked. 'You have probably heard some bad things about me? About Condor, eh?' Hector said, smiling, as he sat down beside Tom. 'Kentucky, the horse racing community. How you say it? They circle the wagons, no? You know how tough this business is? For the last thirty years people have been dreaming, but their dream has become a nightmare. The bubble burst. You cannot go on and on breeding more and more horses, many of them bad, bad horses, just because the market says that if you breed two well-bred horses together their offspring are automatically worth millions of dollars. This is a fallacy, Tom!' He paused. 'So many people here in Kentucky just went on and on, and,' he emphasized 'they got encouragement to do so from the people at the top. The Jockey Clubs, the Breeders' Cup, the Senor Beagles, the NH. What do you call that clueless organization that thinks it can run and regulate horse racing in America?'

'The National Horse Racing Association, the NHRA,' volunteered Tom.

'Yes, the NHRA and greedy thoroughbred breeders. Dreamers, building sand castles. A house of cards, made of bogus acronyms, with every institution propping each other up. It was all a façade. Big sales pitches: be a part of the sport of kings! But behind it all, nothing.'

Hector was making the running, and Tom was listening.

'Senor Delmontez, what happened to my dad?' he asked suddenly, turning and looking Hector straight in the eye.

Hector gulped. Composing himself, all he could manage was, 'A bad business,' as he gazed out the window, his angular features and Roman nose silhouetted against the light.

'What was my dad doing at the foaling barn in the middle of the night with your associate, your manager, Ramon Diaz? Had there been an emergency? Where was the night watchman? You must have known that there were mares due? Why so much silence about this? Why was no vet called? Was there nobody else out there who saw what happened? There has got to be someone who was there and knows what went on,' Tom pleaded, adamantly.

Hector stared out the window.

'Why, suddenly, has this place turned into a fortress?' he continued. 'Where is Margaret? She has run this office since before I was born. I saw Chuck, but where are the staff: Bobby Mattock, Skeeter, and the boys?

'Your father had some financial problems, Tom.' Hector wasn't looking at him, which he took as a bad sign. 'This place was struggling,' he paused. 'A few bad years, you stand a bad horse or two. Then there was the lightning that stampeded those yearlings and the farm lost that good colt, with a broken leg, that he was counting on selling for a lot of money, here at Keeneland, two years ago. It all adds up, Tom. This farm was running on empty. It would have failed by now.'

'But I don't understand. What have you done? My dad is dead. I find out that he'd signed away the farm, and I...' He faltered. 'I, I have nothing. I need an explanation.'

'It's business, Tom. Whether it was his fault or not, your father mismanaged this farm and I now own it.' Hector's tone had changed. Still measured, but it was apparent to Tom that what had happened was one thing, and the situation now and for the foreseeable future was altogether another.

'Tom, I am a businessman. I have to make this farm profitable. My company, Condor, has many interests. Some have served me well. I keep them. Others, if they don't work, I let go.

'You still haven't explained what happened to my father, though. He's dead. Why? How?'

'Well, you will have to speak to the police. They are carrying out an investigation.'

'What about me? This place? I thought that one day it would be mine. Ever since my dad put me up on a pony, I have been dreaming about this farm one day being mine. I was in Europe learning the business. I have worked in every aspect of this breeding operation, with the stallions, foaling, sales. It's my life!'

'You can come here anytime, Tom. What do you want to do?'

'I want my farm back.'

There was a pause as both men looked out the window. It had started raining, and, as the rain ran down the panes, Tom thought about his mom. She always wore a silk headscarf like her mom back in county Cavan, in Ireland, when it rained. What would she say? 'Don't get emotional,' that's what she would have said. 'Think things through. They can't be as bad as they look, on the surface.'

'Well, Senor Delmontez. I'm going to have to think about this. Thank you for your time.' Tom stood up. 'I appreciate your offer. I'll get back to you.' And with that he walked out without shaking Hector's hand, and drove back into Lexington.

◆　◆　◆

Tom realised that he wasn't going to get anything more from Hector and the idea of working for him was repulsive, in the circumstances. Senor Delmontez knew a lot more than he was saying, and the mere thought of being his vassal bothered him in so many ways. And what troubled him the most was the way that everyone seemed to be accepting what had happened so naturally, when there was nothing natural about what had happened or was going on, at all!

Mark was waiting for him. 'How'd it go with Senor Slick? Badly, by the look of you.'

'You're right about the slick part. You look like you're going somewhere.'

'Well, yes. First, though, an FBI guy called. They need to speak to you down at their field office. He wanted to come here, but I told him that you were out. So, as I am just going out to see some folks over near Paris, come along with me. You can call whatshisname from the car.'

'Where are we going?'

'Oh, it's a small farm. I've known these people for yonks. Small breeders, Paddy and Betty McDonnell. The family have messed around with a few mares. I met them at the sales. Nice people, they just need a bit of help when it comes to presenting their stock. They don't want to be sucked into a big consignment shot, where whoever is promoting the deal is looking after their bigger clients and they fall between the cracks. And they don't like the fact that they always seem to draw bum places in the catalogue, as small-time consignors. You know, first few lots to sell or finding themselves in the ring while everyone is having lunch or watching races. It's a game that they're not quite sure they're getting a fair shake in.'

They were back in the Jeep that Tom had driven out to Caledonia, with Mark now at the wheel, speeding along Circle 4. 'This'll be a learning experience for you, matey. And, until you get yourself sorted out, you can make a few bucks between now and the end of the summer.'

'Doing what?'

'Ducking, diving, bobbing, weaving. It's a game! Now, seriously, you better ring that FBI fellow before he sends a posse after us.'

Tom was put through to Agent Mehrtens, new on the Caledonia Farms fire file. And the agent explained that Tom needed to come in with his lawyer to confirm one or two things that his colleagues had not established. Purely routine, he said. And the following morning at 10 a.m. was agreed upon.

'Now then,' said Mark when he'd hung up. 'How about a spot of lunch? I know this little country kitchen where they do a serious smoky B-B-Q sandwich. Paddy McDonnell isn't expecting us until around three, so we have plenty of time.'

The restaurant, down a gravel side road, had the healthy sign of a full parking lot of beat-up pickups. 'The locals sure know their grub,' said Mark, as they parked in the shade. It was a free-for-all inside, with a profusion of burly bearded men, universally adorned with bib overalls and feeder hats that identified the farms they worked on. Everyone sat on benches along crude wooden tables and were served by cheery waitresses wearing brightly coloured aprons. 'This is real country food,' yelled Mark above the loud chatter. 'Help yourself to extra sauce. You can eat as many biscuits as you like.'

Tom hadn't thought too much about food recently, as he'd been so conscious about making the weight during his brief career as a jockey, so this was a welcome feast. The conversation around him was all Derby talk. This was horse country and his fellow diners knew their stuff.

'You get good info in places like this,' said Mark, 'not stuff that's in the *Racing Form*. Having contacts is what it's all about. Come sale time, it's good to have your card marked. You know, stuff like this mare has had no luck, slipped twins, then was barren because some idiot at the lab lost the tests and the dope who owned her never got her recovered. It looks bad on paper, but a word from someone at the source that her latest foal is an absolute beauty, with perfect confirmation, is something that the big boys may miss. That's when you can pick up a bargain.' Between a mouthfull of succulent chicken he added, 'It can work in two ways, though. The first way, you have a client who doesn't have much money and you wise him up to this lot. He buys it and pays you a nice commission for the heads-up. Have to have this sorted out before, though, as some fuckers try to pretend that they knew this, anyway, and you don't deserve to be taken care of. But, it can work the other way, too. Just as we're hopefully going to do today, for Paddy.'

'He says he's got a nice individual, but the paper won't look good in the catalogue. So, he needs me to put the word out to a few people I know: trainers, owners, you know, you've gotta come and see this colt, who is a great athlete… blah…blah…blah. Paddy knows what he needs and anything over that price is gravy. So, if you help him, he'll kick back a few bucks. Paddy's a real straight-shooter, no worries with him.'

As the restaurant cleared out and Mark settled the bill, Tom went to the washroom, or rather a primitive outhouse, behind the building. As he was relieving himself into an upturned aluminum half-drainpipe that was angled towards the corner of the rickety shed, a voice beside him said, 'Ain't you Mr. Bob's son? Over at Caledonia?' Upon Tom confirming this, the man introduced himself as Randy Dobbs. 'I worked for your daddy until just last week. Then the whole lot of us got let go by the new owners. I don't know what's going on out there right now, but it sure ain't good!'

'Randy, I would very much like to speak to you about my dad's farm and what happened to him, but we have to get to a farm right now. Is there anywhere we could meet or a number where I could get hold of you?'

'Right now I'm over at Byng's, getting yearlings ready for the sales and that. So you can find me there. I don't have no phone. But if you give me your number, I can call you from a payphone.' Tom gave him his new cell phone number.

'That was a great place, Mark. Thank you,' said Tom as he got back into the Jeep. 'You know, I ran into a guy in the washroom who used to work out at Caledonia. He's gonna call me. I need to find out from someone, who was there, what went on the night my dad died. Who was working as night watchman that night, what's going on now?'

'There you are! You never know what you are going to hear or find out in places like these. Could get the Derby winner. Could get the number for one of them cute waitresses,' Mark laughed as they set off for the McDonnell operation, which turned out to be a modest but well-kept fifty-acre establishment, at the end of a dirt road to nowhere.

CHAPTER 10

'Kinda locked in here, ain't we?' joked Paddy McDonnell, as he greeted them amongst a pack of barking hounds of various breeds. 'The sheriff comes down that road, there ain't no way out 'cept if you know the back woods, where the boys have their stills. Know what I mean, Mark?' he chuckled.

Mark laughed. 'Paddy, meet Tom. He may need to hide out there one of these days.'

Paddy McDonnell was second-generation Irish, but looked like so many of the men that Tom and Mark had just lunched with: John Deere feeder hat atop his six-foot weather-beaten frame that was clad in khaki pants, a faded blue denim shirt, and stout work boots. He was a Kentucky boy, raised in Bourbon County: an outdoor guy with the omni-tan of constant exposure to the elements that had bleached the fair hair that rimmed his well-worn hat.

This farm had no fancy name, just a rural route number, and the horses on it were their owners' hobby that gave him something to look forward to when he wasn't working in the Ford plant over in Versailles. Paddy's parents had been horse people, but realists who had quickly found out the precariousness of relying upon fragile four-legged creatures for a living. Hence, their children had gone to college and now Paddy, having studied engineering at UK, had a good, steady job and could indulge his little passion without counting upon it to put bread on the table.

This was a small-time operation. The subject of today's visit from Mark O'Malley was to assess the farm's two yearlings, which would be most likely going up to the September sales at Keeneland, and make a strategy to sell them for the maximum. Paddy and Betty had got lucky at a dispersal sale, some two years previous, as the North American bloodstock market had teetered and farms and their stock were sold off, often at bargain-basement prices.

Killyshandra had been her name, and Paddy's wife Betty had spotted her first: the last lot in a complete dispersal at the end of a long day. A five-year-old, and so far not bred mare, she had some black type (graded stakes form) in Canada, on the turf, and what Paddy had liked about her was her strike rate: fifteen starts, six wins, four seconds, and three thirds. In other words, she'd only been out of the first three twice in her life and both those races were Grade 1 affairs, one being the Canadian Oaks, on a sloppy track that obviously hadn't suited her. She had the stamina to win around two turns, had won on the turf, and her dam's sister was a Group 1 stakes producer in Europe.

During the excesses of the 1980s this mare would have made $300,000, but at the end of a hot, humid Kentucky night, the buyers must have been burnt out by the heat and jaded by too many Scotches at the bar, as lot number 879 had been knocked down to B & P Stables for $45,000.

Paddy's father, Seamus, an ex-steeplechase rider back in the day, had always believed that pedigree was fine, but that for a mare to be successful she had to have had some ability, herself, so she had something to pass on; toughness being a quality that, in his humble opinion, overrode everything else. His involvement in this purchase had been key to the deal, as was the selection of stallion. 'He's got to have good confirmation, a nice shoulder with correct angles that act as good shock absorbers,' was what Seamus believed, 'that can stand up to the poundin' they give 'em over here.'

The barn was an old tobacco drying shed that had been converted into four stalls and, upon entering the dark, cool space, the three men encountered McDonnell Sr., sporting bib overalls, wellies, and an old tweed cap. Stooped now by his near eighty years, he hadn't lost the distinct tones of county Kildare. 'Well look here, Mr. Mark, high-flying converted Irishman. Bless my soul, it's good to see you!' Mark and old man McDonnell shook hands warmly and Mark introduced Tom as a steeplechase rider.

'Yes. Did a bit of ridin' myself, you know,' Seamus began. 'Back in the time of Arkle. Now's there's a proper harse. They called him 'himself.' Did you know that? I knew Pat Taafe. When they came to Cheltenham, they looked Mill House in the eye and ran away up the hill. Left him in the dust. Greatest harse I ever saw.'

The ceiling was low, and a dank passage led to the back and dropped down to a small covered arena, with more stalls that had back doors straight out into a paddock. It was a simple but effective setup. As Seamus led them through he whistled and two yearlings, at the far end, in the shade of some trees, picked up their heads.

'Come on, boys!' In one hand he had a leather shank and in the other a small feed bowl that he rattled. The yearlings cantered towards them, stirring up a cloud of dust in their wake.

'Out here, we don't have many luxuries, but I believe that's not a bad thing. If you mollycoddle young stock they can get soft,' said McDonnell Sr. 'A racehorse has got to be tough. From the day we wean these fellas, they're out here on their own. We have great water here, you know: plenty of calcium, good for bones. Strong, good bones. When we send a yearling up to sell, he's an athlete. We don't give them no steroids or hormones. You know, sometimes you look at a yearling that some of those big-time sales operators put through the ring and they look like a two-year-old! I've said this to Pat so many times: you do this to a horse, he gets soft. Then, if you ship him, say to Europe where they don't allow all that shit, he falls apart. It's like a drug addict going cold turkey: they can't handle it and the next thing they've got all kinds of viruses and flus. And they just don't make it.'

Seamus probably could have gone on all day on his pet peeves and beliefs about how a young thoroughbred should be raised, but by this time his two charges were nuzzling up to their caretaker. 'Here Pat, put a shank on the Northern Lights colt and I'll just get this guy to stand over here, so these gentlemen can take a look at him.'

Paddy led the second colt, a dark bay with no visible markings, over to the side, while his father got the chestnut that he was holding to stand correctly. 'Whoa there, boy. These bloody flies, they just drive 'em crazy and it's not even May!'

'What do you think of him, Mark?' asked Paddy.

'Boy, he's got some size, hasn't he? He's the Majestic Knight colt you were telling me about, isn't he?'

'Oh, he's a grand harse,' enthused Seamus. 'You just see how he fills out. By the time he's a three-year-old he'll be standing close to seventeen hands.'

'Reminds me a bit of Curlin. You know, big and tough,' said Mark, referring to the popular classic-winning sire.

'What I like about him, too, Mark, is that he's got really good bone. You know, not too long but robust; a great shoulder and a good, flat knee, standing over a bit. Not bad at all.'

'Lovely hind leg, too,' added Seamus. 'That's where all the power comes from. That's his mammy. She has an arse on her the size of that barn door. I'll tell you, this is the best colt that we have bred on this farm by a country mile.'

'Who is she in foal to?' asked Mark.

'The same harse,' chimed in Seamus, who in this barn certainly was the man in charge. 'We like him. And, if this fella is anything, we then have his full brother or sister on deck.'

'And how about the Northern Lights colt?' Tom asked. 'We used to have him at Caledonia. But he's now down in Ocala.'

'Nothing wrong with him. Nothing at all,' said Seamus. 'It's just that, alongside this guy, anything would look inferior.'

'And, you're sending them both up to Keeneland's September sale?' asked Mark

'Yep,' said Paddy, 'it attracts a wider range of buyers than the July sale. We don't want to be lost behind all that black type.'

'Ok, Dad, thank you for showing them to us,' said Paddy. They bid the old-timer goodbye and followed Pat indoors, to his cramped office off the family kitchen. Betty was away, so he put the kettle on. 'So, what do you reckon, Mark?,

'You mean, what do you think you may get?' He hesitated. 'Or rather, what do you feel that you need? That's the crux of it, eh?'

'Well, this'll be Killy's first foal. We love her, you know that. But they may knock her Canadian black type. You know, running in restricted company with just Canadian-breds.' He poured the boiling water into a large red teapot that, by the stains, had obviously brewed many a cuppa. 'He's a real athlete, Mark. We just need to get some serious buyers. Buyers with money, to have a look at him.' He paused. 'Would a hundred and fifty grand be too much? We paid forty-five for the mare and Majestic Knight's standing for twenty.'

'You just don't know, these days,' mused Mark. 'What I will say is that today's buyer is a lot more discerning. Pedigree alone isn't enough. You have to have the confirmation. You know, look like a racehorse. And this fella will show well. All we can do is to put the word out and try and get him in front of as many players as possible. You just need a bit of competition.'

'Well, we'll talk when the catalogues come out. And, you know that, if you can bring in a buyer for that sort of price, Betty and I will look after you,' Paddy added, as he poured the tea.

CHAPTER 11

Driving home, Mark explained to Tom how he worked with his small clients.

'The game has changed dramatically,' he said. 'All the big-monied farms of the 1960s and '70s, the Calumets, the Greentrees, and Darby Dans, they've all gone. Sure, the slack was picked up by Irish buyers and then the Arabs, but these horses were nearly all exported. Their owners had farms overseas and the people who came in to buy these places in Kentucky, Maryland, Florida, and California just didn't have the money to run them. One minute you have one or two horses and that snowballs, so that, before you know it, you have forty. Then someone suggests that you get a farm. That costs money, and running it a pile more. Then you start breeding your own stock, maybe even stand a stallion. And, if that stock doesn't work out, you end up with paddocks full of worthless horses that are eating you out of house and home. Someone once said to me: don't invest in anything that eats or can die. And I'm telling you that this business will bury you in a heartbeat, if you don't stay on top of it. It's tragic. I've seen people walk away from places, leaving horses unfed and uncared for.'

'No!' said Tom

'I can't tell you how many very smart people, who have made fortunes on Wall Street and in businesses around the world, get into the horse business and think they know it all. In the real world they've made their money by hiring and using experts and expertise. But, on the racetrack, they second-guess their advisers and trainers, changing the latter like they change their socks. And, before you know it, things spiral out of control.' Mark paused, as he angled out to pass a horse van ahead. 'Right now, the business is a lot leaner. Fewer buyers. And those that are left are much more particular. Used to be that you'd focus on a couple of big consignments, identify a few lots that figured to be in your price range, and then hoped you didn't get into a bidding war with someone with much deeper pockets. What I'm trying to do is go around and look at as many horses as I can, often from unlikely sources, and then use my contacts to showcase the ones where I feel that I can make a commission. There are lots of villains in this business, Tom, but if you get a reputation as being a hard worker and, most important, a straight shooter, you can do ok.'

'What happens if you bring a buyer to look at Paddy's colt and he buys it, for say the $150 grand that Paddy hopes to get. Do Paddy and the buyer both pay you? You know, commission on both ends?'

'Good question. There has been a lot of smoke about this recently. So now sales companies require disclosure and the registration of agents and whom they're representing. But, believe me, a lot of stuff still goes on. You just gotta know who you're dealing with. With my little guys, I'm completely upfront. I don't want to gouge them. So, if Paddy's colt makes $150K and he and Betty are happy to pay me 10% for bringing in a punter to buy him, and that buyer is also prepared to pay me for marking his card, I will tell them both that that is the way it is or sometimes go five and five, splitting the 10%, if the colt goes through the ring to the highest bidder, my guy. Now, say he doesn't make the reserve that Paddy and Betty have put on him and a private sale is subsequently negotiated, everything has to be pared down. And, this is where, if you don't know your players and how trustworthy they are, they can screw you.'

'How do you mean?' asked Tom, somewhat naively.

'Well, you have a seller and a buyer who have only met because of your introduction. But some people forget about this and think they can eliminate you and make their own deal. Such trickery gets around and believe me, when I tell you, this is a small and incestuous little business, where everyone knows everyone. They may profess to all be friends, pulling together in a great sport-cum-game, but 99% of them are fearfully jealous of each other. As I say, you need to know who you are dealing with. That's why I stay small. Paddy isn't going to screw me unless I screw him.

'The sad thing is that I know many horsemen who have started out trying to do the right thing. You know, look after the new client. But the new client wants to win immediately. So, what do they do? Tell him that he should be patient and then watch some other trainer come along and pinch the horses off them with a whole spiel of b.s. stories? Or go ahead and burn promising horses by being too hard on them, too soon? Short term gain, maybe. But this nearly always ruins what would have been an otherwise long and fruitful career if patience had only been exercised.

'I've seen it a thousand times: young trainer gets hot to trot new owner, young trainer does the best he can, but his punter is not happy and watches his friends' horses winning with a big-time trainer, who just happens to have a few stalls vacant, should Mr. Hotshot new owner feel like changing trainers. So that's what happens, and our well-intentioned young trainer gets shafted. And this is why many of these big trainers today believe in fucking their clients before they get fucked. Pretty bad, isn't it?'

'I'll say.'

'You look at the top trainers these days. They fire their horses all over the place, like a shotgun. It's a numbers game: the more shots the more chance you might hit something. They don't win because they're good or know what they're doing. They win because they run so many horses, sometimes three or four in the same race. It reminds me of a tout I used to know. He put out a hotline every night. Twenty-five bucks to call in and get Liam's bankers for the following day. His trick was putting out multiple bankers, knowing that some of his victims would always score! Then they'd keep on paying the twenty-five and tell their friends. The others, he didn't care about because he knew there were always going to be fresh mugs out there, and he'd have to live two hundred years before anyone cottoned on, or the supply burnt out. He'd laugh about his lobster pot. "Mark," he'd say, "I chuck this pot out into the sea every night and when I go look-see what I got the next morning, holy cow, I haven't even had breakfast yet and I'm a gino ahead!" Talk about money for old rope. You see Tom, this is a great game, but you have to have your wits about you…Tom?'

He glanced across to the passenger's seat and young Tom was off with the fairies, snoring quietly.

◆　◆　◆

Special Agent Mehrtens was all business. It was only 10 a.m. but he and the air conditioning were already humming.

Tom and Bernie Shaefer sat across the same metal table, as the agent shuffled through a manila file of what looked like insurance claim forms. 'Are you familiar with insurance fraud, Mr. Fraser?' he started. 'Well?'

'What are we talking about, here, agent? Insurance on what?' interjected Shaefer.

'Bloodstock insurance, sir.' Mehrtens was abrupt. 'Taking out substantial coverage on a horse, sometimes for a lot more than they're worth, and that horse then mysteriously dying, or more to the point, and in some people's opinion, being killed. Killed to collect the insurance money.'

'And how do you know that, Agent Mehrtens?' enquired Shaefer, squinting through his glasses at the agent's card, which he had been given and was now lying on the desk in front of him.

'At this point, we do not know anything, sir. But, in our enquiries relating to the two recent deaths here in Bourbon County, at, errr,' he said glancing at more paperwork before him, 'the Caledonia Farms. The owner, a Dr. Hector Delmontez, has filed a claim with Lloyds of London, policy number KY27695, brokered here in Lexington by El Gruppo Services through World Wide Livestock Insurance of London, England, for five million dollars for the mare, Magnolia, who allegedly died in the same fire,' Mehrtens coughed, 'that also killed Mr. Robert Fraser and Mr. Ramon Diaz.'

'So, I guess she was a valuable mare.' Shaefer shrugged.

'And, that's why you are here, sir.' Mehrtens turned to Tom. 'What interest did your late father have in this mare, Magnolia? And what exactly was his relationship with Dr. Delmontez, the claimant?'

Shaefer headed off Tom. 'My client has already explained to Agent Kirchner that he has been away in Europe for over a year and that, even though he did grow up on the farm and knew that Magnolia was the big mare, he was too young to have been involved in or known anything about the business relationship between his late father and Dr. Delmontez, the, err, claimant.'

'We know that, sir. What I'm asking your client is, did your father own the mare that died, this Magnolia mare?'

Tom looked at his lawyer, who nodded. 'As far as I know, sir, my dad owned Magnolia. She was his best mare. A champion on the racetrack, she'd produced a whole bunch of top stakes winners for us, for the farm. She was,' he faltered, 'she was the best.'

'Now, Mr. Fraser, I'm not from these parts and don't know anything about the breeding process. But I need to ask you these questions.'

Tom looked at Shaefer. 'Agent, my client can only tell you what he knows, not what he thinks. So no speculation, ok? Go ahead.'

Mehrtens was reading from a prepared list and asked what Tom thought Magnolia was worth, to which Shaefer objected. 'How would he know? He's already said that he was not involved in the running of the business and, in any case, that would be speculation.'

Nevertheless, the FBI agent diligently continued on: How long do mares live? How many foals do they produce each year? For how long do they continue producing? How old was Magnolia? Why had she been so valuable? How many foals had she had? How successful have those foals been on the racetrack? And, now that he'd established that she had been sixteen and that some mares tailed off before they reached twenty, had Magnolia still been capable of having good foals? It went on and on, with Shaefer interrupting frequently that the questions were speculative or leading. Or just plain irrelevant.

Finally, after everything on his list had been dealt with satisfactorily or just not answered, Mehrtens stood up and stretched. Tom could see dark patches under his arms. 'Do you think that Magnolia was killed to collect five million dollars?'

'Enough is enough, Agent Mehrtens, we've been over this before. You have no basis for assuming that my client had any involvement in this matter. I must insist that you refrain from asking him questions that he simply cannot answer.'

Mehrtens frowned. The clock showed 11:21 a.m. They'd been at it for almost an hour and half. 'Well, thank you gentlemen, for coming in. We will be speaking to Dr. Delmontez and other staff at Caledonia, and we would appreciate it if you could make yourselves available should we need to speak to you any further.'

CHAPTER 12

The Kentucky Derby is contested seventy-odd miles down Route 64 from Lexington, at Churchill Downs racetrack in Louisville. For fifty-one weeks of the year the famous Twin Spires look out silently over a traditional but unremarkable oval racetrack, in a decidedly ordinary part of a far from exciting Kentucky town.

Stark concrete and breeze-blocked barns; empty, old-fashioned, and windswept, wooden duckboard grandstands; harboured a thousand echoes. 'Mint juleps!' the waiters would cry, 'Mint juleps!' There was not a dry eye in the house as the band played "My Old Kentucky Home" and one hundred and forty thousand, including an infield throng of over-fifty, would sing along as they wiped their eyes. And then, after the most exciting two minutes in sport, cheer their heroes home.

Now it was week number fifty-two and for seven magic days, leading up to the first Saturday in May, the circus of thoroughbred horse racing was in town.

Tom had been to Churchill Downs many times with his dad, though never to the big show. Today, thanks to his gregarious host, they were going in style, the whole hog: with lunch, a private box, and the right people. The smart people. The people who ran the sport of kings these days.

Much had happened over the past month in his world, but this game went on and the one thing about Mark was that he never left you time to feel sorry for yourself.

'This is an important stage for us, Tommy boy. Gotta be there and look the part. Gotta be where it matters. There aren't many occasions in our business when the world is watching, but this is still one of them.'

The Porsche had been in for the full works at the car wash and Mark's light blue linen suit, made for him by a tailor in Mumbai during a stopover he'd made visiting an Indian client on a horse charter the previous summer, had been cleaned and pressed. 'It's a marathon,' he said, 'fourteen fucking races! Gotta have deep pockets and plenty of stamina. First race is 11:00 a.m., can you believe that! And, by the time we get to post-time for the Derby, around six, with the humidity, the booze, the suffocating crowd, you'll be drained. We're just lucky that we'll have somewhere to sit down, in the box. Maybe next to some of the lovely ladies that'll be there. I wouldn't want to be in the infield or down in the grandstand for eight hours. Sheesh, shoulder to shoulder, long line-ups at the bars, dumb punters who can't make their minds up or simply don't know how to play, clogging up the windows. And they're paying through the nose for this torture. No sir, not for us. We goin' first class, and as guests. So, it's free!'

Atop the blue-look, Mark sported a nifty panama. And, after much persuasion, he'd convinced Tom that such headgear, beyond keeping off the sun's rays, was actually a cool accoutrement. The roof was down and, as they queued in traffic approaching the famous racetrack, the boys were able to engage pedestrians heading to the same destination, with their fold-up chairs and picnic coolers, and the local house owners, often out in the middle of the road soliciting clients to park on their lawns for the day. 'Twenty dollars! Safe and sound. We'll make sure it's here when you get back! Twenty dollars! Just twenty dollars! The closer you get, the more you pay. Twenty dollars! You can't beat it.'

It was barely ten o'clock, but the sun was high in the sky and it was going to be a beauty. A fast racetrack, thought Mark. So important for the horses to have no excuses, forget the fact that a rainy, muddy, and sloppy day made life miserable for all concerned.

A man in a suit cobbled together with what looked like several Union flags was hawking his tout sheet 'All today's winners! Just ten dollars! They're all here!'

I bet they are, thought Mark. Every sheet a different one!

'Oh, the sun,' sang Mark. 'It brings the ladies out, in their scanty outfits. You see, Tom, today, it's a fashion contest for them. This may be the Derby, but the fillies will be front and centre, too. Oh my, look at that babe.' Mark waved to a young girl in impossibly short white cut-off jeans and what looked like pink jockey's silks, exhorting drivers to park on her patch of grass. 'Hey darlin' you wanna hop in?' he called. The young lady blushed. 'Its twenty-five,' she said. 'And do you come with the twenty-five?' Mark laughed. Tom pulled the brim of his hat down.

Thanks to their generous hosts, Mark and Tom had a sticker for preferred parking and had been issued with special badges that spirited them past a host of officious-looking gatemen and security guards who were manning the turnstiles.

The horses for the first race were leaving the paddock, as the boys ascended in a clubhouse elevator to the sixth floor, where once more their credentials were scrutinized. As they were waiting for what seemed like the hundred and tenth time to be patted down and glared at, the tension was broken by a cry of 'Mark, darling!' and Tom's intrepid escort was engulfed in the very ample hug of a lady in a splendid light green dress and enormous cream hat, from under which he emerged with a blotch of bright red lipstick on his cheek.

'Tom, this is Lucy. Lucy, I want you to meet Tom Fraser.' Tom and Mark had decided not to qualify introductions every time with his unfortunate circumstances, so no mention was made of the association with Caledonia, his father's recent death, or the ongoing scandal that, of course, everyone was talking about.

'Tom, how nice to meet you. Lucy Waldman,' she said, offering her hand. 'Is this your first Derby? We have a runner in the sixth race today,' she gushed proudly. 'It's just so exciting to be here with so many people. So many famous people, on such a big day.'

Tom explained that this was his first Derby and asked Lucy who her horse was.

'Quintessential. He's a five-year-old. My husband Peter – he's over there, I will introduce you to him – he says that Quinty, as I call him, really likes the turf. Last time he ran at Keeneland and finished fourth, but they had taken the race off the turf and our trainer, Jim Graham , says that he's in a good spot today. Oh, it's so exciting to be here!'

They were now being escorted to the box section. So Mark bid Lucy adieu, suggesting that they should meet after the sixth, to hopefully toast a victory.

'How do you know all these people?' asked Tom, as they were led through a narrow passage that took them to the back of the stands, where their box's lunchroom looked out over the paddock below.

'Met the Waldmans at Saratoga a couple of years ago. Lovely people. They're from New York. Peter does something on Wall Street, but don't ask me what. They have a place out on the island, near Seacliff. I was actually playing golf in the horsemen's tournament at the MacGregor country club and Pete was in our four. I then saw them at the sales, and from time to time he's called me, when he wants some advice. But their trainer doesn't appreciate advisers, so I have played it cool. They're good people. No harm knowing them. Might be able to sell them a horse one day. You never know. It's just networking.'

Lunch was spectacular. T.J. Van der Meer's box accommodated eight seats out front and in the lunchroom a table had been laid for twelve, so that additional grazers, as he called them, could stop in for a visit during the afternoon. On a sideboard there was a most inviting display of cold food: salmon, prawns, oysters, and a myriad of salads and cheeses, all of which was dispensed by a team of neatly clad waiters, with Churchill Downs' famous Twin Spires logo on their chefs' jackets.

T.J. sat at the head of the table, with Jos Danvers and his wife Deidre either side. Missie welcomed the boys warmly. After encouraging them to dig in, she suggested that they should sit next to her and give her some winners. Mark didn't know the other guests, but there was all afternoon and another thirteen races ahead to become acquainted.

Doing the Derby in this sort of style required pacing the action. Races went off and some guests would leave the table to place their bets and then go out to the seats, at the front, to watch. Others were quite happy to watch the small closed-circuit TVs that were mounted on the walls, in the corners, scribbling on their programs. This was probably the only day all year that they'd go to the track, so finer points and direct involvement with any one particular race escaped them. It was just a day out: good food and elite company on a marquis occasion. They had no idea who the horses were, the different conditions of each race, nor who was even running in that year's Derby.

Some had cut out a list of runners and riders from their local newspaper as, to them, the *Daily Racing Form* was Double Dutch. So tapping into the many experts that were on hand and playing their hunches was just fine.

Missie Van der Meer explained that she was a hunch player. 'All my dear husband ever talks about is the racetrack. Horses, horses: breeding them, selling them, and of course all his one-track-minded friends. I decided a long time ago that this would drive me nuts. So, it just goes in one ear and out the other.' She smiled. 'I like Keeneland, and we go to Saratoga, and today is special. It's a day out. A chance to dress up. Isn't it just so much fun?' she winked at the boys. 'Billy Beagle, Teddy and their chums can have all their sales stuff, betting handle numbers, and bottom-line bullshit, but I'm happy betting my two-dollar bets. You know, I like to go down to the paddock – at Saratoga you can stand under the trees and watch the horses being saddled – but today the crowd is going to be just too much, so we'll have to smoke 'em out from up here! What do you boys like?'

Mark looked up from studying the past performances for the fifth race in his *Daily Racing Form*, knowing full well what he'd like: a stormy day, rain lashing against the window, log fire crackling, and the two of them snuggling between the sheets. 'Sorry, I missed that,' he said.

'Who do you boys like in the next race? I see you studying away, all that gobbledygook. To me, it's like the *Wall Street Journal* or some financial paper: just meaningless numbers.'

'Important numbers, though,' Mark replied. 'As they say, when you buy a Form - *Racing Form! Racing Form!* All the winners are right here.'

'Well, I like horses with two-word names, starting with the same letter. What do you call that? You know Battling Billy or Mighty Mouse. You know what I mean?'

'I think they call that alliteration,' piped in Tom.

'Why don't we play some Pick 3s. They have them running almost every race. Like here we can play the fifth, sixth, and seventh and maybe, even, the sixth, seventh, and eighth. Then, hopefully, we're always live with something,' said Mark.

'Hopefully is the optimal word,' Tom said, smiling.

Missie laughed. 'This sounds like fun.'

'I'll tell you what,' said Mark, 'on a day like today, with a big crowd of mostly uninformed bettors, the pools for each exotic are inflated and you get much better value, as many people bet on outsiders because they're a big price or they like the jockey's silks.'

'Or think he's cute.' Missie winked.

'Who's cute?' asked Tom.

'The jockey, you fool,' said Mark.

'I just think some of those Hispanic riders are so sexy,' said Missie. 'So handsome, so brave. OOOO-eeee, they're like little bull fighters!'

'Pound for pound, the best athletes in all of sports,' said Tom

'Ha! Ha!' laughed Mark. 'Are you including yourself in that category?'

'Of course! You're a rider, too?' blurted Missie.

Tom blushed. 'An aspiring one. So far, mostly unsuccessful.'

'The man's being too modest,' added Mark. 'He's a budding steeplechase star. Ridden winners in jolly old England, you know,' he joked.

'Oh my, I'm in the best company, then.' Missie beamed. 'I have two personal experts of form here.'

And some, thought Mark. 'Ok. If we budget a hundred bucks per investment, or fifty two-buck permutations that is, we can play three or four in each race or, if there is a banker, play six or seven in the other two races and hope to come up with a longshot. I know it's nice to win. But, if you pick the favourites all the time, we're hardly going to cover our outlay.'

'But I like winning,' said Missie. 'I just love going up to the window and collecting after each race.'

'Well, let's try to win something that's worth collecting,' replied Mark. 'Here, for example, we have full fields of twelve in the fifth and sixth that look pretty open, and in the seventh there are only eight runners and you can narrow that one down to two horses. So, let's pick five horses in each of the first two races and play them on to the top two in the seventh. That's a hundred bucks: five times five times two, equals fifty times two dollars, got it?'

'Your friend Lucy likes her horse in the sixth. Quinty something?' said Tom.

'Indeed. We'll put him in,' said Mark.

'Well, in this next race, I like Burlington Bertie, gotta put him in,' said Missie.

'A push. But we'll put him in. Would be a nice price,' muttered Mark, deep in his *Form*.

'I like the horse from Canada on the turf,' said Tom. 'Phil Britain doesn't ship his horses unless they're well meant. He's a 27% trainer. Gotta put Muskoka Mist in.'

'What do you mean by 27%, Tom?' Missie asked.

'That's his win rate. Anything over twenty is good. You get over thirty and people start thinking you've got the juice. You know, you're cheating, doping.'

'They do that? Really?' asked Missie.

'Too often. Too bloody often,' muttered Mark. 'Your T.J. would tell you that if he wasn't all wrapped up in this image nonsense. You know, denying anything bad, so the people at PETA don't get bent out of shape. Right here, in Kentucky, its as bad, if not worse, than anywhere.'

'It's competition, Ms. Van der Meer,' said Tom. 'If someone's using something to improve the performance of their horses, a trainer I mean, then the owners of other horses will ask their trainer if he's doing the same thing, when they're not winning and the other guy is. It's tough. If you don't take chances, you risk losing your horses to another trainer who will.'

'But don't they get caught?' asked Missie. 'And it's Missie, not Ms. Van der Meer, ya hear?'

'They do and they don't,' said Mark. 'Every state has different regulations. New York, Canada, they're the toughest. Here, not so much.'

'Some trainers are chemists, not horsemen,' added Tom. 'They rely on their vets. Some couldn't train ivy to grow up a wall without their vet's help.'

'That's awful,' said Missie

'Well, let's not spoil a lovely afternoon worrying about horse racing's issues. Let's try and figure out some winners and make some money!' said Mark.

At that moment, a large man in a sickly, pale green suit, carrying an overladen plate of goodies from the sideboard, launched his very substantial frame into a chair opposite Mark. The table shuddered and he introduced himself as George Boyce, from Oklahoma City.

George announced that he and his wife, Janice, who arrived meekly in his wake with a much smaller plate, had been snarled in the traffic. 'One day a year they get a crowd and they can't manage it. Couldn't organize a piss-up in a brewery.' He laughed at his own humour. 'Then those gatemen didn't recognize our passes. Bloody Philistines, that's what they are. Fascists, imported to give us poor hard-done-by suckers a tough time. Missed the first three darned races!'

'Oh, George,' bleated Janice, 'they saved you from losing your money. You know you didn't like the first few winners. Now settle down and enjoy your lunch.'

George fumed and stuffed his mouth.

'Well, hello,' said his long-suffering wife. 'I'm Janice. I guess y'all have met George?' she tittered apologetically. 'It's always the same, but he gets over it. Don't you, George?'

By now Boyce had spread his Form out across the table and into Janice's mayonnaise. Who the hell is this guy? thought Mark, and what have we done to deserve his company.

'Well, it's real good to meet you folks,' said Missie. 'You must be friends of Teddy's?'

'And you are?' spluttered Boyce, with his mouth full.

'I'm Missie, Teddy's wife. As I was just saying to these boys, I don't go to the track often, but today is special. And I'm lucky to have expert advice. This, by the way, is Mark and Tom. Mark is from Ireland. Tom is a steeplechase rider. He's a Lexington boy.'

'Steeplechases. They have all that jumpin' stuff, don't they?,' said Boyce. 'Hard enough to pick a winner on the flat, I say.'

'Well, Mr. Boyce, you must excuse us,' said Mark, 'as we have some bets to commission. It's been real nice meeting you. Come on team, we don't want to get shut out.'

'No way!' boomed Boyce. 'No sir, there's no excuse for that.'

'As if that's never happened to you dear,' said Janice, 'he'll be late for his own funeral, I say.'

'Well, happy punting,' said Mark, hastily ushering Tom and Missie from the table.

Standing in line at the PMU window, he apologised to Missie. 'Please forgive me, but we just had to get away from that guy. That man is a dose. How did he get invited in here?'

'Well, I don't rightly know,' said Missie. 'I'll have to ask Teddy. I'm sure he's some political guy. Maybe a senator or something? Someone Teddy and Billy need to help them with whatever they're doing in Frankfort or Washington. Maybe he's a casino guy?'

Fucking loud a-hole, that's what he is, thought Mark, but in the company of a charming lady he was not about to make a bigger issue out of it. 'Ok, we'll play the alliteration horses for you, Missie; there is one in the fifth, Burlington Bertie, the two-horse and two in the sixth, the two and nine, and we know about the Waldman horse, Quintessential, in the sixth. Any fancies, Tommy boy?'

The lines were lengthy: full of hesitant punters who were unfamiliar with the procedure. But the team had plenty of time, as they heard the bugle announce that the runners were coming out onto the track for the fifth race, with six minutes to post listed on the monitor above the betting window.

Mark placed their bets, collected his ticket, and suggested that they should go out and watch the race from the box at the front, that overlooked the racetrack.

'Boy, this is nice,' said Tom, as he gazed out over the busy racetrack before them. 'We're right on the wire! These are sensational seats!'

'These are Teddy's Bluegrass seats,' said Missie, smiling and waving to friends around them. 'Do you see the lady in the pink hat, two boxes over? That's Melody Chance, her husband is the state's governor. They're in Billy Beagle's box.'

The horses were circling behind the gate, in front of the stands, and the enormous crowd was buzzing in anticipation. Then it was post time: the bell rang, the gate opened, and they were off to the sound of a furious din that far outdid the thunder of hooves disappearing towards the clubhouse turn. The field was then temporarily obscured behind the marquees, screens, and TV towers of the infield as they hurtled down the backstretch, the commentator's drone but a distraction, as close to a quarter million eyes focused on TV monitors.

'How are we doing?' yelled Missie.

The field was by now approaching the top of the stretch. As the horses fanned out and thundered towards them, Mark trained his binoculars on the leaders.

'And it's Burlington Bertie who has come through on the rail, to take it up,' boomed the race caller.

'Go on Bertie, my son!' yelled Mark. Everyone was standing and it was difficult to see.

'Is that my Burlington?' cried Missie. The crowd roared and, in a blanket finish, four horses raced to the wire. It was hard to call. As the cheering subsided you could hear the speculative – and hopeful, thought Mark – calls of those who thought they may have cashed. 'It was the two. The rail got it,' someone shouted.

I bloody well hope so, thought Mark. Everyone was glued to the monitors and infield tote board, as a replay of the closing stages was played. It looked like the two might have held on, grimly. The nine-horse had finished fastest of all, on the outside. He was the favourite. Mark thought that the other two, sandwiched between, were the one and the eight. The team had the favourite, but then so would so many others that they didn't need him. But he was better than the one or the eight, as they didn't have them.

It was close and the crowd hummed in anticipation. Two favourites had already prevailed, pockets were full, and the alcohol was flowing. Then a roar. Not the sort that signified another chalk winner, but one that had a strangulated groan descant: it was 2-9-1-8. The two-horse, Burlington Bertie, had held on, at twenty to one. As the returns were posted, they showed a return of $42.40 for the winner, $16 for place, and $10.20 to show. An upset, and the new team were off to a great start with their first Pick 3.

'What does that mean?' enquired a visibly excited Missie.

'It means we're live. And live with a major player! That $42-winner will have knocked out a lot of people. We need a drink and we must buy some insurance,' said Mark.

'What do you mean insurance?' asked Missie, as they repaired to the lunchroom.

'What he means,' said Tom, 'is that we are now in a position to cash a big

Pick 3 ticket, if our other legs hold up - if the horses that we've selected in the sixth and seventh races win. So, because we could, technically, collect maybe a thousand dollars or more, depending on the prices of the next two winners, we should protect ourselves by betting on the dangers. If we cash the ticket we are rolling, big time. On the other hand, if one of the horses that we haven't played in the second and third legs of the bet wins, and we've had an insurance bet on them, we'll at least cover our stake, if we're lucky.'

'Oh, my goodness, there's so much going on. I love this, it's so exciting!' exclaimed Missie.

'Winning is exciting,' said Tom. 'You can't beat it.'

Back at the table George Boyce was not celebrating. Rather, he was letting anyone within earshot know that Rudy Vasquez was a crook. 'Bloody pinhead,' he remonstrated, 'the nine-horse,' that had presumably carried his money, 'was tons the best. What's he doing going five-wide around the first turn? The man's not got a good post position. So take him back and over to the rail. Save ground. He went fifty yards further than he needed to and gets beat a dirty nose, on the wire. Sheesh! I could have ridden him better!'

Janice looked nervous as she played with a meringue on her plate.

Mark requested wine from the steward and the team toasted a good start.

'So, what's such a big deal?' enquired their angry neighbour.

'We're live in a Pick 3, with the winner, a $42 horse,' said Tom.

'Yes, I picked him,' said Missie. 'I just love those alliteration horses. You know, with two words…'

'Yes, I know. Two bloody words starting with the same fucking letter. Might as well have used a pin. I can't stand it,' moaned George.

'Don't be such a bad loser, George,' said Janice, 'lovely name, Burlington Bertie. I'd have bet a few dollars myself, if I'd known.'

'Well read the bloody program, woman,' snapped Boyce as he flung his own down on the table and heaved himself out of his chair. 'I need some fresh air,' he said as he lumbered out of the room.

'Phew,' said Mark. 'What a game! Now then - let's go down to the paddock and check out Quintessential and maybe chat up the Waldmans?'

This was easier said than done as the large crowd was in full swing. Mark suggested that Tom play the horses they hadn't played in the second leg of their Pick 3 on top of their selections, in $5 Exactas, just in case. There were twelve runners. This meant playing seven horses on top of five, for an outlay of $35. The seven were all longshots. So, if one of them came in, it would be a handsome payout that would more than compensate for the initial $100 Pick 3 investment.

As they neared the paddock a nine-deep throng was basking in the bright sunshine, amidst a sea of hats and perspiration, and Mark suddenly found his hand enveloped.

'Lead on,' a voice whispered. His heart missed a beat. Where to, he thought, smiling. But then the way parted and dead ahead was a member of Churchill Downs' security, guarding the entrance to the paddock with his life. Undaunted he said, 'I'm with Ms. Van der Meer, here.'

Not missing a beat, Missie chimed in. 'Yes. There's Teddy, over there.' And, in the blink of an eye, they were in.

It has often been said that owning a racehorse provides around-the-clock anxiety. Once the hammer falls or your claim is successful the metre starts ticking and the yo-yo of emotions swings into gear. Some owners are entranced by the ride, putting total faith in their trainer and relishing every shot of adrenalin along the way: good workouts, encouraging bulletins from the barn, along with the usual setbacks of coughs, colds, ulcers, and a multitude of different manifestations of lameness. The usual valleys of despair, sure, but always confident of imminent victory. Others make the experience sheer torture by second guessing their trainer's every move, taking bad advice from ill-informed sources, and agonizing over every hiccup. In short, they just don't enjoy the ride. A bit like part-time golfers who blame their clubs for every bad shot.

The former is rarer than the latter, especially if they're not winning. But each trainer has his own MO when it comes to dealing with clients. Today Jim Graham was at his most congenial, as the Waldmans were lapping up their moment in the sun. He was old-school and nothing would have upset him more than to be told he had to run a horse where he knew they did not belong merely to make the owners happy. It would reflect poorly upon him, and the stats mattered. Today Quinty belonged, and a good showing, in front of a large audience here at Churchill, and audiences watching from thousands of simulcast outlets and cable networks around the globe was good for business. Nonetheless, Mark knew better than to get in the way and make fatuous comments at the wrong moment. So, he and Missie blended into the crowd; she checking out the hats, and he what was under them; always conscious that his hand was still being held gently. A good thing there are so many people and everyone is so preoccupied, he thought. Not good for business having T.J. a jealous man.

Jim Graham had Quinty turned out beautifully. A deep reddy brown chestnut, with a somewhat lighter, almost flaxeny mane that had been expertly plaited, he looked a picture. The Waldmans and their trainer were chatting to

Jerry Barton, their jockey from New York, who was in to ride in the Derby, later that afternoon. Since being united with his charge, Jerry and Quinty had never missed the board, on the turf. This was a step up in class. But, if Jimmy Graham felt they belonged, they had to be taken seriously.

The horses were mounted and their excited connections filed out of the paddock. By the time that Mark and Missie got back to the box they were at the post, so they went straight out front to watch.

Quinty ran his heart out, briefly hitting the front as the field turned for home, eliciting loud yells from the Waldmans, two boxes over. But he tired in the final sixteenth of a mile, to finish a good third behind a genuine Grade 1 horse, with top class European form, who was edged out by Tom's selection, Muskoka Mist, at 8/1.

'Let's stay away from the table,' suggested Tom, 'as we don't need Mr. Know-it-All getting jealous.'

'Don't worry about him,' said Missie. 'It's his wife I feel sorry for! We're fine, just here. So where do we stand?'

'Well, we have two horses in the seventh, the third leg of our Pick 3. And I reckon this is strictly a two-horse race. The one-horse, Lightsout Larry, is the speed. He has the rail and, if he gets an easy lead, he'll be tough to catch. But we really don't want him to win, as he'll be odds-on and I'm hoping that there is some competition for the lead, up front, and our other horse, Outboard, who is a closer, can run him down. We have now invested $135, with the insurance on round two. So I think we should let these two ride.'

It had been a sultry and humid Kentucky afternoon. Six races down and six more ahead before the Derby. 'Mint Juleps!' a voice cried. And a jovial waiter proffered those in the box a tray of the delicious local beverages, spilling over with ice cubes and mint leaves. 'Mint Juleps! Celebrate, if you're a winner! Drown your sorrows, if not! Mint Juleps! Mint Juleps! You can't beat 'em!'

'Would you boys like one?' asked Missie. 'They are so refreshing. Here, three please.'

'And how are you today, Ma'am,' said the smiling black face. 'Knockin' 'em dead at the windows?'

'Well, we're hoping,' said Missie, as she handed over $45 for the three amber drinks. 'I'm in good company and we're live, as they say, in this Pick 3.'

'I'll be rootin' for youse'. And thank you, ma'am,' said their amiable thirst quencher, as he accepted her generous tip. 'Mint Juleps! As easy as one-two-three. Get 'em here! Mint Juleps! You can't beat 'em!' And then he was gone, congratulating and consoling, along the way.

Now the horses were emerging onto the track, below. Lightsout Larry was on his toes, prancing beside his lead pony, as his rider Rudy Vasquez perched gingerly above, lightly holding the base of his mane. The combo was listed at two to five on the board. And a lot of chalk players would be looking to collect what appeared to be an easy 40% return on their money, over the next minute and twenty-odd seconds. It was seven eighths of a mile, perhaps beyond Larry's best. But he was three for five when he'd ventured a furlong beyond his preferred distance of three quarters of a mile and, if he got an easy lead, he usually was able to hold on and bring the bacon home.

Owned by a syndicate from Miami, who had claimed him for $50,000 two years before, he'd been a revelation since being turned over to his new conditioner, Frank Fernie. Now a bone fide stakes horse, not only in Florida, but also New York and California, some, including his previous connections, wondered what Fernie was using, which in racetrack parlance meant what magic potion had his new handler introduced to bring about such an amazing improvement in form? Whatever it was, Larry was on a roll and although this was going to be his debut in Kentucky, the local, friendly spit box was not going to be the reason he failed today.

From high above, Mark trained his binoculars on the parade. His little syndicate's fortunes were riding upon the one and two here. And, by contrast, the two-horse, Outboard, presented a completely different picture: seemingly unfazed by the noisy crowd and sultry conditions, he hobby-horsed to post, his powerful dark quarters radiating good health. Today he was being ridden by the wylie Joe Magee. At forty-two, probably past his best. But, with jockeys' titles in his resumé and well over three hundred stakes victories to his credit, punters ignored him at their peril. Mark knew this and, as back-up to the big favourite, he felt he had the bases covered. Outboard was listed at two to one, second choice.

At Churchill, the seven-furlong gate is set back in a chute, partially obscured by temporary bleachers and a large marquee, on big days like today. So when the track announcer interrupted the buzz with his 'They'rrrrre at the post! And they'rrrrrre off!!!' It was a few strides before the field came into view.

'And it's Lightsout Larry,' he called with great gusto and extra emphasis upon the lightsout bit, 'by three, as he breaks sharply.' The annoucer then went on to list the rest of the field, as they pursued the hot favourite through the first quarter mile. 'And Outboard, bringing up the rear, some ten lengths off this fast pace that's being set by Lightsout Larry.'

'What's happening? What's happening?' cried Missie.

'Well, it's good and bad,' said Tom. 'We have the favourite, who is in the lead and will now be tough to catch. But our other horse, who would pay us a much better return, seems to have missed the break.'

'They've gone a half in forty-four and two. Lightsout Larry, on his own, looking like he's gonna wire this field. Lightsout Larry by five, as they turn for home. Valiant Knight pursues him, with What's Up Doc and Outboard picking up the field. Lightsout Larry by five, leading them home. Valiant Knight fading, as Outboard closes fast. Lightsout Larry holding on. Outboard really motoring. Lightsout Larry, Outboard. Too close to call!'

The two horses flew past the wire, locked together. The photo sign went up and Mark, Tom, and Missie let out a cheer. 'Well, we got it, whatever happens. I just hope the two got there. Let it be two,' shouted Tom.

They waited. A good win or a great win?

But no, the numbers flashed on the board: 1-2-5-3. The favourite had held on grimly by the shortest of margins. They were winners. But, before they had time to celebrate or begin calculating what this meant, they were rudely interrupted by an extraordinary noise and they turned to see a slightly inebriated George Boyce, running between the boxes like an excited football player who has just scored a goal. 'Rudy's my man! Rudy's my man! There's only one Rudy Vasquez! All the way Rudy! Ha! Ha!'

'What an absolute turkey that man is,' exclaimed Tom, as the jubilant Boyce continued in circles with his arms out, presumably imitating a plane, 'Lightsout Larry! Shame it isn't Lightsout George from one of my punches!'

'Now, now, Tom. The man is just having fun,' said Mark. 'Probably the first winner he's backed since Lassie was a pup. Let's go in, have a drink, and see what we have made.'

In the dining room, Boyce was exultant, ordering champagne. 'Wire to wire. Made every post the winning post. Never in doubt. That's the way I like it!'

On the monitor the horses were returning to be unsaddled and excited members of the Everglades Stable were crowding into the winner's circle to have their photo taken with Larry. 'I reckon he'll pay $2.80 with maybe an Exactor of $7,' Boyce continued. But no, there was a hush, as the track announcer declared that the rider of number two, Outboard, has claimed foul against the winner. Hold all tickets!

There was a murmur.

'Foul? What's he talking about? My horse went wire to wire. Who is this guy, Magee? Crazy! This number is not coming down!' But Boyce sounded worried.

Just then the voice of the announcer confirmed that 'a foul had been claimed for interference at the break, leaving the gate,' and the monitor showed a head-on shot as the field exited their stalls, from which it was very evident that the horse on the rail had veered out sharply and cannoned into the horse on his outside, the two-horse, Outboard, who was knocked sideways, losing several lengths. This had all been obscured from the stands by the temporary bleachers and maybe the favourite had shied away from the large marquee, just inside the rail? Whatever, it looked serious.

'He's coming down,' said a voice from the rear of the box. 'He annihilated him!'

'Jesus Christ!' Boyce was sweating. 'Fucking pinhead! I don't believe it.'

'George! Please keep your voice down,' exclaimed Janice. 'I'm awfully sorry,' she said to nobody in particular,' he gets so excited.'

'Never mind, Mrs. Boyce,' said Missie. 'He could stay up. You know, the stewards don't like to disqualify a short-priced favourite on a big day like this. It just reinforces the public's notion that racing is fixed. We have both horses. So fingers crossed!' She winked at an anxious-looking Janice Boyce, who wasn't looking forward to her husband's reaction to an imminent reverse.

Boyce paced up and down and released his gut that had been straining all afternoon against the constriction of his waistcoat. The sweat poured down his ruddy cheeks.

Numbers 1 and 2 were flashing on the board. The crowd buzzed. Then an audible groan was heard, followed by muted yells, presumably from Outboard supporters, and the board went momentarily blank. Then it was 2 over 1 and George Boyce pounded his fist into the table, upsetting glasses and coffee cups. Mark looked at Tom. We can't laugh, or this guy might just turn the table over, he thought. But this is hilarious. He bit his lip and winked at Missie, giving her a thumbs-up, below table level, out of sight of their disintegrating fellow diner.

'That's it, Janice! We're outta here! Should never have come. First the fucking traffic. Miss the first three races. Then this fucking spic excuse for a rider. He couldn't ride a sodding tricycle. Then these stewards! Fuck! You can't win!'

'That's racing, George,' implored Janice. 'It's like golf. If you can't deal with the bad shots, give it up.' As her fuming husband exited the box, with his long-suffering wife in his wake, she added, 'If you think this is bad, you don't want to see him on a golf course.'

While this virtuoso meltdown was going on, a security guard had been summoned and he now appeared on the scene, looking menacing. 'There has been a call regarding a disturbance,' he said.

'No worries, officer,' said Mark. 'Mr. Boyce is just leaving. He has a 6 p.m. twilight tee-time.'

Everyone laughed. Such entertainment. Such fun for those three Pick 3 winners of 2-2-2 for $1,400. A net profit of $1,265, or a handy $422 each!

2-2-2! Mark wondered what Boyce would have made of that. Beginners luck, eh!

After the dq (disqualification) kerfuffle things quietened down. Eight races in the books, six to go, with the big one looming. For many it was a day-long, alcohol-fueled extravaganza in the sun, on the one day of the year that the infield was opened to spectators, who often didn't end up seeing much racing but sure drank a lot of booze and had a whale of a time.

In the grandstands those without reserved seats, who had arrived early to claim their vantage points, jostled elbow to elbow as they sought the shade and somewhere to perch. It was, in effect, a marathon test of endurance.

But, high up in the boxes, tea was being served and Missie Van der Meer took her now-flush betting partners through to the NHRA and Breeders' Cup box, where Billy Beagle was entertaining guests from racing jurisdictions throughout North America and overseas, most prominent of whom Tom immediately noticed was Hector Delmontez with his ever-increasing entourage.

'There's your man,' said Mark, provocatively.

'He's not my man and I'm certainly not his,' Tom replied, testily.

'And Bog, too! I wondered what happened to him. Obviously found himself better digs,' Mark continued.

'Well, hello there, friends.' Hector embraced Missie and motioned for her and the boys to join his table. 'I'm sure you know most people here better than I do. So good to see you. Tom, I want to introduce you to Johnny Ward-Clark from England.'

Ward-Clark grinned and extended a hand without rising from his chair. 'Tom has been working in England, where he was an amateur rider,' Hector enthused. 'Johnny is with the Classic Bloodstock Services group out of Newmarket, who are going to be working with me on my new syndicate.'

'That's exciting,' said Tom automatically, without meaning it at all.

'Yes. I'm over here because my bosses at CBS had to pop back for the Guineas Meeting at Newmarket,' Johnny gushed. 'My first trip to the Derby. What a cracking good day! What a crowd!'

Yes, thought Mark, and trust you to have weaseled your way into the holy of holies.

As it turned out, the hot favourite, a hitherto unbeaten colt from California, named Martial Arts, sent chalk players home happy, coming from off a fast pace to win the Kentucky Derby convincingly by three lengths, and set tongues wagging about his chances to land the elusive Triple Crown.

A syndicate made up of a WWE fighter, an ex-NFL football player, and a one-time B-movie and porn star celebrated in the winner's circle; and TV announcers proclaimed that this fusion of sports, indoors and out, was good for the game. And racetrack executives guffawed, deluding themselves that their prayers had been answered.

Or was it just the booze and the guile of the likes of Hector and Bog?

The sun had shone and a festive crowd of 145,000 had set a betting record of just over $250 million during the afternoon. Churchill Downs was a happy place. Billy Beagle and his friends were happy, and Mark and Tom were in pocket, if a teeny bit exhausted, as they made their way through the litter -strewn parking lots to where they hoped their car was waiting for them.

CHAPTER 13

There was no doubting the change of mood at the field office on Monday morning. Gone were Mehrtens, Kirchner, and Company. and in their place a much slicker-looking crew. Different getup, altogether. Better cut suits. FBI.

As usual, Bernie Shaefer had met his client in the parking lot and the two of them, seasoned by previous encounters in the same stuffy, airless room, now sat silently, while FBI Senior Special Agent Chuck Bowman went through the minutes from earlier depositions; the silence only interrupted by the turning of pages and the hum of the antiquated air conditioning as it struggled to mitigate the stale, fetid air.

The distant wailing of a siren could be heard. Which actual division of local law enforcement, ambulance, or fire services, was irrelevant to the matter in hand.

Bowman breathed in deeply and looked up, bridging his hands on the table in front of him, and resting his chin on the platform that he'd created. He, like so many in his profession, looked ex-military. Probably just over six foot of trim muscle, buzz cut, angular and tanned features, and piercing blue eyes. Tom figured him to be mid-forties; probably, after the marines, he'd attended the FBI Academy, advanced quickly through the ranks, and was now a contemporary G-man. Trilby replaced by iPhone. Definitely a twenty-first-century gumshoe. No nonsense here.

'Mister, er, Fraser,' he hesitated, 'thank you for coming in.' His tone was level baritone, akin to his bulk. Probably upstate New York, maybe Rochester or Syracuse, by the sound of things.

'I want to take you back' – he pronounced it almost 'beck,' in the New England-style – 'to your meeting with Agent Kirchner.' He paused while he read through a passage in the notes in front of him, continuing, 'the agent asked you…and I'm just reading here…what would a foal from the mare Magnolia have made at auction, had he or she ever been put up for sale? Is that right?' He looked up, raising his head and disengaging his fingers.

'We have already dealt with this, Agent Bowman.' Shaefer paused before going on. 'This is a hypothetical situation and, as your notes will I'm sure tell you, my client was out of the country and not conversant with his father's affairs on the farm.'

'That may be so, sir. But the forensics results are inconclusive, leading the coroner, our investigative team, and the insurance company's adjusters to wonder what did actually happen, why, and,' he paused, 'whether someone may have taken the mare? There just is no residual evidence: no charred skeleton, no halter. Don't most valuable horses have their names and sometimes pedigrees etched onto brass plates on their halters? If everything was completely incinerated, and I gather that this was an intense fire, wouldn't a brass name-plate survive, or the rings and buckles, perhaps?'

'That I don't know,' said Shaefer. 'But what, if that was or wasn't the case, has that got to do with Mr. Fraser?'

'Well, sir,' again he paused, as if struggling with what he either knew that they didn't know or how he was going to couch his message. 'We have a bit of a problem because Senor Delmontez, the owner of Caledonia Farms, has suggested in his claim that, in his opinion, if there is any doubt about the death of his mare, she may have been stolen before the fire.'

'That is preposterous,' blurted out Shaefer, 'and who do you think stole a heavily pregnant mare and spirited her away, knowing full well that she and any progeny of her's would be worthless without provenance? You need papers to authenticate…' he trailed off. 'Anyway, as we have now said three times, my client, Tom Fraser, was four thousand miles away in Europe when all of this happened. How could he possibly have been involved in, or have had any knowledge of, such an absurdly unlikely scenario?'

'Well, we have interviewed Senor Delmontez and subpoened the farm's bank accounts and it is concerning that Mr. Fraser Sr. was apparently so indebted to his new partners, Condor Bloodstock, etcetera, sir.'

'Agent Bowman, even if I advised my client not to say anything, as is his right, I know he has nothing further to add to what he's already told you. And, I don't think you have any grounds for detaining him.'

'No, sir. But I wish to advise you and your client that this case now involves not only potential insurance fraud, narcotics smuggling, and money laundering, but also murder, in the light of Senor Delmontez's recent testimony and suggestions that one of the deceased, Robert Fraser, may have had accomplices. We will be continuing our investigations that now include Interpol, the USDA, and federal narcotics agencies both here in the United States and in Venezuela, where Condor is registered.'

After Shaefer had left, Tom sat in the jeep. It was mid-morning and the temperature had already risen into the eighties. It was going to be another hot and humid Kentucky day and this heat had combusted the familiar racetrack odour that seemed to permeate the vehicles of all those who frequented such places. Years of dirt, damp straw, moldy hay, manure, sweat, and seasoned leather, pounded by disinfectant and saddle soap, combined into a noxious cocktail. As nursing homes retain smells of urine, disinfectant, and bleach, so stables the world over stink in a standardized way, too. But Tom was oblivious to all of this, in his own little twilight zone.

◆　◆　◆

It was just over a month since his world had been turned upside down. But it seemed like an age. What had happened? What his life was before and the last few weeks seemed part of separate orbits, ones that had spun wildly off course. Everything, recently, had been compartmentalized: living from day to day, buoyed by charitable encouragement and support. But how much of it was sincere, he wondered? And now…now that the dust was settling, what do I do now?

This trance was suddenly interrupted by the ring of his cell phone. The sound startled him, as it was different to the phone he was used to. The caller was not identified, and in his somewhat disengaged mood he answered blankly.

The voice on the other end was local, by the distinctive Kentucky drawl, but sounded nervous too. 'Hello,' a pause, 'is that Tommy Fraser? This here's Randy Dobbs.' The line wasn't especially clear and there seemed to be quite a bit of background noise, as if the caller was in a bar or some crowded location.

'Who?' asked Tom.

'It's Randy…Randy Dobbs. I worked up on the farm, for your daddy. You gave me this number out at Flo's last Thursday. You know, Flo's Diner out on the Versailles Pike? Said to call you?'

'Oh, yes, Randy.' Tom was alert now and sat up from where he'd been slouching, in his funk. 'Thanks for calling.'

'You and me's gotta meet,' Randy went on, 'can we get together soon, as there's some bad stuff goin' on, out at the farm. At Caledonia. Stuff you need to know about.'

'Where are you, Randy? And where would be the best place for you? Do you have wheels? If not, just let me know a time and place that works.'

'This here's a pay phone. I'm down on Courtney Street, at Joe Louis'. It's a bar. Where are you at?'

'Not far at all, Randy. You just stay there, and I'll be with you in fifteen minutes.'

As he hung up and drove out onto Circle 4, the air conditioning kicked in and sharpened his thinking. A few minutes before he wasn't going anywhere, and the more he'd contemplated that the more hopeless his situation had seemed. But here was, perhaps, a lifeline to find out what had happened. It wasn't mid-day yet, but it had sounded to Tom that Randy may have had a few beverages already. His nervousness was a forewarning.

◆ ◆ ◆

Joe Louis' had seen better days and the neon sign announcing Liquor was askew and not illuminated, as all such signs always seemed to be, beckoning twenty-four hour refugees from life's worries. It was on the corner of Courtney and Brown, in a rundown part of town, and the vehicles in the parking lot, out back, were of the beaten-up variety: several sporting gun racks, heavy-duty bumpers, and Confederate flags. This was a workin' man's drinkin' hole: a bit of country music on the juke box, but precious few comforts beyond steel bar stools and tables beside a functional but amply stocked bar, once the eyes got used to the gloom.

Randy was sitting alone in a booth, towards the back. Beyond him a passage led to washrooms and an exit door that had obviously been involved in some serious beatings, adorned with a poster announcing that 'You want credit? You have come to the wrong place!' And some apparently dissatisfied patron, maybe being forcibly ejected via this particular channel, had scrawled 'Fuck You!' on it.

On the table was a packet of Marlboroughs and a half-drunk bottle of Budweiser. Their owner sported a stained white T-shirt atop faded and frayed blue jeans and a pair of grubby sneakers. What little greasy hair he had left was matted to his small head by sweat, and the beady little eyes that peered out from the darkness left little doubt that his current lot in life was a precarious one.

Once upon a time he'd fancied himself as a rider and with his diminutive frame had shown some promise until he'd lost his bug (apprentice weight allowance) about the time his wife realized he wasn't going to make it and had moved on to what she'd hoped were greener pastures. And Randy had slid down the unforgiving racetrack drain into oblivion. The worse things got, the worse were his mounts and frequent falls, and, once the injuries had kicked in and his heart had given out, the opioids had taken over. He was now ground crew, from whence there was no salvation from a state of permanent insolvency and hopelessness.

'There you are,' said Tom, sitting down opposite on the cracked vinyl-covered bench of the booth.

'What'ya havin',' said Randy. 'Me, I'm just nursin' this here Bud.'

A barmaid had materialized and Tom ordered two Buds. His eyes had, by this time, become accustomed to the gloom and he could see that, despite its unappealing exterior, Joe Louis' had a decent clientele: maybe a dozen feeder-hat clad drinkers at the bar and a similar number gathered around a pool table, beyond. Most were watching the highlights from a ball game on the TVs, and the buzz of voices and that commentary meant that their conversation was confined to the booth.

Randy chewed a nail nervously. So Tom made the running.

'How long were you at Caledonia?' he asked.

'Almost three years. I had been over at Turfway and my boss, Harry Green, was shipping to Calder for the winter, so I just said to myself, Randy, you gotta stop chasin'. Tack room to tack room, never gettin' nowhere. So I ran into your daddy one day, at the sales, as Mr. Green had sent up a couple, to unload in the horses-in-training sale they have at Fasig-Tipton, he and Mr. Green being good friends. And Harry, he said Bob, Mr. Fraser, I mean, your daddy,' Randy looked keenly at Tom.' He said, Randy, here, is looking to quit the track and get himself a steady job and a bit of security. And the rest is history, as they say. A fine man your daddy was,' he added, looking sheepish.

'So, what did y'all do at Caledonia, Randy?' Tom sipped his Bud.

'Well, to start with it was just about anything. The best part was that they gave me my own place. A lil ol' apartment in a house down by the back gate. It weren't much. But it was my home. I cut the grass, painted fences. Then, at foaling time, we was real busy. So I was like the swingman: here, there, and everywhere. Even got to take some stock up to the sales. The boss trusted me. Like I bin' around horses all my life, Tom. There ain't nuthin' I ain't seen. Do just 'bout anything.'

'So, what happened? Why are you no longer there? Don't they need you? Who have they got running the place now?'

'It started about two years ago. I guess I must have been at the farm for a year or so. One day mister Fraser brings this Spanish-looking guy around the farm, Dr. Delontez, or something like that; he's from South America, you know?'

'Yes, I've met him. He's from Venezuela, actually.'

'Well, this South American guy, he starts showing up real regular. Then one day I'm sent to Cincinnati with the horse van to pick up some horses that came in on a plane from Chile. Yes, Chile, I think it was. And there were all these Hispanic guys talking Spanish, and I bring two horses to the farm with this guy Ramon. Real weird guy, never said a word, just smoked a cigar. One of them cheap green one's from Puerto Rico. It stunk!'

'So, when you got back to the farm, what did this Ramon guy do?'

'We put the two colts in the old red barn, away from the mares, because of a quarantine thing. And Dr. Delontez was there with your daddy and some other guy who I think was a vet. And the groom who came with them, this Ramon guy, went off with Dr. Delontez. They seemed to know each other pretty well. So, after that we got used to seeing vans coming and going with more horses and their South American grooms, I just thought, at the time, that it was none of my business and that these guys were new clients of your daddy's.'

Randy was now in full flow and, without interrupting him, Tom signalled for two more Buds. 'So, you say that things started,' he paused, 'things started changing. What do you mean?'

'It just seemed that these guys were taking over. You know, giving orders. And Chuck and the men who bin' there all this time were at first confused and then not happy. One time, it must have happened in the middle of the night, this colt that had just arrived from South America got cast and broke his leg. We came in in the morning and he's heading out on the meat wagon. And Curtis wanted to know who was in charge, you know, who came in with this colt and who was watchin' him? You know, after a long trip, to a strange place, this colt's gonna be...,' he hesitated, 'disor-i-ented...is that how you say it?' Randy smiled as he mangled the word. 'It was bad management, like. Yet, you know, the thing that struck me was that nobody made a big issue about it. Nobody seemed to care. Here's this fine-looking colt comes in, breaks his leg, get's put down and carted off, and everyone carries on as if nothing has happened. That ain't normal.'

Tom thought about what Martin O'Sullivan at BGT had said about accidents.

'Anyway, we was just doin' our jobs. And, honest, everything seemed ok. Then, what's it now? Maybe six weeks ago, I hear your daddy and some of the Spanish guys having this big argument, you know, shoutin' like. Your daddy was real upset. But when he saw me he stopped and they left. I don't know what that was all about, but the next thing, I guess it was about a week later, the foaling barn burns down, your daddy and that Ramon guy die and we lose the big mare.' Randy gulped and nervously took out a Marlborough that he lit between stained and bitten fingers. He inhaled deeply. 'They didn't want us nowhere near that barn. There was fire trucks, police, and a whole bunch of them Spanish guys. But we, the farm staff, was told to keep away.' He looked up with a far-away, despairing stare. 'Then they fired us all. Fuckin' let us all go!'

Tom extended his hand and held Randy's, signalling for the check. 'Finally! Finally! I'd found a home. Somewhere where I was appreciated and had some security. Some roots, you know.' he sobbed. 'I weren't goin' nowhere, Tom. I'da spent the rest of my life at Caledonia. Your daddy was good to me.'

The patrons were now engrossed in a game of football on the TV, so nobody paid any attention as the two men in the booth exited into the bright early afternoon sunshine. Tom offered Randy a lift, but he had laundry in across the street and planned on staying in town as it was his day off. Out in the daylight he made for a sorry sight: an unhealthy-looking, pale greyish pallor glistening over his drawn and acne-scarred features. But at least his baseball cap and sunglasses did cover up the mournfulness somewhat. 'Please stay in touch,' said Tom. 'I can reach you out at Byngs, I guess?'

'Yep, but I'll be getting' myself one of them phones soon. So I'll call you.'

As Tom was just about to bid him adieu, Randy reached into the pocket of his denim jacket. 'I almost forgot. I don't know what this is,' he said as he gave Tom a small leather pouch, 'one of them South American guys, that I picked up off a plane one night in Cincinnati last fall, left it in the truck. Maybe you know someone who can tell you what it is?'

Tom opened it and found a 50c.c. bottle of an unidentified clear injectable solution, wrapped in a piece of paper on which had been typed ten six-figure numbers in a neat column. They were as meaningless as the liquid was mysterious. And he drove off with a thousand thoughts on his mind.

CHAPTER 14

Reggie Halpern was up early. It was Preakness day and the Elevator Stable had a runner at Pimlico racetrack, where its unlikely members had met, two years previously.

As he fastidiously tied his bow tie, a new one for the occasion that he'd picked out in a Bloomingdale's three-for-the-price-of-one sale, he wondered for seemingly the thousandth time why fate, that humid Maryland day almost two years ago, had made him do something, so against all his principles, that had cast him into such a bizarre association?

For eighty-four years he'd managed quite nicely, by adhering to his father's mantra of 'looking after your own business and being beholden to none.' At the outset this had been in the family bookmaking business, which had thrived as the fairest and most fearless layers of bets in New York City up until the introduction of parimutuel wagering in 1940, and since then per R. H. Halpern's Wines.

'Provide an honest service, my son,' Solly had always preached. 'Keep the best company, but never indulge in such vices as gambling and drinking, yourself.' Yet somehow he'd allowed himself to get sucked in by a bunch of degenerate racetrackers.

'You know, Reggie,' his wife Linda had said to him, 'you moan and complain, like all the other Jews down at the market, when they feel they've been short-changed. But I'll tell ya, you've been a happier man ever since your elevator experience, and don't tell me that owning a part of a racehorse isn't the most fun thing you've ever done.' And, even though he'd never admit it to her, Reggie grudgingly had to concede she was right.

Those had been halcyon days. Bookmaking and wine were glamorous, and the track was the place to be in New York, with big-time players and stars of the screen and the stage. Belmont Park, and Saratoga in the summer, and Hialeah and Gulfstream, down south in Florida, each winter. Reggie Halpern had been a fixture at all of them.

As the years had passed, though, he'd retreated somewhat into his apartment, on West 67th Street, right across from his favourite dining haunt, the Café des Artistes, where the doorman procured last-minute reservations for hot tips and will calls at the track. And now, in retirement, it was just the New York Racing Association's (NYRA) local circuit. But, even in his dotage, nobody on the racetrack had their ear closer to the ground than Reggie Halpern.

That fateful trip to Baltimore had been prompted by a visit to see his one and only child, Violet; a product of the first of three trips to the altar, who was gravely ill at the time. Extracting extra value from being in town at the right time, he had taken in the second leg of the Triple Crown. It was, he reckoned, a more logical race than the helter-skelter of the Kentucky Derby and he felt that the New York form, that he knew so well, held up well at Pimlico. So why not try and pay for the trip?

As it had turned out, precious little profitable commissions were laid, thanks to the overloading of the already rickety and out-of-date Pimlico electrical circuits on a hot and humid day, when air-conditioning units and refrigeration systems were under the severest pressure. And, clambering into an overloaded and antiquated elevator to take him up to the fourth floor of the clubhouse for the ninth race, the City of Baltimore Handicap, Reggie and fifteen anxious racegoers had found themselves plunged into darkness, as the power had failed and the steel box in which they were encased, cheek by jowl to feathered hat and straining bosom, shuddered to a halt between floors.

First there had been a nervous laugh. Then silence. And then panic, as several passengers realized their predicament and lost control of fragile emotions, related to close confinement. There was screaming and sobbing. Nothing was happening, nor what was worse for those who knew just what a dump Pimlico was, was likely to happen imminently.

For Reggie, the irritation had been more monetary, as this was the race he'd been waiting for: a New York-based banker, at a good price. And now he was facing the possibility of being shut out.

While Reggie's impatience at missing out on a score had distracted his emotions, others expressed their frustrations and panic differently. In the corner, tucked around from the control panel where the emergency phone was not working, Victor Todd had been chewing his short but immaculately sharpened pencil and cursing under his breath at this outrageous interruption. While sandwiched between a divinely scented lady in a wheelchair and a sweaty lump who was standing on his foot, Nils Vigelund had remonstrated with his betting partner, Colin Nightingale. 'We're gonna get shut out! Can you believe it?'

A girl had screamed and burst into tears. 'Y'all shut up. I'm trying to phone for help,' someone had said, which brought a laugh from the dark. 'And you think you'll get through to these arseholes, on a day like this! Ha! I've got a better chance of winning this next race. Fuck!'

When the light had finally come on and the elevator had creaked to the second floor, nobody really knew or cared how long they'd been confined in such purgatory, they were so relieved to be disgorged from it. It had seemed like they'd been there for ever, but it probably hadn't been more than fifteen minutes. And, as they'd poured out unceremoniously onto the floor in a dazed heap, it was those who had had every intention of betting on the just-completed City of Baltimore Handicap, who seemed the most immediately aggrieved or relieved.

Nils and Colin had looked at each other sheepishly, realizing that their temporary incarceration had saved them the fifty bucks they'd have blown on their choices. Reggie had adjusted his tie and after checking out the result realized that he, too, had been most fortunate to have kept his money in his pocket. Meanwhile, the ever-gallant and visibly excited Victor had insisted on escorting the lady in the wheelchair downstairs.

There had still been almost an hour to the Preakness Stakes, and, finding themselves drawn together in the confusion, Nils, Colin, and Reggie had bought some water from a nearby refreshment cart, taken a time out for a chuckle about the absurdity of the whole incident, and walked outside to get a bit of fresh air as the crowd headed down to observe the runners for the Preakness Stakes. Meanwhile, the winner of the City of Baltimore Handicap had returned to the winner's circle, to be unsaddled, and, as they had looked down, they'd observed their erstwhile elevator passengers having their photo taken with the winner.

It was none other than the divine-scented, wheelchair-bound lady, and at her side Victor Todd; with his unmistakeable moustache, polished dome and bowtie he looked like a cross between Oscar De la Renta and Errol Flynn. And Nils confirmed, from his program, that the lady in question was none other than Vera Montagu, owner of Shenandoah Valley Farms and the winner, Indus

Warrior, who Victor had apparently supported at the windows.

'Well, I never,' Reggie had remarked. 'Those people have done it again! It never ceases to amaze me how, just because they train their horses in the back woods of West Virginia, people ignore them. I'll tell you what, whoever is running that operation sure knows what they're doing.'

'They have Basil Foster down on the program,' Nils had said. 'But he's just a front. A program trainer. Apparently, back at their training centre, Ms. Montagu's cousin, Matt Pearson, is doing all the training. You know the story about him? Ex-Marine, in Afghanistan; must have got shellshock or whatever they now call it - PTSD, post-traumatic stress disorder. Whatever. He was training for Ms. Montagu at Laurel, I think it was. A bit of a loner. Strange guy. He got himself ruled off by the Maryland racing commission for beating someone up. I don't know the full story.'

Colin had gone on to say that it was something to do with a jockey. Pearson didn't like the ride he'd given one of their horses. So, he went out onto the track when the boy came back to unsaddle and laid him out with one punch. 'Went away in the ambulance. DNF, vanned off.' He'd chuckled at his own humour; the dreaded racetrack vernacular for those that did not finish.

'And they arrested Pearson,' Nils had added. 'I think he just quit after that, even though he was ruled off. He went home.'

The men had chatted away, as you do when you've been through a nerve-wracking experience, and they'd exchanged stories and cards, so that the Preakness came and went, and they watched the TV monitor without a betting interest.

Reggie had returned to New York and thought no more about the trip to Baltimore until one day, about a year later, his phone had rung and an excited voice on the other end of the line had greeted him with a proposition that he just could not refuse. Or so Victor Todd had said. The gist was that Victor had formed a syndicate to claim a few horses and Reggie was lucky enough to be invited to join this partnership that could not fail. It had taken Reggie longer than it would have ordinarily done to politely but directly decline what he had considered to be a very dodgy endeavour that guaranteed nothing except an endless stream of bills. But Victor was not taking 'no' for an answer, and the only way that he had got him off the phone was to agree with him that if Matt Pearson could be persuaded to train the horse that Victor's syndicate claimed, he might consider getting involved. As he had known only too well that Matt Pearson was: a) ruled off, and b) even if he was training, somewhere in a remote part of West Virginia; it was privately for Vera Montagu, and they certainly were not going to entertain outside clients, he'd reluctantly agreed. He'd thought he was out of it. But how wrong he'd been.

It had taken Victor a while as he and his two partners in the Elevator Stable, as they'd called themselves, Nils and Colin, had made a couple of bad claims and come up against a brick wall when trying to communicate with Matt Pearson. But, on an inspiration, the boys had zeroed in on Rikki Tikki Tavi: claimed him for $50,000 and just shipped him down to Shenandoah Valley Farms, on spec, believing that the elusive owner and her enigmatic trainer could not resist the challenge.

Now, almost a year later, Reggie was off to see Rikki run in the same City of Baltimore Handicap that had proven to be the catalyst of this highly unlikely marriage some two years previously. He'd promised Victor 'get Matt Pearson and I'm in,' and here he was.

◆　◆　◆

After the excitement of the Kentucky Derby, life for Tom returned to reality the following Monday. And, with the doldrums of mid-Summer in Kentucky looming, he did not need to think twice when his Aunt Vera called.

'Dear Tom, I've been wondering how you are getting on and thought, with the Preakness Stakes coming up in just under two week's time, you might like to come down to Shenandoah Valley for a stay? Matt has a barn full of horses and sure would appreciate any help that he can get, it being so difficult to get good people, when you're off the beaten track, like we are.'

The invitation was so timely. And the following weekend he took a flight from Lexington to Washington, Dulles, where he was picked up by Basil Foster.

He hadn't been down to visit his aunt since his mom's death. But he'd heard all about Basil, who was a regular participant in Loudon County hunting circles and a key member of the Shenandoah Valley Farms team, and had spoken to him briefly at his father's funeral.

'So good you could make it down to this neck of the woods, Tom,' Basil had greeted him. 'I gather from your aunt that you fancy yourself as a bit of steeplechase rider, these days, eh?'

Basil Foster was a bit of an enigma himself. Perhaps that's why he fitted in so well at Shenandoah Valley. Originally from Ireland, he'd trained with some success there and latterly in England on the flat and over jumps. But his last endeavour, a private job in Newmarket, had not worked out and, through his close circuit of Irish racing friends, he'd found himself a job in Middleburg, where he'd met the dashing Ms. Montagu in the hunting field. Then, some four years previous, he'd ended up at Shenandoah Valley, as 'official trainer,' as he liked to bill himself, though others, not so kind, variously referred to him as program trainer, general dog's body, jack of all trades, frontman, and swingman. What mattered to him was he was doing what he loved, was being well-paid for doing so and, most importantly, he fit in. Basil liked the limelight that his boss, Matt Pearson, eschewed. They made a good team, if an odd couple.

Now in his mid-fifties, Basil, like many young Irishmen, had taken a stab at riding over fences, back in the day, and kept himself fit. A slim five-foot-six, he joked with Tom that he could still do 140 pounds at a push. 'There's no substitute,' he said, 'to being able to get up on one, every now and then, and get a feel. That's why I love it here. Your aunt just lets us get on with it and Matt, while he can be a pain in the arse with his obsessive, compulsive carry-on every now and then, is only interested in stuff on the farm. He doesn't want to go to the track anymore. I guess you heard about that fracas, up at Laurel?'

'Sort of,' said Tom, as Basil loaded his suitcase into the twin-cab Silverado.

'Well, Matt just lost it, I guess,' said Basil, as they exited the airport and headed west along Highway 15, past Leesburg, in the direction of Berryville. 'He ran a filly, one day at Laurel. In those days we had a dozen at the track. Anyway, this filly, a real nice filly, she didn't like the stick and Matt had told Gene Lovato many times not to abuse her. "She'll try her best", he'd said. "But, the moment you pick up your whip, her tail will go around, her ears will pin back, and she'll back right out of there." And what did the fool do? Only lay a fierce beating on her. I've never seen Matt so mad. He jumped up from the box, where we were watching, and ran down onto the track. And, when little Gene got off the filly, Matt nailed him. One punch, broke his jaw. Laid him out cold!'

'What did they do?' Tom asked.

'Oh, there was all hell to pay. The stewards originally suspended Matt. Then the rider sued him for assault and the Maryland Racing Commission charged him with bringing the sport of horse racing into disrepute. Conduct unbecoming. They've got a nerve, the bastards!' Basil eased over onto the exit to 340 north. 'What a performance. They wanted Matt put in jail. Premeditation, they said. It wasn't spontaneous. He had time, going down in the elevator, to rethink his actions. It was a bit dodgy for a while. But your aunt sorted things out and Matt signed a peace order, agreeing to a one-year suspension.' They were now at the gates to Shenandoah Valley Farms. 'Been here ever since. He ain't going back to no racetrack!'

As they drove up the long drive, lined with walnut, hickory, oak, and maple trees on either side, the neatness of the property reminded Tom of home. There were plenty of fancy places to the east, closer to Upperville and Middleburg, but this little gem, tucked away on the banks of the old river, was pure heaven. No wonder Matt Pearson had no desire to venture too far from it.

The pickup crossed over a dirt track. 'This is our training track,' said Basil. 'It's deep, you know, for legging up and putting a bit of bottom into 'em. A mile and a half around, all the way down behind those woods, you can see over there, and back up in front the house. When we need to breeze 'em a bit, we ship into Charles Town. It's only twenty minutes away. The experience relaxes a horse, so when we get to ship them somewhere, to run, they don't get all het up.'

They drove past a turning, to the left. 'That's the barn, down there,' Basil indicated and kept straight on up to a charming red-brick house, typical of the neat craftsmanship popular in the early part of the nineteenth century, that is seen throughout many parts of Maryland and Virginia and particularly in the Washington suburb of Georgetown. 'A beautiful spot, isn't it?,' he continued. 'Built in 1849, there's a list in your aunt's hall of all the various owners over the years, through the Civil War. This place would have certainly been a key landmark, looking north over there, towards the river.'

They had stopped by steps up to an imposing front door that was opened by a sizeable and smiling black woman in a maroon tunic and consuming white apron. Tom knew her from previous visits with his mom. This was Elsie, and nobody in these parts made better gumbo stew, flaky biscuits, or scrummy brownies. She embraced Tom. As he entered the cool hallway, he thought to himself, At last, some love.

'Ms. Vera's out at the pool, with Mr. Matt. You go on out there, Mr. Tom. You know the way and Basil and I will put your things in your room. I'll bring y'all out some lemonade.'

The main hall opened to the left, where a magnificent maple staircase spiralled up three floors beneath a massive crystal chandelier. Further to the left a passage continued to offices and the west suite, while to the right, past a powder room, a passage took you to the kitchens and beyond to Matt Pearson's study and the east wing. Tom went straight ahead, through the drawing room – where as a small boy he'd run in wet bare feet out to the pool and got a scolding from his mom that he'd slip on the old Douglas Fir floorboards – out through the French windows, past the lily pond to the swimming pool, where his Aunt Vera was reclining under a wide-brimmed sun hat on a chaise longue, looking out over a peach orchard, at the Shenandoah valley below.

'Dear Tom, welcome to sanity.' She gave her nephew an awkward hug from her prone position. 'Did you have a good flight? And was Basil on time?' The accident might have slowed her physically, but she remained a strikingly elegant woman, with a mind as sharp as a whip.

'Yes, yes,' said Tom. 'I'd forgotten how beautiful it is here.' He sat down on a lawn chair and gazed at the pastoral scene before him: bougainvillea, azaleas, and gardenias flanking the low black railings and a wrought iron gate, opening beyond to neatly mown lawns.

A grey mare whinnied and flicked her tail in the nearest paddock, in the shade of a walnut tree. Others around her lay peacefully in the lush grass. It was mid-afternoon, the hottest time of the day, and they were enjoying their siesta.

'Would you like something to drink, Tom?' Vera asked.

'Thank you, Aunt Vera, I would. But I think Elsie's bringing us out some lemonade.' At that moment Elsie did appear with a tray and two small Jack Russell terriers in tow, who charged around the pool to greet their new guest. 'So much fuss! Whoa, you guys,' said Vera as first Monty, then Freda, leapt onto Tom, licking his face clean.

'What a welcome! Now you've met my little family. Thank you, Elsie. Isn't it nice to see young Tom again?' she continued.

Elsie nodded. 'We put Mr. Tom in the Maple Room. Y'all find your things there.' And she withdrew to the house

Tom and his aunt chatted. 'Matt was here just a moment ago. But I guess he went down to the barn. They'll be feeding soon. If you like, I'll get Basil to take you down there in the morning. Would you like that?'

'I would,' said Tom, as he yawned. And the two of them sat in silence. So much to say…but this was not the time.

◆　◆　◆

Dinner that night was served in the library: a splendid room, off the main drawing room, but with the same fifteen-foot ceiling and intricate wainscoting. The two rooms were connected by enormous doors that, when they were open, showcased magnificent marble-faced fireplaces. For tonight, they were closed and, being on the cusp of June, there was no fire. Instead, the bewitching electric violins and mournful piano of contemporary Italian composer Ludovico Einaudi played softly from the sound system, hidden away amongst a thousand books.

While Elsie was the baker in the house, Matt Pearson was, as far as he was concerned, the chef. His past army experience had left him lost in mid-life, upon his honourable discharge, and to balance the relentlessness of the racetrack, a place where for twenty-four hours a day, seven days a week, three hundred and sixty-five days a year, his colleagues and co-workers spoke about nothing else but their horses and in most cases associated misfortunes, Matt had immersed himself in the culinary arts. That, and the kitchen garden behind the barn, kept him sane.

Tonight, he served his cousin Vera and, he guessed, his second cousin, once removed, although he wasn't exactly sure what their relationship really was, Boeuf Jardiniere with tagliatelle. The carrots, onions, and herbs were from the garden and the beef came from the local butcher in Berryville.

Matt Pearson liked cooking because it was a quiet craft. He liked a nice glass of wine, too, and for such a lusty meal he'd chosen a fine bottle of Brunello de Montalcino, a lovely full-bodied Italian, from 100% Sangiovese grapes. And, as it invariably does, the good food had kept the diners quiet, busily consuming the fine meal.

'Well, Tom,' said Matt, finally. 'You are going to meet our new owners tomorrow,' putting emphasis upon the 'our.'

Vera interrupted him. 'Explain to Tom, just how we got involved with these guys.'

'What do you mean, we?' said Matt. 'I had nothing to do with it. It was you who let them in. You know, I don't like dealing with owners. And when there's four of them, that's four times the trouble.'

'I know, I know,' sighed Vera. 'But they've promised not to bother you and just deal with me.'

'We'll see,' huffed Matt, pouring more wine.

'This is a great story, Tom. Where shall I start?' Vera wiped her mouth with her napkin. 'A couple of years ago we sent a really nice colt up to the September sales at Keeneland. Toby, you'll get to know him, he's the in-house expert on such things...Toby said he was the best-looking yearling that we'd ever bred on the farm. Anyway, he went for a lot of money. That IT guy from California, Wayne Stansfield, paid $1.5 million for him and they sent him to be trained by Timmy Trebor at Santa Anita. You know, the Hall of Fame guy - got lotsa horses in California, New York, all over.' Vera took a sip of wine and coughed.

'Well,' she continued 'Rikki Tikki Tavi, as they named him, started out gang-busters. He won his first two starts by wide margins and they shipped him to Saratoga where he won the Hopeful, by five. At that point people were talking about him being a Derby horse. Anyway, to cut a long story short, they went to the well once too often. He was, still is, a big colt, kinda top heavy, with a big old shoulder and massive quarters. He was still growing. When Matt saw him at Saratoga, he said he'd stop on him and give him time to mature, if he was training him. Didn't you Matt?'

Matt had heard all of this before and was in the corner changing the music, from whence he offered up a grunt.

'Where was I?' Vera asked.'Oh yes, they ran Rikki at Belmont, on a bad track, and he got beat. Something was bothering him. But instead of backing off they doubled down for the Breeders' Cup, because that year it was at Santa Anita and the owner wanted to impress his friends. Well, he ran no good and they say they found a chip and operated on his knee. Whatever, when he came back six months later, he was three by now, he just wasn't the same horse. Couldn't make the lead and ran horribly. That guy Trebor, he can be very hard on his horses. I guess he's got so many of them that he doesn't care. Easy come, easy go.'

'Rikki had won close to four hundred thousand by this stage, but his future did not look bright. So, the owner took him away and sent him to Max Meyers at Monmouth. He ran him on the turf and all he did was run off and stop, like he'd hit a brick wall. It was sad, because there was something wrong. So, I guess it was last summer, they dropped him in for fifty thousand one day at Monmouth and he was claimed. And, when I saw that in the Daily Racing Form, I thought that was that. What a shame.'

'I should let Matt take over here,' she said. 'This is the funny part, Tom.'

'If you insist,' Matt replied. 'Vera, here, goes to the Preakness two years ago and gets stuck in an elevator. Then she meets this wacko Jamaican guy from Toronto and the next thing is we're training for him and his buddies!'

'Hang on a minute, Matt, that's not the half of it. Basil and I are in an elevator, going up to watch Indus Warrior run in the City of Baltimore Handicap, and there is a power failure. So, we are stuck there and miss the race, that Indy wins. When we get out, this charming man, Victor, helps us get to another elevator that's working, so we can go down for the win picture. Mr. Todd, that's Victor's name, says he would love to send us, meaning Matt, a horse one day and I think nothing of it. Then, a couple of years later, I'm in bed one morning and I get a call from Toby, down at the barn. He says "You are not going to believe this Ms. Montagu, but Rikki's back." Apparently, a van showed up in the middle of the night and our night watchman didn't know anything about it. So, not knowing what to do, they turned him out in the small paddock by the barn. Toby comes in at five the next morning and there's this handsome head hanging over the gate and he knew who he was immediately. Ha! Ha! You don't want to know the shit that Matt put up when he saw him. I thought he was gonna kill me! He said, "Vera, are you crazy? This ain't something those dumb-ass guys you met in the elevator have done, is it?" And just then Victor calls. It was hilarious, Matt was doing his nut!'

'So that was last summer,' said Tom. 'How's Rikki been doin'?'

'Brilliant. Just brilliant,' said Vera. 'You're going to see him tomorrow.'

'It wasn't always so brilliant,' said Matt. 'When Rikki got here, he was a mess. I had to straighten those boys out right away.'

'But they understood, Matt. They've been watching you. You should be pleased. They've let you take your time. And now Rikki's back.'

'Sorest horse I ever saw,' said Matt, grimacing. 'When we got to lookin' at him, he was sad.'

'So, what did you do, Matt?' asked Tom

'You should ask Mr. TLC Toby that tomorrow, Tom,' said Vera.

'Yeah,' said Matt. 'They don't make horsemen like him anymore. The time he's spent with that horse is just phenomenal.' He drank some wine. 'First, we took his shoes off, turned him out, backed off on everything, and just let him settle down. He was so sore when he got here. He was just mean. Cowed in the back of his stall when he was in, wouldn't eat, and just sulked out in the paddock. Some days the flies drove him crazy. But we got his feet straightened out. And once we'd got some shoes back on him and started riding him about the woods, Toby would spend hours standing him in ice, packing his feet, painting the coronet bands with a mild blister, all the time growing him a new set of wheels. I'm sure this horse had foundered at one point. They'd just overloaded him and he got a fever. Then what happens is they're getting off something, a sore shin or bad feet, and the next thing they've pulled some muscles in behind, getting off those issues. Rather like you have a stone in your shoe, and you take a bad step and put your hip out or something. To be frank, this horse was fucked when he got here.'

'So how long before you could start doing anything with him?' asked Tom.

'Well, I'll have to say, those Elevator guys, whatever they call themselves, have been very patient. Not a word. They've just paid the bills and they know that there is going to be no return. Yet, anyway. So, after Christmas we got him going again, just hacking about the woods. You could see he was happier, rolling around in the snow, when we turned him out, and that the heat he'd been carrying had gone out of his feet. To see him bucking on a cold morning was a sight for sore eyes.'

'I wondered what would happen when we started to turn the screw a bit. And the first time we took him into Charles Town, to breeze, I told Jose, who has spent a lot of time working with him, to just let him do whatever he wanted to. I shouldn't have worried. The plan was to two-minute lick him from the eighth pole a complete circuit around to the wire, nice and easy, well off the rail. Well, when Jose chirped to him, Rikki just took off. I don't think they've seen a horse work like that before at that little bullring. I didn't have a watch on him, but the clocker called me up afterwards and said that he'd gone three-quarters in 1:15, and this with 140-pound Jose just sitting as quiet as a mouse, and right out in the middle of the track! He wasn't even supposed to be working! By the time Jose was able to pull him up, he'd almost gone around again. And he came back bucking and kicking. We had to put the tack on him the next day, he was so sharp.'

'When Matt came back from the track that morning,' said Vera, 'he was not Matt! Far too spirited and upbeat for Matt,' she kidded.

'Well, you know, I had to think twice. My first notion was to ring up the owners and tell them. But then, I thought, let's just play this cool, as many a morning glory has fizzled in the afternoon sun. So, we played it down. Rikki was coming along nicely. We liked the way he was going. And, three weeks ago, we found a little spot for him, on the turf, down at Colonial Downs. Seven eighths of a mile around one turn – they have good turf courses down there – probably a bit short for him, but I knew that, off the lay-off, he would be super sharp.'

'And he won, like a thief in the night,' said Vera. 'It was amazing!'

'Tell me about it,' said Tom, transfixed by the resurgence of Rikki.

'It was so funny,' said Matt, lightening to the story. 'This Victor guy and his friends were ok with the spot but not ok with the rider. I thought that we should try and change Rikki's style. Trebor had him all cranked up and they always sent him to the lead. But, I thought, let's just let him drop out and settle, and then see if he can come from off the pace. The last thing we wanted to do was hurt him again in a speed duel. So, I decided to ride Angela, one of my girls, who comes and rides out here for us, regularly. She's had a few rides, knows the horse, and does what she's told. Plus, we got the ten-pound bug – it was one of those non-winners of a race since forever – Rikki has all the conditions in his favour because he hasn't won in almost two years, so you couldn't find an easier spot.'

'What did the owners say?' said Tom.

'Well, they really didn't know what to say,' replied Matt. 'Reggie, the older guy, liked the weight allowance. I think he looks upon this whole thing as anything we can salvage is better than nothing. Victor, who is a sheets man, wanted the leading rider. But Nils and Colin were ok with the broad, as they said. And she did them proud.'

'How did it unfold?' asked Tom.

'First of all, we rather ambushed these guys. They weren't expecting to see Rikki in the entries. So, none of them could make it, which was great. As for Rikki, he was amazing! Toby took him down with Basil and he was very relaxed in the paddock. He missed the break, which actually turned out to be a good thing, as I'd told Angela not to rush him. So, she just sat on him maybe twelve lengths out the back. Meanwhile, up front they went a half in 45 and change, far too fast, and by the time they got to the top of the stretch they were stopping badly and Rikki just circled the field and won, pulling up by six. His time of 1.22.3 was excellent. He ate up and the next day was tearing the barn down. We couldn't turn him out, for fear of him injuring himself, he was so sharp.'

'So here we are, running in the City of Baltimore Handicap tomorrow, on the Preakness card,' said Vera, 'back where it all started!'

CHAPTER 15

When Tom woke, it was dark and he wasn't sure, to begin with, where he was. Then he heard Matt's voice, for the second time: 'Tom…Tom…are you awake? It's 5:15, see you in the kitchen, in five minutes.'

The house was quiet. When Tom descended, he found Monty and Freda curled up in their baskets, snoring by the Aga stove.

'Here,' said Matt, handing him a mug of tea. 'There's milk and sugar over there. Get what you need, and we'll take it with us.'

By all measurements Matt Pearson was a solid man. Honed from a lengthy army career, he'd maintained his six-foot-four, two-hundred-pound frame in battle condition. In the pre-dawn cool it was draped in a quilted olive jacket, topped by a faded Orioles' ball cap, as they walked to the barn, sipping in silence. Behind them, the sun's first rays were peeking up over the ridge beyond the river, onto the mist in the valley. A chorus of bluebirds in the Osage orange trees nearby announced the arrival of dawn.

The barn was already a hive of activity, with everyone going about their routine chores. The nightwatchman, Jack, had fed at 3:30 and the ground crew of Toby, Slick, and Curtis had been on the scene for more than an hour. Those being turned out were already in their paddocks. The first set of five were tacked up and ready to go, and in the tack room Matt introduced Tom to Jose, Dieter, Angela, and Betsy. 'We have a gentleman rider here today, folks. All the way from jolly old England,' he joked. 'Thinks he's a steeplechase jockey!' They laughed. 'Who do you think we should put him on this morning, then?'

Betsy, who, from under her shamrock-green crash helmet, had already clocked the cute young man from Kentucky, said, 'He can ride Mata Hari and stay at the back with me, outta the way of Rikki and the boys up front.' That suited Matt just fine.

Mata Hari was a four-year-old filly, bred on the farm, that Vera had sent to be trained in England, where she'd won three of her five starts on the turf. By Oriental God out of the homebred mare, French Connection, the naming was typical of her owner's sense of humour. Now back home, the plan was to get some black type and send her off to a good stallion in Kentucky, the following spring. A strapping chestnut with a full-white blaze, she was a lot more refined than the heavier-set jumpers that Tom had been used to. But, as all members of the stables at Shenandoah were, she was well-mannered and certainly not about to eject her new partner.

As the small string exited the barn onto a dirt track that wound around behind the kitchen garden and down to the Meyerstown road at the very back of the five hundred acre property, Rikki Tikki Tavi pranced at the front, his breath misting in the cool air. He was sharp today and Toby had equipped him with four bright blue galloping bandages, lest he knock himself in his friskiness. Up top, Jose had let his irons down and sat quietly, hobby-horsing his finely tuned mount.

The usual plan was to trot back up the hill and walk down again, before setting off onto a harrowed dirt track that wound counter-clockwise around walnut wood, past the house, where Matt would be watching, sometimes with Vera, if she was up, but always with Ripken, his black Labrador, and out to the eastern most extremity of the property: a distance of about a mile and a quarter, rising all the way. Then a walk back through the woods for a repeat.

Today, however, Rikki was only doing one tour and he returned to the barn with Jose for a bath and thence the two-hour van ride to Pimlico with Basil and Toby.

Walking back through the woods, for their second canter, the talk was all about Rikki, who was the undoubted star of the stable. Angela was going to be riding him in a $500,000 stakes race, her first venture into such illustrious company, and Betsy and Dieter were ribbing her. 'You don't get to claim the bug, in a stakes race,' said Dieter, 'maybe they'll let you start early!' he kidded.

Frankly, Angela was very surprised that Matt had ridden her back. He was such an unpredictable character. You just never knew with him, and he certainly didn't hand out compliments. He'd just said, in passing, you will ride Rikki on Saturday and that was that, even though the Elevator boys weren't so sure.

Vera had received a polite e-mail from Victor, expressing his co-owners concerns over whether a young lady, like Angela, could hold her own against the big boys from New York and California. Colonial was ok in a micky mouse race, but this was big time Grade 1 stuff. Vera did not disagree, but she did remind Victor of the conditions under which Matt had agreed to train the stable's horse. 'You know Victor, I have to say that this is an unusual move for Matt. Normally he doesn't like to over-match his horses, and it's a big step up from a bitty allowance race down at Colonial to the very best at Pimlico…on Preakness day. But Matt's a canny guy. He knows his horse and he knows that Angela gets on with Rikki and won't hurt him. And,' she added, 'she can do the weight, as he gets in real light at 108 pounds. So, let 'em run, I say.'

Victor had relayed this rational back to Reggie, Nils, and Colin and got the reaction he'd expected. But what the hell. He'd pointed out, after studying his daily racing form, this isn't a tough Grade 1: there are only eight runners, no Europeans, thank God, and we get weight all around. 'And they pay fifty grand to the fourth, in these affairs,' he'd added.

Angela hadn't even thought what potential financial remuneration all of this meant for her. It was just such a responsibility, in her fledgling career. 'Think. You'll be on TV,' said Betsy. 'We'll all be watchin' yer!'

'Well,' said Angela, 'you don't need to worry about me waving my stick and looking stupid, because you know that would mean it's my last ride for Matt. For a while anyway.'

'I know,' said Tom. 'I made a real fool of myself at Cheltenham, in March. Fell at the last. Too confident. Thought I was Tony McCoy. This game can be a humbler!'

After the second, slightly stronger open canter up the hill, the four returned to the barn. As Tom unsaddled the now sweating Mata Hari, Curtis, her groom, whispered to him, 'That Betsy, she your new girlfriend, young man? Ooooo-eee! I think we're all gonna see a lot more of you round here. Yes sir.' The old groom whistled to himself as Tom held his filly for her a bath. 'Oooooo-eeee,' he repeated, winking at Tom. 'Hear that, Slick,' he said to his colleague, who was doing the same for Betsy's mount and well within earshot.

'You a stirrer, Curtis. You got a lady real embarrassed, here. See, she blushin'!' Slick replied.

Rikki had already left for the races as the riders walked their mounts around the barn, while they cooled out. Then, after returning them to their stalls which had been mucked out and bedded down with fresh straw by the ground crew while they had been out exercising, the riders hopped into their cars and headed off to a normal day of work: Betsy to Winchester, where she was articling for the local law firm of Brewster, Burke, & McFadden, and Dieter and Jose to other farms nearer Upperville, where they were working with various clients' horses, both thoroughbreds and show horses.

Tom headed back to the house for breakfast. It was eight o'clock.

◆　◆　◆

In the kitchen, Elsie was making blueberry pancakes. The smell of bacon sizzling in a pan on the Aga had got the attention of the dogs, who yapped their greetings. Matt, engrossed in the *Daily Racing Form*, grunted, 'Nice filly isn't she,' to Tom, without raising his head from his studies. 'Help yourself to some coffee.'

'Yes, she sure is,' said Tom. 'How many have you in training, down here?'

Matt sipped his coffee. 'A mixed bunch. It really depends on the time of year. We've got five mares that are here full-time. That is, of course, when they are not away being bred. Then we have the foals and yearlings, up until they go off to the sales. As for racehorses, your aunt has about ten in training, at the moment. One in England with Bill Bass, six here – you saw five of 'em this morning – and there's Touch and Go, who is turned out right now,' he moved his Form to make room for a plate of pancakes that Elsie had brought to the table. 'Then we have a couple on the road.' He poured some maple syrup over his pancakes and picked up a piece of bacon in his fingers.

'What do you mean, on the road?' asked Tom, making way for his breakfast plate.

'Well,' Matt paused, while licking the syrup off his fingers, 'I don't go to the track anymore, you know. Got tired of the place. Prefer to just train 'em here. It's quiet, no politics, no owners, no pushy agents. So, we send a few out to where we think they can do some good. We have a great guy in Canada, Ronnie Broadhurst. Real old-school. Has a small string at Fort Erie. Have you ever been there?'

'No,' said Tom. 'I hear it's a great place to train.'

'Sure is,' replied Matt, with his mouth full. 'They've got one of those old traditional dirt tracks. Horses love it. Great cushion. When they gallop by, you can barely hear their hooves travelling over it. Not like some of the rock-hard surfaces they have at too many racetracks these days, where it's all about speed and time. They also have a great turf course, which is unusual for a B-track. So, right now we have a couple with Ronnie that he is going to run on the turf at

Woodbine this summer, and we have a filly up at Belmont that we hope to run in a little stakes race there next month. She doesn't ship well, so we sent her up early to acclimate. She's with an old steeplechase rider I know who trains a few and knows what he's doing,' he added through a mouthful of toast.

'So, Basil is the trainer for the horses that are trained here?' asked Tom.

'Yep,' said Matt, 'on paper, anyway. He likes the track, and I'm fine, just here. Suits us well. He left with Rikki and Toby before you guys got back. They'll be at Pimlico before ten. Basil likes all the media attention. Hell, I can't remember the last time I put on a suit and a tie.'

'You're becoming a real hillbilly, you are, Matt,' laughed Elsie. 'You and your garden. We all gonna start calling you Chauncey!'

Matt chuckled. 'I think you got me confused with our program trainer, Basil. He's our Peter Sellers. But Tom, you are going to be the man today. You have been elected to take your aunt to the races. So, go and get yourself smartened up.'

CHAPTER 16

It was a big day for the Elevator Stable: the first time the four partners would all be present to watch a runner together and the first time they would see their new racing colours, over which there had been considerable debate. Victor, as the progenitor of the enterprise and self-proclaimed manager, had prevailed with his symbolic choice of black, with a white vertical arrow and gold cap. The black represented the inside of the infamous elevator, when the power had failed, the white arrow indicating that they were going up (hopefully), and the gold was the pot at the end of the road. Reggie thought this was idiotic and not at all in keeping with the famous racing silks of the most illustrious owners on the turf. But both Nils and Colin were in agreeance, arguing that the contrast was easy to follow – black, with a shining gold lid.

Reggie's train from Penn Station was full of racegoers, travelling the three hours by rail from New York City to Baltimore. Victor, Colin, and Nils had flown in the night before and were installed in the Mariott Hotel down by the harbour, in the Fell's Point neighbourhood of the city. The arrangement was to meet there at 11:30 and take a cab to Pimlico. It was going to be a long day and, as post time for their race, the one before the main event Preakness Stakes, wasn't until 5:10, they were in no hurry.

Vera Montagu had asked them to join her for lunch in the clubhouse dining room. It was going to be the first time they'd got together since those infamous fifteen minutes.

Basil and Toby had traveled north with Rikki on 340 to Frederick and then east, across 70, to Baltimore. The luxury gooseneck trailor, custom made in Ocala, Florida, for up to four horses, with partitions that could be removed to make one big stall for a mare and foal, had its own living quarters up front. Detailed in the Shenandoah Valley Farms' colours, it was a fancy rig that got many a stare.

Today was a short jaunt, and, being a Saturday, there wasn't the usual heavy commuter traffic; so they arrived just before ten, in time to be inspected by the Maryland Racing Commission veterinarian.

A stall in the stakes barn with the Preakness horses had been offered for Rikki, but Matt felt there were going to be too many members of the press in the way and that he would be better off as far away from this action as possible. So, rather to Basil's dismay, they found themselves quartered in lowly Barn 15, looking out through a stark chain-link fence onto a derelict building site, covered in graffiti and festooned with beaten-up shopping carts. This part of Baltimore was not for the faint-hearted and, on big days like this one, it was not uncommon to see bands of local delinquents pushing these carts around, as conveyors for stolen booty.

Pimlico might host the second leg of the Triple Crown and, in the Preakness trophy, the Woodlawn Vase, have the oldest and largest silver cup in all of American sports. But, as a racetrack, it had seen better days. Today a crowd of close to one hundred thousand would pack the dilapidated grandstands and spill into the infield, where college students would imbibe olympian quantities of beer and hope it would rain, so that they could play touch football and wallow in the mud. But, for the remaining three hundred and sixty-four days of the year, you could fire a cannon through the property and not worry about hitting anyone. This tranquility obviously suited the local wildlife and it was no exaggeration that the rats in the Pimlico barns were bigger than the cats, so plentiful was the supply of grain and ideal the living quarters for vermin.

Basil, or Sir Basil as Toby liked to tease him, may have been down as official trainer on the program, but he knew who was calling the shots. Having experienced for himself what it was like to struggle as a trainer, he had reconciled with the fact that this really was about as good as he could hope for. And Matt Pearson just kidded him that, having already been ruled off, it would be him (Basil not Matt) who took the full blame for any positive tests. In some states they may have been frowned upon for such blatant practices, but in Maryland, Pennsylvania, and even Kentucky, there were ways of circumventing such trivialities if you were in with the right people and Vera Montagu was as well-connected as they came. So, no worries.

◆ ◆ ◆

After Elsie had taken Vera her breakfast in her ground-floor room, she and Mavis, her nurse, helped her dress, selecting a yellow outfit, with daisy-style hat, to compliment the black-eyed Susans after which the fillies' equivalent to the Preakness is named.

Matt brought the customized Range Rover around to the front door and instructed Tom on collapsing the wheelchair, reassembling it, and driving the fine vehicle.

'Usually, Basil drives your aunt to the races if it's a big day or not too far. Otherwise we watch on TV. She,' he gestured to Vera, 'has got every racing network known to man hooked up in her office and bedroom. I'll show you when you get back. We can watch all the races in Britain, France, Dubai, Hong Kong, even Australia. Why would I want to spoil a nice day in the garden by going to a dump like Pimlico, when I can watch it all here?' He shut the door and waved. 'Stay away from dodgy elevators!'

'Isn't this fun,' said Vera as she and Tom set off. 'We have so much to talk about, you and I. Sometimes I just find it deadly being stuck in a car with dear old Basil for several hours. He means well. But…'

Matt had programmed the GPS, so Tom had only to follow its directions, which was a good thing as his aunt made the conversational running. They talked about his mom, and of course the recent fire and terrible loss of his father. 'These things, when they come upon you suddenly, cannot be dealt with the way some people assume. You know, nobody knows how you feel, and everyone has their own way of dealing with the loss of a loved one,' she paused, 'some are never able to do so.' There was a silence as Tom drove. 'I lost my dear Jim far too young. For a long time, I couldn't believe he'd gone and always harboured the notion that it was all a bad dream and that one day I would wake up and he'd be back.'

Tom drove carefully, within the speed limit. 'Then,' his aunt continued, 'we lost your mother, I had my little accident, and now this. When will it end?'

Tom didn't know what to say.

'It's too soon, Tom. You can't possibly have got your head around this yet. They say that time is a great healer. Well, it may be, but even when the reality of what's happened has been reconciled, to a point, you still know that you will never get over it for the rest of your life. You'll think about these things every day.' She paused and Tom could see that she was struggling with a hanky.

'I have my horses. What would I do without them? Having Matt here and running the show has been great: as much for him, as me. When he came out of the army, he was lost. His time in Afghanistan really seems to have left a mark on him. To get over it, he just immersed himself in horses. It was his therapy. And now we make a bit of an odd couple, don't we?' she laughed. 'His being ruled off and settling down here,' she continued, 'was the best thing that could have happened. He's happy here. And so am I.'

'What did happen?' said Tom. 'At the track, I mean.'

'Oh, that. I guess Matt had a moment. Some people get traumatized and it takes years for their frustrations to come out. Dear old Matt was not enjoying the structure of the racetrack: the bad help, the politics, the incestuousness and petty jealousies of highly competitive people all confined within a small space. He just blew a fuse. He shouldn't have done what he did. And it's a good thing that he only broke Gene Lovato's jaw because a big guy like Matt could have killed a hundred-and-ten-pound jock, and that would have been curtains. As it was, they wanted to file assault charges and mentioned jail and all that. But we sorted things out, looked after Gene and, in the end, it was accepted as being beneficial to all concerned that Matt quit the track. Certainly, I'm really happy to have him here. He brought Toby and Slick with him, and the barn and the garden are in better shape now than ever before.'

Vera Montagu rambled on and Tom listened intently. Before he knew it, they were turning into the reserved parking lot for Maryland Hunt officials.

The valet parking crew obviously recognized the Range Rover and its owner, as a host of greeters helped Tom set up the wheelchair and push his aunt into the clubhouse. 'Watch out for them elevators, now, Ms. Montagu,' the chief amongst them joked, as he loaded them into one that was headed to the fourth-floor Jockey Club boxes.

◆　◆　◆

The rendezvous at the downtown hotel had gone well, and the Elevator boys were track-bound in a limo. 'Ever since that episode, I can't stand being squeezed into small hot places,' said Victor. The others, who were all engrossed in their racing forms, grunted.

On the train, Reggie had downloaded the scratches and changes that he read out from his phone. The closer they got to Pimlico the slower their progress became. 'Do you think we should go and visit Rikki on the backside?' said Colin.

'What for?' Reggie fired back. 'We can't help him now. You can make your acquaintances in the paddock.'

'What's the story, Reg?' enquired Nils. 'We got any shot?'

Despite entreaties not to do so, Reggie had lit up a nice Cohiba that he'd been saving for the occasion. He'd do his best not to chew this one into a soggy mess that, with his normal smokes from Puerto Rico and Honduras, usually was the case. 'Eight-horse field. We got in light,' he was brief and to the point, as usual. 'The broad can do the weight, no changes.'

'No European invaders, thank God,' said Victor. 'No real speed, either. Not that I can see, anyway, which may be a problem, as we need something to run at.'

'How about the South American horse?' asked Nils. 'First time on the turf. First start in the US. Maybe he's speed?'

'Not that kind,' said Reggie, dismissively. 'Been running on the dirt. That form, down in Chile, ain't much. He ain't won nothin'.'

'Seven wins from eleven starts, though,' said Victor. 'But it's hard to figure out that form. Just little purses.'

'I know. But it's the Trebor-factor. Gotta give him some respect.'

'Fuck Timmy Trebor. He's no turf trainer. Who are these people?' asked Nils.

'Owned by Haras del Condor, it says,' replied Victor. 'They've brought their own rider, Junior Alvarez. Ever heard of him?'

This discussion had usefully passed the time and with a jolt the limo drew to a halt at the main clubhouse entrance, where it was agreed that the driver would pick up the passengers later that afternoon. 'Maybe we'll be celebrating. So we'll call you,' Colin had said, optimistically.

◆　◆　◆

Bypassing all elevators, the four punters found their way to the entrance to the Turf Club dining room, where their new owners' badges gained them admittance and an escort to Ms. Montagu's table, on the bottom tier, right beside the window and, of course, adjacent to the wire.

'Well, well, gentlemen. Welcome to Pimlico, again,' said their smiling hostess.

'It's so good to see you again, in so much better circumstances, Ms. Montagu,' said Victor, somewhat nervously.

'None of that Ms. Montagu stuff. Victor, it is, isn't it?' and Victor smiled.

'It's Vera and this is my nephew, Tom, from Kentucky. Tom, say hi to the Elevator Stable.'

Tom rose from his seat and greeted the new arrivals, who seated themselves. Vera, by the window, looking down the track, Victor beside her, then Tom – 'A good place,' Vera said, 'for you to run our bets from' – with Reggie, Nils, and Colin facing them.

'What fun this is! I can't remember the last time I went racing and we didn't have a runner. You know, Rikki is yours. I'm just a spectator.'

'I must say that it is a bit of a turn up,' said Reggie. 'I still can't believe that I let this guy,' he said, turning to Victor, 'persuade me to get involved in this caper. All these years I've stayed away from ownership and then – you know what happened – we get stuck in an elevator and here we are. It's like a spell was cast.'

'That's what makes it so irresistible. That's karma,' said Vera. 'Now then, you boys, go and serve yourself some lunch. The buffet is really good, here on Preakness day. And then we'll see if we can pick out a few winners. Tom, if you don't mind, could you please bring me something light. Some smoked salmon, a bit of salad. That would be so kind.'

The line-up at the buffet counter was making slow progress, so Tom excused himself and went to the washroom, where entering the door he bumped into a nattily clad young man, exiting in a hurry. 'Well, hello,' said Tom, but the man was gone. He felt sure he had recognized him, but couldn't think where. Then, returning to the table, with plates laden, he looked across the room and spotted his man seated between none other than Billy Beagle and Hector Delmontez. It was Mark's friend who'd been at the Derby in Kentucky. Johnny something. Mark had given him a nickname. That's right, Bog. W-C, the water closet guy, Johnny Ward-Clarke of the CBS. What was he doing here and, furthermore, how come he was sitting with such illustrious company?

'Have some friends here?' asked Vera, as Tom placed her plate in front of her. 'I hope that's alright?'

'Yes, yes, thank you so much. Who is that guy, over there with Billy Beagle?'

Everyone turned, but nobody seemed to know. 'Well, that's Tim Trebor at the end of the table,' said Nils. 'He's the leading trainer. Has horses all over.'

'Yeah, he's got that South American horse, what's his name – El Cordobes – in our race. Maybe he's the owner?' said Colin.

'No,' said Tom, 'that is a bloodstock agent from England. His name is Johnny Ward-Clarke and he's sitting beside Dr. Hector Delmontez, the man who has taken over my father's farm in Kentucky, the man with the mustache, and Billy Beagle, the head of Keeneland. Dr. Delmontez owns Haras del Condor. So, I guess, El Cordobes?'

'Do you know him?' said Victor. 'Maybe you could ask him about his horse?'

'I do and I don't,' said Tom. 'I have met him, but I really don't know anything more about him, other than the fact that he comes from Venezuela, owns a lot of property and some successful businesses in South America, and now controls Caledonia Farms.'

'What's he doing with Billy Beagle?,' said Nils. 'And is that the guy from Canada, who is with them, too, at the end of the table with the red tie on?'

'That's Calvin Weiner,' said Victor. 'He has a powerful stable of horses in Ontario. And that guy beside him is Mike Rogers, his farm manager. I see them all the time at Woodbine. That Rogers' pretty shifty. I wouldn't want to buy a horse from him. Know what I mean?'

'I guess the one-horse merits a little more consideration, then,' said Reggie, studying the past performances for the City of Baltimore Handicap and particularly those of the South American invader.

◆ ◆ ◆

As often happens on big days, when crowds make it difficult to move about and you find yourself in unfamiliar surroundings, the punters of the Elevator Stable, looking forward to their seminal entry to big-time ownership, spent little time handicapping the other races. Vera Montagu, though, was fascinated by their jargon, carry-on, and different perspectives in race analysis and reasoning for making their selections.

Victor, being an accountant, was a stats man and fan of the sheets, as they call the boiled-down figures on race times, fractional times, trip factors, etcetera, all of which combined for two mysterious numbers that informed the reader of a horse's relative merits and whether it was improving or regressing. He tried to explain this to Vera, and the fact that this was what had attracted him first to Rikki. 'His back numbers, as a two-year-old,' he'd said, 'were exceptional. Then he'd shown a steady decline, until of course Matt Pearson got a hold of him and that last race at Colonial suggested that the tide had turned and Rikki was sitting on a big race.'

'How do you know this, Victor?,' she asked, 'when you have no idea, ordinarily, how a horse is doing in his training? Now you do, because I've kept you posted when you've called or e-mailed me, but, for everyone else, they are just guessing that since their last race a particular horse is going forwards, not backwards? Isn't that right?'

'Spot on,' said Nils. 'The sheets are ok, up to a point. But now they have so many different surfaces, from track to track, and you've got all these horses shipping in from overseas; it's hard to match relative figures.'

'How do you handicap a race, Nils?' she asked.

'The old-fashioned way,' Colin interrupted. 'Nils has favourite combinations and only follows certain trainers. He believes that the trainer and his staff are like mechanics. You know, a car won't run any good if it's not tuned right. And it is this that sets apart the trainers who have a high-percentage strike rate from those who operate under 10%: the guys who run lots of horses all over the place and only win through sheer numbers.'

'It's not very scientific,' said Nils, 'but it makes me selective and that, maybe, is the main reason why I'm quite successful, overall.'

'Tell me. I'm intrigued,' said Vera. 'Do you guys have wives? Is there another side to your lives?'

There was a chorus of laughter. Tom smiled, thinking of Mark. These are his type of guys, he thought.

'Very much so,' said Reggie. 'But mine has other interests: ballet and the arts. She gave up on me a long time ago and does her stuff, and I do mine. My father was a bookmaker. I guess racing is in my blood.'

The boys hadn't really known one another other all that well, other than as occasional acquaintances on the racetracks of the eastern seaboard over the years, until the incident in the elevator. And this had suited them fine, as on the track it was all business and the fewer diversions and needless gossip the better. Each had their own methods that a psychiatrist would have had fun matching with their individual personalities.

Reggie, dour but practical; a show-me-the-money type of guy who was not easily impressed and did not suffer fools kindly.

Victor, more mercurial; his nattiness and attention to detail almost obsessive. Mathematically gifted, he printed out his track bias numbers from his patented computerized formula every day. With great gusto he would whip out the neatly folded sheets from the inside breast pocket of his ubiquitous navy blue blazer and make little notes with his trademark pencil that he'd sharpen to a pinpoint, all the way down to the eraser. His friends called him Shoebox Victor, because he would keep all his win tickets in a shoebox and didn't cash them until just before Christmas every year – when he and his wife Gladys would spend the proceeds on a trip home to visit their families in Jamaica.

Victor wasn't a big player, but he was a shrewd one who, when he'd had a nice score, would excitedly share the good news with anyone within earshot: the joy in his sing-song patois accent only equalled by his ear to ear grin. As punters went, Victor was as happy as they get.

Colin, on the other hand, was a hunch player who felt that, because of his status and friends in high places, he had access to privileged information that gave him an exclusive edge.

Originally from England, where, as a headstrong young man, he'd spent more time in betting shops than at school; he'd subsequently travelled the world on his parents account and ended up belatedly in Canada, as a sort of latter-day remittance man, part-time bloodstock agent, and full-time punter. A fixture at Woodbine, he and Victor were racetrack acquaintances, whose shared love of cricket and sartorial excellence had drawn them together. That they'd ended up stuck in the same elevator now seemed almost preordained. The banter between them was quite comical, with Colin poo-pooing Victor's micro-analysis as not taking into account the 'inside' knowledge he would glean from his well-heeled friends, and Victor good-naturedly mocking Colin's aloofness.

'Do you guys work?' asked Vera.

'I've never worked a day in my life!' said Colin. 'Work is something you don't enjoy doing, it's a chore. I have just been lucky to find sources of remuneration that I consider to be fun.'

'And how about you, Nils? You strike me as a bit of an artist yourself,' Vera continued.

'I'm flattered. Thank you.' Nils smiled. 'Actually, my father was the artist. He was a conductor. His family was German. But I grew up in Buffalo and I guess that music was in my blood. I'm now director of music at the Manhattan School of Music.'

'How wonderful! That is impressive,' said Vera, 'So, is Saratoga your favourite racetrack? You can kill two birds with one stone up there, with the Saratoga Performing Arts Centre. They have some wonderful concerts during the season.'

'Yes, ma'am. I might just retire there one day. They also have good golf courses. It's my kind of town.'

'And did your father take you to Saratoga? Was he conducting at SPAC?'

'No. A much more humble initiation at Fort Erie, just over the Peace Bridge, in Canada. My dad first took me there in the sixties. We saw Northern Dancer break his maiden at the Fort. The rest is history. I now live in Yonkers. There's OTB there and I go to NYRA tracks, but the Toga is indeed my Mecca.'

'This is all fascinating,' said Vera. 'My, oh, my. Chance meetings in life.' She paused, looking out the window across the racetrack, immersed in thought. 'Tom, you're going to love Saratoga. It's one of the few places where I am truly happy these days. I always go up there for six weeks at the end of July. It's a gem. You just can't beat it. I love to have a bet, every now and then. You know, thinking that you know something that nobody else does and getting a good price on a horse that you have inside info on. It's so exciting. By the way, did you guys bet on Rikki when he won at Colonial? I did,' she said with great satisfaction. 'He was so-ooooo good that day. His PPs were so-ooooo bad! I just loved it. He wasn't my horse anymore, but I had the scoop!'

'That's why we sent Rikki to Matt,' said Victor. 'We know, or at least we think we know, what's going on and can handicap races as well as anyone. But it's having that edge, especially coming off the layoff, when all the doubters dismissed Rikki as washed up, that gives you value.'

'Sure. We all bet on him that day at Colonial,' said Reggie. 'It was the one time we had a big edge, despite the bad paper. Those horses weren't much, down there. If he hadn't beat them that day, we'da had a lemon on our hands. As I say, even though he was only 3/1, a 3/1 shot pays the same $8 at Colonial as it does at Belmont Park. Unlike these hunch-sters, though, I played him on the nose and took the 3/1, whereas these wise guys played a whole bunch of Exactas and Trifectas onto horses they didn't know. It worked out for them, but in my book, you should stick to what you know.'

'Ok, Mr. Logic,' said Vera, 'are you going to bet on Rikki today?'

Reggie looked up from his *Form* and took off his glasses. 'I doubt it. This is a completely different ball game. It may not be a really tough Grade 1, but there is no such thing as an easy stakes race. If we hit the board, I will be pleased with the confirmation that the claim was a good one and we have a viable racehorse. You know, we're not stuck paying for one that is one step away from the glue factory.'

'That's an awful thing to say! Rikki's gonna surprise you. You'll see,' said Vera.

◆　◆　◆

A fine lunch and good wine had bonded the unlikely gathering with rapt conversation. They lost track of time. So, before they knew it, the ninth race was upon them.

Over in the corner, there had been a mass exodus of Hector Delmontez and his friends, as they had descended to the paddock. Vera excused herself, saying that as she didn't want to chance another power failure and miss the race, she'd stay at the table and watch from there. 'If you guys get the money, though, I promise I will get these bones down to the winner's circle for the photo. I couldn't miss that.'

None of the syndicate had ever been into a paddock before and none of them had ever met Basil Foster, either. All they knew was that they had the five-horse. So, they gathered under the grandstand, in the indoor paddock, by saddling stall five. A large crowd surrounded the small oval walking ring that was overlooked by a mezzanine above. Not pretty like Hialeah, Keeneland, or Saratoga, but functional.

Rikki Tikki Tavi looked like a prizefighter entering the ring. His deep, dark brown, almost black, coat glowed with a sheen of oil glinting from within his finely tuned muscles. Now a four-year-old entire horse, he'd filled out magnificently, with a powerful bowed neck holding a proud head with intelligent eyes. Toby loved this horse and, as he led his charge around the ring, the bond between the two was palpable. Here they were calm. But calm waters run deep, and any observer could see they were ready for business.

The favourite, at 2/1, was a horse from New York, called Cooperstown. Had he not had a vested interest, Reggie would have made him his logical choice. He'd won his last start at Gulfstream, going this distance of a mile and an eighth on the turf, and he looked solid. Of the others, two were Group 3 winners from Kentucky, one of whom Tom noticed had run in the Quintessential race on Derby day; three were locals representing Maryland, that were stepping up in class; and there was the South American horse, El Cordobes, who was the outsider at 50/1; with Rikki, a 20/1 shot on the board.

The Delmontez crowd gathered around the one-stall with Tim Trebor. Their colt, a four-year-old – which actually made him really a three-year-old per the different hemisphere foaling times; spring in the north and fall in the south – was a rather light-framed and flashy bay, with four white socks. Whereas Rikki plodded round calmly with his head down, saving his energy, El Cordobes was on his toes and Tom could see that his groom had put the chain of his shank over his top lip to get extra control. Between his hind legs, he'd started to sweat, on what was a very humid afternoon.

'Well, now you've seen him, what do you make of him?' Reggie asked Tom.

'Whatever chance he might have had, and I, personally, gave him no chance in the first place, has probably gone. He's too wound up. By the time he goes through the post parade and gets to the gate, he'll be a wreck. I heard them talking about this horse at Keeneland, but he doesn't have the class for this level,' he replied.

Just then Basil Foster showed up and a valet appeared with the saddle. A very small one, indeed, with Angela having to do one-o-eight. Normally Basil would have been playing the Tom role, up in the Turf Club, but today Matt had told him to stay with Toby and his horse. Old feelings in Maryland towards crazy Matt Pearson, as many referred to him after the infamous on track knock-out incident, died hard, and the lower profile any horses associated with him had, the better. Besides, Matt had warned Basil to not let his horse out of his sight, as 'I wouldn't put it past those sons of bitches having a go at Rikki.'

So, it had been a sandwich and cup of tea in the track kitchen. No lobster and smoked salmon.

Rikki pawed the rubber matting, as Basil tightened the surcingle. A quick dose of the magic sponge in his mouth, a wipe down of his forelock, and he was ready. In his early, speed-crazy days, he'd sported blinkers, tongue-ties, patches, and all manner of cumbersome equipment. But now he was running in a standard ring bit, with no nose band. He carried his head low, when running, and, per his new relaxed style of coming from off the pace, that Jose and Matt had spent so much time developing, there was no need to tie him up with restrictive nosebands.

Angela Morris appeared in the splendid new stable colours. In her wafer-thin boots, she seemed even shorter than Tom remembered her from the morning. Nervous handshakes were exchanged and Basil boosted his young rider into the saddle. No need to give instructions, as he knew that Matt had told Angela to do the same as at Colonial: let him settle at the back of the field, save ground, and see what he's got from the half mile pole home. 'And,' he'd added, 'for this race, hug the rail, because they save the best ground down there, next to the hedge, for big days.'

This was a huge day, not only for the Elevator Stable but also their charge's rider. Heading out onto the racetrack in front of close to a hundred thousand raucous and slightly tipsy fans was quite an unnerving experience, as, over the speakers, the Baltimore Colts' now-defunct marching band played "Maryland, My Maryland".

On the way out of the paddock, Tom ran into Hector Delmontez. 'Hola, Tom!' the smiling Venezuelan said, turning to introduce him to his entourage. 'How do you like my horse?'

'He looks great,' said Tom, politely. 'I hope he runs well for you.'

'A fifty-to-one shot. But you never know.' Hector smiled. 'If he's like his namesake, the greatest bullfighter I ever saw, he will be tough. Do you know my friends? My trainer, Tim Trebor? And, of course, you know Senor Beagle.'

Trebor grinned and graciously said that he thought Rikki, who of course he knew well from earlier times, 'looked great.'

The crowd swept them towards the stairs. Billy Beagle smiled at Tom. and Johnny Ward-Clarke pretended to ignore him, as he ushered Calvin Weiner and his wife Samantha into an elevator. I hope he gets stuck in there, thought Tom.

Back at the table, Vera wanted to know if the boys were making a bet. There were four minutes to post time. 'Make your mind up,' said Reggie, impatiently. 'I'm going to watch outside, where I can have a cigar.'

'Ok,' said Tom, remembering Mark's MO from Churchill, 'let's put Rikki on top and bottom for fifty bucks. He's such a big price. That's how my friend Mark would play it: a seven hundred-dollar investment. We'll work things out, after the race,' adding with a chuckle, 'when we collect.'

The horses were advancing onto the turf course that ran inside the dirt oval and was just under a mile around. The start would be slightly to their left, near the top of the stretch.

Cooperstown had shortened to 9/5 and there had been a bit of money for Manxman, one of the local horses who had come in from 5/1 to 7/2. Rikki was steady at 20/1 and El Cordobes, the big outsider, still at 50/1. By now the latter was awash with sweat that his rider, Junior Alvarez, was scrapping off his shoulders with his whip and, to make matters worse, he wasn't taking too kindly to loading into what was, for him, a very different starting gate to the one that he'd been used to in South America.

Once he was in, though, the field loaded quickly and the starter released them to a prodigious roar from the crowd. On the rail, young Alvarez gunned his mount, who shot out of the gate to take up the running. Behind him the field settled, with Rikki Tikki Tavi bringing up the rear, perhaps ten lengths off the lead.

'El Cordobes,' said the track announcer excitedly, emphasizing the syllables with his best effort at a Spanish pronunciation, 'by six, as they go into the clubhouse turn. It's the South American setting a blistering pace. They went the first quarter in twenty-two and one, the field stretched out behind. Cooperstown moving up now, on the outside of Manxman, with Rikk-i-Tikk-i-Tav-i the backmarker by some.'

Up in the grandstand, Reggie lowered his binoculars and took his by-now nervously chewed cigar out of his mouth. 'Too fast!' he spat, 'he's running off with this rider. He's gonna stop bad.'

As the field headed down the backstretch, the commentary continued. 'They have gone a half in forty-five. Up front, it's still El Cordobes blazing away. The field is really strung out with just over three eights of mile to go. El Cordobes continues to lead…in fact, he's drawing away. Three-quarters in one-o-eight and thr-eeee!'

Back upstairs the boys and Vera had been watching Rikki, probably the only people who were, as the longest priced horse on the board stunned the crowd with his front-running performance. The pace had, indeed, caught the field by surprise, but Angela had not panicked and as they exited the back stretch, she asked her mount to make a move.

'Too much to do,' shouted Victor. 'This horse, on the lead, is not gonna stop.'

And that was the way it was. The unfancied invader, the 50/1 shot and longest priced horse on the board, wired the field. 'It's all over!' shouted the by-now hysterical commentator. 'This race is history! At the wire, drawing away. On his own. El Cordobes. A winner by six. Photo for second,' he continued.

The crowd was stunned. A few boxes below Vera and her guests, though, there was a lot of backslapping and hugging going on, as Hector Delmontez and his rapidly expanding bunch of associates streamed off to greet their winner.

Sitting back down at the table, the Elevator boys could see the rerun of the closing stages on the monitor. 'Hey,' said Victor, 'looks like Rikki got second!'

'Yes!' said Vera. 'Good old Rikki – good on Angela – he got up to be second. That's so amazing.'

'Dead right, it is,' said Victor, 'you get a hundred grand for being second in a five-hundred grander: twenty percent!'

'How about the Exacta?' asked Nils. 'Fifty to one on top of twenty to one! We will just about scoop the pool!'

And, so it turned out, the 1-5 Exacta paid $1,335 to a $2 stake. 'So, twenty-five times thirteen hundred and thirty-five equals?' said Colin.

'Just over thirty-three grand,' said Victor, frantically scribbling his calculation.

◆　◆　◆

As is always the case, after Triple Crown races, when a Derby winner extends his streak and looms as a possible champion of that elusive treble, there was great speculation in the trustees' lounge after Martial Arts had bagged the Preakness. It had been a long day and those assembled were well lubricated as they celebrated in the rafters of the rickety old grandstand. Vera had pointed out that traffic exiting the racetrack would be appalling, so they might as well accept the invitation extended to owners of runners in the stakes races that day, and join in the bun fight.

After their bonus exacta winnings had been divvied up, Reggie had bid his colleagues farewell and taken a cab to the station for his 8 p.m. train back to New York. But Victor, Nils, and Colin were not in any hurry, so they accompanied their generous hostess and Tom up to the sixth floor via another dreadfully over-crowded and antiquated elevator. 'Close your eyes and hold your breath,' she'd said, and they'd made it safely.

Amidst the raucous crowd of boozy racegoers, Tom could see the El Cordobes team, whooping it up with Alfred Van der Francis, the ageing president of the Maryland Jockey Club. Billy Beagle was there, too, with Calvin Weiner and a seemingly ever-increasing bunch of bandwagon jumpers, congratulating and fawning over Hector Delmontez.

As Tom pushed Vera's wheelchair into the room, the way parted to a table by the window, where they were able to look down upon the now-dwindling crowd. It had started to rain and the remnants, in the infield, fueled by gallons of beer, were indeed playing touch football in a sea of mud. Tom wondered whether any of them had any idea who had won the races that day.

The guests buzzed with excitement over the possibility of a Triple Crown winner but, so too, the extraordinary performance put on by the South American invader in the City of Baltimore Handicap.

On the way up, in the elevator, Tom had overheard someone saying that the winner 'ran like a horse that had been plugged in. Either that or he was juiced up to the eyeballs. No way, off that form in South America,' they'd continued, to a silence that suggested others found this statement to be risky at least, and actually rather slanderous, had the connections of El Cordobes overheard it.

The Elevator boys had never been to a reception quite like this and lapped up the fact that they were now rubbing shoulders with their heroes and the elite of the turf. However much Tom inwardly despised Hector Delmontez, he felt that it was his duty to congratulate him. After all, he currently represented the continued presence of Caledonia Farms at the highest level of the sport. Because Hector was besieged by well-wishers, it was hard to get a word in, but Tom caught his eye and he happily cut off the correspondent from *Thoroughbred World* magazine, who had been boring him to death with an obscure story about his horse's pedigree, by introducing Tom to the ongoing conversation. 'Tom, how about that? Wasn't that great? Do you know Trevor Gilpin from the, err...I forget...who are you with?'

'TW,' said a heavily perspiring bulbous man in a light grey suit that he'd long-since outgrown.

'Eeeee's an expert in bloodlines. Loves my horse,' said Hector.

'A fantastic performance. I'm happy for you,' Tom said politely, while quietly biting his tongue. 'Was it a track record? Must have been close?'

'No,' said the TW man, '1:47 and two, just missed it by a tick.'

'I'm proud of my country,' said Hector, turning to Billy Beagle and a beaming Cal Weiner. 'Didn't we tell you, in Kentucky, that we were bringing up this horse and Senor Weiner was going to enter into a partnership with Caledonia, to stand him at stud?'

'Well, he's now worth a pile more than he was then,' said a delighted Billy Beagle. 'Just what we need to inject new blood and excitement into our breeding program.'

'Can't have enough good out-crosses,' added Weiner. 'We're, I mean, our new partnership is going to race him this season, maybe even take a shot at The Arc, and then stand him at Caledonia.'

'If he continues on like this, there'll be a long line-up of top mares wantin' his services,' Beagle added.

'And at a premium price,' said the gushing Weiner. 'Could be a hundred grand a pop!'

Tom sportingly wished them well and, as he turned to return to the table in the window, found himself face to face with Johnny Ward-Clark. 'Oh, hello there,' said the rather startled bloodstock agent. 'Didn't we meet at Churchill Downs?'

'Indeed,' said Tom. 'I see that you are in with the right people, again.'

'Yes, the CBS is advising Senor Delmontez. And, as you probably know, we already represent Calvin Weiner and his bloodstock interests. My boss, Jos Danvers, put them together and I'd say it's working out rather well, old chap, isn't it? What's your name? I forget. Met so many people recently.'

Tom had come across this sort of greeting before, during his time in England. So, he understood it and its extraordinarily bogus sincerity. 'It's Tom. Tom Fraser. Good for you guys,' he said, batting the ball back over the net. I know now why Mark calls you Bog, he thought.

'Damn good place, this Baltimore,' Bog continued, 'came up from Lexington on Hector's Lear. Played a spot of golf yesterday, and went to the Maryland Club's Calcutta Night, last evening. Hell of an event! Ever been?'

'No,' said Tom.

'Well, the who's who of Maryland racing, plus of course the internationals here for the Preakness, have a little gathering. Men only. There were about a hundred of us.' He paused, 'Yes, about ten tables of ten, maybe a few more. Who cares - great food, lots of good wine. You buy tickets, at a hundred dollars each. Our table of Hector Delmontez, Billy Beagle, and Cal Weiner put up five hundred each.' Tom was getting nauseated by Bog's over-the-top familiarity with horse racing's supposed heavy hitters. 'The pool was just over thirty thousand, all told. And when they drew for each horse, we got Martial Arts. Ha! Ha! Then there was a guy from the bloodstock sales; I think his name was Laddy something. Well, he auctioned off each horse. And, depending on what chance you give them, you can bid on them. We kept our horse, fortunately. So we got first prize, which Billy Beagle tells me is worth about twenty grand! Ha! Ha!'

Tom gritted his teeth. This was aggravating and Bog was rubbing it in. 'And, if that wasn't good enough, we go and win a Grade 1 with our new horse,' he continued.

'Well done, indeed. So nice to see you again,' said Tom, not meaning it at all. 'I have to go and join my punters over there.' And he saluted Hector as he turned away.

'The only downer,' he heard Bog saying over his shoulder, as he mercifully departed his company, 'was that the five-horse spoiled my forecast bet,' he said using the English term for Exacta. 'Billy Beagle told me that he had no chance, so I left him out! What a bummer, eh? Would have paid a fortune!'

It did. And we had it, thought Tom, smiling with great satisfaction.

It was close to midnight by the time Tom and his aunt made it home. On the kitchen table there was a note from Matt: 'Rikki ate up. Grade 1 placed! How about that! See you in the morning.'

'Looks like you are riding out first set,' said Vera. 'See you at breakfast. I have something to show you.'

CHAPTER 17

As they headed out into the early morning mist, the chatter was all about the previous day's racing. It was a big deal that there was a legitimate contender for the Triple Crown, but Rikki's race and the way that the winner had run was the number one topic.

Dieter and Jose were kidding Angela. 'Got caught napping, eh?' they chided her.

'Well, so, too, did all those fancy New York riders,' she shot back. 'Besides, the word in the room was that that kid plugged him in.'

'You don't really think that anyone would carry a machine on a big day like yesterday, do you, with a huge TV audience all watching? I can't believe that,' said Dieter.

'Just when it works the best,' said Jose. 'Nobody's thinking that you'd pull a stunt like that. Junior's a good rider. He's been champion in Chile and Argentina. Knows how to ride, that kid. Hey, whatdya doin' slangin' us Hispanic jocks, eh!'

Tom listened. 'Maybe you're right,' he said, 'the way horse racing is right now, you know, with all this PETA stuff, they couldn't afford to have a positive test or scandal like that in a big race, on national TV. It would be the final straw, and all those animal rights' wing-nuts would say "told you so", and they'd bury the sport. So, they'd just lose it. Sweep it under the rug. Pretend it had never happened.'

'Maybe he was hopped and plugged in?' laughed Jose. 'What a guy! Ships in. Rides one horse. Gets the money. Ships out. Who's laughing now?,' he continued, chuckling at the thought.

'Well, Rikki ran a big race,' said Angela. 'Without the winner, who may or may not be legit, he's a winner of a $500K Grade 1 stakes races. Not bad for a fifty-grand claim, eh?'

'Gotta be the rider,' joked Betsy.

Back at the barn, Rikki was out on the rubber matting, having the up-tight hosed off his front legs. After he'd cooled out in the test barn, Toby had carefully packed his feet with mud and expertly encased his legs from ankle to knee in the cure-all racetrack poultice. He was old-school and for him there was no compromising, with whites all-round and exquisitely crafted butterfly bandages over his knees. It had all taken a great deal of care and time, as his compliant patient had chomped contentedly on his hay net.

After a graze, during which Silas, his designated hot-walker, had hosed his knees and ankles with cold water, he was released into the rolling ring: a sand-filled and boarded arena about thirty feet across, where he cavorted and his carers watched him with great glee. 'You should have seen that South American horse, in the test barn yesterday, at Pimlico,' said Toby. 'Crazy, man! I thought his eyeballs were gonna burst right outta his head. Rikki and me, we were there for close to an hour and he still hadn't cooled out, when we left. I never seen a horse so crazy-lookin', man!'

Matt Pearson leant over the rail. 'He ok? To turn out when he's finished here?' he asked Toby

'Sure, boss. He's good,' replied Toby.

'Just put some bell boots on him. He's sharp and I don't want him grabbing himself, if he starts running and bucking around his paddock.'

'You got it, boss,' said Toby. 'Your times up here, Mister,' he lovingly addressed his charge. 'We gonna go get you a bit of R&R here in the shade.' With that Rikki was captured and led off to a small and shaded paddock, where he'd spend the rest of the day, quietly grazing.

Matt and Tom headed up to the house for breakfast, where they found Vera in the kitchen, sipping coffee and reading from her iPad. 'They're talking about taking the horse that won Rikki's race to Europe. Gonna run him in the Arc,' she said, referring to arguably the world's most prestigious race, run at the beginning of October every year at Longchamp racecourse in the scenic Bois de Boulogne of Paris, France.

'Won't be able to hop him, there,' grunted Matt, pouring himself coffee and diving into a pile of blueberry pancakes that Elsie had just put before him.

'Do you really believe that?' asked Vera, looking up from her story.

'Damn! I'm only watching the TV. I wasn't there. But he sure ran like he was being plugged in.'

'Do you think a high-profile trainer, like Tim Trebor, would do something like that, though? Too much to lose.' She paused. 'Says here that the owner is syndicating him and that there is interest from Canada and some agency in England that represents powerful Arabs,' she continued reading, squinting through petite steel-rimmed glasses perched on the end of her nose.

'I doubt Tim Trebor has had this horse in his barn for more than a week. And with all the horses he's got, all over, he won't have known much,' added Matt.

'How about the owner?' ventured Tom. 'I have heard some strange stories about Dr. Delmontez and his operation.'

'Yes, of course. He's taken over your daddy's place now, hasn't he? You been out there recently?'

Tom told them about the hostile reception that he'd received when he'd driven out to Caledonia, and the subsequent meeting and conversations that he'd had with his father's erstwhile partner. 'The guy at BGT told me that they were very private and wondered if they were up to a bit more than it seemed on the surface.'

'What do you mean? What did he say?'

'Well, Ramon Diaz, the guy who died in the fire, was on Interpol's radar as being closely involved with drug cartels that they have been monitoring. And the Lexington police and FBI are investigating possible money laundering and insurance fraud in the enquiries that are related to the fire.'

Matt went silent, munching on his pancakes, deep into his *Daily Racing Form*.

'Then,' continued Tom, 'when I went out to look at some yearlings with my friend, Mark O'Malley, we ran into one of the help from the farm. A guy named Randy Dobbs, who Senor Delmontez had recently let go. I met with him, last week in Lexington, and he told me that some really weird stuff was going on. You know they have had a suspicious number of accidents involving recent imports?'

'What sort of accidents?' mumbled Matt, not looking up from his Form.

'Horses getting hurt while in transit, on planes, in vans. Sometimes just turned out in paddocks. Fatal accidents, like broken legs, colics, inexplicable fevers.'

Matt looked up. 'And you think that they were not accidents and that they arranged for these things to happen and then claimed insurance money, eh?'

'Well,' Tom paused, 'I can't say that for certain, but Martin O'Sullivan warned me that, in the industry, eyebrows had been raised. And,' he hesitated, 'when I met with Randy Dobbs, he gave me an unmarked bottle of some injectable that one of the Condor guys left in a farm truck. Maybe it's just some Ace Promazine, but...' he trailed off.

'Where is this bottle?' grunted Matt.

'Back in Lexington,' said Tom.

'Bring it here the next time you come. I'll get Dr. Hyatt to check it out. Those bastards are capable of anything,' he mumbled.

'Now then, Tom,' said Vera, changing the subject and pushing her plate away, 'you and I have a little visit to make. You don't need Tom anymore this morning, do you Matt?' she asked.

'No, we're fine. Only had the one set this morning. The rest are either walking or being turned out. We can manage, thanks.'

'Ok then, Tom. I'll meet you in the hall in twenty minutes.' She looked at her watch. 'Why don't we make it nine o'clock?'

◆　◆　◆

Basil had left early that morning with Mata Hari, bound for Fort Erie, where she was going to be prepared to campaign the Woodbine summer meet's stakes program on the turf. So, it was Silas who brought the Range Rover around to the front door and helped Tom and Elsie load Vera and her wheelchair.

Silas, or 'Stray' as the men in the barn called him, was the resident jack of all trades; happiest in the barn with the horses, shooting the breeze, walking a few, hosing one, grazing another, mucking out a few stalls, or holding one for the blacksmith - available for any menial task, be it mowing, painting or repairing fences. He'd seemingly been around forever, but nobody could remember quite how he'd found his way to Shenandoah Valley Farms or where he'd come from. That was why Toby had aptly named him 'Stray.' 'Just like one of them barn cats, here,' he said, 'you don't know who they belong to or where they've come from.'

Silas had a mysterious past that he never discussed. But it appeared that he'd spent time on the racetrack, and probably a bit behind bars. As Matt said, 'Great guy. But don't put him on the payroll. As soon as you do, he won't show up. The key,' he continued, 'is to pay him by the job or day, piecemeal.'

Like so many others who had worked for Matt over the years, Silas had been a transient for most of his life. 'Movin' on,' as he'd say when asked, 'What's happenin' Stray?', 'Just movin' on.' That was, anyway, until he'd touched down on the banks of the Shenandoah River and found the peace to be to his liking. Rumour was that he had a sister over in Ransom, the other side of Charles Town, and he could be often seen peddling his bicycle in that general direction, along Highway 340.

'A good bench player,' said Toby. 'Maybe doesn't show every day, but when he's here he can play every position. Just don't tell 'im that there's a big ol' hay truck comin' in tomorrow that needs unloadin' or you won't see 'im for a week!' He laughed.

Today Silas was on the ball. He and Toby had helped Basil on his way before dawn. They'd taken care of Rikki, and now he'd washed his boss's car and was playing his car-jockeying role with aplomb.

'We are so lucky, Tom dear, to have such good help,' said Vera as her nephew drove off down the tree-lined drive and turned south onto 340. 'Today we are going to a little farm between Upperville and Middleburg, just in behind Rokeby: the old Mellon estate, birthplace of Mill Reef and Sea Hero, both Derby winners. The former at Epsom and the latter at Churchill. I think that Mill Reef just might be the most perfectly conformed racehorse I have ever seen. What a champion he was.'

Just south of Berryville they turned east through Millbrook, passing lovingly tended hobby farms with neat dirt arenas that featured white-painted jumps and oxers. The banks along the roadside were covered in dogwoods, bluebells, and primroses. 'Roll down the window, Tom,' said Vera. 'I just love the scent of the wildflowers at this time of year. And of freshly mown grass.

'We are going to see my friend, Lorna Buchanan. She and her husband, Jim, who is some sort of lawyer in Washington, live in Georgetown and they have the cutest little hobby farm out in the back of nowhere. You're gonna just love it. It's such a peaceful place. We keep a few mares down here. They just do so well.'

Tumbleweed Farm was indeed tucked away in the woods, with Goose Creek running through the centre of its hundred acres. Tom could see, as they turned in through neat stone gates, that it was a beautifully kept property, with intricate criss-cross fencing atop dry stone walls, around lush green paddocks. The drive crossed over the creek and fanned out in front of a classic, old stone house covered in early flowering wisteria. A mob of small terriers erupted out of the front door, as Tom and his aunt came to a halt.

'These are Monty's and Freda's family,' said Vera. 'I didn't bring them today, because they get too excited and we don't want them upsetting the mares and foals, do we?'

As Tom unloaded the wheelchair amidst the yapping dogs, a commanding voice from within the house brought them quickly to order. 'Enough! That's quite enough you guys! You must be Tom?' said Lorna Buchanan as she extended her hand and then helped him load his aunt into her conveyance. 'What a beautiful morning, Vera dear. So good to see you.'

She must have been in her mid- to late-sixties. Tall and fit, her grey hair combed back and tied in a ponytail above a primrose flannel shirt and blue jeans. A no-nonsense stylish lady, thought Tom.

The two friends exchanged pecks on the cheek. 'Let's go around the back and look at a few horses.'

Tom pushed the wheelchair along a gravel path, around the side of the house, as their host led the way. 'The bulbs have done really well, this year,' she said as they walked past banks of tulips and daffodils. 'Maybe just past their best. But now we've stopped the deer digging them up, they've really established themselves. Like a carpet of red and gold; they're so beautiful.'

This place was, as his Aunt Vera had described, almost like one of those too good to be real Thomas Kincaid paintings, and Tom wondered if he'd see some bluebirds on a bird table, beside an ornamental pond full of monster gold fish.

'Well, here they are,' said Lorna, stopping to lean over the gate of a small paddock. 'We've got French Connection with her Damocles colt.' She pointed to a chestnut mare with a flashy chestnut foal at her side. 'And over there, that's Cleo with the orphan.'

Tom could see a big bay Clydesdale mare grazing beside some willow trees at the far end of the paddock, with a small, dark-coated foal by her side. 'She's taken really well to him,' said Lorna. 'I was a bit worried when they arrived because the little guy looked so tucked up and weedy.'

'Will they come over here?' asked Vera. 'I'd like Tom to see them.'

Lorna whistled and banged her hand against the gate, and without much hesitation the two mares, with their youngsters at their sides, trotted over. Besides the huge Clydesdale the foals looked so delicate, their long spindley legs like young giraffes', looking so out of scale with the rest of their bodies.

Lorna nuzzled the muzzles of the two mares and produced some nuts from her pocket. 'Cleo is almost twenty, you know,' said Lorna. 'What a good mom you are,' she said lovingly to the big old mare, scratching her behind the ear and kissing her on the nose.

'Aren't you worried that she'd sit on her foal, or crush him when she rolls?' asked Tom.

'You'd think,' said Lorna, 'but it's like an elephant with its little calf, the relationship between one so big and one so small and sooooo delicate,' she said, attempting to pat the little dark foal, who sheltered wearily beneath his mother's towering frame. 'They are so gentle. Look at those spindly legs. It's hard to believe that one day they'll propel over a thousand pounds at close to forty miles an hour.'

The little, dark bay colt turned his head towards his admirers and Tom could see a simple white star in the centre of his forehead: a bit like a shamrock or a clover leaf. The symmetry was perfect. 'What's he by?' he asked.

'I think Last Post,' said Lorna, turning to Vera. 'That's what Matt told me, anyway, when he dropped him and his mommy off here.'

'I think that's right,' said Vera. 'You know, I sometimes get these things muddled. We'll have to check with Matt.'

'And who is Last Post, if you don't mind me asking?' said Tom quizzically.

'Ha! Ha!' said Lorna. 'Ask your aunt, here.'

Vera smiled. 'Last Post is a horse we bred on the farm. A very well-bred colt, by Gettysburg out of Southern Belle. We sold him as a yearling for a lot of money at Saratoga, but he never really fulfilled his potential. Won a couple of minor stakes and then broke down badly on a sloppy track at Aqueduct. Bowed a tendon, that day, and that was the end of his racing career. Matt spotted him in a dispersal sale one day and, because he was still an entire horse, we bought him for twenty thousand dollars, to stand down here. With that breeding program they had in West Virginia, because of all the money from the casino at Charles Town, we figured he might get a few mares...' she trailed off. 'Reckon these local breeders didn't think much of him, though, because he hasn't had many mares.'

'Good-looking horse,' said Lorna, 'but things aren't what they used to be. It was such a shame that he died last fall. To be fair, he never really had much of a chance.'

'I know that they can change so much over the next two years, but this little guy has got a lot to like about him,' said Tom.

'Let's go in, and have a cup of coffee,' said their host.

Inside the hall, and what appeared to be an office off to one side, were filled with sporting prints. Tom recognized Herring, Munnings, and Lionel Edwards from his days with Bill Bass in West Ilsley.

As Lorna and Tom steered Vera into the spacious but cozy kitchen she said, 'My husband, Jim, is a bit of a collector, as you can see.' In the corner there was a large, open, walk-in fireplace, with various iron apparati designed to swing pots over open flames. 'Lovely old stone house, this,' she continued, 'dates back two hundred years. When we bought it, just over thirty years ago, it was falling down. Jim discovered the iron shackles that they used to manacle the slaves in, in a cellar under the hall! Seen a bit of history, has this place,' she said, as she filled the coffee pot.

'Lorna was out with me, the day I had my accident,' said Vera, looking up at a collage of hunting scenes and photos of various Buchanans mounted in the field and at local horse shows near Upperville and Middleburg.

'Yes, your aunt was something to behold in the field,' said Lorna, 'those were the days...' she trailed off. 'I'm so sorry to hear about your dad,' she continued to Tom, 'are you now going to be spending some time down this way?'

'Tom hasn't decided,' said Vera. 'We had a nice trip to the Preakness yesterday and he's probably going back to Kentucky to take care of a few things before making his mind up about the next step, aren't you Tom?'

'Well, yes. So much to think about,' said Tom as Lorna poured him coffee.

Returning home, Vera suggested the back roads through what she said was, in her opinion, the best fox hunting country in the United States. A bit like the rolling hills of the Cotswolds, she thought. 'Heythrop country, ain't it?' she suggested to Tom, and he nodded, even though he wasn't familiar with the Cotswolds that his aunt was describing.

'Just pull up over here,' she said. 'This view, looking southeast, may be the finest in all of Virginia.' Tom turned off the engine and they looked across acres and acres of emerald pastures, stretching as far as the eye could see.

Eventually, Vera broke the silence. 'I expect that you have been wondering what happened to your dad?' she said, gazing into the distance.

'Yes. Every minute of every day. I even have dreams, well, nightmares, actually, about it. It makes no sense. And now, the more I find out about Hector Delmontez and what has been going on at the farm, the more I want to find out what happened.'

'That's why I brought you out here this morning. I want to tell you.' She turned and looked at Tom. 'There are only three people who know. And you will be the fourth.'

Tom's jaw dropped, as Vera continued. 'I got a call from your father, back in early March. He had had some financial issues with the farm and brought some new people in, that Billy Beagle said would provide the investment needed to shore things up. But they turned out to be bad people. Your father never told me all the details, but he was very worried about the way they were carrying on and he wanted to protect the farm's main asset, Magnolia. He was concerned that Senor Delmontez might try and kill her for the insurance. Apparently there had been quite a few unexplained accidents since they showed up.'

Tom listened intently, as Vera continued. 'So, as we were sending a mare to near Lexington, to be bred, I said if he felt Magnolia was in danger, maybe we could could bring her down here? Well, everything escalated very suddenly. And, from what I gather from Matt, who'd received a frantic call from your dad, there was a big fight in the middle of the night between your father and Senor Delmontez's assistant, a man called Ramon Diaz, I think. Anyway, your dad called Matt and said that Diaz was going to kill the big mare, and to please come and help him stop it. When Matt arrived the two had had a terrible fight – apparently the mare had foaled and Diaz had injected her with something that killed her – your dad saw him trying to do the same to the foal and hit him on the head with the nearest thing he could find, which was a shovel, and, as Diaz fell, he plunged the syringe into your dad's thigh. Diaz was dead and your father was in a bad way, as whatever drug he'd been injected with took effect. Your dad knew he was dying and begged Matt to take the foal and set the barn on fire.'

Tom looked on, dumbfounded. 'Your dad handed Matt his phone and said to give it to you. You would understand. And he died.'

'What happened then?' whispered Tom.

'Well, Matt realized that he was in a bad situation and I suppose he reacted instinctively. Maybe his experiences in the army helped him. I don't know. Anyway, he scooped up the foal, put him in the gooseneck trailer with our mare and her foal, and set the place on fire. Thinking about it, and his slightly fragile state of mind, it's a good thing he did as he certainly doesn't need to get into any more bad situations.'

The two looked out of the window, in silence. 'The place went up like a powder keg. Matt drove outta there and didn't stop until he was a hundred miles down the road. It's lucky that that barn was on a remote part of the farm and it was one o'clock in the morning, as there was nobody about and he was well away from everything by the time he saw the fire trucks heading out from Paris.'

Vera reached into her purse, pulled out a phone, and handed it to Tom. 'Here it is. I don't know if there is any charge left on it. I haven't touched it since Matt gave it to me. And, in case you were wondering,' she paused, 'that little dark brown colt you saw just now, at Lorna's, is Magnolia's.'

The tears were streaming down Tom's face. He had no need to look because he knew what he was going to find. The last message sent: 'You'll know him when you see him. Just like his mom!'

CHAPTER 18

Johnny Ward-Clarke was on a roll. The trip to Kentucky and Maryland could not have gone better. The agency had landed a new client in Hector Delmontez and he had been assigned to the account. 'John, you know Senor Delmontez and appear to get on really well with him,' his boss, Jos Danvers, had said. 'They are going to send El Cordobes over here for the Arc, and I think it would be a good idea to introduce more of our clients to the syndicate.'

Johnny was the perfect liaison chap for new clients of whom his bosses weren't quite sure. If they proved themselves to be kosher, the big boys would embrace them, but if they turned out to be tire kickers or fly-by-nighters, they'd be Johnny's chaps. It worked well and, in the case of Hector Delmontez, was going spectacularly.

Now Johnny was at Lords cricket ground with Indian media king Ravindra Motti-Singh for the first day of the England versus India Test Match. 'Chat him up and make sure he has a great time,' were the instructions, as he'd been issued exclusive tickets for the pavilion, courtesy of Danvers' Marylebone Cricket Club membership. The intention was to charm Mr. Singh and make sure he bought all his bloodstock through Classic Bloodstock Services.

Johnny had spent considerable time selecting what he felt was an appropriate outfit for his first visit to the headquarters of cricket: cream linen trousers that he'd picked up in Lexington, a pale blue button-down shirt, and a dark blue blazer. The fact that he wasn't a cricketer and had never been to a first-class game hadn't occurred to his bosses. So, the absence of the right panama band and tie was a big deficiency that he very quickly cottoned-on to once he'd looked around the crowded ground and observed that everyone sitting beside him in the pavilion was thus adorned.

Mr. Singh was making his first visit to Lords, too. As a relative newcomer to the English social scene it was just as well for Johnny, because he knew nobody beyond a few members of the touring Indian team and certainly none of the English cricketing elite all around him, resplendent in their colours: red and gold, the MCC; Red, Gold and Black, I Zingari; Red and Green, the Free Foresters. All subtle symbols of belonging.

Ravi, as he'd instructed his nervous host to call him, was totally at ease in the late-morning sunshine, sporting an immaculate taupe-coloured linen suit. A pair of steel-rimmed sunglasses perched on his nose above a splendid military-style moustache. The tie and the band on his panama, Johnny had noticed, had already received nods of approval. 'Tollygunge,' he was told, 'not in this league, at all. But I do play when I have time,' Ravi had confirmed, modestly.

Indeed, on that beautiful early June morning, as India were put in to bat on a wicket that might ask them some questions, according to a man sitting behind them who had volunteered his opinion to all within earshot, there wouldn't have been anyone in the whole ground aware that they were sharing space with a veritable titan of the old colony.

Ravindra Motti-Singh had grown up the youngest of eight children in the Punjab, where his father had been a local jute merchant. Educated at a private school just outside Delhi, he'd won a scholarship to Birmingham University in England, where he'd gained a Master's degree in computer engineering that had enabled him to return to India and start an online education program that streamlined local students for university entrance. This fledgling enterprise had blossomed into Motti-Media: a multifaceted company that had now diversified into news, publishing, the IPL, and online gaming.

Married to a Bengali from Kolkata, named Marisha, the Singhs lived on a farm just outside Bangalore, where he bred thoroughbred racehorses and indulged his passion for cricket and coaching his two sons, Sachin and Bishen, who would be both heading shortly to Eton.

The first period before lunch, in a five-day game, is usually a pretty cagey time and this proved to be no exception, as the Indian openers held off England's pacemen through the first turgid ten overs that produced a mere twenty-three runs. There were a few oohs and ahs as ball beat bat, but the defence was solid and certainly silenced the very partisan crowd in the pavilion.

The subtlety of the strategy was new to Johnny, who was smart enough to resist passing comment on the lack of entertainment. In fact, he found listening to the banter between the dinosaur cricketing establishment around him to be most amusing. It was the first appearance of the year for many, who obviously regarded the first Lords' Test to be a signal that summer had arrived and the official cricket season had started. And their fond greetings to one another, as they apparently emerged from hibernation in the counties and remarks about 'wintering well,' made him smile. This was a different world.

At lunch India was 85 without loss, and there was a murmuring of disapproval as the players left the field. Ravi applauded the stubborn batsmen and got a few dirty looks. All around him picnic hampers were being opened and gin and tonics dispensed to the disappointed members, greatly in need of cheering up.

'We have tickets for lunch in White's tent,' said Johnny, standing and stretching his legs as he ushered his guest up the aisle.

As they walked past the members' lunchroom door, an elderly man sporting the home MCC colours was being helped up the steps. 'Used to be,' he could be overheard growling to a young steward who was holding the door for him, 'that members meant members. Now they seem to let any bounder in. The place is going to hell in a handbasket.'

Ravi smiled. 'I am used to that,' he said to Johnny. 'Sometimes, in India these days, you wonder if you're not in a time warp as there are still clubs and ancient institutions that uphold old standards and the protocol of the Raj even more pedantically than their former masters. It's actually quite funny.'

Bog grinned, not knowing quite what he should say.

The tent, for lunch, was situated on a lawn at the Nursery End, as the opposite end of the ground from the pavilion is called. Johnny could see that, bored by England's lack of success, lunchers had made an early start on the substantial fare being catered by Fortnum & Mason's. Pink gins were being chugged down with gusto, and it seemed that the popular view was that the selectors had got it all wrong. 'Gotta pitch it up on a greenish wicket, like this,' said one man with a deep red complexion that offset a spectacularly carbuncled blue-ish nose. 'Jones is bowling far too short. No length. No line.'

'I would have given Turner an over or two before lunch, if I was captain,' said another. 'We need a breakthrough, right after lunch.'

It was primarily a smorgasbord. And after establishing where their table was and ordering drinks, an IPA for Ravi and a Perrier for Johnny, they found themselves in a lineup for a sumptuous spread of cold salmon, rare roast beef, and a wide variety of salads.

As he helped himself, Johnny was ambushed by an altogether unwanted greeting. 'Hello Bog! What are you doing here?' The voice was familiar and with dread Johnny turned and was confronted by Algy Sinclair. Oh, no! Just when things were going swimmingly, and he was about to reel in his new client. I hope Ravi didn't hear that, he thought to himself.

'Hello there,' said Johnny, with minimally disguised sincerity. 'Do you know Ravindra Singh?' he asked. 'Ravi, this is Algy Sinclair. He's with the competition, ABA. Anglian Bloodstock.'

The two men shook hands. 'To answer your question,' continued Johnny, 'Mr. Singh,' to you, he thought, Ravi to me, 'is looking to buy some mares and we're taking care of him. He came to the right place,' he added with a laugh. 'And Jos just thought he might fancy a bit of cricket, as India is playing. So here we are.'

'Splendid. Where are you sitting?' said Algy.

'In the pavilion stand,' replied Johnny with an assertion that suggested 'Where else?'

'Good show,' said Algy. 'I'm here with my uncle. He has a box, where he's probably drinking far too much, at the moment, with his stuffy guests. So, I thought I'd pop out and join my mates over there.' He pointed to a table, at the other side of the tent, that was full of tall young men who all looked frightfully sporty and were attired in the perfect kit. 'Why don't you join us for tea? If play continues the way these Indian guys have started, most of the guests will have departed or gone to sleep by then.'

It was the last thing that Johnny wanted to do, but he could see that his guest was intrigued. So, it was agreed that, at just after four, they would meet at box number 307.

After a lunch, during which Johnny enquired politely about his client's farm, in India, how many head he owned, and what bloodlines he liked, they returned to their seats and watched the much-maligned Jones remove Salim Gupta with the first ball of the new session.

There was a big roar around the ground, which had filled to almost capacity with fans that had taken the afternoon off from work, as a wicked in-swinger took the batsmen, who possibly was still savouring his lunch, by surprise, trapping him plumb leg before wicket, as he shuffled unconvincingly, neither forward nor back. 'Told you so,' growled the man behind them, whose earlier rhetorical question had finally been answered. 'Pitch it up. Make the blighter play!' he opined to the buzz.

To Ravi's immense satisfaction, that was the only wicket that fell before the break for tea, by which time India was 182 for 1, with Suresh on seventy-five and the dangerous number three, Rahul Bundar, forty.

In the box, the occupants looked somewhat shell-shocked, as Algy greeted them. 'Mr. Singh, I'd like you to meet my uncle, Lord Armscote. And, Uncle Teddy, this is Johnny Ward-Clarke.' He didn't think it would have been fair to introduce him as Bog, although the thought had crossed his mind, as his uncle would not have let it pass and probably would have gone on to tell some anecdote about once knowing a chap called Bog who was in the Ghurkas, and in the end it would have been humiliating for his guest. Good manners prevailed.

'So, you're from India, eh?' said his lordship, standing unsteadily to shake Ravi's hand. 'Your chaps are doing a bit too well, for my liking anyway. Do sit down.' He gestured to his guests to take the seats at the front of the box that had been vacated and now provided the best view. 'And you, sir. What is your game? Play a bit, eh?' he said to Johnny, which was exactly what he had hoped he could avoid: being put on the spot.

'Well, actually, no sir,' said Johnny.

'Played at school, I'm sure?' continued Lord Armscote.

This was hell. 'No,' replied Johnny.

'What did you do? Row? Were you a wet bob?'

'No, sir. I didn't go to Eton.'

Fortunately, this awkward conversation was interrupted by a sudden downpour as the heavens opened. The sky looked ominously black and, even though the wicket was covered promptly, pools of water started to accumulate in the outfield. So, after about twenty minutes, it was announced that play had been abandoned for the day.

Inside the MCC bar, the feeling was that the rain had come just in time. And, if the weather continued dampish and overcast in the morning, this might help the England bowlers. The more drinks that were consumed the better their consumers thought this prognosis was.

Johnny was anxious not to linger in what for him was dodgy territory, as it had appeared that Algy was getting on far too well with Ravi; something that certainly wouldn't please his boss. So, they'd left as soon as he felt it was polite to do so.

◆ ◆ ◆

On the short flight from Washington to Lexington, Tom reflected upon the revelations of the previous weekend. As shocking as what he'd learnt from his aunt was, he was beginning to put the pieces together and, while he could see a potential mine-field ahead, there was now at least a light at the end of the tunnel.

The circumstances of his father's death confirmed the insidiousness of Hector Delmontez. But he wondered who else had been there at the farm that night: the fourth person that his aunt said knew what had happened, and about the existence of Magnolia's foal? She had told him, on the drive back from Tumbleweed Farm, not to mention anything that she'd told him to anyone and particularly not discuss any aspect of it with Matt.

It had been an extraordinary stroke of fortune that it was Matt and not Basil who'd driven the mare down to Lexington. Matt very seldom went anywhere with the horses after the ruling-off in Maryland. But Basil had felt ill and, at the last moment, Matt had volunteered. And thank God he'd had the presence of mind to assess what had confronted him and made a decision that Basil might not have been able to do.

As Matt had related to Vera, when he'd received the urgent call from Bob Fraser, just as he was about to set out on the return journey with the newly covered mare and her foal by her side, he'd driven directly to where Bob had said, knowing the farm from previous visits: something that Basil would not have been able to do. Upon his arrival he'd quickly realized that Ramon Diaz had not only intended to kill the mare and foal, but Bob too. That she had dropped her foal that night had complicated matters. But finding himself with two dead bodies and the dead mare he had acted instinctively, remembering his crisis survival training in the Marines. The fire had consumed everything, but the foal was safe.

Tom had so many questions that he would have liked to have asked Matt. How had he managed to get the little foal all the way back home safely without any help? It was a miracle. He was now, he guessed, his dad's legacy. There was something to look forward to. But what about provenance? The great mare was dead. So, too, as far as anyone else knew, was the foal she'd been carrying. Now they had a foal on their hands that officially didn't exit. How would they establish his pedigree and get papers and a passport?

Vera had rather vaguely answered his questions. 'They were lucky that they were off the radar, down here on the Virginia/West Virginia border, where nobody pays too much attention to what's going on. If it had been Kentucky, there would be too many smart arses and local vets and regulators, never mind people on the farm wanting to know what's what. We'll sort things out,' she'd said.

Mark was at the airport to meet him. As they drove back into town, Tom told him about the Preakness, how Rikki Tikki Tavi had run so well, the extraordinary performance of El Cordobes, and seeing Hector Delmontez and his hangers on. 'Oh, I ran into your friend Bog too. He was there. Apparently, CBS is going to be syndicating Hector's big horse.'

'He says you're a great guy,' said Tom.

'Who? Bog?' laughed Mark. 'He's one smooth operator, I'll give him that.'

'Right in there with Billy Beagle and those Canadian guys. They, apparently, went to some posh men-only sweepstake dinner the night before the Preakness at an exclusive club in downtown Baltimore.'

'Oh yea, the Calcutta Night at the Maryland Club. Great fun. Was Laddy Dance doing the auctioneering?'

'Yes. I believe so,' said Tom.

'Don't make 'em like him anymore,' said Mark. 'I just love the way he stops and talks to the bidders. It's not just that rat-tat-tat stuff – bang, bang, bang – he makes a story out of it. He knows everyone. It's an art form. Sometimes, if you are the last bid, it can be agonizing as he tries to extract one more from whoever is bidding against you. Great guy. We must go, another year.' 'I have a bit of sad news for you,' Mark continued.

'Oh yea, what?' said Tom resigned, as if he hadn't had enough recently.

'You know that guy you met in the washroom of the restaurant? The day we went out to the McDonnell's place, and you met him again in a bar in Lexington sometime after that?'

'Randy Dobbs? What's happened to him?' asked Tom, alarmed.

'He's dead, I'm afraid. It was on the local news. A man found, unresponsive, early last Sunday morning. I think someone was carrying the garbage out from a bar and found him in the alley out back, behind a dumpster.'

'That's awful,' said Tom. 'Did they give a cause? Was he beaten up? Had he been in a fight?'

'Don't think so,' replied Mark. 'From what I read in today's paper it was an overdose. That carfentanyl stuff, they say. There's an epidemic going around. It's supposed to be a hundred times more powerful than heroin.'

'Jesus, that is sad,' said Tom. 'Poor chap was a bit lost. Did they mention anything about a funeral?'

'No. But you could call the hospital or police station, I guess.'

Need to stay away from the cops, thought Tom. 'Let's call the hospital when we get to your place.'

'Don't expect he had much of a family, judging by what you said,' said Mark. 'Sad, indeed. Another promising guy from the racetrack bites the dust.

Sounded like he lost his bug, ended up riding bad horses for bad people at bad tracks, had a few falls, got busted up, got on the painkillers, and went down the slippery slope.'

'I'd like to go to his funeral,' said Tom. 'Not that I really knew him, but I would be interested to see if anyone shows up because Randy was one of the few people who was working with the Delmontez crew on the farm, until he got let go.'

◆　◆　◆

Cheap but hardly cheerful, the short non-denominational service in the institutional funeral home, hidden away in a rundown industrial estate on the lower east side of town, attracted more mourners than Tom had thought would be there.

The Sheriff's department had informed Mark that the body had been subjected to a routine autopsy by the coroner, as was the case with all suspicious deaths. But it had been perfunctory: just another indigent drug user overdosing. No nearest and dearest. In fact, not much of anything, and poor Randy's Ohio driver's licence was even out of date, with an address in a Cincinnati suburb that may have been where he had lived years before. But nobody there knew of him now, just like precious few who had read the short notice in the *Lexington Examiner* remembered his glory days, as leading bug-rider at River Downs and Turfway Park.

Through the Ohio racing commission, an aunt in Toledo had been finally located. But the prospect of perhaps being asked to cover expenses of a funeral had quickly cooled her out. So, the pathetic, cremated remains of Randy Dobbs stood in a small urn on a table, while someone who had never heard of him delivered a monotone eulogy filled with fatuous generalizations about him being a good man who had passed on to meet his Maker. A man who loved the turf. But, as Tom thought, was soon to be under it. What was left of him, anyway.

In the background, a loop recording of cheesy music drowned out the sobs of the only person in attendance who seemed at all saddened by the occasion: a petite woman, of perhaps forty, in a pale cotton dress. She was in the front row, alone with her hanky.

When, mercifully, the sheepish-looking attendant, in his shiny black suit and matching black clip-on tie, looked up and bowed solemnly, following the final prayer, to signal conclusion, she turned to leave, and Tom could see that life had been hard on her.

The last funeral that Tom had attended was his father's, and he'd been in such a daze that he'd forgotten most of what had gone on, amidst the hugs and sympathetic murmurings. Now he was a detached observer, but one with a much keener interest in what had transpired in the deceased's final days and hours than most in attendance appeared to have.

Just off the foyer there was a room where coffee was being served from a metal trolley to about a dozen people. Tom accepted a cup and introduced himself to the woman who had now put on her raincoat and was looking wistfully through the window at the damp parking lot and chain-linked fencing, with the sign Jarred Funeral Services, as the rain poured down.

'A sad day,' he said. 'I'm Tom Fraser. I didn't know Randy well. Well, in fact, I didn't know him at all until just recently. We met at a roadside café, out near Paris. He used to work for my father.'

'Yeah,' she said, 'he used to work for a lotta people. He was a good kid. Could have been a top rider.' She sniffled and wiped her nose with her hanky. 'Got fucked up, like everyone else who thinks the track is where it's at, and that people care. They don't care! They just use you.' She looked up at Tom and attempted a smile. 'I'm Lee-Anne. Randy and I used to go together, back when he was leading rider. Best bug since Steve Cauthen, the kid, they used to say. Now look at him, just a bitty pot of ashes.' She started crying again.

'Lee-Anne,' said Tom with as much empathy as he could manufacture, 'when was the last time you saw Randy?'

'Musta bin three, maybe five years. He quit the track. Couldn't gallop horses no more, the pain was so bad. Just got fed up movin' around. Tack room to tack room. Wanted to settle down and get a steady job, put down some roots, he said.'

'Yes, he told me that,' said Tom, 'when I met him about a month ago. He'd been working at my father's place, Caledonia. But as you may have heard there was a bad fire and two people, including my dad, died. The new owners let Randy go.'

Lee-Anne was unimpressed. 'When I read it in the paper, I thought something bad must have happened, because the last time I spoke to him on the phone he seemed bothered by something. Had been real happy, working for good people, he said, but then things changed.'

'Well, I think he was. But, after the fire, all his friends were let go and the new owners brought in their own people. Mostly Mexicans and Latinos from Central and South America. We met at Joe Louis' and he didn't look well.' He paused, 'Lee-Anne, was he on any medication? You know, opioids?'

'As I say, I ain't seen him in a while. He used to do stuff. You know, all them riders are into shit. After he broke his thigh in a bad fall at Mountaineer Park he was on a powerful prescription for a while. That and the wastin' ain't no good for you,' she drew deeply on her cigarette, 'can get addictive. But, as I said, I ain't seen Randy in a while. So I don't know what he was on.'

'It's just that when my friend spoke to the cops and asked about the cause of death, they said it was an overdose but wouldn't specify what the coroner had found. The cop said he shouldn't be discussing the case with anyone who wasn't family, but he did remark that in the box, where they note these things, it said "unknown", not Fentanyl, for example. And another thing that was strange was that there was no alcohol in his system, which is odd.'

He was about to mention the small phial of an unknown drug that Randy had given him, but was fortuitously interrupted by a small bearded man in a neat grey suit. 'Larry Mullins,' he introduced himself, offering Lee-Anne his hand. 'I represent the Kentucky Horseman's Benevolent and Protective Association, the HBPA. We're so sorry about Randy. Are you family?'

'No. But I guess you could say we was part of Randy's racetrack family,' said Lee-Anne. 'You know, people drift in, drift on out, like the circus, travelling from town to town.'

'Hello,' said Tom. 'I'm Tom Fraser. Randy used to work for my father at Caledonia.'

'Yes. I am sorry about your father and what happened,' said Larry. 'I used to be a rider, myself,' he smiled, patting his tummy, 'many years ago. I guess the track gets into your blood and you never can leave. Galloped horses for a while, when I quit, and then did a bit of agents' work,' he laughed. 'Doesn't make much sense, does it? You can't make ends meet as a rider and you end up trying to do so off 25% of what some other guy makes who can't, either! Crazy! Here's my card. It's not the most glamourous job but it keeps me in the game.' Tom accepted it politely and put it into an inside pocket where it would probably remain until the jacket was next sent to the cleaners. 'My condolences to you both,' he said, taking his leave.

'Do you have wheels?' said Tom.

'No. I got a taxi out here,' said Lee-Anne. 'I need to get to the bus station. They have one to Cincinnati every hour. If you could drop me off, that would be real kind.'

On the way to the bus station, Lee-Anne lit a cigarette and drew in the smoke hungrily, as though her lungs had been crying out for the nicotine shot. Tom could see that once she must have been a fine-looking woman, but the delicate features and high cheekbones had long since been sucked in, giving her mouth a tight, drawn look. Her mousey hair might once have been blond but today it looked greyish and greasy, and her tears had blurred her makeup. What a wreck, thought Tom. She needed a hug and some TLC, but he felt she was too far gone.

'Who were those other guys, at the funeral home?' he asked.

'Oh, them.' She laughed. 'One was Jerry Meyers. JC they call him. And the other guy, the guy with the goatee, he was Sid Dale. Two peas in a pod. Gyp trainers. I suppose I shouldn't be sayin' that, being as they came. Hadn't seen them for ages. Just small-time operators, hustlin' with a few cheap horses here and there. I guess Randy must have ridden for them at some time. Oh! I'm sorry,' she said suddenly. 'I guess you don't like me smoking? I remember one time,' she continued, when Tom didn't say anything, 'Randy rode a horse at Penn National, that Sid was dropping in for a nickel. He was probably worth twenty, but Sid figured that he hadn't run for a long time, after being vanned off in his last start up in Ohio, and nobody would take him.' She drew on her cigarette. 'Anyway, Sid finds out that there's a claim in for him, so he runs out onto the track, during the post parade, and shouts to Randy to bale out. He's acting like a crazy man, wavin' his arms about. Randy falls off. The horse got loose from the pony and ran off. But they caught him. Then Randy said he was hurt and couldn't ride. So they finally scratched him. It was a riot!' She laughed for a moment. 'As I say, good of them to come. It's always the old-timers who seem to care, you know; more than them today who won't do nuthin' unless there's somethin' in it for them.'

Tom dropped Lee-Anne off at the bus station and gave her an awkward hug. 'Take care,' he whispered as she disappeared into the busy terminal.

CHAPTER 19

Johnny Ward-Clarke was in excellent spirits. He'd just picked up a new car: a sporty, late-model Audi that he felt showed taste but not too much flashiness. Not good for people to think he was making too much money, he thought as he drove through the London traffic to pick up his hot new client at the Dorchester hotel in Mayfair.

Today they were going down to Newmarket to meet with Jos Danvers and the directors at Classic Bloodstock Services. Johnny was in his dunn-coloured moleskin trousers, a pink New & Lingwood shirt, and ubiquitous countryman's jacket that the obsequious salesman at Golding's, on the Newmarket high street, had told him was what 'gentlemen wear, when out and about.'

Mr. Singh had spent the weekend visiting family and, with his brother Kulbir, had returned to Lords the day before to watch India mop up the England tail in a famous victory. They had both laughed at the absence of English fans witnessing this calamitous defeat, as they sat in the sunshine, anonymous in their Mound Stand seats.

Jos Danvers's plan was for a tour of one or two select Stud Farms. The first at Six-Mile-Bottom was where he had arranged to meet Johnny, as it was on the way down from London, precisely, in fact, six miles outside Newmarket, and another in Wooditton, after which they would repair to The Three Blackbirds gastro-pub for a light lunch.

Thankfully, for Johnny, the conversation driving down the M11 had been about horse racing and the upcoming Royal Meeting at Ascot, which Ravi was looking forward to attending for the first time, and not about the great Indian victory at Lords the previous day. 'Where we are meeting my boss is a lovely little stud owned by one of our more prominent clients, Sheikh Bhakandar. The Sheikh will have several fancied runners at Ascot next week. Have you ever met him?'

'No,' said Ravi, 'but everyone knows his famous green silks. They're always on TV and, more often than not, in the winner's enclosure.'

'He probably won't be here today. But you are bound to meet him next week at the races. Lovely man. Been a big supporter of our racing.'

Boy, this chap's got the patter, thought Ravi, smiling and enjoying seeing the East Anglian countryside as he was chauffeured to British horse racing's headquarters.

Jos Danvers's Range Rover was parked outside a beautiful old Queen Anne-style house, surrounded on all sides by neat lawns that opened up to the most beautifully maintained paddock fences that Ravi had ever seen. This was a model, he thought, wondering whether palace or mansion were the right words to describe it. No. Manor Stud, as it was called, was perfect.

Ravi and Danvers had not met before, so Johnny, who had picked up their new client from the airport and had been making sure that he'd had a good time, made the introductions. 'Ravi, I would like you to meet Jos Danvers, our director in chief, and my boss, and Eddie O'Reilly, the stud groom here at the Manor.'

Handshakes were exchanged and Danvers, who was sporting his Eton Ramblers tie, just in case his important client should notice, joked about the cricket. 'You chaps gave us a good thrashing, eh?' he laughed. 'I hope John looked after you?'

'Yes, Mr. Danvers, he has been most kind and hospitable,' said Ravi, 'and yes, it was a good result for India.'

'Oh please, please, let's dispense with such formalities. I'm Jos and this is Eddie. He's the chap that makes this place tick.'

'Sheikh Ali not here today, sir?' said O'Reilly, deferentially.

'Not today. He's readying himself for next week's action, I would think,' Danvers replied.

'Yes, sir,' added O'Reilly, a ruddy-faced, short and stout Irishman in a brown feeder coat, tweedy tie, and cloth cap. 'Looks like he could have a big meeting.'

'Well, Eddie, where are we going to start?' asked Danvers.

'I thought we'd go down to the stallion barn, sir. The covering season is almost over, but we may get to see some action. Then we'll go and look at a few foals.'

'Sounds good to me,' said Danvers. 'Here, Ravi, jump on,' he added and the four men got aboard a golf cart.

The tour of Manor Stud went like clockwork, and continued on to Eve Stud in Wooditton. 'This used to be owned by Sir Victor Sassoon,' said Danvers, as they drove up the tree-lined drive. 'They bred St. Paddy here. And a lot of those good horses that Noel Murless had at Warren Place were raised in these paddocks,' he droned on.

Lunch in the charming black-and-white, Tudor-styled Three Blackbirds, afterwards presented an informal opportunity to further impress Ravi with what CBS could do for him, if he was looking for some well-bred mares for his stud in India, and perhaps even a stallion to bring in some new classically European blood to cross with the mares he already had.

Over a very tasty Muligatawney soup and warm homemade bread, straight out of the oven, Danvers got onto the subject of Ascot. 'We have a box,' he enthused. 'Are you ok for kit?'

'If you mean a morning coat and top hat, yes, I am prepared,' said Ravi, wondering whether he was being patronizing and thought he might show up in a dhoti or worse still, a suit. Now that definitely wouldn't be good cricket, he thought, smiling to himself.

'Good man,' continued Danvers. 'The agency is putting together an elite syndicate that will be made up of high profile owners from around the world, and we plan on launching it during the Royal Ascot meet, while all the major players in global bloodstock are in town.'

'We thought you might be interested in getting involved,' Johnny chimed in, on cue. 'It's going to be called Classic Racing.'

'Yes,' added Danvers. 'You've heard the saying about breeding thoroughbreds? You know, breed the best to the best and hope for the best. Well, Classic Racing is going to bring together the best owners and breeders with the best horses in the world's best races.'

'Meydan in Dubai, Shatin in Hong Kong, Narita in Japan, Longchamp in Paris. The very best, like the Royal Meeting at Ascot next week,' chorused an equally enthusiastic Johnny.

The polished tandem had the pitch well rehearsed. 'It'll be a global version of the Coolmore set-up in Ireland,' said Danvers, 'and we are delighted that Dr. Hector Delmontez, who recently took over the famous Caledonia Farms in Lexington, Kentucky, is going to be one of our founding members. He represents South American bloodstock; and you probably read about El Cordobes' very impressive North American debut at Pimlico recently, where he won a Grade 1 stake on the turf and almost set a track record?'

Ravi Singh nodded. 'Just between us, because it's not going to be announced until next week.' Danvers lowered his voice conspiratorially. 'Senor Delmontez is very generously allowing our agency to manage his racing interests in Europe and has sold us a majority interest in El Cordobes, who will be Classic Racing's standard bearer.'

Johnny grinned. 'And we have a top owner and breeders from Canada investing, too. So, Ravi, if you want to get in on the ground floor, this is a golden opportunity.'

'If you would be kind enough to give me a prospectus that explains what is involved and how much this venture is going to cost, I would be happy to get my people to look into it,' said Ravi.

'Good man,' said Danvers. 'We'll see you next Tuesday.'

CHAPTER 20

Since the beginning of the eighteenth century, during the reign of Queen Anne, horse racing has been conducted on what was then parkland around Windsor Castle but is now Ascot racecourse. And every year, in mid-June, the five-day royal meeting is one of the highlights of the British horse-racing calendar.

Situated about thirty miles southwest from central London, the almost two-mile (clockwise) turf racecourse, with an adjoining one-mile straight chute, is a magnet for not only the best horses and most ardent fans of the sport, but hoards of fashionistas and gourmets who swell daily crowds in excess of fifty thousand. On the social calendar it kicks off the summer's must-do list, followed by Wimbledon, Henley, and Cowes.

Today Ascot is ultra-corporate and, some might say, its grandstand now resembles a concrete complex of featureless enclosures, connected by webs of towering escalators, and lacks the charm and exclusivity of bygone days, when the likes of Eliza Doolittle and Henry Higgins, of *My Fair Lady* fame, strolled across its lawns to peruse the horses in the tree-lined paddock. But nobody can deny its star appeal and the aura of big bucks.

Once upon a time, the royal enclosure was so exclusive that admittance was by referral only; divorcees were not admitted and fashion police ruthlessly ejected patrons who were in any way unsuitably attired. In those days, anyone wishing to attend for the first time had to write to Her Majesty's representative and request the privilege of a badge that would admit them to the royal enclosure. And woe betide if your credentials were not top-drawer. It was (then) four days of rare exclusivity. Just six top-class races per day, with invariably big fields that, in the case of the handicaps, run on the straight course, like the one-mile Hunt Cup and six-furlongs Wokingham Handicap, often featured thirty-plus runners that would sometimes add to the excitement by splitting into two groups, racing on either side of the wide-open course.

Nowadays, it is a five-day affair; anyone can get in who is prepared to pay, and the overall quality of the racing has been somewhat diluted, as too much of any good thing tends to do. Nonetheless, its still a big deal, and Ravi Singh was looking forward greatly to the experience.

'Logistics are going to be difficult, with traffic,' Johnny had explained to Ravi, with him setting off from Newmarket and Ravi from his hotel in London. So it was arranged that they would meet at 1:30 p.m. in the CBS box. 'In good time for the royal procession up the course,' he'd added.

The truth was, though, that Johnny had cadged a lift with friends who had access to the prestigious and perfectly located carpark number one, where their picnic lunch would be sublime. Being in the right place with the right people at the right time was so important and, as pompous English occasions went, this was right up there, with no shortage of fine linen tablecloths, crystal, and a seemingly endless supply of champagne.

'Do not let our man out of your sight,' his boss had said. This was a huge day for the newly formed Classic Racing partnership, and by the end of the week Danvers hoped that it could be announced that several of the Turf's luminaries were on board.

As Johnny nibbled on a smoked salmon sandwich and schmoozed with his friends' friends, he felt he'd arrived. Everything was perfect, and he'd remembered to leave the bottom button of his waist-coat undone. 'Don't do that and you'll look like a wanker,' he'd been told by his colleagues at the office on Newmarket's High Street. It's tough, fitting in, he thought to himself, little knowing.

At precisely 1:15 p.m. he excused himself from his fellow lunchers, straightened his tie in its stiff collar, which had been choking him since he'd put it on fully five hours earlier, adjusted his top hat, and set off to fulfill his role as consummate host. The walk through the trees and picnic row felt to him like a model must feel on the runway, his new outfit sleek on his slim six-foot frame. Keep your shoulders back, relax, and look like you belong. A thousand eyes were watching, and he enjoyed being the object of their attention.

Danvers had phoned him several times during the morning regarding Mr. Singh, as he insisted on calling him. 'I do hope he looks the part,' he'd said. 'Make sure you are early, as he might get lost if he finds himself overwhelmed by the crowd. But we don't want him arriving at the box too early. Again, I do hope he has the right kit.'

Johnny crossed the Ascot High Street, milling with purveyors of carnations, roses, tip sheets, and royal souvenirs, and noticed a commotion by the main entrance to the royal enclosure, where a very sleek midnight blue Rolls Royce was decanting its passengers and the ubiquitous paparazzi were snapping furiously away. 'Stand back,' cried the perfectly coiffed chauffeur. And two tall men with beards emerged, clasping their brilliantly groomed black top hats and rolled umbrellas. As they turned and were pointed towards the gate where two large beefeater-type men, dressed in dark green frock coats, stood menacingly checking out those who sought entry, Johnny saw that the cause for the excitement was none other than his man, Mr. Singh, with, presumably, his brother, whose name he had yet to discover.

'Hello, Ravi.' Johnny plunged in as a host of racegoers parted for this grand entry. 'Nice wheels,' he gushed.

Ravi smiled. 'John, this is my brother, Kulbir.'

'A moment, gentlemen,' said a man with a camera. 'Yes. Very nice. One more. There you go.'

'Welcome to Ascot. Come on in,' he said with confidence, belying the fact that this, too, was his debut performance on this stage. Look like you belong, he kept reminding himself, making a mental note that he should follow up with the photographer for a print.

As is the custom, all those granted badges for the royal enclosure pin them onto the lapels of their tailcoats, for men, and somewhere on their dresses, for women, where they can be well-seen. You can have a special one-colour badge for all five days, with which the agency had provided Johnny, making him feel extra important and professional, or have a day badge whose colour is different for each day. Today, Tuesday, being the first day, it was yellow, and on Ravi's someone had neatly written: Ravindra Singh, Esq.

'Lotta nonsense, eh,' he said light-heartedly to his brother, as they made their way through the crowds, past the paddock, and in under the grandstand to the elevators that would take them up to their third-floor box. Johnny had been here often for regular non-royal meets, so knew the layout. 'We'll get our race cards in the box and they will serve you a very nice lunch, I'm sure.'

Like most boxes at major sports venues, guests were fed in a dining room-cum-reception area upon entrance, and then one could walk out to seats in an outside area that overlooked the racecourse. Her Majesty the Queen's horse-drawn landau and the procession of her guests who were in the Windsor Castle house party for the week, was apparently just arriving at the gates at the end of the straight-mile chute, which caused a stir amongst the guests, already lunching. Spotting Johnny and the Singhs, Danvers rose to welcome them. 'Mr. Singh, great to see you, sir. This must be your brother. How do you do, sir. Is this your first visit to Ascot?' he was almost awkwardly formal.

The Singhs smiled and Danvers continued the introductions to a group that were becoming familiar to Johnny. 'I want you to meet William Beagle, from Kentucky, and his wife, Mary-Lou; Calvin and Samantha Weiner from Canada; Hector Delmontez and his lovely wife Patricia; and last, but not least, my dear wife, Deidre.' Everyone smiled and exchanged muted greetings, and Danvers steered Ravi and Kulbir out onto the terrace. 'Cracking good view, isn't it? Right by the winning post. In fact, the course and grandstand just start turning a bit, at this point, and you can look straight down the course. That's the royal party you can see in the distance. Do come in and get a spot of lunch.'

Ravi and Kulbir were served vichyssoise, followed by salmon mousse with prawns. 'You two men are without doubt the most smartly dressed that I have seen,' remarked Deidre Danvers. 'I just love your style. To me, it seems like a sort of frock coat-cum-Nehru Jacket, cut like an old-style morning coat, something you might have seen in Victorian times. I just love it!' she enthused.

'Yes,' chorused the other ladies, obviously charmed by their new guests. 'If you don't mind me saying,' Samantha Weiner addressed Ravi, 'you remind me of Omar Shariff.'

'Bollywood star, perhaps?' Kulbir suggested.

Danvers winked at Johnny. So, he guessed, the boys' kit passed muster.

'Please, tell me what you do in India?' asked Mary-Lou Beagle.

'Well, I have a business that started out in the early nineties as a platform that provided university entrance curriculum, via the Internet, for Indian students aspiring to overseas colleges. From there we developed local high-school level programs, and in fact attracted many mature students who had never had an opportunity to get qualifications before.'

'How wonderful,' purred Mary-Lou. 'And have you been successful?' She paused awkwardly. 'Oh! What a stupid question. I guess you have!' she laughed at her brain cramp.

'He's far too modest,' interrupted Kulbir. 'That small beginning attracted huge government support and now, in India, we have arguably the best trained IT and AI communications workforce in Asia, if the not the world.'

'Good for you,' said Billy Beagle. 'As a Republican I shouldn't really say this, but I'm ashamed of just how poorly educated and ignorant of world affairs many Americans are these days. You can never have enough education.'

'And health care,' chimed in Kulbir, provocatively. 'Motti-Media now co-ordinates over a hundred million cell phone users via a local PayPal money transfer network and, with its latest app, any user can access medical assistance and treatment.'

'Fantastico,' said Hector Delmontez, 'and that's not even ten per cent of your population! Just think of the potential.'

'And you?' Patricia Delmontez hesitated, smiling. 'Meeester Kulbir. Do you live in India, too?'

'No. When Ravi went back to India and made his fortune, stupid me stayed here in the UK,' Kulbir replied.

'And what do you do?' she continued.

'Crunches numbers,' said Ravi.

Kulbir smiled. 'Actually, when I got my degree, I went to Harvard and studied advanced mathematics and computer sciences for my Master's, such as they were in the early days. And now I'm a lecturer in AI at the London School of Economics.'

'So, you're the dumb member of the family,' said Billy Beagle, and everyone laughed some more.

His guests were enthralled by the Singhs, and Danvers could barely conceal his relief that they'd fit in so well. Classic racing needed power players throughout the world, he mused, and Ravi Singh was certainly no lightweight. Got to reel him in. 'Here we go,' he announced suddenly, 'the royal party approaches.' Everyone filed outside as the first landau, drawn by four immaculately turned out grey horses, with their manes and tails exquisitely plaited, and with the leader mounted by a member of household cavalry in his splendid red and gold uniform, turned left off the racecourse and in under the stands. The crowd cheered and hats were raised to greet the monarch in her lilac dress and matching pillbox hat. Horse racing was her passion, and this was a definite highlight, confirmed by her broad smiles.

'Oh look!' said Deidre Danvers, glancing in the direction of the Beagles. 'There is Thurmond Mckenzie with Her Majesty. A Kentucky presence. He used to be the US Ambassador over here,' she said matter of factly to the Singhs as they stood behind her. 'And there's Prince William and Kate in the third carriage.' The sun had come out on cue and the large crowd, excitedly awaiting a great afternoon of top-quality horse racing, applauded generously.

'Can't beat it, eh?' said Cal Weiner.

'Certainly puts the Queen's Plate equivalent at Woodbine in perspective, doesn't it.' his wife Samantha responded, and Weiner frowned.

The first race at 2:30 p.m. was won by a colt owned and bred at Manor Stud by Sheikh Ali Al Bhakandar. As the favourite, he got a big roar of approval from happy chalk players and the bookies smiled wryly, wondering if this might be a painful harbinger of an expensive afternoon.

'Do you remember Eddie O'Riley said they'd have a big week, when we visited Manor Stud last week?' Johnny said to Ravi.

'Yes, I guess it's too late to cash on that one, though,' he replied. 'I'm just joking, of course, because I never bet.'

'Now then,' their host, Danvers, addressed them, 'John is in charge of showing you chaps around. Maybe you'd like to go down to look at the horses in the paddock or take a stroll on the lawn in front of the royal box? Whatever, please treat this box as your base, and we'll see you later, for a spot of tea after the fourth race.'

◆ ◆ ◆

The six races were staggered forty minutes apart and, after round two, Ravi and Kulbir decided it would be nice to stretch their legs and check out the horses in the paddock for the Group 1 Queen Anne Stakes, the highlight of the day, that featured runners from France and Ireland.

'Run over the straight mile, these horses are aged four and older,' said Johnny. 'Some competed in the Classics as three-year-olds, so it's a very prestigious race. I would imagine that Her Majesty will be in the paddock, even though she doesn't have a runner, because she loves to look at top-class horses. Fortunately for us, if we go down with Mr. Danvers,' he was being his most respectful, 'we can probably get into the paddock and have a better view, as he has an owner's badge and, being with Mr. Beagle, they'll let us in.'

The immense crowd swarmed around the many champagne and hors d'oeuvre bars that were cranking out lobsters and magnums of bubbly by the dozen and, at the rail, it was six-deep, with minimum movement and vision due to the proliferation of hats. But Ravi and Kulbir were in the right company and without much ado found themselves flushed out of the mayhem onto the beautifully manicured lawn, around which eight horses were being led on a reddish-brown rubberized track.

This was the crème de la crème, and Johnny pointed out the Marquisse de Montpelier, with her trainer Robert Lefebvre, whose magnificent grey, Espion, was the even-money favourite. The Marquisse's racing silks were pink with a green hoop and cap, and she invariably dressed herself in a mixture of these pastel colours, Johnny informed his rapt guests.

'Our friend, the Sheikh, has another one in here, too.' Johnny gestured, as a handsome chestnut walked past. 'The five, Desert King. And there's the Irish horse, Brian Boru, who won last time out at the Curragh. That was a small Group 3 on soft ground, though, and I just wonder whether he has the class to step up to Group 1 level, on this fast ground.'

Ravi and Kulbir were suitably impressed, as they watched the jockeys emerge from the weighing room and meet up with the connections of the horses they were riding.

'That's the French champion, Jean-Louis Gay, there.' Johnny indicated a jockey in Sheikh Bhakandar's green colours. 'The Sheikh has horses in France with Antoine de Sevigny, at Chantilly, as well as a bunch at Newmarket with Marcus Townsend. That's Marcus over there with Sir Humphrey Edwardes-Jones. They have number one, Fighter Pilot. Lovely horse. Getting on a bit now, he's seven, but a multiple Group 1 winner in the past. In fact, he won this very race two years ago. Might find it tougher here, though.'

The horses were mounted and headed for the parade in front of the grandstand, and the Danvers crowd headed back upstairs to the box. So far Ravi and Kulbir had not recognized a soul, with the exception of the royal family, which was fine by their host. But that didn't last long - as, while waiting for the lift up to the third floor, Ravi heard a familiar voice. 'Hello there. Our Indian friend from Lords,' boomed Lord Armscote. 'Aha! Your chaps gave us a right spanking, didn't they?'

'Lord Armscote, how very nice to see you again, sir,' said Ravi, turning and introducing his brother. 'My brother, Kulbir. And you met Johnny at the cricket.'

'Yes, indeed,' said Armscote, ignoring Johnny. 'I see that you are wearing the Tollygunge tie again. Been checking up on you, you see.' He tapped his nose with his finger, conspiratorially. 'I said to Algy, we should get you down to play for us one weekend. We could do with a ringer, to sharpen up the opposition a bit, eh?'

'I would be delighted, if I'm in the country,' Ravi replied, 'and my brother bowls a mean leg-break, if you are looking for some spin,' he added.

All the time, Algy Sinclair was standing behind his uncle grinning from ear to ear, resplendent in his grandfather's mold-tinged tailcoat, a black top hat that had definitely seen better days, and the most striking purple-and-gold waistcoat that looked like it had been made out of a spare piece of his grandmother's gaudy curtain material. 'I see that Johnny has got you in the right company,' he remarked as the elevator opened and their party entered. 'See you chaps later. We have one in the last race,' he added as the doors closed.

'Who is that chap with your Indian friends? Is that your Bog friend?' Lord Armscote enquired.

'Well, yes and no, Uncle Teddy. He doesn't like people calling him that. Well, not on occasions like this, anyway.'

'Strikes me as a complete bounder,' said Armscote. 'Never played cricket and now he shows up here in a grey hat!'

'Uncle Teddy!' said Algy trying not to laugh. 'He tries. At least his outfit fits him and wasn't a hand-me-down.'

'Humbug!' said Armscote. 'That's not the point.'

◆ ◆ ◆

The Queen Anne Stakes was won by Desert King, in a photo over Espion, with the French horse probably not liking the firm ground as much as the victor. It was another major score for Sheikh Ali and, after the fourth race, he and his manager Hugo Lascelles came up to the box. Also a director of CBS, Lascelles was keen to introduce his boss to the Singhs and the other guests whom he hoped would become key members of Classic Racing.

They sipped tea and watched the fifth race as Sheikh Ali held court, impressing upon the visitors that, had he not been given the soundest advice regarding his bloodstock investments from Jos Danvers and Hugo Lascelles and the very knowledgeable staff at CBS, when he first came to the UK in the late eighties, he would never have had the success that he now enjoyed. It was an impressive pitch.

There was a time and place for business, and Danvers certainly did not want to spoil his guests' day by hustling them into his new venture; that would be very poor form. This was just bonding the players he knew needed to be on board to make Classic Racing a success, and the day could not be going better. He made a mental note to himself to have a word with Johnny about his hat.

The sixth and final race was a two-mile handicap and Johnny suggested that anyone interested should join him in an each-way (win and place) bet on Apple Blossom, a tip that he'd been given by a good friend (actually Algy). The ladies thought this was a great idea, and very quickly forty pounds was raised and proffered to the charming young lady from The Tote, who so far that afternoon had not had much success in persuading the occupants of the box to put their hands in their pockets.

Kulbir had studied his race card. 'Five-year-old mare, trained by Bill Bass at Lambourn for Lord Armscote,' he announced.

'Very good,' said Johnny. 'You're a natural.'

'Tough stayer who has won over hurdles and is a course and distance winner. This all sounds very good,' he continued. 'So why,' he asked, looking at the odds board and then back to the TV monitor in the box, 'is she 20/1?'

'Aha! Another good question,' said Johnny. 'I think the answer is that she is stepping up, here, to tougher competition. She gets in with a light weight, though, at seven stone twelve pounds, and they're riding their apprentice, Jock Manners, who claims five pounds, which means they're getting a fair bit of weight from the better fancied horses at the top of the handicap. Factor in Bill Bass, who has a habit of popping up with a nice-priced winner at big meetings, and I think we'll get a really good run for our money.'

'Ok, I'm convinced,' the mathematician Kulbir said. 'Here's ten pounds.'

'That's great. We now have fifty, so twenty-five quid each way please, my dear,' said Johnny to the girl from the Tote, and ticket was printed on the spot.

Apple Blossom ran a blinder to be beaten less than a length into third. And the Tote paid out handsomely, with the favourites out of the running, returning 8/1 for the place part of the bet, meaning two hundred pounds for the fifty that they'd invested.

A lot of excitement and a dividend. Kulbir was impressed. He and his brother had a lot on their minds as they chatted in the back of the Rolls while it purred up the M4 back into central London. Kulbir counted his forty pounds over and over. A 300% profit. Boneheads in the city beat their heads against the wall every day for ten points per annum!! His brother smiled as he reflected upon the dynamics of the day.

'What's their game?' said Kulbir.

'Whose game?' his brother enquired. 'There were so many different games going on.'

'What do you mean?'

'Well, first there was Danvers and the CBS agency, putting on their own show. They've got their man, Johnny, massaging us. They've got their main client Sheikh Ali giving them some kudos and credibility. They've got his manager, that Hugo guy, bullshitting us. Then you've got the Kentucky guy, whatisname, Beagle? He's putting on his own dog and pony show with all that Bluegrass stuff and his society wife. They're the Kentucky show. Then you've got the guy from Canada who, in my opinion, is a fringe-playing wannabe, and you've got the South American fellow with the trophy wife, whom they are all mesmerized by and who would like us to invest in his great stallion prospect. So, whose game are you referring to?'

Kulbir laughed. 'What a performance, eh? Makes you think. Back in the sixties,' he lowered his voice, 'we'd have been up front and we'd certainly have never made the cut for the royal enclosure. Yet now, they're running around looking for our money. I just loved that guy, Lord something or other; he's still living in the days of the Raj.'

'Take him up on his invitation,' said Ravi. 'Those leg breaks of yours will be lethal here on the green, turning wickets that they have. They'll just love you - maybe even let you bat!'

They laughed and laughed. Up front, their very discreet chauffeur had to bite his tongue in order not to laugh, too.

'Well, what do you make of it all?' asked Kulbir.

'It's simple,' said Ravi. 'They want me to invest in Delmontez's stallion. All that stuff at Lords with Johnny was just softening us up. That Beagle guy is a slick operator. Delmontez is not his type, in my opinion, as those Kentucky folk are not too cool with Hispanics and blacks, but he respects a guy with money and, for that, he'll pay attention, as they've been struggling to find new players for a while.'

'So, Delmontez thinks that getting the heavies in Kentucky and Newmarket on his side is what he needs to make a sale?'

'Yes, that's about the size of it. He's looking for investors and I don't think he cares too much where they come from or what kind of money they have, as long as they have a lot. Watch out for the next move.'

'And what do you think that will be?'

'Well, you know what my main objective is: to launch Real Racing. But, to get there, we have to kiss a few arses. And this, I can assure you, is just round one.'

Kulbir laughed, 'You have come a long way, little brother. Rav-ito! That's what the Latinos call little guys. I'm proud of you. Ha! Ha! Ha!'

◆ ◆ ◆

As the two Indians cruised back into London, parallel to them, but further west and in a much worse traffic jam, as he endeavoured to get onto the M25, circumnavigate the west side of London, and head on up the M11 back up to Newmarket, a sweaty but quietly confident Jos Danvers, now in his shirtsleeves, sans tailcoat, spoke to his partner-in-crime, Hugo Lascelles, on his mobile phone. 'Went pretty well, I thought.'

'That Venezuelan chap is a cool customer,' said Lascelles, similarly mired in stationary traffic.

'It's all about confidence. Having you and Sheikh Ali parachute in, when he's just won two big races, it makes us look like we're where it's at, as our American friends would say!'

Lascelles laughed. 'Who wins the prize? Senorita Delmontez or Mary-Lou Beagle?'

'Actually, if I had the choice, it would be Samantha Weiner. Lovely girl. Gets treated really badly by that wanker of husband of hers, though. Poor girl,' Danvers replied.

'Seriously, John thinks that his Singh chap will buy a couple of mares and, with a bit of a push and shove, will take a piece of El Cordobes. The plan is to get him over to Keeneland and nail him down then.'

'Sounds good,' said Danvers and hung up.

◆ ◆ ◆

About ten minutes behind his boss, Johnny was struggling. The ride down had worked perfectly, but he had let his hosts know that his departure time was up in the air, depending upon what his bosses needed him to do. 'Don't wait for me,' he'd said and, when he got back to carpark one, they hadn't. So, plan B had kicked in per an urgent call to Maltie.

Good old Maltie Haig, the CBS's pedigree nerd with a passion for Malteasers and Malt Whiskey, had the day off and had driven down from Newmarket on his own, in his 2005 Volkeswagen Golf. He'd offered Johnny a ride, but of course John was headed for carpark one, so thank you, but no thank you, he'd said. But good old Maltie was on the same team and, besides, Johnny did not believe that eating humble pie, in this case, could possibly hurt him.

The good news, as far as he was concerned, after he'd ascertained that Maltie had not already left, was that his car was in carpark number eight. So it was highly unlikely that anyone important would see him getting into such a beaten-up old vehicle. The bad news, though, was that it was a hike to get there and it had started to rain.

After making a successful rendez-vous, per phone directions, the first thing that Johnny had realised was that Maltie was extremely pissed and completely incapable of driving his ancient vehicle anywhere, except probably straight into the car parked next to them. So, Johnny took over and, keeping his head down and hoping that nobody recognized him, headed back home to the sound of the maltman's snores.

He hoped that his boss was pleased with the way that he was looking after Mr. Singh. It was quite a feather in his cap that he'd been assigned to this account and, furthermore, the managing of Senor Delmontez. So much to learn! Wish I knew more about cricket. Why was Algy always so cool and I'm not? he thought. He was always in the right place. He and his uncle had looked like Tweedle Dee and Tweedle Dum, with their Dickensian-era outfits and hats that looked like the resident moths had been well fed. But, what was it he'd overheard Lord Armscote mumbling about grey hats? The thoughts percolated through his head as he ground through the gears of the clapped-out Golf. Why was it that Maltie also seemed so relaxed? So unconcerned about what anyone thought about his decrepit tailcoat and dilapidated hat?

Easing in quietly, lest anyone see him, Johnny parked in front of his cottage. And, just as he cranked on the handbrake, Maltie woke up. 'Oh hello,' he said. 'Good job, Bog.'

Seething, Johnny got out of the car and collected his stuff. 'You ok to drive home?' he asked.

'Sober as a judge,' replied Maltie, belching loudly. 'What a great day. Our Place-Pot got a huge boost off Apple Blossom. God bless Algy and his uncle! Lord Armscote looks a bit like Richard Griffiths in the *History Boys*, doesn't he? Top men!'

'Thank you, Malt. You are not going again this week, are you?'

'No. Some of us have to work, Bog, I'm afraid.'

'Well, do you mind if I borrow your hat?' Johnny enquired tentatively.

'Ha! Ha! You want the lucky hat, do you? You wouldn't believe where that hat's been. My grandfather hunted the Quorn in it. My father got married in it. Good grief, it's been in our family since Moby Dick was a minnow. But all who've worn it, dear Bog, would, I am sure, be happy to see it sail into action on your handsome head.' And he flung it out the window like a Frisbee, and sped off.

CHAPTER 21

Ever since the subdued gathering to say goodbye to Randy Dobbs, Tom had been bothered by several things: that the autopsy had shown his stomach to be virtually empty, with no alcohol in his system; that the coroner had dismissed his death as a Fentanyl overdose when the actual substance found was undetermined; and that Lee-Anne had said that, even though he had been disappointed losing his job at Caledonia, he certainly didn't sound suicidal the last time she had spoken to him.

He looked at the 50c.c. phial of clear injectable liquid. Other than a few meaningless numbers, there was no description of the contents. He thought about what Billy Beagle had said about not discussing anything to do with his father's death with anyone, least of all the police. Indeed, he didn't even plan on discussing it with Mark, now that he had heard a version of what had transpired before the fire from his Aunt Vera.

Now Randy was gone, that lead was dead. And, as his sample's provenance could be easily refuted by Delmontez and his staff, just drawing attention to its existence was going to attract a whole pile of heat that he didn't need.

He had two options. Stay on in Lexington with Mark and work the July yearling sales or head back to Shenandoah Valley and work for Matt Pearson on the farm, with the possibility of a few rides in the fall at the local Hunt Meets.

In the end, he decided on a compromise: stay in Lexington until after the sales and then go up to Saratoga with Basil until Labor Day. Then, depending on how things were going, he could decide whether to resume his riding career or make some real money at the fall sales in Kentucky.

Mark explained that the way it worked was that during the months preceding a sale he would be contracted by bloodstock agencies and, in some cases, trainers directly, to look at yearlings that were catalogued to be sold. He worked on a per diem basis, plus expenses, and would e-mail his observations such as big, rangy, small, attractive, awkward, tall, good-boned, back at the knee (a killer), offset (denoting which knee), curby, sickle-hocked, and dozens of other little positive and negative characteristics that would give his clients an idea of what each animal looked like and whether they were worth inspecting at the sale.

Most consignors prepared videos and provided photos from every angle, but there was no substitute for a good, independent eye and, with experience, clients learnt what Mark meant. In turn, he picked up on what they were looking for and which features mattered the most. It saved a lot of time when, at some sales, there were close to a thousand head being sold.

Income from such reconnaissance was bread and butter, but also helped the reputation of the scout. Indeed, just the knowledge that a well-respected agent had been seen looking at certain stock would be enough to draw a crowd. Consignors were always welcoming and propagated their own promotional gossip so that, by the time sale day arrived, those in the know were more than well briefed; not only regarding who was worth taking a closer look at, but who might be the competing bidders. This in turn helped in the making of alternative plans: so and so loves this guy (and his client has a lot more money than ours), so we better be prepared to find something else, more in our price range.

Mark loved the to and fro, and particularly the tire-kicking and interference, that went on while a horse was in the ring, sometimes helping to run up a price for a breeder to what they needed, and then getting a 'thank you.' Such practices and collusion are frowned upon by sales companies and particularly by high-profile buyers who often feel that they've paid more than they really needed. So they, in turn, sometimes revert to 'beards,' or hidden bidders that nobody knows, so competing bidders can't tell how deep their pockets are; or, if they are representing someone, who that person is. It's great craic, Mark thought.

Most states that conduct thoroughbred horse racing will have their own regional sales of state-bred stock. But, by in large, Kentucky and Florida are the two major producers of American bloodstock, with the former the centre of sales activity, highlighted by the Select Yearling Sales in July, when the crème de la crème is up for auction. Thereafter, there is a select sale and a

New York-bred sale at Saratoga in August, followed by the largest Kentucky yearling sale in September and a host of other smaller sales in Ontario (Canadian-breds), Maryland, and Florida, later in the year.

The September sales in Lexington are today regarded as the number one source of good racehorses, and the large catalogue reflects this. However, if a breeder has an outstanding individual that he doesn't want to get lost in these numbers over a prolonged period of up to a week, sometimes they are better off in the select sale in July, where, while they may be a relatively small fish in a very select pond, they will get more attention from buyers with the deepest pockets.

That was the dilemma confronting Mark's clients, the McDonnells. They recognised that they were very small breeders, but were worried that they might get a bad position in the catalogue and they did not want to consign their lovely colt through a third party, even though by doing so would undoubtedly mean presenting him better and more invitingly to the top purchasers. This was their main chance to make a good profit and they did not want to share it.

When he'd first arrived from Ireland, Mark had started by working the September sale for various Irish agencies and their clients, and it had taken him a year or two before he'd established a reputation, as someone with a keen eye, who was a straight shooter and well connected. So, it was no surprise when he'd received a call from Paddy McDonnell, asking his advice.

Paddy was excited. 'They've accepted the Majestic Knight colt for the select sale!' he said with great pride. 'The first yearling from this farm to be so honoured. Betty is over the moon!'

'That's wonderful, Paddy. I bet your Da's happy,' Mark replied.

'Is he ever. He was right all along. This is a real nice colt, Mark, and day by day you can see him progressing. He's got a great presence about him and I can see why those guys from the sales company, who came out to see him, maybe turned a blind eye to his pedigree being a bit light.'

'I know, these Kentucky guys can be terrible snobs when it comes to evaluating class. For them, stuff up in Canada might as well have taken place on another planet.'

'Yep,' said Paddy, 'and that's why I need your advice. Do we go it alone with the big boys, and risk being outshone, or do we pass and wait until September?'

'These days, when top buyers are being so selective, confirmation is king. So, I say, go for it. You were talking about a hundred and fifty grand. Well, if you get the attention of one of the Arabs, you could see twice that here.'

'I'm so glad you said that. Let's just hope we get a good spot in the catalogue. You know how political that is.'

'Fortune favours the bold,' said Mark. 'We'll put the word out and anyone who comes within earshot will, I'm sure, be convinced by your da that here is the chance to buy the next Secretariat!'

Paddy laughed. 'Yes, we might be a one-man band, but Da will sure make a lot of noise.'

When he hung up the phone, Tom told Mark what his plan was.

CHAPTER 22

The headlines of the *Racing Post* and the *Daily Racing Form* both led with stories about El Cordobes, recent sensational winner of the City of Baltimore Handicap, and the plans being made to ship him to Marcus Townsend in Newmarket, to be prepared for a tilt at Europe's most prestigious race, the Prix de L'Arc de Triomphe, at Longchamp racecourse in Paris at the beginning of October.

The release had been timed, post Ascot but prior to the first major yearling sale of the year, so that it would get the attention of international owners and breeders. Now that the renowned Newmarket bloodstock agency CBS had been retained by Hector Delmontez to syndicate his exciting prospect, Maltie Haig had been busy putting together a package of promotional videos, confirmation photos, and pedigree analysis.

After his sensational debut at Pimlico, El Cordobes had been shipped back to Kentucky and was reportedly under light excise at a training centre, fulfilling quarantine requirements. The photographs that had been sent from Lexington showed the same rather light-framed horse that Tom had remarked upon at Pimlico, though there was no indication of whether they'd been taken before or after that race. What was very clear to Maltie, however, was the importance his bosses attached to forming a successful partnership with Hector Delmontez and his Kentucky-based colleagues and marketing him as a unique opportunity to invest in classic bloodlines from South America that would cross perfectly with European mares.

That Maltie was having a hard time finding convincing evidence that this was the case did not seem to be of interest to them. Hector Delmontez was a new player in Kentucky with considerable resources and powerful clients, whom the folks at Keeneland were anxious to do well. It was networking and the old boys club at work: mining new sources of revenue.

Following the Royal Meeting at Ascot, Jos Danvers and Hugo Lascelles had met in London with Hector Delmontez, Billy Beagle, and Calvin Weiner, where it had been announced that Ravi Singh would buy a quarter share of El Cordobes for $2 million and that CBS were on the point of confirming another major investor in the stallion – some speculated Sheikh Ali Al-Bhakandar – making him arguably worth $8 million. In related press releases, it was further speculated that were El Cordobes to win 'The Arc' he would be worth many times more. It was mentioned that there could be a deal in the offing for dual-hemisphere duties, covering mares in the first part of the year in England and the latter part in Australia.

During all of this action, Johnny W-C had been very busy chauffeuring around his boss's clients and making sure that they were well-provided for. The Singhs had only attended the one day at Ascot and Ravi was now back in India. But he'd been in close contact with Kulbir regarding the specifics of the sale, and the agency had kept him busy entertaining their other clients over the five days.

'You look so much better,' Danvers had said, when Bog had shown up in Maltie's weathered black topper on day two; which he was happy to hear, even though the hat was too big and kept dropping over his ears, despite the newspaper he'd wrapped around the inside of the rim. Why, he wondered was it ok for the Yanks, foreigners, and, as far as he could see, a host of celebrities to wear finely tailored, modern tailcoats and grey hats, but, to be part of the right set, a raggedy black one was de rigueur?

'It shows that you own your kit, Bog,' Maltie had joked. 'It's nothing special. Just normal. In your family. You know, you don't have to go to Moss Bros. to rent it.'

The Singh brothers were not easily fooled. Ravi certainly enjoyed his stud farm and the relatively small breeding operation that he had, and it was his intention to upgrade his mares. But buying into an expensive stallion, however ambitious it looked, was secondary compared to the main reason that he had approached CBS in the first place, which was to raise the profile of Motti-Media's next venture: Real Racing. Something which his office in Bangalore planned on launching as a vehicle for major educational fundraising.

While at Birmingham University, Kulbir had done a thesis on the Irish

Hospital Sweepstakes which, during the 1960s (long before the Internet, modern-day communications, and social media), had generated world-wide interest and a considerable amount of money, entirely per cash sales, cheques and postal orders, as credit cards hadn't existed in those days.

The idea had been to sell tickets, at a pound each, for the chance of drawing a horse in a major race. A week or so before the race, when the likely runners were known, those whose tickets were drawn were assigned a horse and rewarded with a prize of £10,000. Then whoever had drawn the ultimate winner, would win the jackpot of £100,000, with the second and third getting commensurate prizes. After taking into account the cost of running the sweepstake and these prizes, the balance was used to build hospitals. So the endeavour had been supported by the Irish government.

Everything had gone well for the first few years and millions of pounds were raised, with people all over the world participating even though it wasn't legal in many jurisdictions. You either wrote off and sent postal orders or cheques; or, if you lived abroad, bought tickets through family in Ireland and the United Kingdom. Ultimately, though, as the venture got more and more popular, there were suggestions of impropriety and sadly it had ended.

What Ravi and Kulbir were now exploring was the possibility of launching a modern-day equivalent via the Internet that would, by virtue of social media and mobile phones, reach a much broader and larger audience looking for real-time entertainment.

As he had done with the creation of the online educational platform, Ravi had worked closely with the Indian government at all levels. His preliminary meetings with officials had suggested that they would be very receptive to sanctioning an Indian-based global sweepstake on selected sporting events, from which proceeds would go towards not only education, but also health and welfare services.

Danvers and his well-connected friends were facilitators and brokers of the so-called sport of kings and, like so many British institutions, their power was based upon connections in the right places. So when the Singh brothers met with the British Horse Racing authority at their Portman Square offices in London, the path had already been prepared. Or so they thought.

Major Alastair Fortescue, who greeted them at horse racing's administrative headquarters, was effusively charming, cracking jokes about cricket and bad weather, as he escorted his Indian guests to the board room. Introductions were made to Lord Jeremy 'Chubby' Magnall, the current senior steward, and about half a dozen other either titled or ranked gentlemen, whose names and roles

Ravi and Kulbir instantly forgot, as they were absorbed by the magnificence of the room and priceless equine art displayed on the walls.

Unfortunately, the outcome of the meeting had not matched the hospitality. As being veterans of Indian bureaucracy and intransigence, the brothers had very quickly discovered that what the English elite might say, in fact, invariably meant something altogether different. And it soon became apparent that their proposal was going nowhere.

Lord Magnall spent a considerable amount of time on extravagant introductions, praising the achievements of Ravi Singh and Motti-Media and extolling the long history of horse racing in India, and everyone present guffawed and offered polite encouragement. But as soon as Steve Norton, of The Tote, a small and wiry-looking man with a prematurely receding hairline and petite steel-rimmed glasses perched on a startlingly pointed nose, cautioned that reviving sweepstakes – even though it was a nice idea, as he put it, and would be so much more easy to promote than back in the '60s – would violate the monopolies laws, as set out in the EU statute regarding gaming licences and, as such, be impossible to administer under the umbrella of The Tote, it became clear that: a) the bookmakers still maintained a monopoly over legalized gambling in the UK, and b) the Jockey Club and its boffins either didn't understand the concept or thought it was inherently bound to be corrupted.

'The Arwish gawt away with it, back then,' said a man with an impressive handlebar moustache and a plumby accent, and his chums chuckled.

Ravi thought to himself, you may not say so, but I bet you're thinking that, if the Irish were fly, a bunch of swindling Indians would be ten times worse.

Even Lord Magnall, who looked like he was about to fall asleep at one point, chimed in. 'Yes, indeed. Can you imagine those hacker chaps, and what they'd do to a thing like that today?'

Kulbir's protestations that Motti-Media would be happy to work with The Tote, as they planned on doing with TAB in Australia and PMU in France, and that the whole venture could be monitored by a reputable firm of accountants to ensure maximum integrity, were all to no avail. Ravi and Kulbir were given the requisite hour and ushered out before the pre-lunch pink gins were poured.

As they awaited a cab, they smiled at one another. 'A penny for your thoughts, brother?' said Ravi.

'You know me,' Kulbir replied, 'want to do things the right way and we shouldn't have expected anything. But,' he smiled again, 'that was something else in there! It still exists. These are the same people who eschewed the study of mathematics and science before the war, who pooh-poohed jet propulsion. It's the same old network, you know, that let the horse out of the stable some seventy years ago, when they could and should have harnessed legalised betting and put a proper levy on bookmakers, and they are now in a position where The Tote handles less than 3% of the action, only half a percent of overall revenue is returned to the sport and the tail, the bookies in this case, is wagging the dog!'

'They don't believe that, though, do they?'

'No, just like Real Racing went in one ear, passed through a vacuum, and straight out the other.'

CHAPTER 23

Keeneland in July was steamy.

After the Kentucky Derby, the show had moved on and the Bluegrass country had eased back to a slower pace, as hundreds of thoroughbred nurseries in the Lexington area nurtured the new crop of foals that had joined the production line during the first six months of the year.

For breeders it was a two-year cycle, begun with immense scrutiny of complimenting pedigrees and confirmation match-ups; mixing one bloodline with another to come up with a perfectly conformed and fleet-footed foal that had the heart of a lion. Then, after selected mares were bred (often several times before pregnancy was confirmed) to the stallion of choice, with many travelling from as far away as California, Canada, and parts of Europe, nature took over and it became a question of safe carriage to foaling, some nine to ten months later, in the spring of the following year.

As an investment, the whole process was fraught with uncertainty, so that by the time the product of a planned mating was conceived, foaled, nurtured, weaned, and raised to the point of being a yearling, costs often far exceeded those originally budgeted for. So, by the time a young thoroughbred enters their second year and heads to auction, the journey has often been tenuous, making it far from certain that, by July, he or she is ready to be presented for sale.

Indeed, there was talk that July was too soon, and unless a yearling had been an early foal from January or February of the previous year, it was highly unlikely that they would have matured sufficiently to be at their best. But breeding is big business, driven by results and returns: the quicker the better – much to the detriment of the sport, in the view of many old-timers.

So the select sale at Keeneland in July is, for thoroughbreds, the latest boat or car show, where the new models are on display and where the movers and shakers of the sport restock. The crème de la crème of precocious American bloodstock is up for sale, with speculators and buyers from across the continent, and England, France, Ireland, Japan, Australia, and Canada on hand and, thanks to the recent successes of Caledonia Farms and its new owner, Hector Delmontez, several new interests from South America and beyond.

Amongst this illustrious gathering, Joss Danvers and Hugo Lascelles had set up their headquarters for the week at the Hyatt Hotel, in downtown Lexington. It was from there that Johnny W-C had been instructed to chaperone Ravi Singh. 'While he is in town, do not leave his side,' his boss had said.

As they breakfasted together, Johnny explained the format of the two-day sale. 'We did our homework on the pedigrees, as soon as the catalogue came out, back in Newmarket, where our chaps identified lots of interest,' he enthused, enjoying the collectiveness of being on the CBS team. 'Then our guys on the ground, here in Lexington, went out to inspect the individuals that we'd earmarked, for confirmation, and took the photos that you will have found in the package we couriered to you in India.'

Ravi nodded. It was his first trip to Kentucky, but he was prepared for the heat and was sporting a pair of loose-fitting, cream-coloured linen trousers, topped by an open-necked pale blue safari-styled shirt of the same material, with sandals and a panama. It was going to be a long and very warm day.

'My boss has a meeting with Mr. Lascelles and Sheikh Ali this morning. We're going to meet up with them for lunch, when it will be confirmed that you have bought a part interest in El Cordobes and are a new member of Classic Racing. We'll then look at a few yearlings that may be of interest this evening,' continued Johnny, detailing plans for the day.

For the occasion, his first at the select sale representing CBS, Johnny was sporting a pair of bright red designer sneakers, turquoise Bermuda shorts, and a pale-yellow golf shirt, with an emblem that Ravi did not recognize, but felt sure was cool. To keep off the bright sun, when they ventured out, he was carrying a red baseball cap, to match his sneakers, which featured the logo of a well-known local Bluegrass sales company, and around his neck a blue pen, on a string, from another important sales-related enterprise, that would always be right there to make important notes.

Ravi smiled at the kit selection, as he glanced around the room where maybe two dozen similarly clad people were muttering in a variety of different languages.

◆ ◆ ◆

As Mark had explained to Tom, the sales are quite a game.

Just one yearling sold at a time. But, all the while, so many people standing around and you just wonder what their involvement is. Who are these people? Are they buyers? Are they sellers? Are they veterinarians, agents for van companies and airshippers, or just tire-kickers and guys that they had talked about who wheel and deal and hustle a living from brokering partnerships, running up sales and other chicanery? A horse sale is a fascinating melting pot of intrigue and Mark was about to introduce Tom and his house guest, Algy Sinclair, to the quintessential American version.

Today, though, his primary objective was promoting lot number 142: a chestnut colt, foaled on February 24, 2016, by Majestic Knight out of the Canadian mare Killyshandra, consigned by B & P Stables. If everything went according to schedule, he would enter the ring around seven that evening.

The McDonnell's had got doubly lucky, with a good spot (time-wise) in the catalogue and, because the leading consignor in the sale, Made-to-Measure Farms, had not completely taken up the most prominently positioned barn, they found themselves assigned a stall right at the heart of the action, in front of which Mark, Paddy, and the ever-present Seamus would spend the day promoting their handsome colt.

Seamus, as expected, was at the helm. His pride and joy looked magnificent with his rich chestnut coat glowing in the sunshine. The time he'd spent personally schooling his charge was evident in his perfect manners, which saw him stand quietly while being examined, showing himself off like a top runway model. As Mark had predicted, it was his looks that were the quality that had got him into this select field. And throughout the day he attracted plenty of attention. Maybe it was just Seamus's infectious blarney, but it did seem that lot 142 had caught the eye of the right people.

'Talk can be cheap, though,' Mark reminded his clients

Johnny and Ravi had arrived just before eleven and spent an hour or so before lunch looking at a few fillies. They were hardly likely to be the sort that the latter would buy for India. But, as Danvers had said to Johnny, 'make the man feel like he belongs, introduce him to the right crowd. Show him, more importantly, that the agency is in with the right people.' It was a huge PR schmooze-off, but Ravi lapped it up and at lunch made a short speech when Hector Delmontez introduced him as a partner in the new Classic Racing syndicate, saying how much he was looking forward to seeing his new acquisition run in the Prix de l'Arc de Triomphe at Longchamp in early October.

At the lunch, Calvin Weiner confirmed his involvement with Classic Racing and promoted a private sale of South American-bred stock that he would be offering in Canada in early September.

The sale had started auspiciously, with two million-dollar toppers in the first session; Billy Beagle and T.J. Van der Meer looked on contentedly.

Meanwhile, back at the barn, Mark and Paddy were discussing the merits of their colt with a short, round, and red-faced man who was perspiring profusely under his bush hat. Larry Smithers was a 'pin-hooker', known for astute purchases that he would then turn around and resell, either privately or at other sales, for a profit. Today, he knew the story on lot 142: great individual, a standout, but light on July select-sale pedigree, something that the highrollers would definitely mark him down on. And he just felt that, maybe, by sniffing around, others might think that the attention he was giving the colt merited their closer inspection and, thereby, perhaps a commission from the consignor for, dare he say it, running him up a bit?

Mark smiled to Tom and Algy, who were sitting in deck chairs in the shade, listening to Larry's spiel. 'Listen, Larry,' he said, 'if you have a serious punter and your guy signs the ticket, we'll take care of you. The McDonnells know what they need, and trust me, you top two hundred grand and we'll be happy to look after you.'

Paddy McDonnell grimaced when Mark mentioned the figure. Before they'd got into the select sale, they'd been talking about one-fifty. 'Is that what you need?' said Larry.

Before Paddy could say anything, Mark replied, 'You may even have to go higher, judged upon the action this colt has seen.' This seemed to deflate Larry, who probably figured he was going to bully some neophytes at this level. 'We're at the high-stakes table, here,' Mark added, 'this ain't no low-level, pin-hooking shot, I can tell you.'

Before Larry could respond, the conversation was interrupted by a familiar voice. 'Hello there, lads. What have we got here?' And they turned to see Johnny W-C and his handsome bearded client.

'Duckin' and divin', bobbin' and a-weavin', tryin' to make a livin',' said Mark. 'You know Tom, don't you?'

'Yes. Met him at the Preakness and again earlier in the year, here in Kentucky. How are you Tom? And Algy, too, I see. What on earth are you doing here?'

'I'm here to pinch your punter,' joked Algy. 'Mr. Singh, sir. So good to see you again. I'm pulling Bog's leg, of course! You will remember, we met at Lords.'

Johnny grimaced and the men shook hands. 'Ravi has just bought into the Classic Racing syndicate,' he announced.

Tom Fraser frowned.

'Yes, indeed, and I met you again, with your uncle. Lord, ah?' replied Ravi.

'Uncle Teddy. Armscote, at Ascot,' Algy helped him.

'He has a stud farm in India and bought some mares through the agency last month. Told him he'd have to check out Keeneland as it's where it's at, as you Yanks say, eh!' Johnny joked.

'Only a few Irishmen, here, I'm afraid,' said Mark, turning to the McDonnells, father and son. 'You know what they say about the bog, eh, Bog?'

Now it was Johnny's turn to frown. 'So, what are you boys peddling here?'

'Nice one,' said Mark. 'I'll leave that up to Seamus, as this is really his show. Tell him, Seamus, about your big harse.'

Lot 142 was brought out for the umpteenth time. And Seamus regaled his latest audience with the same story that he'd been relating all morning, adding that if Vincent O'Brien were still with us, God bless him, this was just the type of horse he'd have snapped up for Robert Sangster, back in the day.

Johnny studied the handsome chestnut; ran his hands across his withers, and pronounced him to be just over sixteen hands, all the time gazing seriously at the yearling. He stood back, squinted, and said, 'can you just walk him up there and maybe trot back? That's it. Now, straight towards me.' He looked serious and hoped he looked like he knew what he was doing.

Under the trees the B & P guys smiled at one another, as Ravi took it all in.

'Where are you staying, Algy?' Johnny asked, after he'd told Seamus that he'd seen what he needed and he could put his charge away.

'With Mark. He's very generously putting me up. The agency didn't send anyone to these sales, as their clients will wait until September. So, I thought, why not just pop over and see how Tom is doing? And here we are. Pretty amazing place. I love the rat-tat-tat style of the auctioneers over here. It's a hoot.'

'Yep, getting Algy a bit of Bluegrass experience. Then we're going down to Virginia and on up to Saratoga,' said Tom.

'Some of us have to work,' said Johnny, rather pompously. 'So, Mark, what does your man expect here?' he added with authority, presumably for Ravi's benefit.

'Well, he's right here,' said Mark. 'Why not ask him yourself?'

Paddy blushed, not entirely sure and certainly somewhat intimidated by the officiousness of Johnny Ward-Clark. 'Well,' he paused, 'this is our first crack at the select sale. So we're a bit reliant upon Mark's advice. But, judging by the interest this fella has generated, we would be disappointed in anything less than two hundred.'

Johnny studied his catalogue, his blue pen-on-a-chain clasped between his teeth. 'Our guys marked him down on pedigree. I see the dam's paper is pretty light: all that restricted stuff. You know, for Canadian-breds only, up in Canada,' he bumbled on, muttering like someone with deep knowledge who was processing vast quantities of data. Finally, he drew in a deep breath and turned to Ravi. 'Can't fault him on confirmation. Just wonder, though, whether he has the quality to be a graded stakes winner?' And he noted down something against lot 142 in his catalogue.

'If you sign the ticket,' said Paddy McDonnell, 'we will look after you.'

'No need for that,' said Johnny, dismissively. A paragon of virtue.

Mark, Tom, and Algy held in their mirth.

'Toodle-oo, then,' said Johnny. 'We'll catch you later.'

'Later indeed,' said Tom, under his breath.

◆ ◆ ◆

In mid-July, it does not get dark in Kentucky until close to 10 p.m. and, even at that hour, nights can be still and sultry. But, that evening, a nice breeze wafted into the Keeneland Sales arena, around 6-ish, and those who had started to wilt picked up.

Seamus and 'Killer', as he'd affectionately nicknamed his four-legged friend (as a son of their mare Killyshandra) were ready. A little oil on his hooves and a last-minute combing out of his mane and rich, reddish brown tail - both of which had been neatly pulled. As the sun dipped to the west, casting shadows through the barns, the dapples still glowed.

Lot 142 would be walked up to the ante-ring, where he would circle with maybe a dozen other yearlings headed along the production line. Around the perimeter, groups of admirers and potential buyers cast last glances. Had they missed something? How was each lot handling the noise and crowds? Could this be a harbinger for future skittishness or the poise of latent stardom?

The lights from the arena shone increasingly bright, and from within came the bark of the auctioneer and shouts of spotters, confirming bids. Then a large man in white overalls and a green Keeneland baseball cap took the shank from Seamus. And, like a loving father watching his young son head into school on his first day, he watched Killer walk calmly into the ring, like a pro.

The McDonnells had situated themselves to the left of the elevated stage, a few rows up, and just behind them sat Mark, Tom, and Algy. The object of their attention stood attentively, ears pricked, gazing out at the large crowd before him. Immediately above them, on a dias, three of Keeneland's auctioneers conferred. The number 142 shone brightly from boards around the arena.

'And now,' announced Walt Dyson, 'we have Lot 142, a chestnut colt by that good young stallion Majestic Knight out of the stakes-winning mare, Killyshandra. What are you going to start him off at?' And off he went: 'Give me fifty, do I have fifty?' and there was a shout from a spotter. 'Yes! Jim has fifty at the back. Gimme sixty, outside?' – There was a 'Yep!' – 'I have sixty. Thank you. Seventy, eighty. Eighty thousand for the Majestic Knight colt.' He paused. All the time the Killer seemed totally unimpressed, as if to say, 'is that all?'

Walt Dyson was one of Keeneland's characters, a real yarn-spinner when he was on his game. 'Now then,' he drawled, 'you folks seem to be dozin', eighty thousand for this handsome fella, you'd be stealing him. His mammy won a bunch of stakes up in Canada. Only off the board twice in fifteen starts! A young mare, with unlimited potential to produce runners. The sky's the limit. Someone gimme a hundred?' - 'Yep!' - 'Thank you, Jim. You're back in sir, well done. I have a hundred. Someone a hundred and twenty, thirty?' - 'Yep!' - 'One hundred and fifty' - 'Yes, sir!' - 'One sixty?' - 'Yep!' - 'One Seventy? Why not make it two, sir,' he said, smiling at a handsome man in a cowboy hat, sitting next to a very cute young lady. 'Take him home for your wife, sir.' The lady, quite possibly not his wife, blushed. 'We have two hundred for the Majestic Knight. Two hundred!' He raised his hammer. 'No? Yes! Two twenty-five! A new bidder! Here we go. Two fifty. Yes! Give me three? I have three! Three hundred thousand for this son of Majestic Knight. Three fifty, sir? Thank you. I have three fifty, at the back, with Joe. Give me three seventy-five, sir?' he said, turning to the previous bidder. 'How about three sixty? You've come all this way. Gimme three sixty? No?' he paused and wiped his brow. 'I'm selling here.' He looked around the arena. 'I have three fifty, and I'm selling. You're gonna lose him!' Bang! The hammer came down.

'Sold to Marcus Townsend. Thank you, sir.' The low murmuring was like a sigh after the emotion of the previous three minutes or so. Dyson noted $350K in his catalogue and turned the page. Down below, Paddy hugged Betty who was crying. Mark leaned over. 'He's going to a great horseman.'

Outside, Seamus was reunited with his budding star who, as if to show off that he was worth every penny just spent on him, put in a little buck and skip as the cooler evening air perked him up. He would return to his stall and arrangements would be made for his removal once the new owner had settled with Keeneland and the McDonnell's. 'You're off to Limey-land, Killer,' Seamus told him, as he himself almost danced a little jig.

Back in the arena, Betty's tears flowed as she was assisted to the bar, where double Jamesons were ordered and toasts proffered to their good fortune, Killer's future career on the turf in Europe, Marcus Townsend, his new owner, whomever he or she was, and everyone within earshot who had anything to do with this great transaction. On his way out of the arena Algy said he'd bumped into Townsend, and reported that his new trainer just loved him. 'A real athlete' he'd said.' Algy wasn't sure for whom the purchase had been made, but thought it might be Sheikh Ali.

'Ha! Ha!' said Mark. 'Bog didn't think he'd have the quality or class to be a Group horse.'

'What the fuck does he know about class?' chimed in Algy, raising his glass. 'To the Killer!'

CHAPTER 24

The morning after brought varying news and conditions. Chez the B & P stable, there were a few sore heads, but it was back to routine, albeit with finances having taken a very welcome boost the night before. On Transylvania Road, Mark sipped his tea in the kitchen, while his two guests snored upstairs. Normally at this time he would put on his dressing gown and come downstairs to play the piano, to get himself psyched up for the day. But today he didn't want to disturb Tom and Algy and, after reading the front page of the Lexington Examiner, he certainly wasn't in the mood for music.

In headlines, there it was: 'Stakes Horse Dies on Paris Pike.' The story went on to detail how, at roughly 11:45 the previous night, the four-year-old, South American-bred, colt El Cordobes, who had recently won the Grade 1 City of Baltimore Handicap at Pimlico, on Preakness Day, had apparently escaped from a barn at Caledonia Farms, where he was quarantining in preparation for shipment to Europe, and had then been killed in a collision with a pickup truck on the highway outside the main gate. The story went on to confirm that the as-yet-unnamed driver of the pickup was in Lexington general hospital, in the ICU.

At the same moment, Johnny Ward-Clark and his client Ravi Singh were absorbing this news over their pancakes in the dining room of the Hyatt Hotel. A room that the day before was abuzz with chatter, today resonated only with mumbles and the clinking of cutlery.

Even though Johnny's prediction regarding his friends' yearling had been way off, which he hoped hadn't sown seeds of doubt in his important client, the previous day had been a huge success. The agency had announced the partnership of Hector Delmontez, Calvin Weiner, and his man Ravi; and at the lunch he'd met Lucy Beagle and was in love.

Now this. For the first time in his life he was lost for words.

'A roller-coaster business,' said Ravi, after the silence had become close to unbearable.

'Mr. Singh. Sorry, Ravi. I don't know what to say. How could this have happened...' he trailed off.

'Well, I guess there is insurance?' Ravi sounded hopeful, rather than optimistic.

'Yep,' said Johnny, without much conviction. 'They'll sort things out. Puts a bit of a sour taste in your mouth, though, doesn't it? You know, you don't feel like going to the sales today, or I don't, anyway.'

'Well, that's okay,' said Ravi. 'I have a meeting, here in town at 10. See how you feel. My plane to New York leaves at 6 p.m., so I'm not bothered about going back out to the sales.'

'Okay, let's chat after your meeting.'

◆　◆　◆

Back on Transylvania the lads were stirring. It had been a rough night. So much energy and expectation had been put into the sale of Mark's first yearling, as official agent at the Keeneland select sale that, when everything had exceeded their wildest dreams, a major Celidh had errupted. They'd left the sales quite early, but had not missed a beat, taking in a number of Irish bars before ending up at the Hyatt Hotel where some hard core drinking was going on and an unusually tipsy Bog had been found carousing with none other than Billy Beagle's very charming daughter, Lucy.

How that liaison had turned out seemed to intrigue Mark and Algy more than the El Cordobes story, as they wolfed down their bacon and eggs.

'Jesus, Bog's a chancer!' said Mark. 'I suppose you have to take your hat off to him? But Billy Beagle's daughter! Really?'

Algy laughed. 'Wait till Mrs. Beagle puts him on the spot. No title, eh?'

'Fuck Bog!' said Tom, from his immersion in the front-page story. 'This whole business with El Cordobes is horrible. I have a feeling I'm going to get another call from my friends at the cop shop.'

'What did Martin at BGT say about accidents?' said Mark, pouring more coffee.

'Yep, the first thing that came to my mind.' He paused, continuing with his reading. 'No comments from Delmontez and his guys. Yet. It will be interesting to see what sort of spin they put on this.'

'Didn't they make some kind of an announcement yesterday? At a lunch reception at the sales?' asked Mark.

'Yes, and Bog's guy was introduced as a new partner, along with Delmontez and that Canadian guy, Weiner. The syndicate is, or was, going to be managed by Bog's people: Danvers and Co. at CBS.'

'Not a good day for them,' said Algy.

Right on cue, the phone rang and Mark answered. The smile on his face told Tom that his prediction had been right on. 'Detective Watson of the Lexington po-lice,' he said, emphasizing the last word, as he passed the phone to Tom.

And sure enough, Tom's presence was required, at his earliest convenience, to discuss recent developments out at Caledonia Farms. Tom suggested the sooner the better, as he was going to be leaving town the next day. So 1 p.m. was agreed upon.

◆ ◆ ◆

Ravi returned to his room and answered a few pressing e-mails. Kulbir had read the *Thoroughbred Times'* website and wanted to know what was going on. Practical and without the emotions of someone wedded to horses, his first question was regarding insurance. Is such an accident covered? And, forgetting about the loss of the horse, were they liable if the guy in the pickup truck died?

So far nothing from Caledonia. The silence was deafening.

As he sat in his cab on the way to 625 Harrodsburg Road, the headquarters of the National Horse Racing Association, Ravi wondered whether his brother was right. Was horse racing a thoroughly disreputable sport and the people involved to be avoided at all cost? So far, he had seen the good side, care of Joss Danvers, Royal Ascot; and the sugar-coating that Johnny Ward-Clark had put upon the so-called Sport of Kings. But, at the same time, wasn't it the agency's idea to get him involved with Hector Delmontez and what was now rapidly becoming a very dubious cast of characters?

His imminent meeting with the movers and shakers of American thoroughbred horse racing, that morning, was going to be quite telling. He texted Kulbir – 'Hold tight, get back to you shortly' – as he arrived at his destination: a six-story modern glass-and-steel building surrounded by a tastefully landscaped parking lot.

The lobby featured surprisingly elaborate security that, after he had been piped to the sixth floor, he mused during the ascent must mean that they occasionally received hostile visitors. Strange for the Sport of Kings, he thought, smiling as he was greeted by a serious-looking Tim Keyser. Very different in stature and dress to Major Fortescue at Portman Square, but as equally obsequious in his welcome.

Billy Beagle's corner office looked east, and the morning sun that was streaming in highlighted the stylish décor and ubiquitous equine art.

As usual 'The Dawg' was beaming and Ravi mused that he would make the perfect politician.

'Ravi.' There were no awkward formalities. 'How nice to see you, albeit in such unfortunate circumstances. What a terrible business. I got a call from Hector this morning. Could not believe it. They've had such bad luck out there, since, you know, the fire…' he trailed off, as he turned to introduce his colleagues, continuing to mutter under his breath: good people, good racing people. 'You know T.J., my assistant in just about everything we do down here.' T.J. Van der Meer stood up from the long table he'd been sitting at with four other men in suits. 'This is Senator Wardle; George Boyce, our new commissioner; and Mike Leightner of Sports Television and Marketing (STVM), our wonderful marketing arm. You met Tim on your way in – he's director of communications, here. Wouldn't know what we'd do without him,' he chuckled.

Everyone sat down around the table and Beagle, again, poured out his dismay at the morning's news. 'Jinxed! First dear, old Bob Fraser and now my friend Hector's big horse. The industry can't afford such losses.'

Ravi sat mid-table, feeling strangely out of place; surrounded by large serious-looking men whose focus was entirely upon his slight and bearded frame. He mused that Kentucky had been on the other side in the Civil War and here he was: an Indian in Dixie, for all intents and purposes.

The meeting didn't have the superficially polite but inwardly insincere feel that Lord Bagnall and his chums had given him in London; that was something uniquely British that they and they alone had perfected. Instead there was a different type of 'let's hear what you've got to say, even though we already don't like the sound of it' feel.

'Mike,' Beagle addressed the STVM man, Leightner. 'As our chief salesman and PR voice, could you please fill in Mr. Singh with what you are doing, so successfully for us, may I add.' Everyone tittered except Ravi, who took in the nervousness of their mirth.

'Thank you, Billy,' said Mike Leightner, pushing back his chair to give his considerable girth more space. Probably a good bit younger than he looked, the man in charge of making horse racing Prime Time Entertainment, as he billed himself, sported an arsenal of gaudy jewelry, from various carbuncle-sized rings to a prominently displayed watch, under his ultra-expensive looking cuff links, which appeared to handcuff a bushy growth of dark hair that flowed out across the back of his hands. While he'd let his sizeable six-foot-plus frame blossom nowhere near a gym, instead of body maintenance it looked like he'd invested in a year-round suntan salon and jarring hair dye. The New Jersey accent complimented his designer–sleeze look.

Where had the NHRA found this guy, wondered Ravi. He looked like a WWE promoter or Vegas carnival barker on steroids.

'As you were saying,' Leightner continued, 'we are making horse racing great again!' Everyone except Ravi grinned. 'It's all about making the experience memorable. Having the right people, who are tuned into today's social media-driven celebrity TV crowd, delivering the message. We now have Bobby Barker as a spokesman.'

The assembled group uttered guffaws of approval.

'Excuse me,' interrupted Ravi, 'but who is Bobby Barker?'

'Bobby Barker!' Leightner exploded with laughter and his chair creaked under him. 'You've never heard of Bobby Barker! Where have you been hiding? Outer Mongolia?'

Ravi could see Billy Beagle grimace at that one.

'Never mind that he hasn't heard of one of our country's great chefs.' Beagle chuckled. 'Tell him about the great TV presence, the giveaways, our loyalty program, and catch slogans.'

Leightner rambled on, using esoteric media jargon and hyperbole that had Ravi baffled, mentioning various sponsors that he'd never heard of and constantly repeating hackneyed slogans, until Billy Beagle called a halt and asked Ravi to give his pitch.

It went better than it had before the British boffins at the BHA, considering he had to explain the whole sweepstake concept in much more detail before it was understood around the table. But, once he'd finished, he was immediately informed that such a venture would contravene interstate laws associated with so-called wire fraud, and it became very apparent that because of the fractiousness of American horse racing, where almost every state had different rules and separate standards, it was going to be nigh impossible to get everyone onto the same page.

'With all due respect,' said Ravi, 'it is gambling that sets horse racing apart from many of your other major-league sports. Yet, you have allowed casinos and lotteries, together with many other forms of cheaper and more accessible entertainment, to take the lion's share of the general public's discretionary dollars. Your total handle on live racing is plummeting, and you guys have not embraced online gaming the way you should have.' There was a silence.

Ravi wondered whether he'd overstepped the mark. But the frustration, of knowing how to solve their problem, yet being rebuffed by idiotic arguments against what he was proposing, was getting to him.

'What do you call your game?' asked Senator Wardle, who had been very quiet up to that point.

'Real Racing,' said Ravi. 'It's an easy brand that rolls off the tongue and will have a global appeal.'

'And how do you think that you are going to promote it?' asked George Boyce.

'Online,' replied Ravi. 'We have Indian government backing, because of the good causes that we are supporting, and some of the best IT guys in the world to run our servers and processors. Anyone can play anywhere.'

'Well, not in the USA,' said Billy Beagle. 'Wouldn't Congress have to pass a bill to change existing gaming laws, Travis?' He turned to Senator Wardle.

'Sure would. And I can tell you that horse racing is not their top priority right now,' the Senator confirmed.

There was a pause. Ravi could see several of his hosts looking at their watches.

'Thank you, gentlemen,' he said, smiling at the circle of obviously perplexed men. 'I greatly appreciate your time. I will leave you with my card and perhaps we can talk again sometime when you have given my proposal further consideration and, perhaps, seen some positive results from the prototypes that we are planning in conjunction with the authorities in Australia.'

There was no acknowledgement and it was left for the great politician and consummate diplomat to usher his Indian guest to the elevator. The sales were on – got to keep drumming up new business – and his parting shot was, 'Mr. Singh, I am so sorry about what happened to your horse. Those are good people in that syndicate. Senor Delmontez at Caledonia, Cal Weiner up in Canada, and of course our good friends in the UK. I hope this setback won't put you off? I think that El Gruppo will take care of things. We need more good people like you in our sport.'

As he rode back to the hotel, Ravi wondered what or who the hell El Gruppo was.

◆ ◆ ◆

Bernie Schaefer turned out to be available for the short notice visit to the local constabulary and he and Tom, as usual, conferred briefly in the parking lot before their 1 p.m. meeting with Detective Watson.

'This whole saga ain't getting any better, is it?' he opined to Tom.

'Let's just listen to what they have to say,' Tom replied, impressing his attorney with the maturity a few experiences with the law had instilled in him.

Watson welcomed them to the same sterile office and laid out the usual protocol, introducing his buddies. 'I think you've met Dewey.' He indicated the tall, gaunt man in the corner whose drawn physique suggested a diet of cigarettes and alcohol, but precious little else. 'This escalation has taken us a bit by surprise,' he admitted. 'So, I'm afraid the Feds, who you've spoken to before, couldn't be here. But Inspector Daniels, from the FDA, I don't think you know?'

He introduced Daniels, a man quite a bit younger than anyone Tom and his lawyer had met before. Obviously, by his softer accent, not from Kentucky; Daniels it turned out was from the narcotics division, which immediately set off alarm bells in Tom's head.

'First, all I can report is that, as yet, we are treating this latest incident as an accident and the driver of the pickup, err, Wayne Jarvis, is expected to survive his injuries. Our people are out there now, investigating. But the reason that we have asked you to come in today, Mr. Fraser, is more to do with our ongoing investigation of the fire, back in March.' Watson read from his notes. 'Before we return to this and I ask you a few questions, I would like Dr. Daniels,' it had stepped up a notch, 'to outline what his department are doing. Doctor,' he said, turning to Daniels.

'Thank you, Dectective. Yes. Further to the department's attention being drawn to Mr. Diaz's involvement with this matter, we have been conducting background checks on all employees at Caledonia Farms and, in particular, Senor Delmontez and any staff related to the Condor Group. As you know, that is the name of the corporation through which Senor Delmontez conducts his business in South America and which, via Condor Air, he has transported bloodstock to North America. Ramon Diaz was a chemist by trade, and his name has been connected in files provided to us by Interpol and anti-narcotics agencies in Venezuela and throughout Central America – Honduras, Costa Rica, and Mexico – to cartels that we know are active in smuggling narcotics.'

The room had gone very quiet as this news sunk in. In the corner, Dewey stood like an agonized plinth, one leg crossed in front of the other, chin resting in a cupped hand. It was early afternoon. He hadn't had a drink yet, but man did he need a cigarette badly.

'Mr. Diaz died in the fire at Caledonia, and we are just trying to figure out what he was doing with your late father, Mr. Robert Fraser, between roughly eleven-thirty and just after midnight on the night of March 18. At a remote barn on the farm.'

'The fire consumed virtually everything. So, it was impossible to do any autopsies,' added Watson.

'Your father,' said Daniels, turning to Tom. 'Had visited South America in 2009.' He looked down at his notes. 'Senor Delmontez and the Venezuelan horse-racing authorities hosted the Racetracks of the America's conference in Caracas that year, and your parents were amongst the guests.' He looked at Tom again. 'Your mother, Mrs. Laura Fraser, died, under suspicious circumstances during that trip. And now that Mr. Diaz's name has shown up on our radar, we have obtained a very interesting list of the other guests that Senor Delmontez invited.'

Tom and Shaefer sat silently.

Daniels paused, while he looked at what appeared to be a lengthy list of names before him. 'Senor Delmontez seems to be well connected.' He smiled. 'Just about a who's who, it appears from our enquiries, of top officials from the horse racing world. You probably know many of them?'

Before Daniels could say anything, Shaefer interrupted him. 'You are speculating, Inspector. We've been through this before. My client was only fifteen years old in 2009.'

'Just saying,' went on Daniels. 'We are speaking to everyone from the United States,' – 'And Canada,' interrupted Watson – 'who attended that conference, because subsequent to it Senor Delmontez began accelerating his bloodstock operations in this country and right here in Kentucky.'

'We haven't decided whether the fire at Caledonia was an accident or foul play. But, as my colleagues have informed you, we are looking into possible insurance issues and, with this latest incident last night, we are extremely concerned that what might have been until then an isolated and completely unconnected matter could be now very relevant. And,' he paused, 'part of a chain of serial insurance fraud.'

'Inspector Daniels is referring to the recent disappearance of Dr. Lawrence Mason, head of the Maryland Racing Commission, who attended the Caracas conference. Dr. Mason has not been seen since he went out fishing on his small boat from the marina in Havre de Grace, almost a week ago,' added Watson. 'And we were due to speak to him two days after his apparent disappearance.'

'What has that got to do with my client?' said Schaefer impatiently.

'Could be nothing,' said Daniels. 'It's just that from what we are learning and, don't get me wrong, I may be an expert in my field, but this horse racing business is a completely different ballgame for most of us,' he rambled on, looking up from his notes for confirmation of what he was saying from Watson and the tombstone-like Dewey, 'when Senor Delmontez's horse,' he looked down again at his notes, 'the one who was killed last night, El Cordobes, won a recent race of some significance; I'm told some eyebrows were raised. You know,' he paused, 'it was odd. A bit of an upset, eh?'

Jesus, thought Tom. I hope these guys haven't been looking into Randy Dobbs' death. Let's just hope that that matter has been dismissed as perfunctorily as his cause of death: just another indigent victim of opioids. But now he was wondering: could Delmontez's men have rumbled that he'd pinched their gear and offed him?

This whole business was becoming more insidious by the moment.

'Well,' said Watson, indicating the end of that particular session, much to the visible relief of Dewey, who was already reaching into his pocket for his smokes. 'We just thought we'd update you, following last night's development, and let you know that our enquiries are ongoing and that we may still need to talk to you again. Depending upon how things pan out.'

The meeting ended and Schaefer informed the desk clerk of Tom's intended plans over the next few months, suggesting that his office be the point of contact.

CHAPTER 25

It was going to be a road trip: some eight hours from Lexington, Kentucky, to Berryville, Virginia – uncharted territory for Algy.

Tom had rented a Jeep Cherokee, on Mark's advice, that could be dropped off in Virginia and, the day after the sales ended, he and Algy set off at the crack of dawn.

The boys didn't have much luggage, but the comfort of a full-sized vehicle on a long journey was paramount. Despite having next to zero experience with an endeavour such as the one they were embarking upon, Mark had advised, 'plug in your GPS and follow your noses. Don't speed and don't pick up hitchhikers, no matter how attractive they may look.'

Travelling at a steady fifty-five to seventy miles an hour, depending upon state laws, could be numbing on the seemingly endless freeways, so his last piece of advice had been for regular pit stops, plenty of water, and driver changes, even though the rental company had muttered about Algy's foreign license.

On such long and often boring trips it does help to be friends, and Algy joked about what it would be like spending all day in a car with Bog.

'You wouldn't need to worry about that ever happening,' said Tom, 'it would be beneath him to drive anywhere when flying was an alternative. Probably in one of his fancy client's private jets!'

'Looks like he may be spending a bit more time in the Bluegrass,' said Algy. 'He and Lucy Beagle were pretty lovey-dovey, the other night.'

'Yep, he sure knows how to schmooze his way into the right circles.'

Algy began. 'So, tell me, now we have a moment, how are you doing? It's hard to believe that it's only four months since you lost your dad.'

Tom, who was driving, stared ahead. 'Yep, that last meeting with the cops sure made me think.'

'How are they doing? What do they think happened?'

'It seems that things were a lot worse than I imagined. You know, you're away and you just presume that everything is okay and the farm is running smoothly. But it obviously wasn't, and,' he paused, almost tearing up 'it bloody wasn't!'

'Oh, I'm sorry,' said Algy. 'I didn't mean to upset you.'

'No, it's all right.' He blew his nose and gulped. 'The show with the cops just confirmed to me that the mess is far from over.'

'What do you mean?'

Tom paused. 'It seems that there is a lot more that went on that night than what's come out so far.' Algy listened, intently, from the passenger's seat on his right, as Tom drove on for some minutes before continuing. 'What I'm going to tell you is between us.' He sniffled. 'According to my Aunt Vera, where we are going, my dad was very troubled by what Delmontez had been doing on the farm. You know, he'd put a lot of money into propping things up because, as I now understand, it had been struggling financially. Anyway,' he continued, 'Delmontez sent one of his henchmen, a guy called Diaz, to kill our good mare, Magnolia, to collect the insurance. It's a long story, but my dad and this Diaz guy got into a fight and the upshot was the fire in which they both died.'

Algy listened attentively. 'How do you know this?' he finally said.

'Well, as luck would have it, Aunt Vera's cousin, Matt, was in Lexington with a mare that they'd brought up to be covered and my dad apparently called him to come over and help him deal with Diaz. When he got there, Diaz was dead, and my dad was fatally injured.' He blew his nose again. 'The mare was dead, but she'd foaled and Dad told Matt to take the foal, a colt, and get out of there, because Matt has some history with the cops and no amount of explaining would have got him out of that...awful,' he choked, 'awful...thing,' he said, holding back a sob.

'So, what happened? How could Matt take a newborn foal? It must have died.'

'I haven't told anyone this. Well, not until my Aunt Vera told me the story. But, before he died, my dad sent me a text, the night after the fall. You remember? It said: "You'll know him when you see him. Just like his mom!"'

'Is that all?' said Algy.

'Yes, and I wondered what it could have meant. That was until Aunt Vera...'

'You mean he's alive!'

'Yes, yes.' Tom burst into tears. 'We're gonna see him. He's a beauty.'

The Jeep droned on as silence prevailed, only interrupted by Tom's sniffles.

'Oh, my goodness, Tom. What are you going to do?' asked Algy, eventually.

'What can I do? I certainly can't go and tell the cops what I now know, as Matt and Aunt Vera would get into terrible trouble. I don't know. I guess we have to lie low and see what happens.'

Algy thought. 'Just thinking...your Aunt Vera and Matt have got a foal with no provenance. How are they going to get around that? We know that he's worth a fortune. But, without papers, he's useless. And besides, if he surfaces, all hell would break loose.'

'Well, Aunt Vera seems to think that they have all of that covered. But I agree, that is a big problem. You know how they have all that DNA testing now. Once, you had all sorts of skullduggery going on – people switching foals. You know, you get a well-bred one that's crooked, got a lot of faults, and you exchange him with another that's got perfect confirmation, but nothing like the same pedigree. Then some dope goes and pays a million dollars for him, in the sales, because his advisers tell him that its rare to come across such a perfect specimen with such an impeccable pedigree. It used to go on a lot more often than you would like to think. According to Mark, anyway.' He paused. 'You ask Mark, he'll tell you that I'm not making it up. Aunt Vera says that because they're in Virginia, well actually almost West Virginia, where everyone is half asleep and nobody pays any attention to the local West Virginian foal crop, they will be able to come up with some papers.'

'All the same. If such a fraud was ever uncovered, it would be very serious for those involved.'

'I know, I know. But we're in this. Not you. I mean my Aunt Vera and Matt are, and all we can do is play the hand very carefully.'

'This is incredible. I still can't believe how this little guy survived.'

'It's an amazing story, made all the more so by the circumstances and how the mare that Matt had in the gooseneck nurtured another foal. Matt is a very experienced horseman and Dad, apparently, showed him how to give the foal the medication that new foals need. And then it was just a question of keeping him warm and not trampled by his surrogate mom. When they arrived, they put him with a dear old Clydesdale mare that they've had on the farm for such emergencies, and they took to one another. I've been out to see them. She's been a great mom and he's growing up without a care in the world, completely oblivious to all the drama.'

'So, we have a lost prince. An exiled prince. Some hard-done-by hero of a Hans Christian Anderson fairy tale that needs to be reunited with his kingdom and princess,' said Algy.

'Yep, that about sums it up,' said Tom. 'He doesn't exist, officially, right now.'

'I can't wait to meet him,' said Algy. 'I've come across a lot of people like that who have gone through their lives without so much as a care. So nil desperandum, no expectations or pressure, my friend! There we go!' He suddenly changed the subject. 'The golden arches. I feel a Big Mac attack coming on!'

'You are incorigable. A glutton for punishment! But we need a break and its lunchtime. Just a word. When we get to Aunt Vera's, we'll not discuss our lost prince. And particularly not with Matt. Just between you and I at this point. Ok?'

◆ ◆ ◆

As with all fast food, it tasted good and went down readily. But twenty miles down the road the drowsiness from the sugar-shock kicked in. 'Time for forty winks,' said Tom and they pulled into a rest area.

'I have something to tell you, too,' said Algy as he dozed in the reclined passenger's seat. 'Not as dramatic as your story, but something Mark will be pleased to hear.'

'Come on, let's have it,' said Tom. 'You have the full story on Bog?'

'No. But, speaking of Bog, he's not going to be at all happy and I'm sure his bosses won't be, either, when they find out.'

'So, what's Bog been up to?'

'Well, it's what he hasn't been up to that is his problem. You know, I told you that Marcus Townsend said he'd bought the McDonnell's colt for Sheikh Ali?'

'Yes. Well, didn't he?'

'No. I told him to say that, for public consumption, because the buyer did not want to be identified. Marcus buys a lot on spec and Sheikh Ali is his default position.'

'So how do you know who the real buyer is?'

'Because he's my new punter. That's why.'

'For God's sake, Algy! Who is this mystery man? You're spoiling my nap!'

'Mr. Singh. Bog's ex-client, I guess.'

Tom sat up suddenly. 'Jesus! Does Bog know?'

'I doubt it. Sheikh Ali often doesn't discuss these things with Lascelles and them until after the sales. And, besides, Bog is so infatuated with Miss Beagle at the moment, the last thing on his mind is Ravi Singh.'

'Gee, Danvers will blow a fuse when he finds out. As if the death of El Cordobes wasn't a bad enough bit of news!'

'Maybe not. You see, Bog's one of those guys who could fall into the shit pile and come out smelling of roses. When he finds out that he's let Mr. Singh slip through his fingers, he'll play the Beagle card. You know, I'm now well in with the people who run Keeneland, got all kinds of new connections. Mr. Singh is just a lightweight. Don't worry about him.'

'How did this all happen? I mean, how did Mr. Singh make this decision and who introduced him to Marcus Townsend?'

'Well, it's a long story.'

'Go on, we're stuck in this car for the next three hours. I have the time to listen.' Tom was fully awake by now and started the car. 'You've got me wound up now, Algy, so I'll continue driving. Tell me what happened.'

'We met, by chance, at Lords. You know, the famous cricket ground in London? England was playing India, in a Test Match, and Bog had been instructed by his boss at CBS to take their new client, Mr. Singh, to the game. They, of course, had the best tickets and access to the pavilion, as Danvers is a member of the MCC. I ran into Bog and his new client at lunch and I asked them to join us in our box for tea. My uncle Teddy is also a member of the MCC and he got on like a house on fire with Mr. Singh, as they talked cricket which is something Bog knows nothing about. Afterwards, Uncle Teddy told me he thought Bog was a bounder and that I should pinch his client. But that was after many pink gins and I told him that that wasn't cricket, which made him laugh. He thinks I'm far too nice to be a bloodstock agent. They're nothing but second-hand car dealers and chaps who can't find gainful employment anywhere else, according to Uncle Teddy.

'So, we met again at Ascot and I gave Mr. Singh and his brother a tip that they made money on. Now, fast forward to the sales this week and Bog is marching Mr. Singh around, holding forth about his new client who has just bought into the Classic Racing syndicate, blah blah blah, and I guess Mr. Singh gets rather bored with this carry-on. Anyway, Bog and that ghastly pretentious idiot from the Jockey Club, Geoffrey Gilligan, the pattern race coordinator and official handicapper, and Patrick Waley-Brown, the bloodstock insurance guy who seems to be a big buddy of Hector Delmontez's, were looking at the Made-to-Measure consignment, right next to where the McDonnell's were showing their colt, and I guess Mr. Singh felt a bit left out, because Bog was so into Gilligan's b.s. and of course the Made-to-Measure spiel put on by that loathsome veterinarian, Dr. Loveridge.

'Those guys are consummate salesmen, with all their pretty girls in the matching outfits showing off their stock, plus videos and all kinds of other gimmicky stuff. Did you know, by the way, that you can always tell which of Loveridge's girls he's cranking, because, once in his stable, he arranges for them to have braces put on their teeth! Weird, eh? Anyway, I digress. Where was I? Yes, Mr. Singh felt a bit left out and the next thing he knows is that he's corralled by Seamus McDonnell, who puts on the Irish charm and tells him that the greatest trainer in the history of Irish racing, possibly the world, Vincent O'Brien, would be buying his colt, if he was still with us today. Then Mr. Singh hears Bog and Gilligan dissing him because he doesn't, in their opinion, have sufficient black type to suggest he'll be top class and, remembering what Uncle Teddy said, he thought I'm going buy this colt.'

'Easier said than done,' said Tom.

'Well, that's it. He asked me whether I could bid on his behalf. But I told him that our agency had not established credit for this sale.'

'So, how did he meet Townsend?'

'Well, I know Marcus and I know he buys a lot on spec and has credit arrangements set up with all the sales companies. Besides, they know him as a top trainer. I introduced Mr. Singh to him, at a quiet moment, when very few people were about.'

'How did he know that Mr. Singh wasn't just a tire-kicker?'

'Good point. But I guess he's known me for a while and he trusts me. That's what it boils down to. And besides, if Mr. Singh does a runner, he has plenty of other owners who'll jump in, if Marcus says he has a yearling that he likes.'

'Well, well, this is a big move for you. Are you going to act privately for Mr. Singh or steer him to your guys at Anglian?'

'It's up to him. He was anxious that the whole thing be kept very hush, hush. In fact, he hasn't even told his brother, who was very anti the El Cordobes and Classic Racing deal, and got him to promise to never make any more rash decisions without his approval.'

'What a trip this is turning out to be,' said Tom. 'I thought I'd steal the thunder!'

The drive from Lexington, through eastern Kentucky into West Virginia and across to Highway 81, which runs north south from the Canadian border, just below Montreal, all the way to the Gulf of Mexico and New Orleans, had been monotonous. But, in just under eight hours, they arrived at the gates of Shenandoah Valley Farms. It was close to 5 p.m., local time, and, as they drove up the long, tree-lined driveway, Algy could see that this was a very fine property, equal in every sense to those he'd seen in Kentucky and Newmarket.

◆　◆　◆

Mid-July, in these parts, brought extremes of heat and humidity and the paddocks were already showing signs of distress. But the trees were magnificent and, under groups of hickories, oaks, walnuts, and Osage oranges, mares and foals could be seen relaxing in the shade, flicking away the flies with their tails.

Matt was at the helm for dinner on the patio by the pool, starting with a perfectly chilled gazspacho, garnished with chives from the garden. All around the fireflies danced as the sun set behind them and he filled the diners' glasses with Sancerre.

Vera Montagu raised her glass. 'Welcome to Shenandoah, Algy. We're a bit off the beaten track here. But we manage okay, don't we Matt?'

'I'll say,' said Algy. 'So generous of you to invite me.'

'Wait 'til we get ya workin' tomorrow,' quipped Matt.

'I can't wait,' Algy replied. 'It's just a shame that I can't stay longer, because Tom has told me so much about Saratoga.'

'Ah, Saratoga,' said Vera. 'Basil is taking four up there on Saturday. Tom, you'll be interested to hear that we're sending Rikki up to Canada to run on the turf at Woodbine, a week from Saturday.'

'How's he doing?' asked Tom.

'Great,' said Matt. 'Of course, his owners have been champing at the bit to run him. But there haven't been many good spots. I thought about a race at Belmont the other day, but I reckon that the big sweeping turns of Woodbine will suit him perfectly. Their turf course is outside the dirt track, a mile and a half around.'

'Yes,' said Vera. 'It's the King Edward Gold Cup, a mile and an eighth. A good purse. The boys are keen for me to go up and watch him run. Did I tell you that I am now an official member of the Elevator Stable?' she beamed.

'No! That's incredible,' said Tom. 'Tell Algy about these guys. It's a great story.'

Over dinner Vera recounted the tale of getting stuck in the elevator and the extraordinary chain of events that had led to a horse that she'd bred and sold being claimed and returned to Shenandoah.

'It's a shame that you won't meet these guys,' said Tom. 'Are you warming to them yet, Matt?' he asked.

'You have to understand, Algy, that Matt is my private trainer,' said Vera. 'For many reasons that are too complicated to go into here and now, Matt doesn't like dealing with outside owners. Anyway, these guys are an exception, aren't they Matt?'

'Well, Algy, I have to be honest and say that against my better judgement they somehow weedled their way in here, and the rest is history.'

'But, Matt, tell the truth. You love Rikki, eh?'

'Yep. I have to say that Rikki made the deal. But, to be fair, Victor and those guys have been very good. I get the occasional text or e-mail, suggesting races for him. But they know the rules.'

'Matt calls the shots,' Vera said to Algy, 'but these guys are way ahead. They claimed him for fifty and he has a win and a second in a Grade 1 stake, meaning over $100K in prize money, so they aren't complaining. And especially so, now that I'm in the syndicate, the training fees are less.'

'So, what do you make of the news about El Cordobes?' Tom asked Matt.

'Something not right about that horse. I told you that I thought they plugged him in at Pimlico. Well, by the sounds of things, they may well have hopped him, too. We had a mare dropped off here the other day by BGT, out of Lexington, and the van driver told my man Toby that when they took the horse back to Kentucky, after that race, he was crazy. Kicked out the panel behind his stall and threw a fit, on Highway 81. There is something very fishy going on with those South American guys. So I can't say that I was surprised when I heard the news.'

'A friend of Algy's had just bought a share in him,' said Tom.

'Well, he just blew his money then, didn't he,' said Matt.

'Isn't there insurance?' asked Vera.

'Probably,' said Matt. 'But,' and he paused, 'there have been too many suspicious things going on around that farm and the people involved, recently, and I can't believe they'll pay out without asking questions.'

Tom saw Vera frown. 'Well, we've still got Rikki and I guess he now has one less opponent to worry about. Oh, how nice,' she said, as Elsie served the salmon in aspic, with Matt's homemade mayonnaise and crab mousse.

◆ ◆ ◆

For Algy, riding out on the farm wasn't all that different to back home in England, at many of the little permit-holder's stables he was familiar with in the Point-to-Point and National Hunt racing world.

The small string of six filed out of the barn into the early morning mist, just before 5:30 a.m. It was a soft time of the day, as the first rays of sun crept over the ridge to their east. Jose was leading the way on Rikki, who must have known that his next racetrack assignment was nearing, because he was on his toes.

It had been over two months since his last race at Pimlico and he was sharp between his rider's slender legs. Jose had beautiful light hands and, like with so many talented Hispanic riders, his mounts got a good message the moment he alighted upon their backs. Dieter followed on Touch and Go, who, after almost a year off the track, was getting good again. His vacation had seen him put on the pounds and Matt had been careful to bring him along ever so slowly. Blessed with electrifying natural speed that needed to be conserved, this had meant many miles of jogging and slow, long gallops, before any serious work.

'What's your friend's name?' enquired Dieter. 'Algy, eh? Ain't that some kind of slime? Like a scum on top of dirty water? A sort of breeding ground for germs?'

'That's algae: ae, not with a y,' said Tom, laughing. 'He's been called a lot worse than that, though!'

Algy blushed, but in the subdued light nobody noticed. 'Is that helmet of yours square, Dieter? Or is that just my imagination?' he gave back, and the girls laughed, even though they probably didn't appreciate the inference.

'Matt gonna let you ride Rikki in Canada, Angie?' the German asked Angela, who since her Grade 1 cameo performance at the Preakness meet, on the stable's star, had won two races at nearby Charles Town.

'Dunno,' she replied. 'Matt don't say much. But we'll see. Somehow, I think he might go with a local rider. I hear they're a bit cliquey up there, you know - like to keep things for themselves. Don't like outside riders shipping in. Wouldn't surprise me if Matt takes Joe, as he was the leading rider up there five times back in the '90s and they won't give him no guff.'

The mist had risen by the time they had trotted up the hill twice and walked in a circle before their studious trainer and his ever-present canine companion, Ripkin. 'Jose, you can let Rikki run on a bit today, let him blow a bit. Dieter, just nice and slow, three times. You girls,' he said, gesturing towards

Angela and Betsy, 'come up together with Tom and Algy, upsides. Just let 'em get nice and balanced. But don't let them run off.'

Like many trainers of animals, Matt was perpetually tuned into a different wavelength while in their company, trying to think like them. It's like a mother with a child, before it can speak and tell its mommy its needs, he thought. You need to watch every little mannerism and nuance. They're all individuals and the mark of a great horseman is knowing his horses and spotting things before they tell him something is wrong, via a bad work or race. An ounce of prevention is worth a pound of cure, he believed, valuing his rider's feedback. But nobody could fool him.

At the racetrack he'd had little time for so-called horsemen. Condition book readers he'd called them, who spent their whole time in the clocker's stand, bullshitting with their cronies, or in the racing secretary's office sparring with jockeys' agents. They trained by numbers, in his opinion.

Back at the barn, the ground crew were ready, joking amongst themselves and ribbing the two guest riders. 'Your lady's happy to see you back,' said Curtis to Tom, once again embarrassing Betsy. 'Don't know how she survived without you,' he continued to catcalls from the other men who were busily bathing their charges.

Matt leaned over a saddle horse, chewing on a stem of Timothy as Ripkin rolled in the sand ring. It was the day before shipping to Saratoga, and veterinarian Ralph Hyatt was busy with Coggins and health certificates which were required for the journey north.

Doc Hyatt was a Floridian, from just outside Palm City, near Stuart, from whence he split his year between Payson Park training centre in the winter months, and the Middleburg-Upperville area of Virginia during the summer. He figured, that way, he'd get the sun all the time, but not too much of it, and his deep tan reflected a perfect balance. Indeed, standing just over six feet with broad shoulders, a shock of grey hair under his bush hat, he had a look of Indiana Jones about him. He had once been married, he told enquirers. But no lady had been able to get between him and his horses, since then, and he prefered now to pick his company, when he felt like it. Not that there weren't nearly always good-looking women either in his fold or on his staff. Techies, they called them, and Doc Hyatt had a knack of picking the prettiest.

'Hey, Doc!' shouted Toby. 'You gotta tell these boys the secret to gettin' all them good-lookin' women! Yes siree, the good doctor'll write y'all a prescription.' The boys laughed.

Dr. Hyatt smiled. He and Matt talked the same language, and he liked his trips to Shenandoah Valley Farms.

'Doc, I want to introduce you to Tom. Tom Fraser, Dr. Ralph Hyatt,' said Matt. They shook hands and Tom introduced Algy.

'You remember the fire at Caledonia back in the spring, Ralph. When you've finished up here, I know that Tom would like to have a word with you. Come along Algy,' he said, letting out a whistle for Ripkin, 'we gonna go get us some breakfast.'

Tom had wrapped the leather pouch that Randy Dobbs had given him in a plastic bag that now sat on a table in the middle of the tack room.

'I believe that Matt may have mentioned the troubles at home,' he began, and Dr. Hyatt nodded. 'There's a lot gone on in the last few months and,' he paused, 'it seems that the people who have taken over are up to no good.' Looking Dr. Hyatt straight in the face, he continued, 'How much has Matt told you?'

Hyatt looked around. They were alone. 'Pretty much everything. We've known each other for a long time, and he knows that he can trust me. I helped keep that little foal alive, as it was touch and go when he got here.'

Feeling that going over the story one more time was unnecessary, Tom pressed on, assured that the doctor was well versed on the subject. 'Doc, I wondered whether you could check out what's in this phial?' he said, removing the small glass bottle from the leather pouch and handing it to Hyatt.

Dr. Hyatt held it up to the light. The seal was unbroken. So a sniff was no good.

'Standard 50c.c. injectable. Nothing on the label but a few numbers. Maybe some sort of distributor's barcode. Hard to tell,' he mused. 'What's this?' he asked, removing the sheet of paper that had been folded tightly and tucked into a corner of the leather pouch.

'Oh, that. I don't know,' said Tom. 'Just a bunch of numbers.'

Dr. Hyatt unfolded the sheet of paper. 'Ten six-figure numbers. Very strange,' he muttered to himself. 'Gotta mean something. Let me see if we can find out. First, what is in the bottle. I have a buddy in Gainsville, at the veterinary college, who has been doing some work for the USDA. He may be able to help us out here. Leave it with me.'

'Doc, I'm sure I don't need to tell you this. But, no mentioning of where it came from. And split this sample. I mean keep some, because, you know, things can get lost and we need our own sample, just in case there are any disputes.'

'You've got it, no worries,' said Hyatt, replacing the bottle and paper in the leather pouch and placing them in a drawer of the customized medicine cabinet in the back of his white Lexus SUV with the distinct orange-and-green Florida plates. 'I wasn't born yesterday. Leave it with me. We'll get to the bottom of this.'

Later in the day, Tom drove Algy to Washington for his flight back to England. On the way Algy begged him to stop off to see the Lost Prince, as he now referred to him. But Tom felt that any unnecessary attention might only arouse suspicion. After all, there was nothing special about this no-name colt, just that he was an orphan. So best to leave him alone.

Back at the farm Basil Foster was loading the gooseneck to the gills with webbings, rubber mats, boxes for coolers, boxes for linaments, boxes for bandages, and enough tack to equip a troop of cavalry. The journey to Saratoga, scheduled for departure at 5 a.m. the following morning, would take between seven and eight hours straight up Highway 81 to the New York state freeway, 90 East, and then off at the Amsterdam exit 27, and across country through Balston Spa to The Toga; a special place where, for over a hundred years, New Yorkers have retreated every August, for cool breezes, medicinal waters, and the best thoroughbred racing in the land.

CHAPTER 26

The Saratoga of the twenty-first century barely resembles that of the golden era of the roaring twenties, when horse racing was the sport of choice for film stars and celebrities of the day, with enormous, colonial-style houses built off Upper Broadway, and barns filled with regally bred bloodstock owned by the scion families of American business and banking: the Mellons (Rokeby Stables), Vanderbilts (Sagamore), Whitneys (Greentree), and Galbraiths (Darby Dan). But the racetrack itself remains an undisturbed haven of tranquility: a quiet monument in the trees to famous horses and horsemen gone by.

Curtis and Silas had driven up the previous day to prepare the small private barn on the Oklahoma backstretch, adjacent to the training track. They would check out each stall for nails, protruding screw eyes and any holes, or faulty boards that could cause the slightest injury to their priceless occupants-to-be, and bed them down with the finest straw.

Oklahoma was quieter, separated from the main track by Union Avenue, so that during the afternoon races the roar of the crowd did not disturb siesta time. Even today the services are minimal, with limited electricity and water. But Matt liked it this way because the horses' happiness was all he cared about, with round-the-clock TLC and long grazes in the shade at feed time.

The Montagues had a house in town, off Upper Broadway, to which Vera would move with her entourage of Elsie and Mavis, her private nurse, for the duration of the six-week-long meet. A place had been rented just off Park Place, within walking distance of the racetrack for Basil and Tom.

Curtis and Silas, meanwhile, had bagged basic but functional tack rooms on the Oklahoma backstretch close to their barn. And, for them, the latter would be their home around-the-clock for the next forty or so days: attending to the small stable during the day, cooking themselves corn in the fifty gallon oil drums that were heated each day by the barn's propane burners, drinking beer and shooting the breeze long into the nights. It's often said that too much of a good thing can spoil it, but Saratoga may be one of the rare exceptions.

The trip north, across the border, was the first objective upon their arrival. And, after a couple of days settling in and getting used to the track, the gooseneck was back on the road again, with Rikki in the back, Curtis driving, and Tom riding shotgun. Their destination Fort Erie, just across the Niagara River from Buffalo, and the barn of veteran horseman Ronnie Broadhurst.

Fort Erie is an old-style dirt track, not unlike Saratoga, that is very different to the sandier ovals and modern all-weather surfaces of other racetracks in North America; the reddy-brown loam providing a beautiful cushion, under perfect conditions. Perhaps its best feature, though, for a B-graded racetrack, is the unique and scenic turf training track across Gilmour Road: often referred to as the Canadian Saratoga.

Like so many of North America's racetracks, today Fort Erie has seen better days and is now mostly the domain of cast-offs from Woodbine, a hundred miles up the Queen Elizabeth Highway in Toronto, where Rikki was scheduled to perform that Saturday. But, as a training centre, it is still hard to beat.

Like Matt Pearson, Ronnie was old school. A Yorkshire lad by birth, some said he had a Romany background before serving his time in one of the best yards in Newmarket, England, and then setting sail for Canada and the legendry Windfields Farms, where his quiet way with horses had been noticed and, eventually brought him to Woodbine to ply his skills.

Never able to get the stalls he needed at The Woodbine, as he called it, he'd graduated to Fort Erie, built his stable up, and never returned to Toronto, when the opportunity presented itself: so contented was he, off the radar, training his horses on his terms.

For Vera Montagu, Ronnie was the perfect choice, as he and her cousin Matt saw eye to eye and there were no ego issues. Everyone knew Matt Pearson was in charge, even though his name never appeared on a program at any licensed racetrack. Foster was the program name in the USA and Broadhurst in Canada. The two men seldom communicated with one another and their boss just let them get on with it.

Rikki, being a veteran traveller, greedily ate up upon arrival. It was a bit cooler in Canada and Tom had a tough time holding him, as they blew out the next morning. Running down the lane, the clockers caught them for a half-mile in a handy forty-eight seconds, but few noticed that Tom had a great deal of difficulty pulling him up, and he and Ronnie (watching quietly from his pony at the wire) knew that this could have been very much quicker with a lighter and more energetic rider.

Someone who had, though, was Colin Nightingale, who was at the barn upon Rikki's return. Since the excitement at Pimlico, almost three months earlier, the Elevator Stable had been anxiously looking forward to their star's return to the track. Heeding Matt's caution to not interfere in the process, they had waited virtually incommunicado until the word had got out that Woodbine was the next target. So, being just down the road from Toronto, Colin had been unable to resist a barn visit. He knew Ronnie Broadhurst was a softer version of Matt and hoped the reception would be, perhaps, a little more welcoming.

Colin had learnt from Vera that Joe Magee would ship in from Saratoga to ride. He had his advanced copy of the *Daily Racing Form* and was anxious to get the word from the horse's mouth, as he put it, that he could relay to his colleagues.

'Mr. Broadhurst!' Colin, sporting a pair of bright green trousers and a yellow golf shirt, topped by an Elevator Stable baseball cap, which he'd proudly designed, effusively introduced himself. 'Colin Nightingale, the Elevator Stable. I hope you don't mind my intrusion?'

'You're paying the bills, so you have a right to be here,' Ronnie responded bluntly in his broad and direct Yorkshire brogue. ''Tis a fine horse you have here,' he commented as Rikki was walked past, now bathed and sporting a bright red cooler.

'Yes. We like him,' gushed Colin, nervously enquiring, 'What do you think?'

'About what?' asked Ronnie gazing down the shedrow where one of his charges was walking towards him, watching, as usual, every little detail.

'Well, this morning's workout?' said Colin nervously, 'and the race on Saturday?'

'He looked sharp. Any stakes race at The Woodbine is tough. They don't give away their brass up there,' he added.

'I know, I know. We're so pleased he's here. Ran a big Beyer figure (Andrew Beyer's DRF pro-rating) at Pimlico. If he runs back to that number, he should be tough,' Colin ventured.

'Never been a big believer in fancy numbers,' said Ronnie, dryly. 'First past post gets the money. That's what I say. Bugger the time.' And he headed off to the feed room.

Curtis was walking Rikki and this gave Tom, who hadn't wanted to interrupt Ronnie's views and comments, an opportunity to say hello.

'Mr. Nightingale. Tom Fraser, Vera Montagu's nephew - we met at Pimlico.'

'Indeed. Indeed we did,' said Colin excitedly, feeling that Tom could, perhaps, be more informative than his dour trainer. 'So good to see you again. We're excited that your aunt has joined the syndicate.'

'As she is,' replied Tom. 'She'd have loved to have been here, as Woodbine is one of her favourite tracks. But it just wasn't possible with the move up to Saratoga. But she'll be watching on TV, and betting, I'm sure.'

Colin got the lowdown. Rikki was in fighting form. Matt's decision to ride Joe Magee over Angela was because, as he put it, 'the locals can be hostile to ship-ins' and Joe, being well known at Woodbine, would get respect. As for the race, Rikki had drawn the outside post, but in a field of eight it was no big deal. The locals weren't up to much, but there were two horses from Europe: one a colt owned by Sheikh Bhakandar from France and another South American invader of Condor Racing's increasingly widespread enterprises, that was now trained at Woodbine by leading trainer Danny Johnson.

◆　◆　◆

In deference to his major patron, Ronnie made a rare trip to Woodbine. Leaving his beloved barn was not something he enjoyed at all, as it interrupted his strict regimen. But someone had to put the tack on Rikki.

Curtis and Tom had set out after breakfast, aiming to avoid the Toronto rush-hour traffic and get into Woodbine at about 10 a.m. They had missed all the preliminaries and draw and, being now identified in the program as in the care of Ronnie Broadhurst at Fort Erie, the local *Daily Racing Form* correspondents had, much to his owners' disappointment, dismissed Rikki with a byline of 'Will have trouble repeating last.'

Reggie Halpern had flown in from New York City, now firmly on board the bandwagon after the Pimlico race. As the four partners looked down onto the racetrack from their Turf Club dining room table, he observed that this might indeed be a tougher race than the last. The French invader was a Group 1 winner in France and, as Ronnie had pointed out, these top turf races at Woodbine were never easy. All the same, he'd said, if we hit the board there'll be a good cheque: always conscious of his investments paying for themselves. And there was good news that there had been a late scratch, and now only seven would go to post, as the five-horse Marinello, a Delmontez runner, was a vet scratch (considered unfit to participate by the Ontario racing commission's veterinarian).

Tom had spotted someone in the backstretch kitchen whom he was sure he recognized, but just couldn't remember from where until a very worried-looking Hector Delmontez had arrived on the scene and, after a heated conversation in Spanish, Tom realized that he was one of the men who had denied him entrance to Caledonia back in March. Whatever the issue was, Hector had been, for him, unusually angry, and his staff were getting the brunt of it.

The King Edward Gold Cup was just one of several Stakes races being run on what was, locally, a big day and a decent crowd surrounded the picturesque, willow tree-filled paddock behind the grandstand for the ninth race. Tom had walked over with Rikki, and the first voice he heard was immediately recognizable with the familiar laugh. It was Bog, with Hugo Lascelles, Antoine de Sevigny, Sheikh Ali's French trainer, and young Lucy Beagle, all being escorted by Mr. Woodbine, Calvin Weiner. They were gathered in the shade of a willow tree and did not see team Broadhurst enter. And, Tom thought, probably wouldn't have put two and two together; which was the right assumption because the next thing he heard, as they circled, prior to the jockeys coming out was: 'Tom! What on Earth are you doing here?'

'I thought we might lock horns with you again,' he said, 'but I see that your horse failed to make it,' he added with a dig.

'Dreadful shame. A bad reaction to a pre-race medication,' Bog blurted out, realizing instantly from Hector Delmontez's reaction that he'd said something he shouldn't have. 'Never mind,' he continued. 'We have. Rather, the agency has, an interest in the favourite, per Sheikh Ali. Are you going to the sale?'

'What sale?' said Tom.

'Oh, don't you know about the private sale that Cal Weiner and Mike Rogers put on every year, at their farm in King City? This year they're consigning some of Hector's exciting South American breds. It's a gas event, from what I hear. They sell about thirty horses of various ages. You should talk to Mike about it, he seems to be in charge. We're all going up there after the races. It starts at about seven. You should come.'

Just then Ronnie Broadhurst, Joe Magee, and the four members of the Elevator Stable materialised beside Tom and the riders-up signal was given.

As they walked out of the paddock a much more relaxed-looking Hector Delmontez intercepted Tom. 'You get about, my friend,' he opened. 'Unfortunately, our horse will have to wait for another day,' adding, 'maybe we would have surprised you again, no?'

'Yes. Tough luck,' said Tom between gritted teeth.

'Theeese-is-a fab-ulous racetrack,' said Hector with exaggerated emphasis for the benefit of Cal Weiner, who was walking right behind him. 'We will see you at the sale, no?'

'No,' said Tom. 'We're heading straight back to Fort Erie after the race and then to Saratoga tomorrow.'

'Oh, Saratoga!' said Hector. 'We will be there, too. For the sale in two weeks, no? And we have a couple of nice horses, with Timmy Trebor, that will be running before the end of the meet.'

'Well, we'll see you then,' said Tom. 'I must go and watch this race with the owners. Hasta luego.'

With a small field, there was never much pace in the race. And, in a sprint to the wire, the favourite prevailed in a photo, with Rikki a close fourth. Bog and his lady may have been deprived of watching Hector's horse, but were still all smiles as they, along with Hugo Lascelles, accepted the King Edward Gold Cup on behalf of Sheikh Ali, from the very lovely Samantha Weiner.

The Elevator boys were a little quiet. Their horse had run a big race, but circumstances had been against him. Joe Magee had held him up, off the slow pace, and then, when he'd tried to save ground and come through on the rail, he'd been shut off at a key point. He'd run on well, but by then the race was over. It was another cheque, Reggie pointed out, and their investment continued to pay for himself.

After Rikki had cooled out and Tom was grazing him while Curtis wiped down his legs in preparation for an uptight poultice, Ronnie came by to say that his ride up from Fort Erie had left early and he'd travel back with them. 'Just watched the rerun. He didn't run badly at all. Sometimes things just don't work out the way you want them to.'

'What's the story on the sale tonight, Ronnie? Are you going?'

'No. Not me. Are you kidding? That's a bunch of bullshit, if you ask me. I stay out of the way down at The Fort, for good reason.' He paused while he drew on his cigarette. 'Let's put it this way: the people up here run this racetrack as if it's their own fiefdom. I saw you talking to someone in the paddock with Weiner. Now, there's a winner. His daddy made a fortune in the meat and frozen foods business and loved his horses. Sonny, though, he's a real piece of work.'

'What do you mean?'

'Well, after daddy died, that was Jerry Weiner, not a bad guy,' Ronnie continued, 'they got involved with the lottery and casino guys and brought slot machines to the tracks - not just here, but throughout the province of Ontario. With the new racing fans casinos were supposed to generate, and a sizeable take from the slots' revenue, they were getting close to a million dollars a day, back in the late '90s! Horse racing in Ontario received over $4 billion in direct subsidies during that time.'

'What happened?' asked Tom.

'Well, that money was supposed to be spent on marketing horse racing to a new and younger audience, to stimulate betting on horses and, with this new interest in the sport, it was hoped that new owners would appear and so the market for Ontario-bred horses would improve. But all management did was to boost the purses to ridiculously high levels to serve existing owners, and then paid themselves huge salaries for effectively doling out this public money. I mean, the taxpayers of Ontario were paying for a few people to enjoy horse racing, while hospitals and schools were not built. It was a scandal! I mean it is a scandal!'

'I can see,' said Tom. 'But who let this happen? Wasn't somebody in the government watching where the money was being allocated?'

'You'd have thought there should have been someone, but it's just another government cock-up and the person who should have been in charge, the head of the casino corporation, Larry Gerber, got quietly moved out, before the public got wind of what had happened.'

'So, what's happening now?' asked Tom.

'They're struggling. Purses have been cut. The Canadian, and particularly Ontario, foal crop is lower than ever. No new money or new owners are coming into the industry, and media coverage and public interest has disappeared altogether. Now these clowns expect the government to keep on subsidizing them. They're like druggies complaining about going cold turkey. But their paymasters have finally seen the light and don't want to throw good money after bad.'

'So, who is going to go to this sale, this evening?' said Tom.

'Good question. I've been asking myself that quite a lot recently. Weiner gets in trouble – he really should be in jail, if people knew how he effectively stole public money – but he gets himself this new partner, this South American guy who seems to be involved in a lot of rather dodgy things everywhere he goes. My contacts, in the know, tell me that they are bringing bloodstock up from South America. Mediocre stuff, and selling it to themselves and their friends – Weiner and some shifty people from Montreal, drug guys – to legitimize the cash that they have been making for their drug sales. You've heard of the opioid epidemic that is sweeping the country? I have even heard that this South American guy owns his own insurance company, El Gruppo. What they appear to be doing is to insure some of these horses through the company that they own and then, when they've been killed or mysteriously died, they honour the claims, thus making their money legit. I guarantee you that there will be a whole bunch of Russian people at this sale tonight They're just churning cash – all of it dirty money.'

'So, in a sense, they're double dipping. Delmontez brings up the drugs, he flogs a few cheap horses and his customers pay over-the-top prices (really for their drugs) and then he washes his own money per the insurance swindle. Well, not exactly a swindle, because he's doing it with his own stock. But he's making his ill-gotten gains, mountains of cash, into legitimate money. That explains quite a bit,' said Tom.

'I'll bet you dollars to donuts,' said Ronnie, 'that the horse who was scratched today was juiced and, with the adverse reaction, they had to scratch.'

'But wouldn't he have come back with a positive, if he'd won and been tested?'

'Ordinarily, yes. But this is where our Senor whatever-his-name is is really turning the screw.' Ronnie blew his nose and cleared his throat. 'We have had some very strange results up here, during the past year or so, that have raised more than a few eyebrows. And, there have been horses from certain barns that have run way better than anything they've ever shown before. And the one common denominator is Delmontez. You know that horse who won big down at Pimlico on Preakness day?'

'Yes, El Cordobes.'

'That's him. Well, the word was that the rider plugged him in and that may have happened. But I also hear that he was very distressed after that race and did not cool out forever. Indeed, I gather that he never really recovered and that story about him escaping from his stall and hitting a truck is very dodgy. Now, couple the suspicious death of Dr. Mason, the head of the Maryland Racing Commission, and the cops are starting to put together the puzzle.' Ronnie paused. 'It seems that around 2009 an international conference or get-together of racing commissioners, major owners, breeders, and stewards from the Americas, which was held in Caracas, Venezuela, was where Delmontez compromised a few of the attendees.'

'How? What did he do?' said Tom, listening intently to this extraordinary explanation.

'Well, Weiner, to start with, has always had a cocaine and crack problem: everyone here on the track knows that. Once they had to lock him in a tack room because he flipped out, and he's been in rehab a bunch of times. So, he wasn't hard to recruit, especially as he could see the slots money running out. And the others were had in the old-fashioned honey-pot way, with hookers and in an infamous nightclub that Senor Delmontez owns in Caracas, called the Anaconda. Anyway, he's waited, moved some drugs up here on his planes, along with dubious livestock, and he's compromised a few people in important positions.'

'How? Where?' said Tom.

'Well, how about extorting information from the state laboratories assigned to test post-race urine and blood samples? You know how it works? They can't test for everything because it would take forever and be far too expensive. So, what they do is to decide upon random lists of drugs that they know people are using or have used recently. Every horse's sample is split, and they pour sample A, from each of the day's races, into one jug and, if it tests negative for the drugs they are looking for, they know that everyone is clear. So they save time and money. But, if there are traces of anything suspicious, they have to then go and test sample B individually for illegal levels.

'Now, just imagine if you knew what they were testing for and, more important, what they are not testing for. Wouldn't that put you in a very powerful position?'

'I'll say,' said Tom.

'Wouldn't put it past them scratching that horse today because they found out they'd changed the list of drugs they were going to test for, at the last minute.'

'So, it's happening here, too?' asked Tom.

'I'll bet you all the tea in China that Delmontez has Weiner under his thumb. Maybe even someone in the racing commission, too, through him?'

Tom was stunned, wondering, then, just what was in the phial that Dr. Hyatt was testing, and, after what Ronnie had just said, what did those numbers mean? Did they correspond to drugs? Drugs, perhaps, being tested at a certain racetrack at a certain time?

Curtis drove them back to Fort Erie, while Tom ruminated.

CHAPTER 27

Vera Montagu could live at Saratoga year-round, she thought, as she sat out on the balcony off her bedroom, having breakfast and reading the *Racing Form*. It was sales week and the small upstate New York spa town was buzzing in anticipation.

On the front page of her *Form* was a picture of her good friend, Billy Beagle, at a recent private sale on a farm in Canada, where, contrary to all recent trends, record prices had been paid for a limited and mixed offering of yearlings, horses-in-training, and brood mares. Beagle was grinning from ear to ear and beside him were two Russian buyers, Senor Hector Delmontez of Lexington's famous Caledonia Farms, and the sales' host, Calvin Weiner.

'The Russians, Messrs. Yuri Bragovski and Maxim Jirkhov, represented exciting new players in the industry,' Beagle was quoted as saying, going on to praise the enterprise of his good friends Delmontez and Weiner as, 'two pillars of our industry.'

Vera loved the sales, particularly at Saratoga. There was so much quality. All the smart people were there, and the two nights just complimented perfect days at the races. For her, that meant a lazy morning reading sales catalogues and studying form. Then she and her nurse, Mavis, would be driven to the racetrack, where they'd have lunch on the terrace, chat with her racing friends about all matters related to horses: breeding them, selling them, buying them, racing them, jumping them, and hunting them. Sometimes she'd even have a little bet on them, and Mavis would be dispatched to the Mutuels.

Every now and then Shenandoah Valley would have a runner, and, on those occasions, Vera would insist upon visiting that horse in the barn, to wish him or her well, on her way to the track. Everyone knew Vera Montagu; she was one of the last of a dynasty of influential American women with a lifelong passion for thoroughbreds.

Today, Billy Beagle and his charming wife Mary-Lou joined her for lunch, as Beagle was in town for NHRA meetings at the Reading Room and, of course, the sales.

'I see that the Russians are coming!' said Vera, as Beagle and his wife approached.

Attired in a fine, pale blue and white pinstripe linen suit, topped by his regular panama hat, Beagle was his usual charming self, kissing his host on both cheeks and making small talk with Mavis about how he was relying upon her to give him some good tips as Ms. Montagu had told him that she was an excellent handicapper.

Mary-Lou Beagle, relishing the fact that at Saratoga you could wear those lovely clothes that there were, regrettably, fewer and fewer occasions for, looked positively delightful in cream, with olive green piping under a large orange straw hat.

'Yes, that was quite something,' said Beagle as he helped his wife into her chair, with a good view looking down the track. 'I take my hat off to Cal Weiner and his guys: not only putting on such a good show but rustling up some new players. They've got a lot money, those Russian guys. Just gotta get 'em to spend some of it in our business,' he chuckled.

'Well, it sounds like they did,' said Vera.

'Amazing chap this South American; he's done wonders for racing.' And her guest droned on like the corporate PR schmoozer and inveterate booster of the sport that he was.

That night, at the sales, a record was set when Hugo Lascelles, acting for a new Russian client, paid $3.4 million for a filly by Stratospheric from a family rich with stakes winners. And none other than Johnny Ward-Clark signed the ticket for a million-dollar purchase, on behalf of Caledonia Farms and Senor Hector Delmontez. It seemed that the death of El Cordobes had not dampened anyone's enthusiasm. Indeed, quite the contrary, as Delmontez and Weiner bought several other choice lots, confirming that their new America's Stable, as they now rather strangely called the Russian members' syndicate, was blossoming.

Johnny, still unaware that he was no longer his client, had been disappointed to learn that Ravi Singh could not attend the sales. But that hadn't spoiled his fun, as the agency had made him their pointman in dealings with the Americas group that Delmontez was establishing with Cal Weiner. Johnny had been at the sale in Canada, along with his belle, Lucy, and her father, and was drinking the Kool-Aid greedily, with the complete backing of his employers.

◆　◆　◆

In the wake of the El Cordobes setback, despite the fact that El Gruppo had settled the insurance claim remarkably quickly, Ravi was feeling somewhat chastened.

'I hope you've learned your lesson, brother,' said Kulbir, as they spoke on the telephone.

'I know. I know, you were right,' Ravi replied. 'But,' he emphasized, 'we didn't get burnt. We got our money back.'

'This time, yes. You are lucky. My friend Satish, you know, who sold his software business in Florida a few years ago, he bought into one of those fancy syndicates. It turned out all they wanted was his money. I think ten million to buy in. Then they gave him the run-around, taking him for a complete fool. You know how it works? You invest in the syndicate and are then responsible for monthly costs, with the other shareholders. Well, Satish got a thirty-two grand charge one month for what was described as 'a private jet.' But, when he consulted his records, he saw that the day he'd been billed for he'd travelled with his trainer to the races in a car! When he asked what was going on, and suggested that it must be a mistake, he was told that a plane had been standing by, just in case his trainer, the great man, needed to get anywhere in a hurry. Do you hear me, Ravi? These high-falutin' guys'll take you for what they can and there's something not right with the El Cordobes deal. They just seemed so matter of fact. You know, as if they didn't care and this was a perfectly satisfactory result.'

'What are you saying?'

'Well, there's something fishy with that insurance deal. My friends in the city tell me that El Gruppo is not what it appears on the surface. That it's a front for laundering money.'

'And how do they know that?' asked Ravi.

'Just an accumulation of improbable events. You can pull the old three-card-trick once in a while, but these guys seem to have got greedy and they've raised some red flags. And, as a result, there are now a few people being investigated by the SEC. That Gilligan guy and a chum of his who is in insurance and has been brokering some of this stuff. I think his name is Waley-Brown. Watch out. And just count yourself fortunate that you got out before you did get burnt.'

On the end of the line in Bangalore, Ravi bit his lip. He hadn't told Kulbir yet about his Keeneland purchase. 'Well,' he said, changing the subject, 'let's focus on the Real Racing project. At least we've got a little bit of a feel for how the authorities in the UK and USA are going to react. Not!'

'Yep, no point wasting any more time on them.'

Instead of attending the sale in Canada and making a visit to Saratoga, as Johnny and his colleagues at CBS had suggested, Ravi had flown to Australia to meet with Larry Thompson of TAB. Tommo, as his friends called him, had proven to be a breath of fresh air who was altogether much more receptive to his overtures.

Expertly juggling a cricket ball and occasionally going through the motions of making what he called a 'belter of a delivery,' all for Ravi's benefit, Tommo was all on board. 'Crikey,' he'd said after Ravi had explained the maths in Kulbir's polished package. 'I like the sound of these Society Lotteries, mate. The more tickets you sell, the less, percentage-wise, you have to pay out in prize money! Stone the bleedin' crows,' he said, and he'd jumped up and actually did bowl his ball into a net in the corner of his office, where the wall behind evidenced some pace from a few of Tommo's previous deliveries, per the red scuff marks. 'Leave it to me,' he'd said, as they'd headed off for a spot of golf and a few brewskis, as he called them.

CHAPTER 28

The Saratoga meet had yielded three wins from eight starts for Basil's small string, highlighted by Rikki's return to the winner's circle in the Spa Stakes: a two-hundred grander that had ended up going a mile and a sixteenth on the main track.

Calling from the farm, Matt had pointed out that, with the weather forecasted to be rain all week, the race would probably come off the turf and there would consequently be a bunch of scratches. So it was that a small field of five blazed away in the deep slop, cutting each others' throats, and allowing the wily Joe Magee to lie way back off this suicidal pace and swoop by at the wire. In the excitement, Reggie, in the process of embracing his new racing partner, Vera, had tripped over her wheelchair and ended up, rather ignominiously, face down in the reddy brown soup. But that hadn't wiped the smile off his and his colleagues' faces as they not only picked up another hundred and twenty thousand, but made a nice little score at the windows, thanks to Rikki being ignored on a surface that the experts had, inaccurately, predicted he could not handle.

Saratoga had been good, too, for Hector Delmontez. In the wake of the successful sale in Canada, further regular Air Condor flights bringing in new stock had been arranged. Calvin Weiner and Mike Rogers were turning out to be spectacular recruiters of customers for his wares and they had even brought their new Russian acquaintances to the Spa, where they were treated like royalty by Billy Beagle and the sales company.

The budding Americas partnership, under the management of Hector and, by extension, Hugo Lascelles and Johnny Ward-Clark, had expanded rapidly. When the Hopeful Stakes, the marquis race for two-year-old colts at the end of the meet, was won by a colt owned by America's Stable and trained by Tim Trebor, anyone standing near the winner's circle celebrations could have been excused for thinking that they were in downtown Moscow, so thick was the air with Russian.

Trebor, furthermore, made a rare foray across the border into Canada, for the Grade 1 Woodbine Mile in September, setting tongues wagging with the electric performance of his four-year-old, Beachcomber, who had, until that point, never shown form at anything like that level. It had been well known that the record-setting Trebor barn stayed away from jurisdictions with such tough medication regulations and the word was that Tim Trebor did not like Ontario 'spit boxes,' as he referred to local testing. Regardless, no flags were raised, and the seemingly unstoppable fortunes of Hector Delmontez continued, unchecked.

However, as much as the architect of this onslaught might have enjoyed the generous media coverage of his arrival on the Toronto racing scene, he would not have been happy to read a late-August two paragraph article, buried on page five of the *Toronto Star*, titled 'Body Washes Up on Lake of Bays Shore,' that described the mystery surrounding the discovery of what appeared to be a Hispanic-looking male of approximately thirty years on Dwight Beach, near Huntsville, Ontario. The body, which showed signs of extreme trauma, was being held at the coroner's office in Toronto, pending identification, and the matter was being investigated jointly by the Ontario Provincial Police (OPP) and Royal Canadian Mounted Police (RCMP).

◆ ◆ ◆

The summer was coming to an end. In Virginia this meant a short season of hunt meets, at which Vera Montagu loved to see her colours in action. The prize money wasn't always the greatest, but this was where she'd once indulged her passion and on an early October afternoon the view from the elevated ground near the winning post at the Glenwood meet was as fine as anywhere in the land. This was point-to-point racing, American-style, and even Matt Pearson found the informal atmosphere agreeable, standing beside a jump, satisfyingly incognito.

At Tumbleweed, the foals had been weaned. A heart-breaking process for many, whereby they are taken from their mothers and put into their own paddocks in small groups, while their distraught moms whinney and gallop up and down in the distress of being parted from their babies. For the foals, which are known as weanlings at that point, until the following January 1 when, irrespective of their foaling date, they all collectively turn one on the same day and are then referred to as yearlings, the separation isn't so traumatic. And Rocky, as he'd been nicknamed by Winston, the farm manager, soon forgot his surrogate mother after a few squealing and bucking gallops with his new mates around their new home.

Lorna and Jim Buchanan had spent August and September in Provence and, when they had returned, it was assumed that the paperwork for that spring's crop of foals was all in order.

Beside Goose Creek, in the small paddock that bordered the driveway, young Rocky, the dark bay colt with the perfectly formed, shamrock-shaped star, was growing like a weed. Now officially a Virginia-bred, he was listed on his foal papers as being by the local sire Last Post (recently deceased) out of the mare Curtain Call (also dead) who had been by Stage Director. There was nothing remotely suspicious, as the real Curtain Call had, in fact, been bred to Last Post and then, conveniently, died. Certainly, nobody on the farm, including the owners, had any reason to believe that the timing had not exactly coincided with the arrival of Cleo and her surrogate foal.

At Shenandoah Valley, just over the ridge, Matt had marvelled at how his cousin, Vera, had somehow acquired provenance for their secret.

She had first suggested that he be registered as bred in West Virginia. But Matt snuffed that idea out quickly, as this would make it all the harder to explain his performance on the track, which they were convinced would exceed by far that of any West Virginia bred. So, Virginia, the state that had produced the immortal Secretariat, had been opted for.

Additionally, in lieu of her nephew, Tom Fraser, being now parentless and with limited prospects, Vera had gifted the colt to him, in a blind trust, and decided that on the eve of his entry into training, as a two-year-old, a year hence, she would lease him to the Elevator Stable for a down payment that covered his first two seasons on the track, until he turned four, thereby guaranteeing Tom an income. She had explained to Tom that this would have been something his father would have approved of because it was all there was to be left to his son. And that, for obvious reasons, the colt must always stay in the hands of 'folk who are friendly,' as she rather quaintly put it.

'We don't need anyone checking this guy out too carefully. He's never going to be put up for public auction, where there might be suggestions of deception, even though any buyer would be so lucky,' she went on to say. 'And, down the road, if he turns out to be no good, nothing will be said. But, on the other hand, if he does develop into a serious racehorse, any suspicion that he may not be the real thing will be, by that time, moot, and, actually, cream on the top of his achievements. But nobody will ever need to know,' she'd added.

This was all stuff from which Matt stayed well away. What concerned him a great deal more was Dr. Hyatt's confirmation that the drug in the phial that Tom had brought from Kentucky was, in fact, a new and much stronger version of Coramine, a heroin-based derivative, considered a hundred times more powerful than morphine that had not been used, as far as his contacts at the veterinary lab in Gainsville knew, for over thirty years. Its existence, and in such a potent strain, had truly shocked them. Furthermore, his colleagues agreed with him that the coded numbers on the sheet of paper likely corresponded to drugs. Which drugs and in what circumstances, though, was impossible to determine unless they could compare the slip of paper with comparable samples from testing laboratories, and then ascertain which ones matched. This would be a delicate matter to investigate, but the boys in Gainsville were still digging.

◆ ◆ ◆

Ravi was back in London. On Algy's advice he'd transferred the necessary funds to Marcus Townsend immediately after he'd returned from the sale in Kentucky. He had confirmed that his wife, in whose colours he would run, would like to name their colt, who had arrived just before Christmas, on a BGT charter from Cincinnati to Stanstead airport, just north of London, Java Raja.

After the sale, he had been broken and ridden away at a farm near Lexington, so was ready to go into training immediately at Townsend's Newmarket-based Bury Castle Stables. There, his new master, who prided himself on matching his new arrivals with lads and lasses (grooms) whose characters he felt would compliment one another, entrusted him to a lad named David Burns.

Townsend had a good feeling about this colt and David, a diminutive Geordie old-timer, who had spent time stateside, struck him as the perfect caretaker who would not only 'do him' as they say in British racing, but also, because he was so light, ride him in his fast work. Townsend valued such a bond very highly in the search for perfect chemistry that he felt was the key to getting the best out of his charges.

Java Raja settled in with the minimum of fuss, just one of eighty-five other regally-bred yearlings, all about to turn two upon the arrival of the new year – many owned by the stable's chief patron, Sheikh Ali Al-Bhakandar.

A YEARLING

CHAPTER 29

Kulbir Singh had never adjusted to English winters. The dampness got into his bones and no matter how many hot water bottles, electric blankets, bed socks, and his wife's hugs at night; he found the dark short days, long nights, and pervasive grimness unbearably dispiriting. So, he did not need to think twice before accepting his brother's invitation to Bangalore.

Ravi had been buoyed by the enthusiastic reception that he'd received in Australia and the boys at Motti-Media needed his input on the exciting project on which they were working.

So, on a frozen January morning, the Singhs happily shut the door of their damp Clapham townhouse and flew east into the sunshine.

As Kulbir stepped off the plane and breathed in his first breath of warm air, with that unforgettable whiff of dust after a rain, combined with curry and generic shit, he felt like he had never left. As New York is sometimes described as the city that never sleeps, India, he thought, as he and his wife Marisha fought their way through suffocating crowds of porters, bearers, taxi drivers, rickshaw operators, and a sea of endless hustle, is in so many ways a contradiction today: the vast majority stuck in time, yet nowadays a new minority moving forward so fast.

All around him buzzed the mayhem of commerce in a country where over a billion people (close to 90% of the total population) have yet to be provided with the basic conveniences and comforts of the twenty-first century. Yet, within a few hours and not many miles away, he would be in the modern and air-conditioned offices of some of the savviest IT and AI guys in the world: the new and ultra-prosperous face of India.

Motti-Media had come a long way since the first rudimentary online international education programs of the nineties and now controlled a continent-wide network of cable and TV stations, reaching an ever-burgeoning audience of mobile phone users hungry for new content and entertainment.

Bollywood and IPL cricket had created homegrown superstars and their achievements and endorsement, beyond breaking through cultural barriers and ancient taboos, had franked the country as a serious place for investment and business.

Ravi Singh knew how to stir this cocktail with a combination of modesty, charm, and philanthropy, as he'd danced his way daintily through the minefields of bureaucracy to the very top; reckoning, quite accurately, that nothing for an Indian was beyond the realm of possibility, if those in charge of its promotion and administration were taken care of sufficiently.

When it came to gambling, he had his own reservations. But, as he'd explained to every authority that he'd come across in the long process of acquiring licenses in each state, 'on-the-street gambling is going on all the time and has done so forever.' So, almost like a self-inflicted tax, why not harness it to help righteous causes, such as improving health, welfare, and education?' It had been a compelling argument.

After Kulbir and Marisha had spent a comfortable first night at Ravi's latest mansion, the former found himself sitting at a large glass table in Motti-Media's conference room at 7 a.m. the following morning. The brothers had risen at five and swum in the olympic-sized pool before the sun had come up on a blisteringly hot day. Now, attired in comfortable linen dhottis, they listened to Rupe Dhindsa, the leader of the new Real Racing project, as he outlined its concept and launch.

The plan was to target the substantial but very disorganized and informal lotteries that existed in markets right across India, which constantly seemed to shoot themselves in the foot due to institutional corruption. 'Motti-Media,' Dhindsa pointed out, 'would corner the mobile phone and online market, with the assurances of a corporation with the highest reputation for integrity. And,' he hastened to add, 'in this world of omnipotent hacking, the very latest and safest cyber protection would be used to ensure transparency and fairness.' He went on to outline setup and operational costs and what percentage of the balance from sales would go to prizes and philanthropic causes, emphasizing the fact that, as Tommo Thompson had pointed out at Ravi's meeting in Australia, the more sales you make, the more the latter increases proportionately.

'And, if we are as successful as you project, what is to stop someone copying the idea?' asked Rahda Sigtia, Motti-Media's CFO. 'Not just here, in India, where everyone copies everything, and jealousy is rampant. But what about the Chinese or Russians? Or even the Europeans or Americans?'

'Not going to happen,' Kulbir interrupted, 'for a whole bunch of reasons. First, in the local market we have the brand and reputation of MM, plus government sanction and support. Second, when we expand to include major overseas races, it will be in partnership with local authorities, such as TAB in Australia. Besides, who would want to play in any game run by the Russians or Chinese these days, as they can't even lie straight in bed. The level of trust would be zero.'

'Maybe,' continued Sigtia, 'but in Europe they have serious racing, and in the US, too, don't they?'

'Forget about them,' said Ravi. 'Maybe we can do something with the PMU in France, when we show them the potential, but Britain is hamstrung, with bookmakers taking all the gravy and the sport run by dinosaurs.'

'What about the Yanks? They could try and steal the idea. And what about the name?' continued the ever-cautious Sigtia.

'All taken care of,' said Kulbir. 'Our solicitors in London, Cooper, Bailey, Hood & Hall, have patented the concept worldwide and copyrighted Real Racing and realracing.com. I was just speaking to Tony Palgrave-Brown of CBH&H last week and he said that, while they might complain about one of their races being used, if the server is in a jurisdiction beyond their legal reach they would be powerless. And, with the monopolies issues that would govern such an endeavour, no one entity could ever get such a motion passed by Parliament, as it would give them an unfair advantage. So no need to worry about them.'

'And the Yanks? They're very litigious, aren't they?' asked Sigtia.

'True. But, even if they ever got together on a national basis and ran an American version, they would fall foul of their own regulations regarding wire fraud and local restrictions upon online gaming. Like the Brits, they would have no jurisdiction. Not gonna happen,' said Kulbir with immense satisfaction.

'Well, this will all be at the outset,' said Ravi. 'In the long term, what we really want to do is work with these guys, as we will be with the Aussies. You see – we send TAB a big cheque after the first Real Racing sweepstake on the Melbourne Cup and everyone will want a part of it. And the beauty is that, with each race identified with a special cause, there will be no malice. For example, if we run a Real Race on the Grand National, which is our tentative plan in the future, and make the Invictus Games Foundation the beneficiary, do you honestly think that Lord Snooty of the Jockey Club or some conscientious bean-counter in Whitehall is going to object? You'll see, they'll be begging us to cover more of their races.'

'So, when do you anticipate this being ready to test?' asked Sigtia, apparently coming around, albeit slowly, to the notion that this concept might just hold water.

'Its all up to these guys,' said Ravi, turning to six young Indians who, so far, had been conspicuous by their silence. 'What do you think, Rupe?' he asked their team leader: a young man with thick black framed glasses, who looked like he was barely out of high school.

'Probably take us six months to write the codes and set up a format that is simple to access and use. Then its just a question of ensuring the security and integrity of the draw, the barcodes being the identity of each ticket holder, and a mechanism that makes the draw transparent and irrefutable. Building this thing will not be as hard as convincing people that they are getting a fair shake. Then it's just up to promoting it in an inviting way that offers dramatic entertainment.'

'We are talking to an outside monitor: people like KPMG or E & Y to run the draw, to make sure that there is no suggestion of tampering,' said Kulbir.

CHAPTER 30

The year 2017 had been a good one for Hector Delmontez. He had broken into an elite circle and now had some of the most powerful people in the sport eating out of his hand.

In Kentucky, the resurrection of Caledonia Farms and injection of new money into the local breeding industry was music to Billy Beagle's and his colleagues at Keeneland's ears. North of the border, in Canada, Calvin Weiner had proven to not only be a prodigious promoter of his bloodstock but also the best broker for El Gruppo and consumer of Condor Aviation's sundry services, by far. And, to cement his rapidly increasing global reputation as a major player, his new America's Stable was now managed by the prestigious CBS agency of Newmarket, per two pillars of British racing, Jos Danvers and Hugo Lascelles, and endorsed by their main client, the most successful owner in the world, Sheikh Ali Al-Bhakandar of Dubai.

Sometimes, though, the smoothest of operations come unstuck for the slightest and most unlikely of reasons. The Delmontez juggernaut certainly had not been bargaining on: a) one of their grooms falling out of the plane on an Air Condor charter from Caracas to Toronto, and b) a particularly vigilant member of the Ontario Provincial Police (OPP) correlating this strange event with reports of a large plane flying unusually low over his region of Muskoka, several nights prior to a body washing up on Dwight Beach.

Sergeant Blane Webster and his colleagues in the OPP's Huntsville detachment were at a loss as to how the severely traumatized body of a Hispanic-looking male could have ended up on a local beach. And, once the Toronto coroner's office had taken over, it was thought that that would be the last either he or his office would hear of the unfortunate gentleman from some far-off South American country.

Gossip, though, had livened up the sleepy residents of Muskoka and at his weekly curling match the jokes were all about the one that got away and a wall certainly wasn't going to stop this guy. As was always the case, at such events, the beer had flowed freeley and the stories become correspondingly taller, until big Greg McKinnon, fueled by his seventh beer of the evening, had launched a stone that was supposed to be a takeout, but, after it hit the lead rock with alarming speed and became airborne, almost exited through the community centre's south wall, crashing with a thud into a pile of Ski-Doo snowmobile suits. 'That's my Dam Busters takeout,' he gleefully announced to much laughter. 'I reckon that plane that buzzed us last week must have been practicing when that spic fell out. Ha! Ha!'

Webster, who was skipping the now very inebriated McKinnon, had escorted his teammate to a table. While the story he'd heard had sounded far-fetched, he'd noted down the time and night and subsequently made a few enquiries with local airfields. Nobody at Bracebridge, Gravenhurst, Huntsville, nor Port Carling had been able to help him. So, on a whim, he'd checked with Pearson International in Toronto and discovered that on the night of Friday, March 12, an Air Condor cargo charter had circled, north of the City of Toronto, outside its set flight path for longer than instructed. There was, on the face of things, nothing particularly unusual with this because often foreign-based planes were confused by local beacons and landmarks. But the thing that had alerted Sergeant Graham was that, upon arrival, customs and immigration had discovered that on the manifest there was one passenger missing.

The flight crew and purser, none of whom spoke fluent English, had dismissed the discrepancy as being a clerical error and the fact had merely been noted without any investigation opened. However, what Webster had been able to discover, through a contact at the Royal Canadian Mounted Police's (RCMP) Interpol desk in Ottawa, who'd acquired a flight list from Caracas under the auspices of routine background checks, was that a certain Juan Moreno had apparently either missed the flight, been erroneously put on the flight list, or somehow disappeared between Caracas and Toronto. He'd called the Toronto coroner's office on Grenville Street and spoken to Dr. Andrew Dixie, the head of forensic pathology, where he'd learnt that the contents of the stomach of the body found washed up on Dwight Beach contained traces of what appeared to be a rice-and-hot-pepper type meal, consistent with Mexican-style food. Furthermore, the one thing that had surprised Dr. Dixie was that, for someone who appeared of humble origin, his dentistry had been of the highest quality; something, he'd remarked on in his notes, that would have cost a great deal of money wherever he'd come from, and on his wrist he'd sported an expensive Rolex watch that had survived whatever had befallen its owner a lot better than he had.

Sergeant Webster had filed a report to OPP headquarters in Toronto and from there the file had been forwarded to the RCMP's international crime squad which, in turn, had contacted the FBI in Lexington. So, when an FBI cruiser had arrived at the gates of Caledonia Farms, and the news of its arrival had been radioed up to his office, Hector knew that he had a problem.

It had been almost a year since the FBI had last interviewed him in the wake of the fire. The way things had gone so well for him since that time when he had convinced his interrogators that he was blissfully ignorant of any criminal intent, had lulled him into the belief that all this was ancient history. But perhaps things had been going a little too well? And he knew right away that this visit wasn't going to be a friendly one.

Caledonia was an imposing place to visit at the best of times and now the increased security presence gave it an even more daunting feel. But Hector Delmontez knew the game and welcomed Special Agents Brad Kirchner and Jimmy Kestler into his spacious office, as though he was delighted that they'd stopped by, turning on the charm and putting his vistors immediately at ease.

'Gentlemen, this is a surprise,' he greeted the two FBI agents. 'Please tell me that you have come out to visit us because you would like to purchase one of my magnificent horses.'

'I wish we could afford to,' chuckled Kirchner, whom Hector had motioned to sit by the window. 'A fine piece of property you have, here, Senor Delmontez.'

'Indeed, indeed. I tell myself that every day. I say, "Hector, you are a lucky man." You know, officer, luck, or suerté as we say in Spanish. Buene suerté, good luck, in fact, is all you need for a good life. La vida dolce, eh?'

'True. Very true,' replied Kirchner, getting right to the point, 'but one of your employee's buene suerte, as you say, seems to have run out.' He looked the good doctor straight in the eye and said, 'We are here to ask you about a gentleman by the name of Juan Pablo Moreno.' And he took a photograph out of the small folder that he was carrying and placed it on the coffee table in front of him. 'Do you know this man, Senor Delmontez?'

Hector picked up the eight-by-ten photo that showed a smiling Moreno, in a suit, at what appeared to be a wedding. 'He is a handsome man, your friend.' He hesitated.

'Juan Pablo Moreno,' Kirchner prompted him, 'and sir,' he continued, producing several more photos of Moreno, including one that looked like a police mugshot with a number under it and another in which he looked very dead, indeed, 'he is not my friend. Senor Moreno, or his body, rather, was found last week, washed up on a beach in cottage country in Ontario, Canada. And the reason we are here today is that we believe that he worked for Air Condor or,' he turned to Kestler, who'd been standing behind his boss and added, 'Condor Aviation, sir.'

Kirchner continued, 'Yes, this man was, we believe, on an Air Condor flight from Caracas, Venezuela, to Toronto, Canada, on one of the planes your company or companies own, and he somehow ended up very dead in the middle of nowhere in Ontario.' He paused and looked up at Delmontez, who had been sitting opposite him, listening intently while gazing out of the window at the mares in the nearby paddock. 'What do you make of that, sir?'

Hector smiled. 'Agent, I have thirty men working for me on the farm, here in Kentucky, and even now, after several years, I don't know all their names. Back in Venezuela, where I come from, I have hundreds, maybe even thousands of people who work for my companies, of which Air Condor is just one division. I do not doubt your story for one minute and its awful to hear about Senor Moreno. But I wouldn't be lying if I told you that I have no idea whether he worked for one of my companies or not.'

Kirchner frowned. Hector Delmontez was a slippery fish and his profession of ignorance wasn't all that different, in its unsatisfactory evasiveness, to the one he'd recounted in the wake of the fire and the deaths of Ramon Diaz and Robert Fraser. 'Well, it is our intention,' he continued, 'to work with Interpol and the authorities in Venezuela on an audit of all flights made by Air Condor, cargo and otherwise, between South America and all points, including the United States.'

'And Canada,' added Kestler.

'The fact is, we have a dead body. We know who that person is, and we know that that person is known to the authorities, Interpol, and narcotics agents at the FDA.'

This last revelation Kirchner hoped might touch a nerve. But the consummately cool Delmontez never missed a beat. 'Sounds like you have a bad hombre. How does your president say it, eh? A bad, very bad hombre on your hands, officer.'

Kirchner hated being mocked and addressed incorrectly. 'We'll see about that,' he responded, getting up from his chair and putting the photographs back into his folder. 'Thank you for your time, sir. You will be hearing from our office. We can see ourselves out.'

After they had left, Hector sat, staring out the window at the early spring morning. It had started to rain and everything that had looked so green before this unexpected intrusion suddenly seemed rather grey. This visit was worrying, but he was smart enough to not jump on the phone or start texting. If the FBI suspected him of involvement in any of their enquiries, he didn't need them monitoring his communications or subpoenering any of his devices. What the fuck are Cal Weiner and his Russian friends up to?' he mused. It was never a good idea to be a user; it never ended well.

CHAPTER 31

At Bury Castle Stables, the inhabitants who hadn't been shipped down to Dubai had spent the winter months in the virtual hibernation of an indoor ride.

Since his arrival, the chestnut colt, in the third box/stall on the right of the American-style barn at the back of the stable's ten acres, had not put a foot wrong. Sometimes shippers from the United States were the most vulnerable to the dampness of English winters and the change in feed and water, often succumbing to flus and viruses or, as their trainer would tell guests after a glass or two of good Port at dinner parties, because going cold-turkey off all the steroids the Yanks had them on to build them up, for the sales, they just fall apart when it's back to good old oats, hay, and water.

Whatever, Java Raja, as he was now officially named, had been very fortunate that Seamus McDonnell had eschewed all that 'bally-hoo', as he called it, and Seamus's young protégé had adapted to English conditions with flying colours.

Marcus Townsend, even though he'd bought on his new client's instructions, had clocked lot 142 and admired his athleticism. He'd thought that CBS would buy the colt for Sheikh Ali – however, somewhere along the way, that idea had got nixed. So it had been a welcome surprise when a last-minute alternative purchaser brought one, that he'd coveted, to Bury Castle, and he made a mental note to thank Algy Sinclair.

Over at CBS, Bog had been uncharacteristically quiet when he'd found out that his supposed client, Ravi Singh, had purchased a yearling from the

Keeneland July Sales, apparently off his own bat. And it was most embarrassing, that he was now in training and, technically, in competition with the agency's main client, Sheikh Ali.

'What on earth happened?' had been Jos Danvers's first comment. 'Bad enough that you let our man slip through your fingers, but it appears that Algy Sinclair and Anglian have now pinched him,' he'd thundered.

But Bog always seemed to have an explanation. This time he explained that Geoffrey Gilligan had not rated the colt classy enough. And, besides, Mr. Singh may just have been miffed by the whole El Cordobes affair. In Bog's opinion, Singh was a lightweight and the agency should concentrate on Sheikh Ali and people like Hector Delmontez and Calvin Weiner; mentioning that the latter had come up with some Russians with deep pockets. 'We should focus on the heavy hitters.' And, as an aside, he could not help mentioning his burgeoning romance with Lucy Beagle. 'Nothing like being in with the right people,' he'd added.

Aboard Java Raja, that first morning out on Newmarket Heath, David Burns was brimming with excitement. Many years previously he'd experienced a similar thrill when Greentree Stables' regally bred two-year-olds had come up from Aiken, South Carolina, and acquainted themselves for the first time with the rich, dark dirt of the famous Saratoga racetrack. Tucked away in their private barn in the woods, their emergence for public scrutiny had been always keenly anticipated by rival horsemen and clockers, checking out future Classic contenders.

Back in those days, trainer Jack Gaver had forbidden his staff and particularly his exercise riders from discussing the barn's horses. Because he knew that David not only had experience of such high-quality stock from that time and over the past twenty years with his current governor, Townsend knew that Burns and Mr. Singh's newly acquired colt were the perfect match.

As it was the two-year-olds's first foray beyond the confines of their stables, Townsend's senior men, Cockney Lines and Noel Boston, led two groups of about twenty youngsters on older horses, as they stretched their legs up the all-weather, along the bottom of Bury Hill. Nothing more than a slow canter of just under half a mile. Then they walked back to the bottom and did it again.

This year's crop was unusually well behaved and all eyes were on the handsome bay colt, Prince Ali, named by the Sheikh after his favourite son: such high hopes had he of him, being a son of his Epsom Derby winner Aurora Borealis out of his unbeaten 1000 Guineas winner Desert Maiden. This colt was described by his owner as a gift from Allah and anything short of winning at least one classic would be a disappointment. As he watched him go through his paces, Townsend was well aware of the high expectations, musing to himself that such horses bizarrely seem to be prone to freak accidents, while those that aren't worth tuppence could get loose and run down Newmarket High Street without sustaining a scratch.

Townsend liked owners like Ravi Singh, who deferred to his judgement and interacted with him through a third party who, in this case, was turning out to be Algy Sinclair, who self-deprecatingly billed himself as the 'default manager' of his one and only client's one-horse stable. Like many practitioners with deep-pocketed and egotistical clients, Townsend knew that, while every one of his forty or so owners deserved equal attention, his operation was the success it was largely due to just one or two who needed to be handled with every bit as much care as their fragile stock.

Sheikh Ali wanted only the best and this had meant not only retaining the finest trainer but also the best jockeys. Thus, three-time champion Pat Donnelly had been contracted by Bury Castle Stables, with the Sheikh paying the lion's share of the retainer, in return for first claim on his services. This, Townsend knew, could sometimes be tricky, if he ran several horses in the same race and he and Donnelly knew that the Sheikh's entry wasn't their strongest contender. But both men were pros, knowing fullwell who buttered their bread.

So it was, as the weather improved after the Guineas meeting at Newmarket in early May and the stable's more precocious two-year-olds stepped up their training, that those paying attention to the development of the new crop began to realize that, while it was still very early, one individual stood out. Java Raja was not only bigger than the other two-year-olds in the yard, but apparently better in every regard.

Looking altogether far more mature than the rest of the class, his stride was all-consuming. And, in his workouts, he never turned a hair, cruising past his rivals as though they were standing still. Townsend reflectively congratulated himself that he'd assigned his budding star to the low-key Burns, who wouldn't be touting his apparent wonder horse in every pub in town.

Every now and then Hugo Lascelles and Jos Danvers would observe an important work or go around evening stables, to keep abreast of their main client's horses. Their observations would then be subjects of weekly reports sent to Sheikh Ali's PA, Ahmed Al Sheiky – Speedy, as he was referred to on the racecourse – for his flamboyant appearance, and sometimes 'the procurer' because of his omnipresent entourage of 'trim craft,' as Townsend referred to them.

In turn, Algy Sinclair would brief Ravi on how his first and only racehorse was coming along.

Since acquiring his first personal client for the agency, Algy's stock had soared. Ravi Singh might be considered small fry for Bog and the boys at CBS, but he represented somewhat of an international breakthrough at Anglian and it gave Algy reason to go out onto the heath, to watch Java Raja go through his paces, and even attend some of the excellent Sunday lunches that Townsend's wife Rachel served up to owners every now and then, when the stable didn't have a runner in France.

When your main client lives abroad and his only relation in the country, brother Kulbir, was not really into horse racing at all, the vicarious position of being the only local agent came with its fringe benefits and, like many small owners, its feeling part of a greater team, in a powerful stable, with inside knowledge of what the other horses are doing, that is a special part of the 'craic,' as the Irish would say.

Whether they were watching work on the Limekilns gallops, where the turf had not seen a plough since the seventeenth century, at a time when King Charles II had decided that Newmarket heath was the best place for racing his horses and indulging in debauchery, or lunching on roast beef and Yorkshire pudding in the grand dining room at Bury Castle, being part of the most exclusive thoroughbred racing operation in the land was quite fascinating for Algy.

While little mention was made of Java Raja, on such occasions, there was no doubt how friendly his usually cool and business-like host had become. Indeed, Townsend had even invited Algy to ride out first lot, before he started work at the agency. And it was returning home from the gallops one morning that the governor, on his pony, had first conveyed his burgeoning hopes for their mutual charge.

Not a man of many words and certainly not someone to get unreasonably excited about a two-year-old so early in his career, after all the great horses that had been through his hands over the years, Townsend had confided in Algy that they might have something special.

'We've had some good two-year-olds and no shortage of well-bred stock, thanks to Sheikh Ali. But this colt impresses me,' he'd said, going on to add, 'horses mature at different stages and, as you stretch them out, some relish longer distances. But, nearly every top-class horse I've been around or been lucky enough to train, has shown speed as a two-year-old. You may not ask for it, but it's just there. Such horses have gears. And the mark of a really good one is the ability to relax, conserve energy, and be able to deliver that turn of foot at a key moment in a race.' He'd paused for quite a while, Algy remembered, and then, before he'd cantered off to the head of the string, had added, 'I may be wrong. It wouldn't be the first time. But we're gonna have a bit of fun with this fella. Just don't get the owner too revved up. Keep him in the dark. Like a mushroom, feed him plenty of shit, and I'll deal with Sheikh Ali.'

And so it was that not long after that conversation, when Java Raja made his debut in a six furlong maiden at Yarmouth, the occasion was upstaged by a more important one at Newbury, on the same day, where Sheikh Ali had runners and Pat Donnelly was riding. And very little attention was paid to number twelve in the last race, down to be ridden by Frank Coffey, a reliable lightweight journeyman rider whom Townsend used regularly when his main man was busy elsewhere.

Algy had alerted Kulbir, who hadn't been impressed by the diminutive prize of five thousand pounds. Ravi was in Australia, on business, he said, and he, too, would be too busy to attend. So, their manager had driven the fifty or so miles to the east coast and watched his owner's orange with green stripped sleeves and white cap (a variation of the Indian flag) carried to a handy score, at the surprisingly good odds of 6/1.

The odds meant little to the owners, but pints were raised that night by a knowledgeable few in the pubs of Newmarket. Frank Coffey appreciated the crumbs from the big table at Bury Castle and had ridden to orders: nothing flashy. And the two-length margin of victory was just what his boss had ordered.

Algy duly passed on the news and, hearing nothing back from the Singhs, assumed that they had more important things going on in their lives. The following Sunday, not a word was passed on the stable's first two-year-old winner of the season; the previous week, as Bog, Speedy, Lascelles, and Danvers gobbled down their roast beef, congratulating themselves on a good day at Newbury that same day, and how they were going to make a killing at the upcoming Royal Ascot meet.

As he'd expected, the trip to Yarmouth hadn't fizzed on Java Raja. Sometimes, especially with fillies, a first race could prove to be a very unsettling experience, with the change in routine, trip to the races in the horse box, crowds, noise, and, if the race didn't go well or, God forbid, (as Townsend would have skinned the perpetrator alive) the jockey had given them a hard race or several unwelcome cracks of his whip, a horse would go off their feed and lose condition. But Big Red, as his lad had taken to calling him, had devoured the occasion.

◆　◆　◆

In Kentucky, Mark was deep into sales reconnaissance and giving piano lessons to his latest pupil, Missie Van der Meer. The hot and humid weather had set in, so he was up early, for the cool of the morning, when he got the call. 'Mark. Howa-ya?' Algy teased him with his effort to sound Irish. 'Crazy man, what-y-ya doin' up at this hour?'

'You know about the early bird?' quipped Mark.

'Well, talking about early birds, I think you, or at least your friends, the McDonnells, may be interested in some early action?'

'How so?' said Mark, buttering his toast while he kept his cell phone clamped between his left bicep and ear.

'Well, you saw that the colt won first time out at Yarmouth last week?'

'Yep, I saw that. And I've been meaning to give them a ring. Just a little maiden, eh?'

'Ya. But, between you and I, this might be a pretty good two-year-old. So his trainer says, anyway. And, when I spoke to him, he said that maybe we should see if we can buy his full sister off your buddies?' There was a pause on the line. 'They are going to send her up to the September sales, aren't they?'

'Yes. As far as I know, they are,' said Mark, 'but you won't be able to steal her from them. They're not idiots, you know. They read the results. They know what she's worth.'

'Yeah, yeah, I know. But they don't know what we know. And that is that this colt, Java Raja, could be one of the best two-year-olds that Townsend has. And he's got some good ones of Sheikh Ali's, you know. Anyway, Marcus whispered in my ear to the effect that his next race, in a few weeks time at Newmarket, may show him to be above average and that now could be the time to buy the filly. As you know, the owner is looking for a few broodmares, for the future. Whatever. Judging by the way her brother is training, she might be a pretty useful performer herself.'

'All right. So, you want me to smoke out the McDonnells about a private sale?'

'Now ya talking. Woke up have yer? My client, Mr. Singh, buys the filly now, so there is no need to pay any commissions to Keeneland - the sales company stuff, you know.'

'And what do you think your client will pay?'

'Gotta be at least the three-fifty he gave for the colt.'

'Well, what if they want more?'

'Come on! This is money in the bank. You know they run a small operation and they got a lot more than they thought they would for the colt. Do you remember when we went out there, this time last year, and they were talking about one-fifty! Hey, a bird in hand, you know. Anything could happen between now and September. Good things maybe, but equally possibly lotsa bad things.' Algy was at his most persuasive.

'Ok, let's see. Maybe I'll just call in, unannounced, and have a chat with Seamus. But don't get too excited. These are my clients, remember. And I have to look after them. Can't have them thinking that we're trying to steal her from them. That would be bad and could ruin future trust.'

'I'll leave it up to you,' said Algy. 'But, if we're going to do something, it has to be in the next couple of weeks before the colt runs again, and all the wise guys start knocking on their door.'

'Maybe that's just what they'll want? Maybe someone like Bog?,' laughed Mark. 'Talking about Bog, that reminds me. I got a call last week from Martin O'Sullivan at BGT. He wanted to speak to Tom. Something about that South American guy, Hector Delmontez.'

'He's one of Bog's main guys now. Didn't think Ravi was a serious player. What did the guy at BGT have to say?'

'Not sure, but I put him in touch with Tom. I think it was something to do with an accident at Cincinnati airport. The police got involved. I read something about it in the local paper.'

'I'll give Tom a call, right now, before I forget. In the meantime, get on to your people about this filly of Killyshandra's.'

◆　◆　◆

Tom had been down at Shenandoah Valley Farms for almost six months, living with Matt Pearson in the cottage at the back of the property. His Aunt Vera felt Matt needed the company to stop him drifting off into an increasingly isolated and anti-social life and, as the latter gradually let the former into his world, the residual effect was mutually beneficial: Tom getting a few rides at the Virginia Hunt meets and Matt getting much needed muscle in the garden, which he further rewarded per his culinary skills.

Indeed, the way things were working out, Tom was making Basil increasingly redundant and the latter found himself away, more and more, at one racetrack or another, which suited him fine, too, as being responsible for a couple of horses on the road wasn't exactly the most taxing work.

The stable had been purring along at a 27% win clip, with seldom a runner off the board. Rikki seemed to be getting better, the older and wiser he became. Definitely the star of the barn, he lapped up the TLC. Having now more than paid his way, his owners were quite content to wait to hear from Matt when they might see him next in the entries.

Vera had opened a Betfair account that she taunted Billy Beagle about; knowing full-well that it was completely illegal and anathema to him, but that he couldn't do anything about it. So, when Tom had told her that Algy's clients' horse was in at Yarmouth, she'd helped herself to the 6/1, and some.

The arrangement for Rocky, as the now-yearling over at Tangleweed had been temporarily christened by his handlers, had been settled without a hitch and the young colt listed in a blind trust. He would not be going to any sales, which in a way was a bit unusual for a colt bred on the farm, as Ms. Montagu was known to sell all her colts and only sometimes keep a filly or two. So, to keep him out of the way, it was decided to leave him at Tanglewood until the fall and then Matt, Toby, and Curtis could break him in (put a saddle and bridle on him) down at the barn. At that time, she planned on proposing that the Elevator Stable lease him for his first two years, commencing the following January. To that end, it had been agreed that they'd meet at Saratoga, to discuss future plans on the racetrack.

When Tom had received Mark's call from Kentucky, the boys had spoken about Java Raja, who had set tongues wagging with a very impressive victory in his second start; moving up considerably in class from Yarmouth to horse racing's UK headquarters. It had been a field full of highly regarded youngsters and just by chance Marcus Townsend had finessed the Sheikh's schedule, so that he did not have a runner, and Pat Donnelly had been able take the ride.

The boys remembered their first encounter with the handsome chestnut colt, just over a year before. And Mark confirmed that Ravi Singh, after a great deal of arguing with his brother, had purchased the yearling full sister from the McDonnells for the same three hundred-and-fifty thousand price plus an incentivized add-on that, should her very promising brother win a Group 1 race, there would be an extra fifty thousand plus a free service for lifetime, if and when he retired to stud.

It was a creative deal, thrashed out between Ravi, Algy, Mark and her breeders; with the final decision cemented by Seamus, who had pointed out that they still had Killy, who was a young mare, and who were they to turn down such money when, or if, anyone had approached them a year before with three fifty for both of them, they'd have snapped their arm off to make the sale.

Algy confirmed that while Ravi was quite happy to trust his trainer's intuition, the wily Kulbir, who had suddenly become a form expert in the light of his brother's horse's two victories, having never expressed any interest whatsoever before, now felt that maybe they were being made to play second fiddle to the Sheikh.

Marcus Townsend would now have to draw upon his diplomatic skills.

So enraptured were the boys in this success story that Mark had almost hung up the phone without mentioning the main reason for his call. Indeed, it had only been when Tom had joked about what a fool Bog must feel, now, that he remembered Martin O'Sullivan's call. 'Speaking of Bog, his main man is apparently under a bit of pressure.'

'Oh, really,' said Tom, 'I thought Hector could walk on water. What has Senor Slick been up to now?'

'Well, maybe nothing,' said Mark. 'It's just that Martin called and said he'd mentioned to you about Air Condor having accidents and that, a week or two ago, a horse had been killed aboard a Caracas charter to Cincinnati. He wants you to give him a call. From what I gather, the dead horse was taken away to some rendering plant, where I guess they turn 'em into pet food, and something weird seems to have happened. He said he'd explain when you call.'

According to Martin O'Sullivan, there had been quite a stir when the latest Air Condor charter had arrived in Cincinnati, with the plane immediately surrounded by FDA and FBI agents. A swat-like team had boarded, conducted a complete search, and escorted everyone, including the pilots, off the plane to immigration processing. Then a team of veterinarians and agents had unloaded the horses and literally torn the plane apart.

Martin had added that, according to his source, there had been an issue with a missing passenger on a charter to Toronto in late March, which hadn't seemed like a big deal at the time. But the subsequent discovery of the body of a Hispanic male washed up on a Northern Ontario beach had puzzled authorities. And particularly so, when, further to an autopsy and enquiries made by Interpol through Venezuelan police, DNA and photo evidence had identified the man as Juan Pablo Moreno, a Colombian known to drug enforcement agencies.

FBI agents in Kentucky had spoken to Hector Delmontez, the owner of Air Condor, who had denied any knowledge of Moreno. Nevertheless, they must have suspected that something was going on, as there was no mistaking the seriousness of their intentions the next time that Air Condor flew in.

Tom had asked if anything untoward, any drugs perhaps, had been found? But everything seemed to have been in order, except the dead horse.

Reportedly, it had thrown a fit and had to be euthanized when it looked like it was breaking out of its stall. 'This happens every now and then,' Martin had said, 'and, after the carcass was removed, not much was made of it, until the rendering company called to say that it had disappeared. It was weird.

'Because rigor mortis had set in, by the time they'd got the poor wretched horse back to their yard, they'd just left it in one of their trucks as it was the middle of the night. The plane had come in about 8 p.m.,' Martin had continued. 'Anyway, when they came in the next morning the truck had gone! It had been stolen and they found it abandoned in an old warehouse down by the Ohio River two days later. And get this: whoever had stolen the truck had cut the horse up with a chain saw!'

The more Tom learnt about Hector Delmontez the more he realized that what his Aunt Vera had told him about the fire and his dad had to be true. He just couldn't fathom, though, how Billy Beagle, his late father's best friend, and all the other respected leaders of horse racing were being so taken in by someone so unscrupulous and callous. 'You think they were Hector's guys?,' he asked.

'Well, I don't think that it was a random act, by someone who, all of a sudden, got hungry,' Martin joked. 'Have to think they were looking for something.'

'Drugs?' said Tom.

'We phoned the police and they sent a bunch of forensic people over there and took away what was left. But they're not saying anything.'

Tom thought about the phial that Randy had given him, and about the strange incident in Canada. 'Have you noticed any increase in the number of Condor charters, lately?' he asked Martin.

'Funnily enough, we were just talking about that the other day. When they first started coming up here, maybe seven or eight years ago, there would be one or two a year. Then they became more frequent. The one into Toronto, in March, was the second they've sent up to Canada and I hear there is another planned for later this summer.'

'And where are all these horses going to?' asked Tom.

'It seems that Delmontez has got something going with two guys up there, Calvin Weiner and Michael Rogers. On the last flight to Canada there were a couple that we subsequently vanned down here, through our affiliate in Toronto, Van Bergs, as they were mares they wanted to get bred quickly in the season. But the rest were, I think, sold to some clients of the shipper.'

'And the shipper was?'

'I'm not really meant to know this, but a mate of mine who works for Ivan Van Berg, told me that Senor Delmontez covered all costs. That's unusual. Usually the receiver, in this case Weiner and his buddy, would have paid.'

'And what became of the plane?'

'Well, they didn't find anything. The crews' and handlers' papers were all in order and, of course, because the fate of the dead horse was unknown until two days later, they really couldn't hold anyone. So, it left. I believe, headed back to somewhere in Venezuela.'

Tom thanked O'Sullivan for the heads-up, hung up the phone, and decided it was time to visit the horse that never (supposedly) was.

CHAPTER 32

The drive south from Upperville, on a sunny late June day, was idyllic. Tom had the windows down so that the unmistakably sweet scent of newly mown hay wafted around him. The closer he got to Tanglewood Farm the lusher and more enveloping the roadside grasses, cow parsley, and wildflowers seemed to be, and he mused just how well-named his destination had been.

Turning through the stone gates and up over the small bridge that spanned Goose Creek, the drive was now shrouded with the willows in full bloom. The creek but a trickle. If I was a horse, he thought, this would be my heaven.

The Buchanans were away, travelling. So he parked in front of the house and walked across the lawn to the paddock where he had been told he'd find what he was looking for. It was early afternoon, siesta time, when the buzz of bees, busily swarming the Buddleia bushes, was amplified by the haze of tranquility. On the far side, under the bordering Osage orange trees, whose huge boughs hung out over the fencing to provide a perfect canopy from the sun, he could see three yearlings stretched out in the lush grass amongst the flowering clover and dandy lions, their tails occasionally swishing away flies. They looked so peaceful that Tom just lent against the railings and watched, pulling a large head of Timothy and sucking on its sweet stem.

These guys were now about fifteen months old, separated from their mothers and enjoying their blissful independence, completely unaware of their destiny.

'They restin',' said a voice from behind. Tom turned and saw Rufus, the Buchanan's Man-Friday, as Lorna liked to call him because he could do anything, standing by the gate to his left. 'They don't know what lies ahead, the racetrack and all that shee-et. When that bell rings, they gonna wish they was right back here.'

'They're lucky,' said Tom and he wondered if Rufus had any idea just how lucky the one he'd come to see was. They stared out across the meadow. Conversation would have been a spoiler, an intruder on this peace.

'Ms. Buchanan said you'd maybe come by. Do you want me to call 'em over?' Rufus offered.

'Well, I hate to disturb them, but...'

Just then one of the three yearlings got up, stretched, yawned, and looked around at the two men. 'See, they done heard us,' said Rufus. 'Come on over here, you guys.' And the other two got to their feet and trotted over.

'They know I've always got somethin' in my pocket, see.' The yearlings gathered around Rufus, nudging his smock. He patted them on their necks and ran his hand over an ear. 'You Ms. Montagu's boy, eh?'

'No,' said Tom. 'I'm her nephew. She's my mother's sister.'

'Well, your aunt sure breeds some nice horses. They quality,' Rufus continued. 'I'm just a farm boy. Never bin' to no racetrack. But I'm tellin' ya, these three are runners.'

'How do you know?' said Tom.

'Just somethin' about 'em. The way they're put together. They got good blood. I know that, because no horse of Ms. Montagu's comes from cheap stock. But they just have a way about them. I guess it's class, you know. They gotta a way of walkin'.'

Tom rubbed the nose of the dark bay colt with the shamrock-shaped star, dead centre between two large and intelligent brown eyes. 'That's the Last Post colt,' said Rufus. 'We had his daddy here at one time, but he don't look nothin' like him.'

Tom smiled.

'Now. If I was to have my pick, he'd be the one,' Rufus continued.

'And why is that?' asked Tom.

'Y'always have a leader, you know what I mean? These guys all start the same. When they get weaned from their mothers and they're turned out in a field with their brothers, everyone is the same. But you watch 'em and you'll see, the cream comes to the top. One will become the leader, others will follow. And this little guy,' Rufus gave him an affectionate pat, 'he's the man! Ain't you? Go on now, shows us your moves!' Rufus clucked to the yearlings and they cantered off. 'See, that colt don't touch the ground. He flies, man!'

As he drove back to Shenandoah, Tom reflected upon how fate was guiding him and the legacy that his father had left him. Thinking back, after someone is snatched from you so suddenly, its difficult to remember your last meeting; the last time you spoke and never realized you'd not get a chance to say goodbye. It had been over a year and time was healing, but moments such as this quickly brought back tears. Concentrate on what you can do, Tommy, he remembered his father often saying to him. Just try and give it your best shot. Keep your head down, boy. He'd dealt Tom his last card and he was going to play it as well as he could.

CHAPTER 33

Bangalore, monsoon season. Heat and humidity all day long, building and building, and then the heavens would open late every afternoon and life would drink.

The programmers at Motti-Singh had been working around the clock on the platform for Real Racing and the prototype was speculatively scheduled for launching in the local market, per a test race at the local racecourse.

Not the most auspicious place to start. But before the concept was launched to players around the world as the greatest live audience participation sporting event, the kinks needed to be ironed out in a backwater, where criticism didn't sink it before it got off the ground.

Ravi Singh had worked together with local politicians, at the advent of the Internet in the late '90s, to develop the online educational programs that had been the foundation of his company. Now these same wheels were put in motion on his latest project: turning an old idea into cyber gold for beneficial causes, not just in his native India but soon on a global scale.

India had taken vast steps since the advent of the Internet, becoming the largest market of cell phone users in the world and expanding exponentially to replace old-fashioned ways and methods (that relied on cash) with the latest and most accessible and secure forms of online banking. Now, over five hundred million Indians were totally dependent on their mobile phones, due to improved satellite services and reach, and Ravi knew only too well that providing content and entertainment for this hungry new market was a potential gold mine.

The model that Kulbir had built in London and, in conjunction with the young team in Bangalore, was simply accessed by the Real Racing app. All a player had to do was download this app and set up an account that would be debited automatically for every ticket purchased and credited for any prizes won.

Players could purchase as many tickets as they desired for the equivalent to US$1 each, up until the televised draw for each race, with each ticket featuring eight numbers and a unique barcode. At that time, players could then watch a computer select random barcodes from total ticket sales, that would correspond with runners in the designated race. Those that were fortunate enough to have their barcoded ticket selected would win the equivalent in rupees to $20,000. All ticket holders, per the eight numbers on their ticket, would then have a chance to win $1 million, if their eight numbers corresponded with the saddlecloth numbers of the first eight finishers in correct order, and whoever had drawn the horse that ultimately won the race would win a further $1 million, with $500,000 for second, $200,000 for third, and $100,000 for fourth. Discounting one-time set-up costs, the ongoing split on ticket sales up to $100 million worked out to approximately 30% for operations and marketing, 20% for prizes, and 50% for whatever cause each race had been identified with.

In the case of the Bangalore race, which would have country-wide exposure but probably generate a smaller local pool due to the novelty of the project, Motti-Media conservatively forecast sales of around that figure, fully appreciating that once the server and host management hub had been set up, its operational costs would not increase for handling a potential global pool in excess of one billion dollars.

The local authorities, for their goodwill and, as Ravi and Kulbir appreciated only too well, protection against competition for their own little cash-cow, had decided that the first 'good cause's' proceeds would go towards building a new and much-needed hospital in Bangalore.

Apart from the technical side of the equation, Ravi had been a little surprised at the scepticism of local politicians (even though they'd all been well-taken-care-of over the years by Motti-Media), because, as soon as those involved saw how much money was involved, they worried that it would spawn all manner of skullduggery and race-fixing. But, as Kulbir had been at pains to point out, while an individual such as a corrupt jockey, trainer, or bookmaker might try to effect the result, the draw was so random that, even if you had someone trying to fix which tickets were selected, it would be impossible to do so. Besides, just so nobody thought that the whole endeavour was an inside swindle, the entire operation would be guarded by ironclad cyber security and the oversight of a team of fastidious accountants.

After several delays, it was decided by the Bangalore Jockey Club that the first race would be a handicap over a mile and a half, featuring a twenty horse field on September 1, the opening day of the Monsoon meet, and that India's patron saint of cricket, none other than Sachin Tendulkar, along with Bollywood celebrities and IPL stars, would preside over the draw three days before on DD National television.

It was, on the face of it, not exactly a revolutionary idea. But times had changed since the Irish Hospital Sweepstakes of the 1960s and Ravi was quietly confident that, per the new vehicles of twenty-first century communications and social media, and the sheer scale of a hitherto untapped market in his burgeoning homeland, he could put the genie back into a bottle.

Motti-Singh was big enough in India to make this work without outside help. And a deliberate effort was made to keep it relatively low key, though Tommo Thompson had persuaded his erstwhile partners to let him be an observer.

The point, Ravi believed, was that the sweepstake be separate and have no bearing at all on the race. In fact, as he planned to prove when the venture went world-wide, it could be run completely independently in every regard except for accessing entry information and TV coverage. All those running the event had to do was card a race with the requisite number of horses on the agreed day in a time slot that generated maximum viewership. The game would then unfold on its own.

Thus, on September 1, 2018, at Bangalore racecourse, the first Real Racing sweepstake took place.

Looking down the road, Ravi and Kulbir envisioned a race every month, somewhere around the world, leaving three-plus weeks to generate sales between races. Thus, preliminary promotions had been started approximately three weeks prior and the hype had steadily increased via popular Indian social media platforms as the day drew closer, to a point where it became apparent that Bollywood matinee idol Tandeer Pataudi owned one of the likely runners and the whole event went instantly viral, causing great alarm at Motti-Media that the servers might crash.

The draw took place in Bangalore's jam-packed Sheraton hotel, with Sachin Tendulkar reading out the barcode numbers of the lucky twenty winners who were immediately credited $20,000 on their cell phones and invited to contact Motti-Media to arrange attending a banquet on race day and the race itself, in three five-star boxes that the company had reserved for their viewing.

As a result of the attendant stars and viral coverage on social media, a record crowd overflowed the grandstands at 5032 Racecourse Road in the Gandhi Nagar neighbourhood of downtown Bangalore to see 20/1 longshot, Mohan Maestro, prevail in a four-horse photo that yielded a 5-11-2-16-17-3-1-7 eight-horse super-fecta, returning one million to the holder of that lucky ticket.

The ticket-holders of runners had turned out to come from all walks of life, much to the satisfaction of the organizers, who hoped this would convince the lowly that they were at no disadvantage because of their caste or economic disposition. And the ultimate winner had turned out to be a rickshaw driver from Madras.

At the end of the day, a most unremarkable horse race had taken place at a small racecourse in a country not known for its horse racing. But the sport would never be the same again.

On the build-up there had been the malfunctions and confusion expected with all new ventures. But the audience had cottoned on very quickly that here was a cheap form of entertainment and, as it had been promoted, realized that you can't win if you don't buy a ticket.

When, having been so nervous as the race drew near that they'd thought about uninviting Tommo Thompson from Australia, the much-relieved board of Motti-Singh sat down the following Monday morning and crunched the numbers; Ravi and Kulbir were left speechless when total sales figures of $126 million flashed up on the large video screen.

The company had spent twenty million developing the software and about the same setting up the servers and hosting offices. They paid out a total of $3.2 million in prizes and just over $80 million was left over for building the hospital. 'We love our cows here. We deify them, indeed,' said the venerable Rahda Sigtia, 'but holy smoke! This is a special cash-cow, indeed!'

CHAPTER 34

For Marcus Townsend, the season had gone better than he had expected. But now he was faced with a serious test of his diplomatic skills. His main client Sheikh Ali's self-proclaimed wonder horse, Prince Ali, was unbeaten in his two starts and being touted as a future Classic winner. The logical and traditional course to attaining that honour led through the seven furlong Dewhurst Stakes at Newmarket in October, over the exact same course, but a furlong shorter than the first classic for three-year-old colts: the one-mile 2000 Guineas at the beginning of the following May. The only trouble with this was that he knew that he had a better colt in his yard.

Java Raja had gone on, from his second facile victory in late June, to win the prestigious Richmond Stakes at Goodwood, in commanding fashion from a small but classy field. The stable's first jockey, Pat Donnelly, had been in the irons again on that occasion and, like his boss, he knew that the winner was very useful.

So far, Townsend had kept his two talented colts apart and was blessed by the fact that Ravi and his wife had yet to appear on a racecourse to see their horse run; merely receiving encouraging messages from their local representative, Algy Sinclair, and statements of earnings from Kulbir.

This suited Townsend well, for he knew that horses are like strawberries: they can get squashed and go off overnight. No point, therefore, agonizing over or making unpopular decisions before he had to, as, for any number of reasons, the showdown might never happen. He figured he'd 'punt,' as his

American colleagues would say, when they hadn't really got a clue what they were going to do.

Fortunately, in Algy, he had someone who understood his predicament. So it was, really, just a matter of massaging Sheikh Ali and feeding his entourage what they wanted to hear. It amused the two immensely that Bog never spoke about Java Raja.

In the end, his story for Sheikh Ali was that Prince Ali looked more like a Derby horse and Java Raja, who might not train on and stay (just fluff for the Sheikh's consumption, to justify this move, but certainly not for the Singh team's ears) could be a Guineas' horse. Therefore, the former would go for the seven-furlong Dewhurst and the latter for the shorter six-furlong Middle Park.

This temporary wisdom of Solomon was lapped up by the Sheikh's men who, thanks to Bog and his chum Geoffrey Gilligan's assertion that Java Raja was an overrated two-year-old who'd had his day and wouldn't train on, hadn't given a second thought to their burgeoning champion even having a rival, let alone one in his own stable.

When Algy went around evening stables the week before the Middle Park, he had to bite his tongue when they came to Java Raja and Gilligan airily announced that he was a nice little horse (hardly, he was close to 17 hands by this point) with slightly dodgy *Time Form* numbers. He'd turned to Townsend and said, 'Marcus, doesn't he belong to your Indian chappie?' which was so comically inappropriate that even the normally unemotional Townsend laughed, as he gave Big Red a carrot, patted him on his neck, and winked at David Burns.

Few stables anywhere maintain the traditional evening stables' routine today, because, with EU working standards, there simply aren't staff who are prepared to work the long hours anymore. But, when there was racing at Newmarket and owners were in town, Townsend liked to revert to the old ways that he'd learnt from his mentors, during the days when straw litters were neatly arranged in walls around each box and twisted-in, as they used to say, at the entrance, with sand sprinkled on the floor; the brass on head-collars shining and grooming tools laid out on top of stable rubbers (cloths) on a little stack of straw in the corner.

Lads in those days had spent a lot of time strapping and grooming their charges, but such over-attention had been proven to have adverse effects, sometimes turning colts savage and fillies stubborn and mulish. Townsend preferred that more emphasis be put upon basic horsemanship: focusing on feet always being well-cared for and a lads' observations of appetite and general mood, which he relied upon them to relay to him.

In a business that can at times be obsessively superstitious, Prince Ali, as the star-apparent, had been assigned a box in the main yard that had previously housed numerous Classic winners trained over the years at Bury Castle. And upon arrival at the Prince's home the buzz noticeably increased, with head lad Wally Mills in his tan smock and tweed cap, regaling the touring owners like a slick maitre d' at a Michelin-starred restaurant.

Algy stood back and smiled as first Gilligan, and right behind him Bog, effused over the sheer brilliance of the four-legged animal before them. To be fair, Prince Ali looked wonderful, as all of the horses at Bury Castle did. But, to listen to the hyperbole emanating from his management team, one could have been forgiven for assuming that here was Pegasus, Champion the wonder horse, Black Beauty, Eclipse, and Frankel all rolled into one.

'Outstanding!' said Gilligan. 'Twuly magnificent,' he went on to say, rolling his 'r' into a garbled 'w.' Turning to Townsend he said, 'Marcus, you've done a splendid job.' Prince Ali's trainer smiled, leaving Algy wondering what self-assumed authority Gilligan had bestowed upon himself to pass such judgement?

'He's coming along well, aren't ya laddy,' said Townsend as he gave the handsome bay colt a slap on his rump and asked his lad to bring him over, so that the gathered observers could see his offside.

'Look at that power, in behind,' said Bog, to nobody in particular. At which, maybe knowing a fool, Prince Ali pinned his ears. And Algy wondered whether he'd do everyone a favour and kick Bog and Gilligan out of his box and into the yard.

Finally, the dog and pony show was over and Townsend invited his guests into the house for drinks. He'd already briefed Algy and, as Prince Ali's connections had never considered otherwise, the toasts were to the Prince and the Dewhurst being just another stepping-stone on the way to numerous classic wins and immortality. By round three the Sheikh's men were talking about a Triple Crown winner and the fact that their horse was going to end the almost fifty-year drought since Nijinsky had landed British horse racing's Holy Grail.

They had no idea that, far away in Dubai, their paymaster was, all the while, meeting with Ravi Singh and that the reason for their meeting had nothing to do with Prince Ali or Java Raja.

◆ ◆ ◆

The Bangalore launching of the first Real Racing sweepstake had been a huge success and Ravi and Kulbir were now ready to reach out to a larger market. As

Tommo Thompson had pointed out, when the figures had been broken down, this first race had been marketed to a largely ignorant, albeit enthusiastic, audience. For them, the appeal had been buying a ticket for a chance to win a lot of money and it wouldn't have mattered what the vehicle was, real or computer-generated. Yet the celebrity involvement, per social media, had made the event a great deal more than the sum of its parts.

Indeed, while the local involvement had generated close to 20% of the total and on track attendance had broken a record, it was participation by online players across India that had fueled the final figure. As Tommo again had observed, per TV ratings and an analysis of the patterns of ticket buying, per the GPS tracking of players' phones, the concept had so far only reached about seventy five million people, or around 6% of the population of India, and probably quite a bit less, when you factored in those who had bought multiple tickets.

At a post-race board meeting, the ever cautious Rahda Sigtia had again pressed Tony Palgrave-Brown about how airtight the patent was on Real Racing and been given the same answers to his original query: that litigating such an issue would be far too costly and pointless. And for all the reasons they had already discussed, nobody else would be able to compete because of regional regulations and those that flaunted such matters would not have the credibility to encourage large global audiences to play their games.

'What we have, here,' said Ravi, 'is a phenomenon that harnesses the Internet, as a provider of entertainment and generator of benevolent revenue: if you will, a sort of entertainment tax. Not one that will penalize the most vulnerable, but rather will promote horse racing, which the sport badly needs, while also funding urgent matters that could save our planet.'

It had been agreed with TAB that the following year's Melbourne Cup, on the first Tuesday of November, would be a Real Race down under, as Tommo Thompson had touted it. In between, there would be a race in March, in Dubai, and one in England, perhaps in August. TAB and Motti-Media had drawn up a revenue sharing management contract, in the belief that TAB's involvement would further confirm the enseavour's legitimacy.

Now Ravi and Kulbir were lodged at the Burj Al Arab hotel in Dubai, as guests of Sheikh Sultan Al-Bakshish, brother of Prince Ali's owner, Sheikh Ali Al-Bhakandar, and a cousin of the ruler of the Emirate, for a meeting to discuss a Real Race during the upcoming Dubai World Cup meeting in March.

The meeting of Sheikh Ali and Kulbir, unbeknownst to their host's UK-based managers, had occurred in the most unlikely of circumstances:

at a cricket match, the previous summer in England, arranged between the Armscote Ramblers and Sheikh Ali's All-Star XI, at the delightful private ground on Algy's uncle's Cotswold estate.

Lord Armscote liked to win and, fearing the All-Star team, which included several semi-pros, might embarrass him, he'd instructed his nephew to round up a few ringers. Having met the Singhs at Royal Ascot, Algy had had a brain wave: recruiting Kulbir.

The one-day 50-over game, which had started at 11:30 a.m., had seen the home team struggling at 100 for 6 at lunch, during which refreshment their generous but equally cunning host had attempted to get the All-Stars drunk. Sitting apart from this revelry, the Ramblers' number nine batsman, padded-up and expecting to be called upon soon after the resumption of play, had been introduced to the All-Stars' non-playing captain. Soon the conversation had turned to horse racing and then progressed to the Real Racing project that Kulbir's brother, Ravi, was planning on launching that fall.

That afternoon, Kulbir had saved the day for team Armscote by putting on a hundred and twenty for the ninth wicket, with a personal contribution of seventy-five, which had left the All-Stars chasing a respectable score of 245.

This total had looked very gettable, though, as the visitors raced to 150 for 2 after just twenty-five overs. But the home team had a surprise up their sleeve. Bringing on Kulbir Singh to bowl his legs breaks, as the sun set, proved to be Teddy Armscote's master stroke, as the beguiling Indian spin bowler had skittled the last eight All-Star wickets for sixty. Man-of-the-Match, the modest Kulbir, had stayed in touch with his new-found friend and here they were discussing round two for Real Racing in Dubai.

'The interesting thing, for me,' said Kulbir, qualifying himself, 'someone who is not an expert of form or really a fan of horse racing, is that to arouse interest you don't need the best horses, as our race in Bangalore proved. It's not like tennis or golf, where people only want to see the Federers and the Nadals, or Tiger Woods and Rory McIlroy. As long as you have a big and competitive field that has been well handicapped, the layman will feel that he has the same chance as the so-called experts.'

'So true,' said Sheikh Sultan. 'We attract the best horses to Dubai each winter because the prize money is good, and I think our top races attract good-sized fields for that reason. But so often, in Europe and North America, the top Stakes races, which feature the best horses, have pitifully small fields. And the fact is that the public is not interested in betting on these contests, when there is often a very short-priced favourite.'

'Yes. We studied the PMU's Quinté races in France and some of the big handicaps in Hong Kong,' Kulbir continued, 'and, even on a regular Saturday in the UK, it is the races with large fields and wide-open betting that appeal to the minimum-stake punter the most.'

After the meeting, Kulbir had flown on to Bangalore and it was there that he and his brother heard the great news that Java Raja had won the Group 1 Middle Park Stakes at Newmarket by an impressive six lengths. Retired for the season, unbeaten in his four races. On the phone Algy had sounded truly excited about his prospects as a three-year-old, even mentioning him as a legitimate contender for the 2000 Guineas, although he cautioned them that Sheikh Ali had a similarly talented unbeaten colt, also trained by Marcus Townsend, who, after a facile win in the Dewhurst Stakes, would be a formidable foe.

◆ ◆ ◆

Hector Delmontez was a puzzled man, as he sat in his office at Caledonia Farms. It was late fall and what was left of the colour had been swept off the trees by the October breezes and was now lying, like a pale-yellow carpet, in the paddocks outside, occasionally dancing in a gust of wind. During the past eighteen months, since the fire, his fortunes had soared. He was the man about town, and he and his very charming wife were always first on Billy Beagle's party list: ever-reliable sources for community fundraising.

Indeed, so welcome had the Delmontez's been made, by the Lexington in-crowd, that he was beginning to wonder about all the stuff he'd been told about their feelings towards minorities; especially Mexicans, which he'd realized very quickly was what most Americans collectively referred to all people of Hispanic origin.

Yet, as the chilly wind that swirled outside was a harbinger of worse weather to come, something was not quite right.

It had started with the Juan Moreno incident. And he was beginning to realize that his Canadian partners, and specifically Calvin Weiner, were not only getting too greedy but were taking too many chances. Indeed, he'd had to cancel the November charter, in the wake of the episode in Cincinnati and the apparent increased police interest in his affairs. Now, according to his main man in Caracas, Conrad Aqueno, who was a Russian-speaking Cuban, someone was squeezing Weiner and he did not like the sound of what he was hearing.

Prior to Glasnost and the collapse of the Russian support of Cuba, Aqueno had, like many of his countrymen, been sent to study engineering in the Soviet

Union; in his case, at the Belarus tractor factory in Minsk. There he'd learnt the lingo and a whole bunch of unsavoury tricks, earning himself the fearsome handle of Arko, for his trademark weapon of persuasion and not-too-subtle intimidation: the arc welder.

Not a particularly imposing figure, standing a squat 180 pounds of chiselled muscle and sinew at five-foot-six, Arko could have been a fighter. However, his disproportionate weight and height hadn't matched any Olympic category that would have brought success. And, along the way, the loss of his left eye, in an altercation that had left him with a livid scar across where his eyeball had once been, had dimmed such aspirations.

Russia had hardened Arko. And when the time had come to return to his native land, he'd decided otherwise and disappeared from both Russian and Cuban radar, eventually showing up in Central America, courtesy of a Venezuelan freighter carrying steel from Vladivostok to Panama City.

Nobody could remember exactly how he'd ended up in the Condor network, but, over the past twenty years, he'd established a reputation for getting the job done, no matter the fallout.

Arko had a sixth sense that Hector trusted implicitly. There had been something about Juan Pablo Moreno that wasn't right. His hands were too well manicured. His teeth were too straight and white. Ever since he'd started working Air Condor charters, he'd had this feeling that he could be a rat. He just wasn't sure whether it was for the cops or another cartel.

Luckily for Arko, the Canadians were too polite. Of course, they had yet to find Moreno's body when the plane landed in Toronto, so being a man short, according to the manifest, was relatively easily explained. But, they'd never actually searched the plane for Senor Moreno, and had they done so and found Arko, instead, there would have been a lot more explaining to do.

The inescapable fact was that Moreno should have been let go, or at least reassigned to the respectable side of the company and certainly not put on as important a flight. Arko was mad at himself. First the pilot had circled too high, so the wind blew the drop off course, and then that fucking idiot Moreno had got his foot caught in a cargo strap and gone out the door with the shipment. When they had landed in Toronto, Arko had hidden away inside a compartment that had been ingeniously disguised between the galley and small toilet at the tail of the plane, and everyone got home safely before the body had washed up on Dwight Beach. But a big mistake had been made and, through the most unlikely combination of a curious OPP officer and a drunken curler, the cops were now nosing about: far too close for Arko's boss's liking.

Indeed, the word was out in Caracas. Arko's contact in the local police, who was on the Condor payroll, had warned him that the trail had been picked up. So, the Cincinnati shakedown had hardly been surprising. Hector was just relieved that his guys had acted quickly and retrieved the goods from the rendering yard before a whole bunch of dogs had expired from overdosing on Carfentanyl.

Hector had smiled grimly. That wouldn't have been funny. But seriously, while things had gone very well over the past two years or so, and nobody had rumbled El Gruppo, despite the El Cordobes business, this latest news that someone was turning up the heat in Canada was concerning.

Earlier in the fall Calvin Weiner and Mike Rogers had put on another of their elite sales, where only specially invited guests had the opportunity to bid for a small and select offering of bloodstock, which had largely included horses that Hector had shipped to them from South America. The sale had again been held on Weiner's farm in King City and, using Hector's Lexington connections and the endorsement of CBS in the UK, a rich and rare bunch of potential buyers were flown in for three days of decadent entertainment.

Billy Beagle had had his reservations, but the amount of money dropped by the two Russians he'd met at Saratoga that summer had been most impressive. He knew only too well that the sport needed this new investment. And, if the UK had allowed its racing to be propped up by Arab despots so successfully for so long, who really cared who these people were or from whence they had acquired their wealth?

Mike Rogers had always been a shameless self-promoter and, having inherited a farm from his hard-working parents, had managed to convince many Canadians to part with their money for his mediocre and grossly overpriced stock until he'd emptied out just about everyone in town. His only salvation had been Calvin Weiner, another reprobate, who'd inherited rather than made his money. At the same time that Rogers' fortunes were going south, Weiner had realized that the deal he'd made with provincial casino officials to subsidize horse racing, and his own pockets, was also drying up. So the two, through their urgent need for cash, had got together with Hector Delmontez to form an unlikely but very profitable enterprise.

At the outset Weiner, like Beagle in Kentucky and Danvers and Lascelles in the UK, represented the establishment that was essential to give the whole scam some gravitas and credibility. Hector had had no intention of burning any of these key men. But at the convention in Caracas, he'd spotted a serious flaw in Weiner: he liked the product too much, which was a real no-no. But

Patricia, his wife, had been charmed by the Canadian duo and Weiner had fixed the Ontario spit box so Tim Trebor could win a Grade 1 Stakes race, and their elite sales were the perfect place to launder money. You ship the dope and you make the transaction clean by over-selling mediocre horses to willing buyers who know they are in fact paying for something else. Then, and this was the clever part, you whack those that are totally useless and claim their inflated value through your own insurance company, El Gruppo. Bingo! Cleaning more money. Double-dipping!

Of course, Beagle and his mates had no idea what was going on and were blinded by their loyalty to 'good people,' like PLUs – people like us – who run the sport. Things had been going very smoothly, but now Weiner's unfortunate habit and his new punter's greed was threatening to destroy a very lucrative pipeline.

What we should do, Hector pondered, as he gazed glumly out into the rain, is back off and let things settle down. But the Canadians, if Arko was to be believed, were having the pressure put on them, so this might be more easily said than done.

CHAPTER 35

Roman Weiner had, like many post–WWII immigrants to Canada, arrived from a shattered Poland with just a suitcase and grand ambitions.

Relieved to be in a free land, he'd changed his name from Wilynski. The Roman had somehow become Jerry and the 'sausage man,' as he became known as, and had dived into the only thing he knew he was good at: hard work.

Founding Weiner Meats in Kitchener, about an hour's drive west of Toronto, in 1950, after four years of slogging at nearby Canada Packers, he'd settled into the Eastern European expat community and soon married his Ukrainian wife, Maria, and produced six children, of which Calvin, the oldest, was his pride and joy. Over the next forty years Jerry the Sausage Man had proceeded to make Weiner Meats synonymous with quality throughout Ontario supermarkets and across all of Canada.

Calvin Weiner had grown up on the farm that his father had bought near New Hamburg. Driven by his parent's pride and ambition, he had attended the best schools before studying law at McGill University in Montreal, and that was where he had gone off the rails.

McGill was young Weiner's first experience away from his rigorous upbringing and the temptations and endless partying, in a city that in so many ways is more European than North American, had proven to be irresistible with the late seventies drug culture, glamour, and seemingly endless loose women.

Jerry Weiner had started out by buying a few cheap standardbred horses that he remembered his father training on his small holding near Krakow before the war. Soon Weiner Stables' stock were featuring prominently, not only at local fairs, like Elmira just down the road from their farm, but against the best on the continent at Mohawk and in Toronto at Greenwood and the new Woodbine racetrack. But Cal Weiner despised his father's humble upbringing and work ethic, aspiring to much bigger and better things. So, it was hardly surprising when, as a young lawyer on Toronto's Bay Street, he'd got in with the smarter thoroughbred crowd who were riding the wave of E.P. Taylor's great successes at Windfields Farms. And it had been at the thoroughbred yearling sales at Woodbine, in the fall of 1973, that the fateful meeting with Michael Rogers had taken place.

Rogers came from a well-to-do Ontario family that had always bred thoroughbreds. And young Michael was known in racing circles to be a consummate promoter of family stock and anyone else's that he felt he could make a buck off when it came to sales time.

When Weiner and Rogers had met, the latter's father had just died and young Mike was 'the man' when it came to thoroughbred bloodstock and sales matters. So, combining his skills of persuasion with Weiner's weaknesses and family money was a foregone conclusion.

Woodbine racetrack in the '70s was on a roll. The first British Triple Crown winner in years (and, in fact, ever since), Nijinsky, had been bred at Windfields Farms just outside Oshawa, about an hour east of Toronto, and the mile-and-a-half Canadian International Stakes, run over Woodbine's famous Marshall turf course, had attracted the great Secretariat for his swansong appearance in 1973.

Meanwhile, down at Keeneland Sales in Kentucky, the first great European invasion of buyers, spearheaded by Nijinsky's trainer, Vincent O'Brien, had driven prices for North American bloodstock sky-high before Arab buyers arrived in the '80s to set records that today seem completely crazy.

Calvin Weiner liked this action. He also liked the partying, the women, and the drugs. And, in Mike Rogers, he had a very willing co-conspirator, as they formed a partnership that would dominate Canadian thoroughbred horse racing throughout the '80s and early '90s. Then the rot set in and now, after twenty years of mismanagement and greed, E.P. Taylor's goose had finally stopped laying its golden eggs.

While Weiner and Rogers had ridden roughshod over the local racing and breeding scene, nobody had paid attention to the burgeoning competition for the discretionary gaming dollar, as casinos and lotteries, particularly of the online variety, had eaten into horse racing's profits.

Betting on the horses had once been a monopoly for those who ran the sport in Ontario. But now there were so many cheaper and more accessible alternative forms of entertainment and, because those running the show had sought to enrich themselves without reinventing their sport and catering to newer and younger audiences, racing was in a major decline.

First, Mike Rogers' dog and pony show collapsed. He then left his long-suffering wife and ran off with his son's girlfriend, further compounding his problems. And Weiner, who'd resumed the bad habits he'd picked up in Montreal, where the local mob always had an abundant supply of good gear, spiralled out of control, ending up in rehab even as he struggled to run Canada's top racetrack and keep up a positive appearance.

Then, along had come the Ontario Casino Corporation (OCC), which some misguided politician had felt needed to expand its reach, in a reciprocal way with horse racing, to generate more players. The deal, whereby OCC operated slot machines at existing outlets for gaming, (racetracks throughout the province) had subsidized the sport to the tune of twenty percent of net profits that, at the outset, had meant close to $1 million a day. Weiner and his mates, at the top of the thoroughbred food chain, had fed greedily at this trough.

For a time, the prize money at racetracks in Ontario was as high as anywhere in North America. The trouble was that only those already in the business had benefitted from this windfall and no effort was made to use these funds to promote the sport to a wider and younger audience that, through its patronage, would, supposedly, increase media exposure and thence the desire to breed and own racehorses.

During this self-serving orgy, Weiner and Rogers had lived like kings and so it was hardly surprising that they had shown up on Hector Delmontez's radar and been invited down to the now-infamous Racetracks of America convention in Caracas back in 2009. Hector knew they controlled horse racing in Canada, but he also knew that their lucrative source of funding was soon going to run out when the contract with OCC ended, and he knew how he could get to Weiner.

That whole week in Caracas had been one big string of excesses, as horse racing's high rollers had indulged themselves at the expense of Hector Delmontez. And Cal Weiner had realized that, in Hector, he had come across a new and potentially very lucrative business partner to keep him afloat, when the tap from the slots was turned off.

But dependency can be fickle. As Hector rued recent negative developments and the increased attention of the the FBI, he began to realize that Weiner was becoming a problem. His customers, the slick Russians whom Mike Rogers had procured upon their arrival on the ultra-prestigious and obscenely expensive Bridle Path in Toronto, were turning out to be a major source of embarrassment.

The horse that had died on the Air Condor charter to Cincinatti had been scheduled to be vanned to Canada. As Hector had pointed out: you had to mix things up and not be too predictable. Indeed, after the Juan Moreno incident, he knew that the RCMP would be all over the next plane to Canada. But a horse, arriving by van from Kentucky, would not have got the same scrutiny that he was sure future air shipments from Venezuela would.

Having been tipped off by their man on the ground, by text, just as the plane had touched down, that there was a reception committee awaiting them, Hector's men had saved the bacon through their quick thinking. But the salvaged shipment of Carfentanyl was still on the wrong side of the border, as far as the clients were concerned. And because Messrs. Grabovski and Jirkov had already paid for it, per their recent grossly inflated equine purchases, they wanted to know where their gear was.

This was a completely different ball game for the boys, and the seriousness of it was brought home to Weiner when two men had arrived late one night at his Muskoka cottage to put the frighteners on him and his wife Samantha, with a very clear message that failure to deliver the goods within a week would result in another visit that would not be so friendly.

The word that the expected shipment had not arrived on schedule had filtered back through the Russian mafia community all the way to Arko's ears, in Caracas, where, in turn, it had been communicated to his boss. A simple encrypted message: 'The Canadian Russians are not happy punters. You need to deliver the goods.'

Hector had thought that he could control Weiner, appreciating that he needed to keep him as an asset when it came to cementing trust within the old boy's network of horse racing's elite around the world. At the same time, he knew that Weiner was also, potentially, a huge liability, with his personal issues, who had to be kept at arm's length with as little overt communication as possible. No phone calls. No e-mails. No texts. No connective trail.

So the message, when it came, had been simple and he had to admire Weiner's chutzpah. The more brazen, the less likely anything would be rumbled.

There was a horse show the following week in the town of Aurora, just outside Toronto, where several Kentucky-based horses would be competing in the dressage competition. And Weiner felt that, if the goods were properly insulated and stored in an innocuous stable wallbox or ottoman, without the knowledge of those travelling with the horses, they would be highly unlikely to be checked at the border. The key was, as he knew only too well, complete innocence. You know you have something, and you get nervous. But, if you don't think that you have anything to hide, your body language is normal.

It was taking a big risk and, if the consignment had been discovered by customs, those on the van would have found themselves in very hot water. But it had worked, and Weiner had dodged a bullet.

This time, thought Hector. But he knew it wouldn't be long before the heat was on again for further supplies.

CHAPTER 36

Fall in Virginia meant fox hunting around Middleburg and Upperville. Local steeplechase meets entertained horse lovers and, on the farms, young stock were being introduced to a steel bit in their mouths, the feel of the long-rein driving them, and then the weight of a passenger on their backs for the first time.

At Shenandoah Valley, the procedure was done the old-fashioned way. Matt Pearson was in no hurry. Indeed, of all the many aspects of training thoroughbreds, this was probably the stage he enjoyed the most. It was the bonding and establishment of trust and respect between a horse and his master. Like a good grounding in manners for a young child, he felt this very first stage, on the way to being a racehorse, was the most important.

'So many good things in life require a foundation,' he said to Tom, as they watched Basil Foster lunging the young dark bay colt by Last Post, nicknamed Rocky.

'I remember an old Italian chef talking about making a great tomato sauce. He said, "Eeets-a-lika you builda a 'ousa. Or you-a maka lova to a woo-man,"' he related, as Toby and Curtis listened intently and giggled. "You-a taka your tima. You-a builda the foundations slowly and properly."

'That's the way I like it,' said Toby, 'nice and slow…oh, yea…nice and slow.'

'Trouble is,' said Curtis, 'you so slow, man, you can't catch up with no woman!'

Everyone laughed. It was a late-November morning, the training had been done, the barn raked, the horses fed, and now the guys were shooting the breeze, watching a newcomer go through his first paces.

'These days lots of people don't bother with the long-reining,' said Matt, as Basil steered Rocky in figure eights, changing direction with just the very lightest of touches on his precocious charge's mouth and the jiggling of the long-reins down his flanks. 'They just cinche 'em up, like they're at a rodeo, and stand back, letting them buck themselves into submission. They don't have the time, and a lot of those horses go to the track with no mouth on them at all.'

Rocky had been brought over from Tanglewood the week before, along with his two paddock mates. On the surface, he looked put together right. But he was just a son of Last Post; nothing to get excited about. Toby, who'd been at the farm the longest, remembered his dad: what a good-looking colt he'd been and how exciting it had been when he'd sold for all that money. But things hadn't worked out and the old saying, 'handsome is as handsome does', did rather sum up his career, although Matt blamed the connections for mishandling him from the get-go. Just too impatient, he'd said, and, in Matt's opinion, they'd made him speed crazy. A bit like Rikki: but a sad story that unfortunately didn't have his good ending.

Rocky was acting like a pro. He had eaten up since his arrival and seemed to enjoy the lunging and long-reining routine that was his daily staple for an hour each morning, after the other horses had been trained, and before being turned out in a paddock beside the drive, in the shade of the hickory and walnut trees.

When finally, after a week of steady work, first walking, then trotting, and then cantering slowly, on the left lead, then the opposite direction on the right and finally, in the long driving-reins, Rocky had first a saddle placed on his withers, then the girth tightened. He'd never flinched. It was, it seemed, quite natural: a piece of cake. And so, having a rider put their weight across the saddle and then swing a leg over was nothing to worry about.

Rocky had arrived at Shenandoah Valley to commence his training with the minimum of fuss, and come Christmas he had not put a foot wrong - exactly the way Matt and Vera wanted it.

Convincing the Elevator Stable that they should invest some of their earnings from Rikki's successes in him proved to be a little harder than they'd expected, though.

From the start, bearing in mind his dubious provenance, Vera had wanted to distance herself and the reputation of Shenandoah Valley Farms from the Last Post colt. And Matt had even thought about running him through a local sale and buying him back cheaply. But they'd decided that, until such time as he'd proved his worth beyond his pedigree, it would be courting disaster to put him in a spot where anyone might feel deceived.

So, his dubious pedigree was the main reason why the so-called experts of bloodlines within the syndicate baulked at getting involved with a young horse who would not start to generate a return on their investment for a year or more and then might never turn out to be any good.

Reggie had reminded the syndicate members that they'd got together – most successfully he'd added – because they'd identified a horse that they could claim, that was racing, without incurring all the expenses that now confronted them. But Vera had snuffed that out by saying that, when Rikki had got to Matt he was in such a bad way, they had actually paid training fees for almost a year before they'd seen any return on their original outlay.

Colin, enjoying association with the 'bluebloods of the turf,' felt that, as they were effectively playing with the house's money, this was a freebie which would hopefully provide more opportunities for schmoozing in the right places.

In the end, Vera had prevailed by using a sales pitch that even Mike Rogers, at his most persuasive, would have admired, saying that she had such confidence in the colt that she'd take a share, herself. And, after further consideration, the vote was three to one, with Reggie the only dissenter.

The Elevator Stable, including Vera, was now the leasor of the Last Post colt for his first two seasons on the racetrack, for $50,000 plus training expenses, to be split five ways, between the syndicate members.

At the end of the lease, the arrangement could be extended, or the horse sold: again, by vote of the five members. Additionally, a provision was put in that, if at any point prior to the colt turning four, a sale was negotiated, the leasers would get 10% of anything over and above the original $50,000.

This last part seemed like a very unlikely scenario, which nobody attached much importance to, and the minor details were thrashed out without further delay.

Then it was time to name him and various inappropriate suggestions were made before Vera took charge, once again. 'Last Post was a son of Gettysburg,' she said, 'which was really just about the Confederate Army's last stand. His dam is Curtain Call and, as they are both, regrettably, deceased, this is their last issue. Therefore, let's call him Last Hurrah.'

There was a silence and Reggie said, 'If he's a dud, it may well be ours too!' Everybody laughed.

'So, it's Last Hurrah,' said Vera, and that was that. The Elevator Stable now had a two-year-old to dream about and worry about. 'You know what they say?' she added.

'I can't wait to hear?' said Reggie, resigned.

'Well, if you own a yearling, you never commit suicide because you're always wondering if this could be the big horse!'

'Ha! Ha!' said Nils. 'If this guy does half of what Rikki's done for us, we'll be so lucky.'

AT THE TRACK

CHAPTER 37

The second Real Racing sweepstake, held at Kolkata racecourse in January, went off without a hitch. The audience now knew what was coming and that their investments were in a legitimate operation. The word had gotten out.

Tommo Thompson was in town again, taking in the second Test Match between India and Australia at Eden Gardens. 'A bit of R&R and a belter of a curry', he'd said. Officials from Meydan Racecourse in Dubai were on hand to observe the event on behalf of, Sheikh Sultan, as Ravi and Kulbir prepared to expand overseas and include a race at the March World Cup festival, for round three.

Again, IPL stars and Bollywood celebrities lent their support to the cause, which this time the local authorities and the Indian federal government, that now wanted a piece of the action, decided should be put towards Prime Minister Kumar's 'indoor toilet in every house' program. This had spawned a whole bunch of juvenile jokes about 'Real Dumping,' and other lavatorial humour.

Undaunted, Motti-Media had approached Sky, TVG, and other sports-related cable networks, regarding coverage, but found that only Channel Nine in Australia was able to circumnavigate legal restrictions. 'You see,' Tommo had most appropriately said, 'these suckers will be begging to cover future races, when they finally get the shit outta their eyes.'

Rahda Sigtia had blinked, then smiled when he thought about the noble cause that the second sweepstake would be supporting. As the lucky winner this time just fortuitously turned out to be a janitor from the Taj Mahal Tower hotel in Mumbai the result could not have been more fitting, as far as convincing a once skeptical public that this was indeed the real deal.

When the dust had settled and Motti-Media and its accountants had done their final sums, a healthy increase over round one was declared, with total sales of $186 million, from which $125 million went to the Khasi Project, as it had been named by Tommo Thompson.

'Stone the crows,' was his initial reaction. 'You know, Kulbir,' he said, 'you're bleedin' right, mate. The more races you run, the less the start-up costs factor in. And you don't need any more bean counters to run a billion-dollar operation than a ten-grander. And,' he exclaimed excitedly, 'the more you sell, the less (percentage-wise) you have to pay out in prizes! This is a winner, pal!'

'Indeed, indeed,' Kulbir responded, pinching his beard as he absorbed the figures and realized that Motti-Media's Real Racing project was just that.

◆ ◆ ◆

Ever since the bookmakers had started to post prices for the following year's Classics, David Burns had been quietly backing the now three-year-old colt he was looking after at Bury Castle Stables for the 2000 Guineas. And, as Marcus Townsend started to crank up his string for the upcoming season, Java Raja was now listed as a 12/1 shot by most firms.

At the outset, he'd got 33s and now, having put on twenty pounds a week or whatever he could afford after his wife had relieved him of his paycheck, had five hundred pounds invested.

In the opinion of most pundits, Townsend's other colt, Prince Ali – the bookies' favourite at 3/1 – was the logical choice. It was generally felt that Java Raja would not run at Newmarket in the 2000 Guineas against his supposedly superior stablemate and be directed, instead, to maybe the French or Irish equivalents. But Burns had confided his investment to his governor, who'd assured him that, if the two colts trained into the Newmarket race in good shape, he'd probably let them both run.

Townsend knew that they would have to meet at some point.

He'd hardly spoken to Ravi Singh since he'd acquired him as an owner, almost eighteen months before, at Keeneland sales. Now, while he was attending the Dubai World Cup, he was quite surprised to bump into him and Algy Sinclair in the Burj Al Arab Hotel lobby.

'My goodness, Algy. What are you doing here?' was all he could muster.

'Looking after my client,' smiled Algy. 'You met Mr. Singh at Keeneland.

Very briefly, I know, when you signed the ticket for Java Raja.'

'Yes, of course! You, sir, are the best owner I have.' Townsend, the consummate diplomat, shook Ravi's hand warmly, continuing, 'Actually, I better be careful saying that here in case Sheikh Ali hears me. But, seriously, not a single phone call. You never bother me. Your horse does nothing but win and you pay your bills on time. It would be an easy business if every one of my owners was like that.' He smiled as he recovered his composure.

'I am glad to hear that,' said Ravi. 'So far, this has proven to be a very productive experience.'

'And what brings you here, to Dubai?' Townsend enquired.

'Well, a bit of business, actually,' Ravi replied. 'My company, in India, in conjunction with Sheikh Sultan, is running an online sweepstake on a race here at Meydan on Saturday night.'

'It's the last race on the card. A handicap, going two miles on the turf,' said Algy.

'Oh, yes, that race,' said Townsend. 'Please forgive me. I have a lot on my plate, and I hadn't really been paying attention to the races that I'm not running horses in.'

'No worries,' said Ravi. 'Tell me how my colt, Java Raja, is doing?'

'In a word: fantastic! He's never put a foot wrong since he arrived. I have Sheikh Ali's horses here, for obvious reasons. He, or his family, rather, own the place. So, Prince Ali will prepare for the 2000 Guineas here and we'll give him a run before the Guineas. I decided to leave your horse at Newmarket because his lad is married and didn't want to come out here. And I value the understanding he has with Java Raja, whom he rides in all his work. They are a very important partnership.'

'How about the Guineas?' said Algy, inquisitively watching to see Townsend's reaction.

Always the polished politician and, Algy thought, shrewd poker player in this instance, Townsend replied, 'Nothing is set in stone. I'll evaluate both horses when we are back at Newmarket. A lot can happen between now and then. And then, we'll make a decision. Both horses are versatile. I don't think the ground will make any difference.'

'Sheikh Ali's not listening,' quipped Algy. 'If your life depended on it, which one would you pick?'

'Aha! Luckily for me, my life does not depend on such a decision,' said a dodging Townsend as Ravi smiled.

◆ ◆ ◆

The Dubai race for Unicef might not have featured the highest-quality field, but the draw, on top of the Burj Al Arab Hotel, conducted by the very popular Saudi Rapper, Al Fhuku, turned out to be a sensation, with the Dish-Dashing F-U, as his fans called him, being lowered on a throne from a helicopter.

In a jurisdiction where gambling is against the law on religious grounds and all betting is conducted offshore or online, there was no shortage of interest amongst the twenty thousand local Emerati fans on hand and millions of TV viewers around the world in the twenty-two-runner field that went to post while the victorious connections of the world's richest race – the $10 million Dubai World Cup, run forty minutes earlier – were still celebrating.

In order to be prepared for the increased action, the IT guys in Bangalore had dramatically boosted the capacity of their servers and, for the first time, TV networks broadcast video of all the ticket holders who had drawn runners who, as it turned out, came from as far afield as Iceland and Borneo with, as Ravi was glad to see, eight Indian-based winners.

In Dubai, because they cannot place wagers on the racetrack, racegoers fill out a form before the first race, with a selection for each one – a sort of free-entry jackpot or Pick 6 bet – and whoever selects the most winners wins a car or prize of a similar value. So, being also able to engage in Real Racing proved to be a big bonus. And to the enormous delight of the patrons of Dubai racing, a new record of $257 million, from all sources, was recorded with a record prize of $5 million awarded to a lucky winner in Dogashima, Japan, who became an instant viral celebrity of Japanese social media and TV talk shows.

Just over $200 million was donated to Unicef by the beaming Bhakandar family, and Billy Beagle of the NHRA and Chubby Magnall of the UK Jockey Club gulped; especially when they overheard a very inebriated Tommo Thompson boasting, 'Just wait 'til we run this beauty down under! And watch out Grand National and Ken-turkey Derb-eeee!'

CHAPTER 38

After the excitement in Dubai, Newmarket seemed cold and lifeless, as the fabled turf turned reluctantly from greyish yellow to green and the pace of workouts increased.

Prince Ali was still in Dubai, where he had murdered a small field in a prep race, specially put on for his benefit. He was enjoying himself so much in the gulf sunshine that his trainer had decided to leave him there and only ship him in at the last moment, when the weather had improved, for the first classic of the British flat racing season, for which he'd now shortened in the market to a warm 6/4 favourite.

Java Raja had always been a tall and rangy individual. Now, with the winter behind him, he'd filled out to be a very handsome three-year-old. His coat maybe wasn't as sleek as Prince Ali's, due to the difference in temperatures between sub-zero Newmarket in winter and the semi-tropical temperatures of Dubai. But underneath his finely-tuned exterior his engine and muscles were charged and ready when he came out and demolished his rivals in the traditional local prep for the 2000 Guineas, the seven-furlong Craven Stakes at Newmarket. That day he was ridden by the stable's retained jockey, Pat Donnelly, and the ease of his victory not only saw his odds cut drastically to 6/1 for the Guineas, but set tongues wagging, with the *Racing Post* headline of Prince verses Raja?

At lunch, two weeks before the potential showdown, Team Ali, as Marcus Townsend referred to Jos Danvers, Hugo Lascelles, Johnny Ward-Clarke, and company when they weren't in earshot, were in boisterously good form as they discussed the formality of Prince Ali's task and his chances of becoming the first Triple Crown winner in almost fifty years. Townsend had not asked Algy Sinclair to lunch that day as he didn't want there to be any reason to debate a result other than a resounding victory for the already anointed one.

There was now no doubt that, whatever his main patron might think, he had to run Java Raja. It wouldn't be popular, but he figured that as Bog had already dismissed him as the bridesmaid who would wilt in the heat of top-class competition, not much would be made of it.

Pat Donnelly was committed to Prince Ali, even though he knew that the stable's other runner would most likely be his main rival and could quite easily beat him. He knew who paid his bills, and kept his trap shut.

This left Townsend with the task of finding another rider. Frank Coffey had done the job admirably first time out at Yarmouth. But this was big-time and there was a huge amount of money and prestige at the stake. So he recruited the services of the French champion, Jean-Louis Gay, who flew over to ride Java Raja in his final tune-up, four days before the big race.

Of all the people keenly following the Java Raja story, the one least seemingly preoccupied with the internal drama at Bury Castle appeared to be his owner, Ravi Singh. The Real Racing phenomenon had taken off and, as he'd hoped, Motti-Media was now being approached to feature races in Japan, Hong Kong, and even one at Garrison Savannah racecourse in Barbados, where the Caribbean island's minister of tourism, in charge of rebuilding after recent hurricane damage, felt their cause deserved consideration.

It was, as Kulbir's model had always indicated, a case of credibility and then scale. First, you convince people that you are not going to scam them and run off with their money. Then, as you develop your product into real-life drama, its the sheer volume of sales that makes the return unbeatable. Kulbir had likened it to a game of Bingo at the village hall, with fifty players and a pot of two hundred pounds, compared to a thousand such games, all connected. Running a thousand, online, cost no more and, because you could offer bigger prizes, the players came to you, like moths to a lone light bulb. It had always been his contention that lottery companies deliberately made sure that early pools were not won outright, so that the accumulation over time drew in extra players, dazzled by carry-over jackpots.

Amidst all this deal-making that had Tony Palgrave-Brown at CBH&H working harder than he had done in the thirty years he'd worked for the venerable firm of London-based solicitors, Algy persuaded Ravi that he and

Kulbir had to be at Newmarket on the first Saturday in May to watch their splendid colt perform on the highest stage.

Now trumpeted as a duel between The Prince and The Raja, the racing press had begun pestering Algy for background information on the latter's hitherto virtually unknown owner of the horse they had cast as 'the spoiler.'

This fact, though, had not been missed in rural Kentucky where, buoyed by the sale of the Raja's now two-year-old full sister, Begum Princess, the McDonnell family had decided to make a long overdue trip back to Ireland which included taking in the Guineas meeting at Newmarket and bringing Mark O'Malley, the man who had made it all happen, along as their guest.

Seamus McDonnell had never been to the headquarters of British racing. However, a small article in *The Blood-Horse* magazine, about the unbeaten colt from Bourbon County taking on his regally bred Arab-owned stablemate (fueled almost entirely by Seamus's partisan input) had caught the eye of the Racing Channel.

With Java Raja now the 7/2 second favourite to the odds-on Prince Ali, Bog had been experiencing midnight sweats and sleep interruptions. Even the normally outspoken Geoffrey Gilligan had gone quieter than usual, covering himself with the announcement in his blog 'G-G' that, in his humble opinion, Prince Ali was more of a Derby-type.

◆ ◆ ◆

Dawn on May 5 in Newmarket crept over the horizon, as head lad Wally Mills made his rounds to check that the runners that day had eaten up. Being based in Newmarket, there was no long van-ride to the races. So, both Prince Ali and Java Raja were ridden out, first lot, to stretch their legs and prevent them from fretting over any changes in routine.

As they made one short, pipe-opening canter up Warren Hill, under the studious gaze of Marcus Townsend and a group of Prince Ali's boosters, David Burns felt nervous shivers for the first time since, as a young apprentice aged sixteen, he'd had his first ride, twenty-five years before. He had now invested just over a thousand pounds at odds from 33/1 all the way down to 16s on the horse beneath him, to land that afternoon's big prize. His wife would have had a fit had she known, he thought, as he let down his stirrups a couple of notches; can't fall off and let the big hoss go, now, he thought. It was irresistible and, when he got back to the yard, he couldn't eat breakfast. He was not letting his breadwinner out of his sight.

In London, the Singhs had chartered a limo to take them the hundred or so miles to the east Anglian racecourse, where Algy Sinclair was to meet them for lunch. He had pointed out that while this was a big day, no tailcoats. Just a comfortable suit with a trilby option, maybe even a light mack, as being such a wide-open expanse Newmarket Heath could be chilly and there was a forecast of showers.

During the month of April, as temperatures had risen, the grass had turned emerald green and the fabled Rowley Mile unfurled before twenty thousand enthusiastic fans like a magic carpet, a mile and a quarter dead straight into the distance. Undisturbed in over three centuries, its springiness was as inviting a surface to race over as God could ever have dreamt of providing.

Whereas the Royal Meeting at Ascot in June was as much a social occasion, with the pomp and ceremony of processions, top hats, tails, and endless champagne, Newmarket is a much more austere venue, with its grandstand like a jagged rock sticking up amidst a ten-thousand-acre lawn. All the races are run dead straight towards these lonely stands, affording very poor viewing for spectators; but the assembled crowd was oblivious to all of this in its appreciation of the sport in its purest form, at the highest level.

The 2000 Guineas, to be run at 3:45 p.m., was the fourth of six races carded. And the two juggernauts from Bury Castle Stables were greeted by a large crowd as they emerged from the racecourse stables, approximately an hour before their denouement.

Marcus Townsend's horses were always beautifully turned out, with their navy blue and gold-trimmed paddock blankets keeping their sleek coats snug from the cool spring breeze. He didn't favour plaiting manes, especially with fillies, as he felt it was just another piece of stress when he wanted his charges to be most relaxed. So both colts' manes had been expertly pulled and lay neatly on the right (off) side of their arching necks.

David Burns had bought himself a new suit from Golding's in the Newmarket High Street and he sported an orange tie to match his owner's silks. Big Red was a dual course winner, so this was nothing new for him and, as for a few extra people, the way he walked around the pre-paddock before being saddled, he did not appear to be unnerved in any way.

Townsend had told Algy to explain to the Singhs that Sheikh Ali expected maximum attention on such occasions and not to be put out in any way if they felt he was ignoring them. The Singhs, visiting Newmarket's Rowley Mile racecourse for the first time, were completely understanding and so absorbed in what was going on that such a slight had never even occurred to them.

Just as in the stable yard there had been a Prince Ali faction and a Java Raja faction, so each horse was attended to by his direct support crew. Townsend even joked to Jos Danvers that it was like being corner man for both fighters in the ring: going on hastily to say, when ambushed by a TV microphone, that, of course, he realized that this was a Group 1 race and he should not underestimate the rest of the field. Even so, the punters had decided that this was a two-horse race and the odds reflected that, with Prince Ali 4/7, Java Raja shortening to 2/1, and 10/1 bar, the rest of the field.

When pressed by the Channel 4 TV presenter for what he would tell his jockeys, Townsend had merely replied that Pat Donnelly knew his horse, so needed no instruction, and that Jean-Louis Gay had watched video of Java Raja's races. 'He's a top jockey. He doesn't need me to tell him what to do.' What he didn't impart was that he'd given David Burns a simple message. 'Burnsy,' he'd said, 'you know this horse better than anyone. Just tell the Frenchman to follow Prince Ali. He'll know when to make his move.'

Watching proudly, but totally anonymously amongst the large crowd that had gathered around the paddock, the McDonnells admired their homegrown star. That morning Seamus had got up early and paid his old friend a visit at Bury Castle Stables. Separated for close to eighteen months, almost half of his young lifetime, the colt had nonetheless immediately recognized the man who had nursed him from his foaling, whineying excitedly, and the tears had flowed down the old man's face as he put his arm around his buddy's neck, gave him a little scratch behind his ear and whispered to him in Gaelic.

Now, as twelve of the best three-year-old colts in Europe paraded before them, Paddy McDonnell reminded Mark of the day that he and Tom Fraser had come out to inspect their colt. 'Hard to believe that it was almost two years ago, when you and Tom came out to the farm.'

'He's come a long way,' said Mark. 'You were right: he's special.'

'Always was,' chimed in Seamus, looking very different in his tweed suit, rather than the overalls and wellies that he'd sported that hot and dusty day back in Kentucky.

'It was meant to be,' said Mark. 'You know, ending up with a good trainer. You and Betty must thank your lucky stars that night you stayed until the end of a long day at the sales and got Killy. What was it you paid?'

'Forty-five thousand,' said Betty, sounding almost apologetic.

'A real money-spinner she's turned out to be,' added Paddy.

'And it's not over yet,' said Mark, as the call was made over the PA system for the jockeys to mount.

In the paddock, the Bhakandar supporters were out in force, with the Sheikh looking supremely confident, as they surveyed the odds-on favourite. Off to the side, the Singh brothers chatted with Algy while Townsend conferred with his two riders.

Often, on such occasions, when the stable ran two or more horses in the same race, they were owned by his main client and it was just a question of instructing the pacemakers of what their role was and to pay attention to how the race was being run. Today, with the cameras on him, Townsend smiled for their benefit.

Featuring just a long straightaway, for every race, the horses have to make their way the full distance that they will travel back over a few minutes later, at a much faster pace. So punters usually have more time to place their bets and position themselves in advantageous places to watch upcoming races from than at many other tracks. Thus, as the owners and trainers made their way out of the paddock, Sheikh Ali was able to greet his new partners from the Dubai Real Racing sweepstake of six weeks before. 'My friends,' he said warmly, 'we lock horns. You, with your amazing and unbeaten one-horse stable, and I, with the jewel in my crown.'

Ravi and Kulbir smiled and exchanged handshakes with the Sheikh and his supporters, and the cameras flashed. Much had been made of the Prince versus the Raja and now the protagonists were getting into the ring.

Walking out onto the course for the mandatory parade that always takes place before Group 1 races, David Burns was comforted by the fact that Jean-Louis Gay spoke such good English: his message would not be lost. Out from the protection of the grandstand, the breeze had picked up and put Java Raja on his toes, as up in the saddle Gay sat quietly, holding a clump of his mane, just in front of his diminutive saddle. 'The governor says,' he said, turning to the Frenchman, just as they reached the head of the parade, 'Follow Prince Ali. And I say, you'll beat him,' he added. And they were gone.

Some horses, confronted with such a wide-open space before them, with the buzz and roar of the grandstands behind, have been known to bolt in such circumstances. With very little to stop them between the Rowley Mile and the English Channel. Such a disaster would definitely have resulted in a scratch. And up in the stands, Townsend focused his binoculars on his two colts, going to post kindly, remembering how many years ago the French jockey Jean Cruguet had been run off with by the filly Hurry Harriet, who'd well and truly bolted a full mile, only to be loaded in the stalls and come back even faster for a memorable upset over the great filly, Allez France, in the Champion Stakes. But that sort of thing was so rare, and the master of Bury Castle was happy to see that all the work his staff had put in was being rewarded by his colts' good behaviour.

Being a straight mile at the beginning of the season, with the ground fresh, the stalls were situated on the stands' side. The field loaded quickly, as in the distance, one mile away, twenty thousand pairs of eyes focused their binoculars or studied the nearest video screen.

No bell, when the gate opens, in England. So, from the stands, the field's exit was silent, as the twelve horses quickly formed into a tight bunch. The commentator, whose voice would occasionally be drowned out by a gust of wind that blew the roars of the crowd into the microphone, announced that the longshot Isle of Arran, the grey, was setting a brisk pace from Prince Ali, with the rest of the field tucked in behind.

Glancing at the screen in front of him, Algy could see that Jean-Louis Gay had got Java Raja relaxed nicely, as the field approached halfway and the rails loomed on the left.

Newmarket looks like the simplest of tracks: dead straight, wide open. Easy. But jockeys unfamiliar with it can easily misjudge where they are, unless they are familiar with subtle markers along the way that enable riders with experience to gauge pace, where they are in the race, and when they should be making their challenge. About three furlongs from home there are The Bushes, as they're called. Nothing more than a bit of scrubby blackthorn on the heath to the right of the course itself, which mark the spot where, they say, King Charles II used to enjoy watching races from, which is the stage in a race when things start getting serious.

Up front, Isle of Arran was spent at this point and Prince Ali surged to the front, on the bridle, to a huge roar from the crowd. Behind him the field was coming under pressure, and, as Isle of Arran dropped back, Java Raja loomed.

With just under two furlongs to run, the undulating track runs slightly down hill, into what is known as 'the dip,' and from that point the run to the wire is slightly uphill. Excitedly the commentator yelled, 'Prince Ali is going clear, as they run down into the dip, with just over a furlong to run.' The crowd roared.

In the stands, Algy was relaying his reading of the race to Ravi and Kulbir, who weren't sure whether to watch through their binoculars or via the video screen. 'He's cruising. We're cruising!' he shouted.

Jean-Louis Gay knew his horse was a real miler. And, if what they were saying about Prince Ali was true and he would be better stretching out to a mile and a half for the Derby, he figured that Pat Donnelly would make as much use of his stamina as he could. And that is how it had worked out, with Donnelly sending on the favourite with fully three furlongs to run.

'Follow Prince Ali', was what they had said. But he was too good a judge of pace to take on his rival too soon. When the Prince had hit the dip, Donnelly had given him a flick of his whip down his right shoulder and he'd veered down to the rail on his left, with a lead of three lengths. Behind him Gay kept his mount balanced and, as they hit the rising ground, he pulled his whip through to his left hand and gunned Java Raja, whose response was electric. Changing legs onto his off-fore (right) lead, the big chestnut colt ranged up on the outside of Prince Ali. The crowd roared. Algy dropped his binoculars and yelled. For a moment it was neck and neck, and then he surged by.

The distance at the winning post was just over a length, but the manner in which he'd slain his rival was breathtaking, as the hush of beaten chalk players blended with the gasps of those who knew they'd witnessed a stunning performance.

Up on the third tier, Kulbir and Ravi beamed, not entirely certain what their colt had just achieved. 'Come on!' said Algy. 'We've got to get down to the winner's enclosure for the presentation.'

Further along, and a level higher, Team Bhakandar watched in silence as the field galloped out, turned, and made their way back to be unsaddled. The first to speak was Marcus Townsend. 'He ran a huge race. Look at the time, a minute thirty-four. That's amazing, here. And they finished fifteen lengths clear of the field.' But his words were of little consolation. 'Gentlemen, we'll chat about this later,' he added. 'We must go down and see the horses and congratulate Mr. Singh.' Had he bothered to look, he would have seen Bog gazing off into the distance with a perplexed smile on his face: when you are used to winning, something like this is hard to take, even if your home stable is on the winning side.

When the horses return to the winner's enclosure, many owners like to lead them in. But, for Java Raja, his weren't quite sure what they should do. So, when Seamus McDonnell appeared through the crowd with the colt, to a huge cheer, they hadn't the heart to steal his thunder.

Marcus Townsend wasn't one for photo ops, allowing his owners to bask in their glory while he conferred with Pat Donnelly. Prince Ali's team looked on like the bemused parents of their only child's wedding to an unknown quantity. Meanwhile, their ever-sporting boss congratulated Ravi and Kulbir and announced loudly to anyone who was listening that their's was going to be a great partnership, which would have seriously worried his advisers, had they heard.

❖ ❖ ❖

On that same first Saturday in May, approximately four thousand miles west of Newmarket and about seven hours later, a worried Billy Beagle excused himself from his guests in the NHRA box at Churchill Downs and took a call on his cell phone, away from the madding crowd.

The voice on the other end of the line spoke at length while Beagle frowned. This was supposed to be the highlight of the American thoroughbred racing season and the large crowd was in partying mood, but what he was hearing rocked him to the core.

It was approaching 6 p.m., local time, and the horses for the 145th Kentucky Derby were in the paddock, which called for a personal appearance. Beagle took a swig of bourbon from his personal flask, straightened his tie in the mirror, and rejoined T.J. Van der Meer and his guests.

This year's Derby was dominated by four horses from the all-conquering stable of Tim Trebor, headed by a coupled entry from the America's Stable of Hector Delmontez, Calvin Weiner, and a bevvy of Russians: the ladies looking ravishing in their finery and the men serious and a tad shifty.

Usually a pretty open affair, with a full field over a distance that none of the runners had ever competed as far as before, this year's race was nonetheless considered by most pundits to be done and dusted.

In the paddock Delmontez and his entourage were already in a celebratory mood. 'Ah! Senor Billy. El Jeffe!' Hector gushed as Beagle tried to avoid engagement but was corralled anyway. 'Theee-se ees incredible,' enthused the South American, resplendent in a large panama hat that matched his very lovely wife's stunning cream outfit and equally impressive headgear. 'My dream, to 'ava a 'orse ee-n the Kentucky Derby,' Delmontez went on, 'and now I-a-ava two!!'

Beagle shook Delmontez's hand politely and smiled as the cameras flashed. Good for business, he kept telling himself, wondering if the race was being televised in Venezuela and beyond and wishing he had not just received the most damning news he could ever have imagined.

As he attempted to play the roll of charming host, he felt ready to vomit.

'Mr. Beagle, sir,' the voice of a young man with earphones and a microphone jolted him back to reality. 'NBC. A few words?'

Beagle summoned his game face. 'Of course, lead on.' And the eager young man led him over to the corner of the paddock where NBC television's ubiquitous all-sports presenter, Merv Bigley, was holding court with a pretty young lady in a black-and-white hat that looked like a combination of a chequered flag and a Neopolitan sponge cake. Without breaking conversation, the slick Bigley introduced his illustrious guest. 'And here we have Mr. Horse Racing himself. Come on in, Billy Beagle, sir. Ladies and gentlemen, this is the man who stirs your mint juleps, around here, so to speak.' And he laughed at his own pretty puerile joke. 'Having fun, sir?'

Being the old pro that he was, Beagle smiled amiably. 'You never get tired of this, Merv. Thanks for having me on.'

'A record crowd. They just seem to get larger every year. Am I imagining things?'

'Maybe you've been listening too much to the president,' Beagle quipped.

'Ha! Ha! Nice one,' said Bigley, not losing out on the fact that Beagle was as GOP as bourbon was the local poison of choice. 'Seriously,' continued the irritating NBC anchor, 'we are about to witness what still is…still is, ladies and gentlemen,' he repeated himself as so many people on TV seem to think they have to, to get attention – as if what he'd just said might be fake news – 'the most exciting two minutes in sport. I'm telling you, folks, you can't beat tradition and we've got buckets of it for you here today at Churchill Downs. Buckets of it. And we'll be right back in a moment with the lovely Nancy, who is going to find out from none other than Charles Barkley who he likes in today's 145th Run for the Roses. Stay tuned for Sir Charles!'

Bigley put down his microphone and listened to whatever was being piped into his ear. 'Right, right, ok. Thank you, sir. What can I say? May the best horse win.'

I guess that's what someone like Luke Skywalker would say if put on the spot to pick a winner, thought Beagle as he eased himself out of the clutches of NBC and headed back up to bullshit with his guests. He felt completely empty and lost and wished he could have got on a spaceship at that moment and beamed himself almost anywhere else but Churchill Downs.

They say that it is never good to count your chickens before they're hatched, but Hector Delmontez was one of those guys who seemed bullet-proofed from superstition. On the roll that he was enjoying, he appeared to be literally able to walk on water, as his Fully Loaded broke on top, sped over to the rail, and proceeded to make the 145th Derby into a procession, crossing the wire well clear of his toiling rivals.

The winner returned $4.20 as favourite, at odds fractionally over even money, and chalk players reloaded their glasses.

Mercifully for Billy Beagle, the governor of Kentucky took care of the winner's circle presentations and speech. It was supposedly the best of times. But he knew that, unless he handled things very carefully, the worst could be just around the corner.

◆　◆　◆

At Shenandoah Valley, Derby day was a ritual. The staff had contributed $20 each to the farm's sweepstake, making for a total pool of $240, and Toby had drawn the winner, Fully Loaded, to collect the top prize of $140.

Matt Pearson, whose runner had finished dead-last, pooh-poohed the result from about the three-eighths pole to the wire, grumbling that the winner was 'juiced' and everyone had laughed and chided him as a bad loser and all-round Grinch.

'It's a good thing your name ain't on no program with our horses,' Toby had joked, 'as they wouldn't win nuthin', with your karma, man!'

Matt grumbled some more and muttered under his breath. 'I'm well rid of those bastards! That horse of Trebor's is only sound one day a week. How he even passed the vet to run, beats me. And he went off favourite. Crazy!'

CHAPTER 39

Last Hurrah had trained since the new year at Shenandoah Valley and then been vanned up for the opening of the Fort Erie meet on May 1, along with two three-year-old fillies and Tom Fraser who, it had been decided, would spend the summer working for trainer Ronnie Broadhurst.

Like Matt, Ronnie eschewed the limelight. And the locals, while admiring his way with horses and the resulting strike-rate of winners to runners, nonetheless dismissed him as a bit of an oddity; labelling him a 'homesteader' because he seemed to spend all his time around the barn - raking his shedrow, mowing the lawns, and constantly micro-managing his operation.

During the '60s and '70s, the racetrack had been a major employer. But now, as little more than a subsidized outpost and refuge for those who could not get stalls at Woodbine, it was a shell of its former self. And Ronnie's main issue was getting skilled professional help: veterinarians and blacksmiths.

Tom was a welcome addition to team Broadhurst; in the form of a cheap groom, hot walker, exercise rider, and general dogsbody.

No mention was made of the fact that his aunt was now chanelling him a stipend each month, from the Last Hurrah trust fund. Both men were blissfully content.

The Broadhurst Stable, in Barn 7, was, by design, a small-time operation, with never more than eight horses: a number that Ronnie felt he could comfortably manage himself with just the assistance of two loyal grooms, Gail and Pam, who'd worked off and on for Ronnie for close to ten years. They were Fort Erie locals who worked at the track from May to the end of October, when everything closed for the winter, and then collected unemployment and ducked and dived in various cash-paying jobs until their beloved horses returned each spring.

Jockeys at Fort Erie subsisted on the small purses, from three days of local racing each week, and were more than willing to make an extra few bucks, exercising in the mornings. So, Ronnie made use of their services and he and the girls took care of grooming and hot-walking duties. Having an all-rounder like Tom on board was a luxury that he might not ordinarily have been able to afford. But he realized that he came with the Shenandoah Valley horses and, as they were what made him get out of bed each morning, Tom was an essential part of the package.

How the marriage had been formed had been supremely providential, with Basil Foster experiencing problems with the gooseneck trailer on the way back from Woodbine some years before. Being temporarily forced to lodge two horses overnight in Barn 7, he had been surprisingly impressed with the way in which the sage old man in charge had managed his little stable.

Upon returning to West Virginia, he'd mentioned this to Matt and Vera and the latter had checked the stats to find that Ronnie's win strike-rate was consistently close to thirty per cent – certainly no juice involved, Basil had assured her – and so it had been decided that this would be a good place to stable a couple of horses for the turf at Woodbine, which was also within striking distance of Saratoga, just four hours down Interstate 90.

Fort Erie racetrack was a great place to quietly develop a nice young horse. And Tom appreciated the laid-back culture of the backstretch, taking Rocky to the paddock each day, letting him stand quietly to watch the gardeners mowing the lawns and planting the flowerbeds. Here only he knew the secret of what he was sitting on and, as the partnership settled in for the summer, he knew this was the perfect place to stay under the radar.

This solitude did, however, have its pluses and minuses. There were the quiet times for reflection and tears. Two years had sped by in a cloud of confusion and introspection. When cast adrift, with no warning, it had come as a shock that, with his main mooring gone, so many acquaintances – that's all they were it had turned out to be – just drifted away.

There was Vera and her lifeline. But now there was Pinkie, too. He guessed it was her chaps that had got her that moniker, but it was what was between them that had caught his eye.

The stock, on show at Fort Erie, might not have been top-drawer, but for

Tom, confused and alone, Pinkie was a bright light that had him lingering out on the racetrack, trolling her cuteness.

'Stay away from that one,' a voice had interrupted his stupor one day, on the way back to the barn. 'Take it from an old man. That smile could get you into a lot of trouble,' Ronnie had cautioned. 'Don't think I haven't been watching you.' He smiled as he drew on his cigarette. Tom looked down and patted Rocky, trying to hide his blushes.

'The lads call her Pinkie,' Ronnie had continued. 'She knows she's a tease. You know that she's Guy Curcione's niece? The fellow from Buffalo, with the pork-pie hat that you see around Nicky Niro's barn? Word is that Guy's mob from Boston. Moved to Tonanwanda some years ago. Now he's the man in town. I would be very careful messin' with little Miss Pinkie, if I were you Tom. Just sayin'.'

The trouble was that what Ronnie had told Tom about his crush only made her more alluring. When one day, not long after, she followed him into the paddock on his routine walk back from the racetrack on Rocky, their collision had been inevitable.

'Them flowers are so—ooo pretty, don't you think?' she'd opened, letting her mount graze the grass border, taking her long, pink-clad legs out of the stirrups and letting them dangle beguilingly.

Tom found himself pleasantly trapped.

'Boy, you're handsome, ain't ya?' his new riding friend continued, as Tom blushed. 'Don't see class like that down here too often.'

Tom didn't know what to say, mumbling, 'Thank you,' before being brought back down to earth by, 'He a two-year-old? Don't say. He's outstanding!'.

'Well, thank you. He is kinda special.' Tom composed himself and wanted to say, 'as are you,' but thought better. 'Yes, we like him.'

'Well, we'll be seein' ya,' Pinkie purred, picking up her mount's head and giving him a tap in the ribs with her well-polished boots. 'We gotta get back to the barn, mister. It's sure been nice meetin' ya!'. And much to the horror of the onlooking gardeners, she trotted away across the middle of the beautifully manicured paddock lawn.

Tom thought to himself, 'They ain't gonna say nuthin', to a chick like you.'

◆　◆　◆

Pinkie became a fascination. She'd never mentioned her name. But now he knew her and she knew him – and had apparently gone out of her way to make contact. Tom was obsessed, but wise enough to not bother Ronnie for more information. Maybe Gail or Pam would know? The former lived in Buffalo. Indeed, she was Italian, too, thought Tom. Maybe she'll know something about the Curciones?

The morning routine became much more fun, as Tom stalked his muse. The smiles and 'hiyas' cheered his visits to the track and accelerated slow gallops to trail that sumptuous pink apparition. She was hot and she knew it and, for the first time in over two years, Tom's primary thoughts were for something other than sad reflections.

Unfortunately, Ronnie's time-consuming requirements in the barn meant that, by the time he'd finished his chores each morning, the object of Tom's increasing desires had always fled the track. Gone to where? No one seemed to know. Pam suggested that her dad only allowed her to indulge her aspirations of one day being a jockey provided she passed her accounting exams. So, it was off to school when the track closed at about 10:30 – but somehow Tom didn't see Pinkie as a future bean-counter. She was far too glamourous for that.

'I know she drives a black Mustang,' Gail had said. 'Saw her with her dad around Nicky Niro's barn, after the races one day. Pretty sleek-looking car. I guess she's somebody's baby?' she'd added, which riled Tom.

The more Tom learned about Miss Pinkie, the more fascinated he became. He started hanging out with two exercise riders he'd met who worked the starting gate in the afternoons, hoping to get the story, but being too shy to profess his intentions. Everyone knew everyone in the small community of Fort Erie, it seemed, except the object of his attentions. And Ronnie, wise old Ronnie, was not doing anything to help the cause.

Maybe he was just too innocent? But sometimes forces have a way of saving souls, even if they do not want to be saved. Despite Ronnie's wise counselling, it had taken too much beer one lazy afternoon and a bunch of salacious tales before the lights went on.

Bruce Hammond and Crazy Bob, the Pony Boy – the latter likely did have a real name but nobody on the track called him anything else which, with his dubious past, was probably just as well – worked the gate and when consecutive races were run out of the chute at the three-quarter-mile pole, the lads would pop down the bank, between races, to grab a brewski in the Grand Trunk Tavern, just across Gilmour Road. The GT was a typical roadhouse bar, rumoured to be owned by bikers, that featured a regular cast of strippers to entertain bored locals, and it was after spending a rare afternoon off, there, that Tom's hopes had been dashed.

Bruce galloped horses for Nicky Niro and, with the races over and his sixth Molson Canadian on the table, he was letting everyone know what he thought about the afternoon's action. 'You know,' he began, 'you guys haven't figured out my man, Nicky, yet. The man's a genius, pullin' the fuckin' wool over youse guys faces, and nobody messes with him, right?'

'Yeah, but I hear he had a bit of trouble at Commodore last week,' Crazy Bob laughed. He pronounced the grim Ohio racetrack on the southern shores of Lake Erie 'Co-mo-door,' like a porcelain Victorian chamber pot. Nobody in the GT had ever heard of one of them, but they knew what he was talking about. Tom's ears were on stalks and the beer was making the stripper, who was winding herself around a pole on the stage to the beat of some monotonous hip-hop sound, start to look very inviting.

'Yeah, actually, his man, Beetle, is a bit lucky to be alive. He and Birdie only just made it out of there. Curcione's people call the shots down there, or think they do, anyways. And, at feed time, this guy comes in the barn and asks, "Where's the runner in the fourth, tonight?" and Beetle says "Who are you?" Bob laughed at the thought. "Never you mind," the guy said, "We're Guy Curcione's people, the boss said to give this to the runner in the fourth", and Beetle did what he was told. Can you believe that dumb fuck?' He laughed again. 'Now it's time to take Cheap Trick over – that's who it was. That classy old son-of-a-gun that Nicky took off Frank Passero for a nickle, last fall – and CT, that's what they call him in the barn, is lying down asleep. He don't wanna run in no race. He's out for the count, with whatever Matey's given him.' Tom listened, fascinated, as his gaze kept being drawn to the writhing form to his left.

'Cut a long story short,' Bob chugged more beer and continued, 'Beetle drags CT over to the paddock. Poor CT's leanin' on 'im. Now his boss comes into the paddock and says, "What the fuck? What's goin' on with CT? He looks like he wants to lie down." And Beetle tells him that his man came by. And Nicky says "What man?" By this time Bob was laughing hysterically and went to choking. 'Gawd. Gotta give up them smokes – anyway Nicky's pissed, so he runs over to Gus Sciola, their guy in Cleveland, and says, "Who's on the lead?" and Gus says, the two-horse. So, what happens? Everyone bets on the two-horse and CT falls out of the gate and trails the field. Easy as pie. But then the two-horse looks like he's run into a brick wall, at the top of the stretch, and starts stopping and, to make matters really bad, CT seems to have woken up. The stuff they gave him must have numbed his pains. Anyway, CT comes runnin' down the lane and gets up to win in a photo. Nicky heads straight for the parking lot. Beetle gets back to the barn and there's two guys there looking for Nicky, and they don't look too friendly. Beetle says that Nicky's gone home. And they say, "What the fuck." But I guess they only had instructions to take care of Nicky – so Beetle, Birdie, and CT got out of there, by the skin of their teeth.'

The table burst into raptuous laughter, envisaging two thugs with baseball bats and Beetle and Birdie wondering, 'What the fuck?' Tom could not believe what he'd just heard and excused himself for a leak. Then he saw her.

In her chaps she was a stunner. Now, as she gyrated her curvaceous naked form in front of a table of lecherous patrons, he gasped and ducked into the bathroom, hoping that she hadn't seen him.

'Hot as hell, ain't she?' said a gruff voice at the urinal beside him. 'Calls herself Brandy Wine. Boy, I could sure drink some of that.'

Tom was appalled – hopes dashed – and looking for an emergency exit. The only solace was that Brandy Wine had disappeared from the stage when he returned to the bar. It was time to leave.

The worst thing was that the next morning Miss Pinkie was there again, bobbing her cute backside in front of him as they galloped down the lane. 'Hello boys,' she said cheekily as Tom came alongside on Rocky. 'Boy you're looking good today.'

Tom didn't know what to say when he pulled up and returned directly to the barn.

'I hear you had a few beers in the GT,' said Ronnie, just in passing, as he made the feeds up later.

'Yes,' said Tom meekly.

'I hear those boys were telling you about the fuck up at Commodore?'

Nothing was further away in Tom's mind. 'Yes,' was all he could say, as the image that he had seen in the GT played over and over in his mind.

'That tells you something,' said Ronnie. 'At a track like Commodore you have two types of horses. Them that once could run and are now at Commodore because it's the end of the road and they are being patched up with whatever drugs their trainers can find to squeeze the last few dollars out of them, before they head off to the glue factory. And those who can't because they are so slow they don't run fast enough to hurt themselves. It's a bit like the first group, the old stakes horses, are Ferraris, E-Types and Lamborginis who had and still have big engines, but their shocks are fucked and their tires flat so they don't run so sweetly anymore, or very rarely without the maximum help. The others, the cheap bastards that have no ability, are like ride-on lawn mowers and golf carts, by comparison. They may chug along, but they have no gas. No class. So when you get an old guy like Cheap Trick and he gets given a dose of the good stuff, to numb his pains, he suddenly feels good. And whoosh, he gallops along and passes all the little cheap guys, because his big engine is still better, even though it might now not be running on all cylinders, than their little two-stroke motors. I love classy old horses like CT. You put the work in, give them a little TLC, and don't race them too often or where they don't belong, and they'll reward you, big-time.'

Tom was staring off into the distance, thinking about Brandy Wine. Maybe that was what the mob guys at Commodore had given dear old CT?

'I don't want to say this again, Tom. Stay away from the GT. Give guys like Bruce Hammond and Crazy Bob a wide birth. They may think what happened the other day was funny, but its stuff like that that gives our sport a bad name. They're not horsemen. Think about it. PETA would love a story like that, to support their notions that horse racing is cruel. I hate to see a classy old horse like CT in the hands of clowns like Niro and his crew. As much as Matt despises guys like Trebor, he and your Aunt Vera would not be happy to hear that you are involved with people like that.'

'Our sport is under the microscope. The antis would like to ban it, like they have fox hunting in the UK and greyhound racing in Florida. These people don't understand the horse business, for whatever reason. They don't understand farming, how meat gets on your plate. You have livestock, you know, so you're gonna have to deal with deadstock, ok? It's that simple.'

'Nobody who loves animals likes to see them get hurt or, in extreme cases, get put down, but that's the way it is. Your Aunt Vera and Matt, particularly Matt, they can't bear to lose a horse. I think Matt actually prefers horses to people. Do you hear me, Tom?'

'I guess,' Tom muttered.

'We all want to win. To pay bills and get ahead. And there are some guys who will sail very close to the wind, to get an edge. You can't blame them for trying. But doping to stop a horse from winning is not only dangerous for the horse and rider, but dishonest and, in fact, criminal.' Tom grimaced. 'Focus on what we're doing, ok? And stay away from those people I was telling you about. That type of disregard for animals is unforgivable. Such people should not be allowed to be around horses.' Ronnie drew hard on his cigarette, as he rattled on. 'Oh, and by the way,' he continued, 'there's a new girl coming tomorrow, to gallop horses for us. Her name is Sara. A figure skater, I believe, from Buffalo. Comes from a good family, I hear. Now there could be one for you to set your sights on.'

'What sights?' said Tom, thinking about his next trip to the GT.

◆ ◆ ◆

Following their big day at Newmarket, Ravi and Kulbir had received an invitation to meet with Sheikh Ali at his house in Belgravia. The Sheikh had been so gracious after the 2000 Guineas and they now found him at his most charming, as he welcomed them into his beautifully appointed drawing room and introduced them once more to Jos Danvers and Hugo Lascelles.

'We are here today for two reasons,' he started the conversation. 'First, I have asked my two friends,' and he indicated Danvers and Lascelles, 'to enter into discussions, on my behalf, to purchase a part of your wonderful horse, Java Raja.' The unexpected news made Ravi blink. 'We know that we have a very special colt, in Prince Ali, and that he will go on and, God willing – Inshallah – win the Derby at Epsom in a month's time,' he continued, 'so we fully realize just how special your horse is to have beaten him in the manner that he did.'

'Indeed,' the two bloodstock agents muttered in harmony, 'a splendid performance. Really top class.'

Ravi smiled, remembering Bog's and Geoffrey Gilligan's assessment of their horse: wondering if Bog had been consigned to the doghouse?

'We won't be so vulgar as to discuss any numbers, at this time,' the Sheikh continued. 'I leave such things up to these chaps to figure out.'

'Best to talk to our man Algy Sinclair, as he knows more about Java Raja and what he's worth,' said Kulbir, cutting to the quick and eliciting a wry smile from Danvers, as the latter ruminated over the fact that they could have had all of him for three hundred and fifty thousand dollars. Bog would be made to suffer for this.

'That's settled, then. You gentlemen will liaise with Algy?'

'And what happens if he says that we shouldn't sell him? He's not for sale,' asked Kulbir.

The Sheikh looked up, a bit startled, regained his composure, and smiled. 'Oh, he'll persuade you to sell a part of him. Just think how much fun we are all going to have together, not to mention the fact that he'll earn himself a nice little commission, me thinks,' he said with a wink. 'Now then, the other matter, Real Racing. My brother Sheikh Sultan and I were very pleased with the positive feedback we got from the sweepstake at the Dubai World Cup meet. In fact, it was the highlight of the entire spring meeting. Our local fans are still buzzing about it and wondering when there will be a follow up. When is the next race?' he glanced at his two guests.

'I think we have another one planned for Bangalore in the fall,' said Ravi.

'That would be going backwards,' insisted the Sheikh. 'I know you guys have a deal worked out with the Bangalore authorities and the Indian government. But, having made the big jump to Dubai, you must now press on and get bigger and better.'

'Well, yes, we do have plans to do this and we will be featuring the Melbourne Cup in early November, in conjunction with our original partners TAB,' said Kulbir.

'How about here in England?' the Sheikh gushed. 'How about a race at the Royal Ascot meeting next month? The Hunt Cup, for example?'

'We met with Lord Magnall of the Jockey Club and people from The Tote last year, and they told us that such a concept would be unworkable here, in England, because of objections from monopolies regulators and, of course, the bookmakers,' Ravi replied.

'That was then, and this is now,' the Sheikh rolled on. 'And that is where these two gentlemen come in. They know the people you talked to. How should I put it?' He hesitated. 'They went to the same schools as these people. They speak the same language. They have a network. That's how it still gets done, you know. Amazing, actually, that anything gets done when you see just how dim some of them are,' he added, laughing heartily as Danvers and Lascelles sat meekly on a sofa, their hands clasped between their knees, looking down at the floor and grinning sheepishly.

See, thought Kulbir. 'The old boy's network; if it's not their idea they want no part of it, especially if it comes from two Indians. Two bounders from the colonies.'

'Chubby Magnall has got racing's best interests at heart,' Danvers volunteered, after an awkward silence, 'and after hearing from him about the great success in Dubai – indeed he was there, so he saw it for himself – the Jockey Club would, I'm sure, now be very interested in sharing a piece of your pie.'

'Exactly,' said the Sheikh excitedly, 'this is a cyber property, it could be hosted from anywhere, but India is perfect for so many reasons. You had the scale to get things going. You have the technical knowhow, and now, after several races that have just got bigger and better each time, you have the confidence of the general public to administer and manage the process in a trustworthy manner. We – ha! ha! – my brother and I count ourselves very fortunate to have got in at the ground level. We believe, from our perspective, as owners who have profited greatly – not just monetarily but from our own personal pleasure, too – that this is a way to give back to racing and the punters. I know that these sweepstakes are generating millions for great causes, but the rekindling of the flame is also important. Horse racing has been losing its customer base. By making it into a form of cheap and easily accessible entertainment for the masses, we are introducing a huge new audience that will generate increased media coverage and you know that that attracts sponsors and advertisers.'

'So, do you think that the BHA and The Tote would be interested in revisiting our proposal?' asked Ravi.

'You bet,' said the Sheikh. 'That's why these two gentlemen are here. I'll let Jos tell you how to approach them.'

'Thank you, Sheikh Ali,' said Danvers. 'The Sheikh is right. Racing does need a shot in the arm. Simply put, there is not enough money being returned for investment in the future from profits made on gambling and particularly from so-called offshore operators. You could say that the Motti-Media endeavour, with Real Racing, is in effect one of those, but you have done wonders in a very short time with proceeds and it would be stupid of the BHA not to work with you because your pool concept bypasses bookmakers who have always been the scourge of our sport.'

'Yes. And getting regulators to approve popular charitable causes is a lot easier than, say, merely propping up a sport that many people consider to be elitist,' added Lascelles.

'Indeed,' said Kulbir. 'But, as Sheikh Ali has just said, the benefits to racing come through raising the profile of the sport to a new audience and further residual revenues generated from TV advertising. And, actually, increased betting all round, because once the new audience starts to understand the sport, they are likely to participate more in it, go to the races, and have a bet.'

'And,' Sheikh Ali butted in, 'on a race-by-race basis, as total global sales increase, each contract can include licensing or management fees for local hosts.'

Ravi and Kulbir had gone into the meeting unsure of what it was all about and when they left, just over two hours later, it seemed like their business on the turf was about to change dramatically.

The following day, Tony Palgrave-Brown of BCH&H and the firm's senior partner, Sam Hall, accompanied them to Portman Square, where the reception from Lord Magnall and his chums was altogether different. They were now the owners of a Classic winner, no less, and in Hall and Palgrave-Brown they were in the right company. That their little enterprise, that had been summarily and humiliatingly dismissed the last time they had been there, had since then become a global phenomenon that had generated hundreds of millions of dollars, was keenly appreciated. Ravi and Kulbir knew why they were there and enjoyed the moment, as Magnall's revisionist chatter maintained that they'd always thought it was a brilliant idea, but 'our hands have been tied by the bookmakers.'

'But, if you can't beat 'em, you might as well join 'em,' a supporting voice had guffawed.

'Well, actually, not,' Sam Hall had interrupted him. 'You can't do that off your own bat, here in England,' and, he thought to himself, you wouldn't have a clue how to start or promote such a concept, anyway, but continued, 'We now live in a world that is more closely linked than ever before. However, in so many ways such connection that should make doing business easier is, in fact, shackled by local and regional regulations and laws. And that is why my clients represent a unique way to bypass all of this in a perfectly legitimate manner that will be beneficial to all parties.' He went on, 'This is not a new concept. People have been running sweepstakes seemingly forever, some legit, many fraudulent. What is special about Real Racing is the vehicle. And the management, security, integrity, call it what you like, is key at a time when people are so concerned about hacking and the security of their own personal information. Thanks to the incredibly bright IT staff running this whole operation, from their offices in Bangalore, we believe that it is beyond reproach.'

'Can't someone just start up a rival endeavour, in Russia or China?' someone asked.

'Theoretically, they could,' Hall continued. 'But it will come down to two things: scale and credibility. That is why my clients are interested in forming partnerships with horse racing's authorities, in countries where the sport is best established. Neither Russia nor China have any history or a reputation for top-class racing and, to be perfectly fair, I don't think the man in the street trusts either to run an operation like the one we're talking about, either properly or free from corruption.'

There were quite a few 'Here, heres,' and it was agreed that representatives of Motti-Media, the BHA, and The Tote would get together to discuss staging a Real Racing sweepstakes on a future race.

As they left the meeting, Kulbir announced, 'So much for a race at Ascot next month. Sheikh Ali will be disappointed.'

'Progress, brother. That was a big move forward,' replied Ravi.

'Indeed,' chuckled Hall, 'the dinosaurs were moving. You set their tails on fire. You did well!'

◆　◆　◆

Prince Ali duly won the Epsom Derby at the beginning of June, franking the Guineas form. When his Newmarket conqueror extended his unbeaten streak to six, in the Group 1 St. James' Palace Stakes at Royal Ascot, the big news was that Sheikh Ali Al-Bhakandar had purchased a fifty percent interest in the classic-winning colt for £12 million pounds from his Indian partner and the founder of Real Racing, Ravi Singh of Bangalore, India.

The deal had been expertly brokered, with inside guidance from Marcus Townsend, by Algy Sinclair of Anglian Bloodstock. When asked to handle this far from insignificant deal, Algy had been simultaneously flattered and terrified. But the cool hand of Townsend, and sound advice and reminders from Mark O'Malley in Kentucky, had ended up making what could have been a drawn out and awkward process very straightforward. Acting on behalf of his main client, Jos Danvers had kept Johnny Ward-Clarke well out of the way.

Townsend, who knew Java Raja better than anyone, had suggested to Maltie, at the CBS agency, to put together a package for Sheikh Ali that confirmed that his Canadian pedigree traced back through some of the best mares at Windfields Farms all the way to Northern Dancer, as he knew that the Sheikh was a big fan of that bloodline.

Kulbir had wondered about twenty million and asked about a second opinion. But Algy had pointed out that that wasn't the way such deals were transacted, and that, in the current climate, £12 million pounds for half put a value of around $30 million on the colt. Which was, he reminded him, a good return on an initial outlay of $350,000. Besides, both he and Townsend had pointed out the not inconsiderable fringe benefits of being part of Team Bhakandar.

CHAPTER 40

It was now mid-June and Ronnie Broadhurst had started letting Rocky run along a bit, in company. The colt had thrived over the past two months and shown signs that he would have the speed to win over three quarters of a mile.

Like Matt Pearson, Ronnie believed that speed was inbuilt, you couldn't instill it. It was just a natural talent. So his early workouts were very much controlled affairs.

Tom was lean. All the same his five-foot-nine frame, while being ok for a steeplechase rider turning the scales at 135 pounds, wasn't ideal for serious work. But Ronnie preferred keeping the same riders on horses because they got to know one another. For him, someone with good hands and a quiet temperament mattered a lot more than a few pounds.

Rocky had a long and steady foundation under his belt before a series of three-eighths and half-mile breezes at Fort Erie, in modest times of 37 and 50 plus seconds. On the face of it, as a son (purportedly) of Last Call, whom no one at Woodbine or Fort Erie had ever heard of, he had attracted no attention. Ronnie was none the wiser and Tom, as Matt had warned him to, kept his head down and passed few remarks about the handsome colt.

He had dropped into the GT a couple of times, on the off chance of having a word with Pinkie. But she had disappeared. Gone to Toronto to make more money, he'd been told. So no more distractions, to his boss's relief.

Clockers at Woodbine appreciated that runners sent up from Fort Erie by trainer Broadhurst had a healthy strike rate and should not be ignored, regardless of their past performances and pedigree. So, it was with keen interest that observers watched the colt, Last Hurrah, when he was shipped in early one morning for a half-mile work out on the main track.

Woodbine, with sixteen hundred horses in residence, was a much bigger and busier racetrack than little Fort Erie, with an all-weather surface. But the dark bay colt with the prominent star took it in his stride.

◆　◆　◆

Whatever issues he might have been experiencing off the track, Hector Delmontez's good fortunes on it continued. It just seemed that wherever horses owned by Haras del Condor, Caledonia Farms, America's Stable, or whatever other partnership he was engaged in, ran, they figured prominently. And a major part of this success was put down to Hall of Fame trainer, Tim Trebor.

Trebor had started out training quarter horses in Arizona and had graduated to the California circuit, with a few thoroughbreds that, over the years and his many successes, had expanded to over a hundred: at sometimes as many as five or six racetracks. His main bases were Santa Anita, in Los Angeles, and Belmont Park, on Long island, New York, with satellites in Kentucky, Chicago and, each winter, Florida.

A slick promoter who made sure that his name was always prominent in racing circles, regardless of the season, and how his string might have been performing at any one given time, when it came to the sales he was at his most effective – reeling in new clients.

Critics decried his 'send 'em and burn 'em' methods,' and his overall shotgun approach. And the mere mention of his name to horsemen like Matt Pearson and Ronnie Broadhurst sent them into hysterics, but nobody could argue with on track earnings, where perennially he topped all lists.

The partnership with Hector Delmontez's horses was ideal: an absent owner, who always paid his bills on time, sent him a seemingly endless supply of horses, and never complained about the occasional breakdown or euthenization. Furthermore, those in his syndicates, and particularly the newer members from Russia, were turning out to be welcome new fodder when it came to sales time, with deep pockets and apparently not a great deal of caution or knowledge.

Fully Loaded had landed Trebor his fifth Kentucky Derby earlier in the year and, although side-lined indefinitely with an undisclosed problem, the Trebor train continued rolling along at an even, for him, higher pace of close to a 30% win rate.

Trebor had even ventured up to Canada and won a Grade 1 stakes race on the turf at Woodbine for Delmontez the previous year, though, in principle, he'd stayed away from Ontario because, as he put it, 'they were too tough up there.' Quite what that meant had perplexed some people. But those that were not his greatest fans maintained that it was because local regulations for race-day medication were far tougher than at most American racetracks. That was, anyway, until Hector Delmontez had come along and now the Trebor express was enjoying surprisingly regular success north of the border, where his small satellite operation of twenty horses was superintended by Danny Johnson.

Canada's top race for Canadian-bred three-year-olds was coming up. And the Canadian, or rather Russian division, as Hector was increasingly becoming aware that it had become, had high hopes for a lightly raced colt bred by Calvin Weiner and Mike Rogers, called Pravda. So Hector decided that this would be a good opportunity to combine a little business with pleasure.

Held almost two months after the Kentucky Derby, towards the end of June, the Queen's Plate is one of the oldest continuously run Stakes races in North America. And, along with a one million dollar purse, the winner gets 100 guineas from the sovereign and often the chance to meet royalty, if they happen to be in Canada and attend the races.

This was an occasion for Senora Delmontez to dress up and party with her husband's ultra-rich clients that she could not miss. Even Hector, upon the advice of his host Cal Weiner, donned a top hat and tails for the big day.

Of complete insignificance to Hector and his smart crowd, who'd flown into town a few days early to party with Cal Weiner at his cottage on Lake Muskoka, was the fact that finally Ronnie Broadhurst had picked out a spot for Last Hurrah (Rocky) to make his debut: a two-year-old maiden (for horses who have never won a race), going six furlongs for a purse of $52,000, carded as the first of twelve races that late-June Sunday.

It had been a big surprise for the Elevator Stable – except, of course, Vera, whom Tom had kept abreast of developments – when Last Hurrah appeared in the entries.

'So exciting,' she had said upon receiving a barrage of texts. 'Sometimes it's best not to know what's going on, because usually it's bad news. And then you fret over stuff that invariably doesn't turn out to be as bad as you thought, and you then wonder why you lost sleep over it and were so worried. You know what I mean?' she'd said.

'Nice try,' Reggie had joked. 'We are like the proverbial mushrooms.'

'Well, aren't you excited?' Vera had gone on to say, 'Debuting on Queen's

Plate Day. Are you going to go? You'd look very dashing in a topper, Reggie!'

Humbug, thought Reggie. 'Too short notice. Can't make it up there. I'll rely on my partners to represent me.'

The headlines of the *Daily Racing Form* proclaimed Pravda as the one to make news in the Queen's Plate. In the first race, the nine-horse in a field of twelve, Last Hurrah's byline from the resident Woodbine handicapper merely stated, 'Fort Erie Shipper. Watch Once,' with morning line odds of 20/1. The workouts were promising but not spectacular, even though he'd had a Woodbine trial about a week previously, with Joe Magee up, in which they'd motored a rapid 59 and change from the gate. Magee, a man of few words, had been impressed. But this was traditionally a pretty tough race, where some of the best local two-year-olds often debuted. So 20/1 was fair enough for a colt by a horse nobody in Canada had ever heard of.

In the receiving barn, the Ontario racing commission veterinarian, Dr. Blender, checked out Rikki, who had an engagement on the turf, and the debuting Rocky upon their arrival; examining their passports, confirming their lip tattoos, and asking Tom to trot them up, so he could observe how they travelled and that they were, in his opinion, fit to race.

For Rocky, the increased hustle and bustle was exciting, and he stood attentively at his webbing, looking out at the action around him, as other horses shipped into the receiving barn. Rikki the veteran, on the other hand, after his inspection was over, lay down for a nap on his bed of peat moss. Nothing to eat before races. So he figured he might as well save energy.

Ronnie and Tom then went over to the racing secretary's office to confirm their arrival and check the latest scratches for the day, which is where Tom ran into his old nemesis.

Holding court with Wally Wood, the *Daily Racing Form's* chief Canadian correspondent, Hector was, as usual, surrounded by his designer entourage. Amongst the local crowd of largely unkempt trainers, owners, and jockey's agents in their jeans, flannel shirts, and cowboy boots, they stood out a mile.

Hector's year-round tan appeared deeper, set off that morning against the pastel colours of his neatly pressed beige khakis and a pale yellow golf shirt: his greying hair swept back over his ears, under a pink baseball cap with the bold black letters PRAVDA.

Tom spotted him immediately and his first reaction was not to make eye contact, but he'd been unable to ignore the bevy of trim ladies and was inevitably spotted by their genial host. 'Hola!' Hector exclaimed loudly. 'Mi amigo, Tom! Tom Fraser.'

Tom smiled. The entrance and gathering area to the racing secretary's office, where so much of the liaising regarding which jockey would be riding which horse and all other manner of racetrack business is traditionally conducted, was full with about fifty people, all chatting at the same time. So the buzz somewhat drowned out his response.

'Senor Delmontez, great to see you, sir,' said Tom shaking the South American's hand and smiling warmly at his friends. 'I'm spending the summer up here in Canada at Fort Erie racetrack with some of my aunt's horses. We run two today. A two-year-old in the first and Rikki Tikki Tavi, in the stake, on the turf.'

Hector took his program out of his pocket and looked at the two races. 'Oh, Rikki. I remember him. Eee-er finish a-seconda to my horse at Pimlico, el Matador, El supremo Cordobes. Oh, what a tragedy! Such a great horse.'

'Yes,' said Tom, hoping that Hector would not enquire about Rocky. And, fortunately, he didn't get a chance to ask that question, as Wally Wood wanted to know more about Rikki, now making his second appearance at Woodbine. So Tom gave him the usual spiel and touched on Victor Todd and Colin Nightingale being natives of Toronto. Across the room he could see Ronnie signalling that he was going to the kitchen to get something to eat, which gave Tom the excuse he needed to disengage himself.

'Gotta go, I'm afraid. So nice to see you, your horses and Caledonia are all doing so well.' He turned to the ladies. 'One day I want Senor Delmontez to tell me his secret.'

'And what secret is that?' said Hector, frowning ever so slightly, which Tom did not miss. 'Oh, just how to get so many pretty girls all the time!' The girls giggled as their host recomposed himself and grinned.

'Ta luego!' said Tom, with a wave aimed at las senoritas.

The Plate, as the locals call it, is still a relatively big deal, even though horse racing receives minimal coverage from the Canadian sports media these days. And as luck would have it, there weren't any other sporting events taking place in the city that weekend, with the Blue Jays out of town. So, with a fine day forecast, a good crowd of around thirty thousand was expected, despite the fact that no royalty would be on hand.

Many would be once-a-year visitors, with wives who saw the occasion as a rare opportunity to don a hat. With five stakes races, twelve full fields, the handle would exceed $10 million, roughly four times that of a regular day.

This last factor appealed greatly to the members of the Elevator Stable who, despite being somewhat blindsided by their trainer, still had high expectations for their debuting two-year-old. It was, as Reggie said, a good day for value because such a high percentage of the money bet on track was from ill-informed sources. Back on the farm, Vera thought the same. But she knew something that her other fellow syndicate members did not: they were running the ultimate ringer in the easiest spot he'd ever find himself. Once people had seen this son of Last Call perform, she knew, his pedigree wouldn't put off anyone in future races and he might never start at twenty to one again.

Ronnie Broadhurst was an all-round horseman. Nonetheless, fans at Woodbine had never really considered him to be someone who had his two-year-olds ready to win first time out. So, when Tom took Rocky over to the large Willow tree-lined paddock behind the impressive Woodbine stands, it wasn't all that surprising that he was still listed at twenty-five to one on the odds boards.

Tim Trebor's local rep, Danny Johnson, had the 2/1 favourite, Mayan Warrior, who had run a good second in his first and only start. Tom spotted him with Hector, two tall men with beards whom he didn't know, and the girls he'd seen in the racing secretary's office that morning, along with Senora Delmontez and Samantha Weiner, all dressed up to the nines.

Calvin Weiner, resplendent in top hat and tails, also had a runner: King's Comet, who had run twice, and been a good, closing third last time out and was equipped with blinkers for the first time. Tom could see Cal talking to his trainer, Jerome Lavigne, and a tall, thin man in a light grey suit and reflector sunglasses.

The first race of a long afternoon featuring twelves races, with the Queen's Plate scheduled for a 5:45 post time, had attracted a good crowd around the paddock, despite the fact that many were still enjoying their lunches in the fourth-floor dining rooms of the Turf Club.

Victor Todd was doing something he never thought he'd do: escorting Gladys, his wife of thirty-five years, to the races. While theirs had been a long and happy marriage, the racetrack had always been his exclusive domain. Victor had been a good husband, successful in his accounting business, and generous to a tee. So Gladys figured that he deserved his indulgence, even though she had no time for gambling.

Today, though, was a tradition in the Toronto social calendar and, what the heck, the Todd family having an interest in two runners on Queen's Plate Day, that was something she could not miss. No matter that Victor had poured cold water on the event and impressed upon her that she'd have a miserable time amongst a crowd of drunken and immoral people, and on a Sunday!

For the day, Gladys had on her best beige twin set, that she kept for special church outings, offset by a rust-coloured, wide-brimmed straw hat. The meticulous Victor sported his standard racetrack outfit with a special yellow polka-dot bow tie, and a small yellow rose in his buttonhole. Colin, not to be outdone, had thought he'd look stupid in a 'claw-hammer,' as he'd referred to a morning coat, amongst a crowd of people dressed from jeans and T-shirts to top hats and tails. So his yellow trousers and pale blue jacket complimented the colourful scene.

Ronnie, whose wife Brenda had bullied him into putting on a jacket and tie, grinned grimly as he shook Victor and Gladys's hands.

The horses, who had now been saddled, walked around the attractive paddock, their coats gleaming in the bright sunshine. Leading Rocky, Tom's mind wandered. Here they were, just over two years after the fire. So much had happened and the two of them had come so far. They were, he mused, all that was left. This was it. We're going to find out in a few minutes, mate, whether there could be a happy ending.

So relaxed were the pair that, when Ronnie called him to stop so that Joe Magee could mount, they could well have been back at Tanglewood: Rocky dozing in the shade and Tom chewing on a stalk of Timothy, to the tune of the buzzing bees. It's a long way that you have come, little man, he mused, thinking back to what it must have been like during the frantic ride from the blazing barn in Kentucky to the tranquility of Shenandoah.

'Riders up! Riders up!' called the paddock steward as Joe Magee popped aboard, his long legs straddling his mount while he tied a knot in his reins.

Ronnie's regular pony girl, Rita, took Rocky from Tom and he and Ronnie retreated to a small stand for grooms, not far from the winner's circle. Tom had no idea whether Ronnie had had a bet, as he never let on whether he liked his horses or not: usually just mumbling generalities like 'nice horse, gotta chance,' to all solicitations. And eventually people gave up asking because they knew he always said the same about every horse, whether he liked them or not. But, in this case, his standard observation would have been a fair one, as he honestly didn't know the real story. And Tom, feeling the butterflies in his tummy and realizing just what an important moment was approaching, decided to let Rocky run without his money, as a win would be more of a reward in so many ways than any bet he might cash.

Upstairs, on the third floor, Victor excused himself from Gladys and made his way from the clubhouse down into the grandstand, where he hoped no one who knew him would see him. He needn't really have worried because the crowds swallowed him up and any association between him, the Elevator Stable, and the nine-horse, Last Hurrah, was lost amongst the din. When he called out his Daily Double wheel on the first and second races, the noise was so drowning that even the mutual clerk had difficulty picking up his soft, Jamaican-accented voice.

Back in their seats, the Todds waited nervously as the horses were loaded. Colin, who had placed his own bets, relayed back commentary as he studied the field through his binoculars, circling behind the gate. Mayan Warrior had shortened to 6/5, as the boisterous crowd loaded up on the first favourite of the afternoon, looking to play thereafter with the house's money.

One floor above, outside the Turf Club lounge, Hector, Tim Trebor, and Danny Johnson trained their binoculars on their colt. He'd looked very on his toes in the paddock and had now broken out into a light sweat. Loaded first, into the one-hole, he waited for the rest of the field while his connections fretted.

The bell rang. The starting gate's doors slammed open onto their magnets and the crowd roared as the track announcer, Daryl Walker, bellowed for the first time that afternoon: 'And they're off!!'

Bang! As the handler standing beside Rocky in the gate (who'd been holding him straight) suddenly released him, his head went instinctively up and collided with the side of the door. Up above, Joe Magee was hanging on to a handful of mane to allow him to exit without harsh contact with his mouth, so the result was that he very nearly pitched over his frightened mount's head, getting a rude smack in his mouth.

From where he was watching, Ronnie cursed. The announcer confirmed that Last Hurrah had broken slowly and was now trailing the field. 'Mayan Warrior,' he barked, 'by 5, as he sprints to the lead, along the rail.'

Fully fifteen lengths adrift, both Rocky and Joe had mouths full of blood. Rocky had knocked out a tooth and Joe had a broken nose, from which blood was now trickling down into his throat. To compound their misery, the former was getting dirt kicked in his face and the latter found his goggles being sprayed with the blood from his mount's freely bleeding mouth.

'Mayan Warrior turns for home, on his own!' exclaimed the excited announcer. 'They're not going to catch him today. Mayan Warrior by six, from King's Comet and Niagara Nick, with Last Hurrah, rallying along the rail.'

After their disastrous start, it had taken Joe Magee almost a quarter of a mile to settle his startled mount and get him running on his left lead. By that time, they were last by a clear margin, so he was able to track over to the rail. Always mindful of how a first experience was so impressionable upon a young horse, the veteran had not hustled his mount nor given him any wake-up cracks from his whip. This was just six furlongs and their race was, effectively, over. So there was no point making a bad situation worse.

In two-year-old races like these, most horses run scared. Frightened by the bell and the shouting and cracking of whips, they run on one breath for about three-eighths to half a mile and then blow up. The first quarter is covered in about twenty- two seconds and change, the second maybe 23 and change, the third 25 plus. So those up front either hang on grimly or burn out. And, if it's the latter, any impression that those behind are making big moves is only because those in front are stopping.

When it comes to assessing performance, the final quarter is a key indicator: any horse that runs it in 24 seconds or less, particularly off a fast first half-mile, is one to be reckoned with.

Here, Mayan Warrior had run like a typical Tim Trebor special. Cranked up with blinkers after his promising debut, he was ready, broke on top, was not contested, and sped off, blowing the rest of the field away. On the other hand, Last Hurrah had broken in a heap, banged his head, and had a miserable introduction. Yet he had rallied from a hopeless position to finish a closing third, beaten less than three lengths at the wire, and had galloped out so strongly that Joe Magee had had difficulty pulling him up.

When the somewhat beat-up combination had finally returned to be unsaddled in front of the stands, most of the other horses were being led away and Hector and his friends were having their photos taken with the winner. Dismounting, Magee muttered through dried blood and no teeth (having removed his false ones, as he always did before races), 'they won't beat him again,' before heading off to weigh in.

Tom took a sponge full of water and doused out Rocky's mouth. Blowing profusely, the latter's bloodshot and dirt-caked eyes stared bewilderingly at him, as if to say, 'What the fuck?' and Tom gave his charge an affectionate pat. 'You'll be ok, pal. Let's get you back to the barn for a bath and a bit of TLC.'

The large crowd, charged in their wallets by a winning favourite, turned their attention to the second race.

Meanwhile, Victor Todd had been uncharacteristically quiet. After thirty plus years, Gladys knew better than to insert herself at such moments. He wasn't a big bettor by any stretch of the imagination. But like all punters, took a reverse, like the one he had just sustained, very personally. Over the years he knew only too well that its much harder to chase losses than be ahead, playing with the house's money.

Back at the receiving barn, Ronnie watched Rocky walking around the shedrow under his blue-and-white cooler. His number hadn't been called to the test barn, so they were able to inspect their charge, cooling out in the peace and quiet of their own quarters; next to Rikki, who watched on, seemingly without a care in the world.

'That made him blow a bit, didn't it?' said Ronnie, as they watched Rocky gulp from a large bucket of water.

'I know you don't crank them up like some,' commented Tom. 'Even so, no amount of work is quite like a race, especially the very first one.'

Ronnie lit a cigarette and looked around in case security was watching. He was out on the lawn, not actually in the barn, but was always conscious of setting the right example. 'I watched the rerun. They ran fast. That horse of Trebor's was ready today. I think they went in 1.10 and 3. A good time for a two-year-old on this track.'

'What were the fractions?' asked Tom.

'22 and 2, 45 and 3,' Ronnie read from the notes he'd made on his program. 'So, based upon a tick for a length over three quarters of a mile, and five ticks in a second, with our horse at least fifteen lengths adrift of the leader at the half mile pole, to close twelve of them, he had to run the last half-mile in under 46 seconds. And I bet you the last quarter, when he was making up a lot of ground, he would have run close to 23. That's a very good effort. I'll be interested to see what sort of number the speed guys give him and how this time compares to others over this distance today.'

'Yep. Well, all things considered, he's back in one piece. Well, minus a tooth. But it could have been a lot worse,' said Ronnie.

As they headed off for a graze, Tom spoke quietly to his friend. 'If only they knew, buddy, they wouldn't be half so surprised.'

◆　◆　◆

The afternoon unfolded predictably, with TV commentators focusing between races on ladies' fashions, while conducting interviews with local celebrities and stars of the Toronto sports scene, drawn out by the good weather and high-quality racing for their annual visit to Woodbine.

By the ninth race, the mile and an eighth York Stakes on the turf, four favourites had obliged and the crowd, fuelled by these easy plays and a not inconsiderable quantity of alcohol, were basking in the sunshine as Rikki was brought to the paddock.

Sporting what was already promising to be a shiner of a black eye, Joe Magee conversed with Ronnie, Victor, Gladys, and Colin under a willow tree, while Tom led Rikki around the paddock.

'Last time,' Victor suggested to Joe, somewhat tentatively, wondering just how he and Ronnie would take the observation, 'you mentioned that there was no pace and that this hadn't suited Rikki's style of running?'

'Yep,' said the Irishman. 'We'll see how the race develops. But I won't be caught napping this time.'

'He's a bit sharper today,' said Ronnie, 'as he hasn't run for a while. So, you may be able to stay a bit closer?'

'Different ball game, today,' added Joe, as Tom brought Rikki over and he gave Joe a boost into the saddle. 'That was around two turns. This is one. With the long run down the backstretch, they get motoring there and I don't think we'll need to worry about lack of pace today.'

On the board, Rikki was listed at 6/1, in a small-ish field of seven. Being the end of June, there weren't any invaders from Europe, as they presumably had plenty of other targets at home at this time of year, and it appeared that the shippers from the US, one from Kentucky and one from New York, were not top-class. Having licked his wounds in silence, since the first race, Victor boxed Rikki in some Trifectas.

As expected, the race turned out to be right up Rikki's ally. Having saved him, down on the rail, off a good opening three quarters of a mile, Joe brought him through with a big move to take it up inside the eighth pole for an easy score. As he'd hit the front, Victor threw off his inhibitions and turned to bellow to all within earshot, 'Bring 'im home, Joe! Money in the bank! I have Rikki on top, in every combo!' much to Gladys' embarrassment.

'Do you really behave like this, all the time, when I'm not here?' she'd asked.

'Unfortunately, I don't always get the opportunity, woman! But I would if I did!'

'Well, I'm just glad that I don't come that often,' Gladys retorted. 'You're a crazy man, Victor Todd!'

But Victor didn't care. Rikki was his champion and winning on Queen's Plate Day in front of a big local crowd, what could be better than that?

In the winner's circle the trophy was presented by the lovely wife of Toronto Maple Leaf's star Finnish centre Max Glokinnen and Victor, Gladys, and Colin lapped up the moment and even spotted Ronnie smiling. Rikki was his type of horse: you looked after him and he fired every time.

Barring the unfortunate start to Rocky's first race, it had been a good day.

As Tom grazed Rikki after his return from the test barn, and drank a beer that Ronnie had procured from a backstretch bootlegger, they could hear the buzz of the distant crowd in the grandstand, as the day's headliner approached.

Rocky, all done up in four, antiphlogistine applied and feet packed, was munching at his haynet, while surveying the scene. The plan was to put Rikki back in his stall and, a few minutes before post time, pop over to watch the Queen's Plate in the racing secretary's office.

But when Tom and Ronnie arrived there they were met by unexpected silence in the ordinarily busy room. 'Holy fuck!' said someone, 'Jesus! Jesus! Who is that?'

Looking at the TV monitor, it appeared that a group of people were attending to two people who were lying on the ground: both appeared to be men, dressed in tailcoats.

'What happened?' asked someone.

As the gathering crowd watched, the horses could be seen circling in the background. They were saddled and ready to be mounted. Yet all eyes were on the people in the middle of the paddock, where it appeared that security and ambulance personnel were attending to the two stricken men on the ground.

Just then a voice came over the loudspeaker system. 'Ladies and gentlemen, we regret that the races have been suspended. I repeat, there will be no more racing this afternoon. We would appreciate it if you could please leave the grounds as soon as possible.'

'What the hell happened?' said a voice.

'I've just heard from Rob Patton, who is in the paddock, that there has been a shooting.' Everyone listened intently. 'He's not sure who got hurt but thinks one of the people down might be Calvin Weiner.'

A murmur went around the room. 'Rob says that the cops are there and that they've surrounded the paddock and nobody can leave.'

'What a fucking disaster,' said another voice. 'Who would do a thing like this? It makes no sense.'

'We don't know, yet, who it actually is. Whether it's one person or two, or possibly more. Do they have the shooter? If that's what it was. Or did they get away?'

Everyone was riveted to the screen until it suddenly went blank and there was an announcement that the races were cancelled and everyone, who hadn't been told otherwise by the police and Woodbine authorities, should go home.

CHAPTER 41

Toronto is the only city in North America that still has four daily newspapers and the headlines on Monday, June 29, of every one of them featured but one story, 'Assassination at Queen's Plate,' with the news that, as the horses were being paraded at Woodbine racetrack prior to Canada's most feted horse race, an unidentified man had entered the paddock and shot Ontario horseman Michael Rogers, 63, four times from close range, before calmly jumping over the railings on the north side of the Rexdale racetrack and departing at high speed on the back of a waiting motorcycle.

The shooting had shocked the racing community, in which Rogers was a prominent local breeder. Original reports had suggested that there had been two victims, but it turned out that the other man, Calvin Weiner, the CEO of Woodbine, had in fact only fainted and had now been discharged from Etobicoke General Hospital.

Toronto police sergeant Gord Morrison, of 23 Division, had issued a statement confirming the victim and circumstances, but refused to speculate on the motive.

Meanwhile, being the cesspool of gossip that it always is, on the backstretch at Woodbine tongues were wagging. A message had been sent, in broad daylight in front of a large crowd on the biggest day of Canadian horse racing that was being broadcast across the nation and to millions around the world. That anyone would invade such a sacred occasion in such a brazen manner baffled the Canadian public. But, within the tightly knit and incestuous racing community, there were those who were not all that surprised.

It was a bit daring to take out someone so publicly and certainly a shock to law-abiding Canadians, who prided themselves for living in the safest large-scale metropolitan community in North America, that anything like this could have darkened their doors. But Rogers had made his enemies on the racetrack and was known to be a business partner of the highly unpopular Woodbine CEO, Calvin Weiner, whom many blamed for the demise of horse racing in the province of Ontario, per his gross mishandling of the recent CART (Casinos at Race tracks) deal with OCC, the Ontario Casino Corporation.

One unidentified source, who had been standing close to the victim, had told a reporter for the Toronto Star that the shooter had said something to the group in which Rogers had been standing, before making his escape. The police, however, merely confirmed that they were interviewing everyone who had been in the paddock at the time of the shooting and had no further comment to make until their enquiries were completed.

Down at Fort Erie, too, there was only one subject on everyone's mind. As Rikki and Rocky were walked around the shedrow, speculation was rife.

'Mike Rogers got what he deserved,' commented Noel McGovern, as he chatted to Ronnie outside his office. 'You burn enough people, the heat will finally catch up with you,' he added, pulling hard on his cigarette.

'Gee,' said Tom, as he walked by with Rocky, 'I thought you Canadians were so polite. So, so incapable of doing anything like this. This is something only gangsters do. Something you might have seen in The Sting. You know, when the Newman character fucked with Doyle Lonnigan…' He trailed off.

'When it comes down to money, there are no niceties,' said Ronnie. 'It doesn't matter if you are Canadian, American, fucking Russian. You screw someone and they'll get mad. I know Mike Rogers shafted a bunch of well-meaning people over the years and it's stuff like that that puts people off getting into the game, which is a shame. And then there was that stuff of him leaving his wife for his son's girlfriend. Not a nice guy.'

'The more I get to know you, Ronnie, the more you sound like Matt Pearson, back in Virginia,' laughed Tom. 'Maybe you're not too far off about the Russians,' he continued. 'I read in The Sun this morning that Rogers and Weiner were with a group of people that included Hector Delmontez and a couple of his Russian friends.'

'It'll all come out in the washing,' said Ronnie. 'They'll take their time, but the cops'll get whoever did this.'

'I'd like to know what it was that the shooter said before he left,' said

McGovern. 'It sure seems to have frightened the shit out of Weiner. Now there's a scumbag for you. Maybe they got the wrong target,' he added, flinging his butt into the ditch and spitting after it in disgust.

Tom was coming around again. If they'd whacked Hector, I wouldn't be losing any sleep, he thought.

'A bad bunch,' said Ronnie, 'we haven't heard the last of this.'

◆　◆　◆

If the previous afternoon had ended badly for the fans at Woodbine, the trip to Toronto had been a big success for the Elevator Stable. Last Hurrah had run a huge first race and according to the reports texted back from Fort Erie, by Tom to his Aunt Vera, at the helm of inter-stable communications, Rocky had eaten up, sore mouth and all, and was bouncing around the barn the next day, looking angry and ready for a fight. A good sign, Tom had indicated.

In Toronto, Victor received this good news as he and Gladys were finishing their breakfast and he had just enlightened her of the avails from a mega Trifecta payout that had been sleeping quietly in the shoebox in his small office. Rikki was a money winner and Nils and Colin had also both profited handsomely.

In New York, Reggie, too, had made a good score, courtesy of Rikki, but was even more pleased when he'd calculated his personal ratings on Last Hurrah's race: a complicated formula involving a measurement of a race's time against the track record and then a plus or minus allowance against other times over the same distance on the same day that took into account wind conditions. In his group e-mail, he pointed out that the winner, Mayan Warrior, had run a 99: a phenomenal figure for a two-year-old at this stage in his career. And, of the three races run over the three-quarter mile distance, on the card, his was the fastest. With Last Hurrah the only closer in the race – who had in fact run by far the fastest last half mile – his number of 96 was theoretically – considering the trouble he'd experienced at the gate and ground lost – the best number and a superb number for a horse on his debut.

Typical of his curmudgenous character, though, he added a caution that he would be highly likely to regress or 'bounce,' as the term is, off this very promising first number.

Victor smiled when he read the e-mail. Here was a guy who had to be dragged kicking and screaming into the partnership and was now completely hooked. His own local track variants agreed with Reggie and the only thing that had him perplexed was the style of running, as the few runners that Last Post had sired were out and out front-running speedsters and Last Hurrah had made a big move, from off the pace, suggesting that, if that was his style, he could, maybe, go around two turns. Maybe this guy might be a bit better than we thought? he mused.

CHAPTER 42

The incident in the paddock at Woodbine had really shaken up the normally unflappable Hector Delmontez. He'd seen plenty of people die: many killed at his behest. But this was a little too close for comfort. While he had a good idea what it was all about, if it was what he now suspected, this was very bad news.

The afternoon had been going so well. The America's syndicate had seen their promising two-year-old colt, Mayan Warrior, win the first race in style and his party had been enjoying the generous hospitality of Calvin Weiner and Woodbine. There they were, in the beautiful tree-lined paddock in the warm late afternoon sunshine, well-fed and more than adequately refreshed with good wine, looking forward to Pravda completing a perfect day. Then bang – in an instant everything had fallen apart.

Mike Rogers had been standing behind him, talking to Cal Weiner and Pravda's trainer, Danny Johnson, when a man in a suit and reflector sun-glasses had squeezed past him in the crowd. And then pop-pop, pop-pop. Four shots, in rapid succession, followed by what had disturbed him the most: 'Watch out, or you're the next,' and whoever it was who'd said those words had vanished into the crowd as quickly as he'd appeared.

Hector had turned to find Rogers stricken and Weiner collapsed beside him, with Samantha Weiner shrieking, as someone he didn't know tried to administer CPR to the former, unbuttoning his collar and covering himself in blood, in the process.

Pandemonium had ensued and a horse had got loose and charged through the crowd of onlookers, creating further chaos. The police had appeared quickly to cordon off the area and make sure that nobody in the paddock at the time of the shooting left without giving a statement.

The fact that there would now be no race, no Queen's Plate victory that day, hadn't really dawned upon Hector. Though he knew that his horse would have another day, his future in Canada now looked doomed and he realised that he needed to distance himself from Calvin Weiner and his dubious associates more than ever.

Anticipating winning the Queen's Plate and participating in the post-race ceremonies and parties, Hector and his wife had planned on staying the night with the Weiners at their farm in King City, to discuss a bit of business. But, with their host having departed in an ambulance and his wife in hysterics, that wasn't going to happen. So, because the police had indicated that they needed to speak with him before he left the country, the shaken Delmontezs checked into the Four Seasons Hotel in Yorkville, central Toronto.

◆　◆　◆

At 9 a.m. on the Monday morning, while the world of horse racing absorbed the shocking news from Toronto, detectives from the homicide squad of Toronto Police Service's 23 Division commenced interviewing the eighty or so people who had been in the paddock at 5:23 p.m. the previous afternoon – the moment that the shooter had opened fire.

By lunchtime, all but a dozen had been dismissed and Detective Raymond Baines, leading the investigation, announced at a press conference that Mike Rogers had died as a result of being shot four times: two bullets to the head and two to the heart. It had, he added, been execution-style, bearing the hallmarks of a professional hit by someone who had specifically targeted the victim. When asked about what the shooter may have said, Baines declined to discuss such particulars or a motive. He concluded by saying that his officers were interviewing witnesses who had reported seeing a man in a light grey suit hurrying from the paddock, moments after the shooting, and then getting onto the pillion seat of a waiting black, possibly BMW, motorcycle. No. No one had followed the motorcycle and there had been no reports from Toronto police or the Ontario Provincial Police of any motorcycle speeding or acting in an unusual manner. Detective Baines pointed out that for five miles around the racetrack there were thousands of warehouses, where the shooter and his accomplice could have quite innocently ridden, and then continued in alternative transportation.

The trail had gone dead.

For Hector this was one more encounter with law enforcement that he did not need. Furthermore, he knew that once the local police had run his name through the channels they would want to know about his other interactions with the authorities in the US, not to mention the Interpol, FBI, USDA, and South American narcotics issues that were bound to surface.

Unlike in the US, the enquiry, right from the get-go, had been orderly: almost too little drama and certainly no vigilantes pulling out guns in the paddock. Effectively, the Teddy Bear's picnic had been ambushed and the ensuing melee was almost embarrassing. Who could have done such a dastardly thing? Indeed, Hector was quite taken aback by the politeness of the Canadian police. Maybe these are the proverbial 'good cops,' he thought, just trying to get me at ease, so that I'll drop a pearl and, in the informality of the situation, incriminate myself by being so off-guard?

'Senor Delmontez,' Detective Clarkson had opened, 'I hope you don't think that this is the wild west?'

'Not at all, Detective,' Hector had replied.

'What a shame, for you sir,' Clarkson continued, 'I guess your horse was the favourite for the Queen's Plate?'

'Yes, Pravda was. But, at times like this, such a thing is not important. We have lost my friend, Mike,' Hector looked and sounded convincingly distressed.

'That is what I wanted to ask you, sir. How long have you known or, rather, did you know the deceased, Mr. Rogers? And how did you meet him?' asked Clarkson.

'Let me see,' said Hector, scratching his head and adjusting his sunglasses. 'I met him through Calvin Weiner, just over two years ago, when they were down in Kentucky for the sales. No. Actually, I remember, it was at a pre-Derby cocktail party with William Beagle at the Iroquois Hunt Club.'

Clarkson noted all of this down. 'And since that time, what business have you done with Mr. Rogers?'

'Hard to say, really,' said Hector, stalling. 'I think Cal Weiner brought Mike into the El Cordobes syndication,' he glanced at Clarkson who looked puzzled. 'That was a good horse I'd brought up from South America. He won a big race at Pimlico and we were in the process of syndicating him before he ran in the Prix de l'Arc de Triomphe, in France. That's one of the most prestigious races in Europe. Anyway, Mike was involved and through his contacts here in Toronto and some new Russian owners that he'd got involved with, we put together the

America's Stable. The owners, actually, of Pravda, the horse we were running in the Queen's Plate yesterday. You know what happened…'

Clarkson interrupted, not really interested in the fate of horses, but the mention of Russians. 'You say that Mr. Rogers was involved with Russians. Do you have any names and where they come from? I mean, where they are domiciled here in Canada?'

'Cal Weiner would be the one you should ask about that. He and Mike ran a private sale at Cal's place in King City and I think it was there that they first showed up. You know, it was by invitation only. High rollers, celebrities, the like. You have some pretty rich Russians here in Toronto. I'm sure you know that Detective?'

'Yes, sir. We do. We do indeed. Did you recognize anyone? I mean any Russians you may have met with Mr. Rogers or Mr. Weiner, yesterday at the races?'

'Well, yes. Mr. Bragovski and Mr. Jirkhov were there to see Pravda run. They are members of the America's Stable.'

'Yes, we know them and have taken statements from them,' said Clarkson, looking at his notepad. 'Anyone else?' He paused. 'Did you see the shooter? How close were you? Did you overhear anything?'

'I wasn't actually aware of it, at the time and in the crowd. There were so many people milling around, as there always are for big races. So, although the shooter must have passed right by me, I wasn't really paying much attention,' he lied, because the moment he'd seen the man in the grey suit with wrap-around reflector sunglasses he'd thought 'mafioso gangster.' Then bang, bang, bang, and everyone was screaming.

'Did you hear anything said?' Clarkson continued.

'No, sir. I was so shocked. My friend. All this blood.'

'You didn't see the shooter leave?'

'No, I'm sorry Detective, it was all such a shock,' said Hector, faking distress.

'And what are your immediate travel plans, sir?'

'Well, I was planning on flying back to my farm in Kentucky today. But, if you need me to stay, I guess I will. We need to get to the bottom of this,' he said, rather insincerely, which Clarkson duly noted.

'Do that, sir,' Clarkson finished. 'You can be reached at the Four Seasons,' he looked at his notes, 'and this 606 number. That's your cell phone, right?'

'Yes,' said Hector, much relieved that this phone was the one he travelled with, stripped of all features that might link him to other numbers and the type of people that he definitely didn't need the law knowing about.

◆ ◆ ◆

Calvin Weiner felt a complete fool. He'd come to in the ambulance taking him to Etobicoke General Hospital, just a few miles up Highway 27 from the racetrack, and the first thing he realised was that he'd fouled his trousers.

The paramedic in attendance smiled. 'You're back with us, eh?' She had seen it all. So a little unpleasantness wasn't going to phase her for one moment. 'Here, I'm just going to take your blood pressure,' she said, as she wrapped the familiar cuff around his arm and it inflated before letting out a sigh and slackened off.

Someone had removed his tailcoat, waistcoat, and tie. As he lay on the gurney, he could feel the sweat on his back seeping through his white cotton shirt onto the grey vinyl. There was a nasty smell.

'140 over 84. You'll live,' the paramedic continued, matter-of-factly, holding Weiner's wrist as she took his pulse.

At the hospital it had all been routine. No siren, by the time it had been established that the occupant of the ambulance was not about to expire. So Weiner was able to gingerly excuse himself to the bathroom before a consultation with the doctor on duty.

'Had a bit of a fright, eh?' said Dr. Rogan. 'Could have been worse, though, I guess?' he continued, as he checked the clip board that he'd been given. 'No need for your friend to come here, sadly. What a shocking business, eh?'

Weiner lay still, disinterested but fearful, deep down. Somewhat cleaned up, his pallor was an unhealthy grey, his brow glistened, and the unfortunate stench endured.

'Well, there's not much more we can do for you here. So I'll get your wife to come and help you get ready to go home. Your number, apparently, isn't up yet,' Rogan chuckled, as a fraught-looking Samantha Weiner rushed through the swing doors and embraced her husband.

'Oh! My darling! What a terrible, terrible thing. Oh!' she cried, 'it's so good that you're ok.'

As she wept on his shoulder, Weiner lay impassively with his eyes closed. He'd maybe dodged a bullet this time, but he knew that this wasn't the end of it and that he had a serious problem.

A police officer had been stationed outside the entrance to the emergency ward and, as Samantha Weiner wheeled her dishevelled husband out, his blood-spattered tailcoat across his knees, two plainclothes policemen approached from across the hall, where they had been drinking coffee.

'Mr. Weiner, sir. Just a few formalities.'

Weiner didn't look up. 'Yes, of course,' said his wife.

'Thank you, ma'am,' said Fred Woolley, a veteran of the nearby 23 Division. 'You'll be staying at home, won't you, sir?' he enquired politely to no response.

'Yes, yes,' Samantha answered on his behalf. 'I will make sure of that, detective. You know where we live. And I gave one of your colleagues all our contact information, back at the racetrack,' she added.

'Yes, ma'am, we have all that, just want your husband to know that we would like to take a full statement from him tomorrow morning. We will come up to the farm.'

I bet you will, thought Weiner.

As Samantha drove him the twenty-odd miles home to the farm, just outside King City, he stared aimlessly out the window as she rattled on nervously about how terrible Mike Rogers's death was.

'Poor Joan. And the kids,' she bleated, 'it was so sudden. So brutal. So cruel. He never had time to say goodbye to anyone.'

'To whom?' growled Weiner, angrily. 'He didn't care about Joan. He didn't care about anyone, except Mike. Left Joan for his kid's fucking girlfriend. Nice guy, eh?' Then he started sobbing.

'Oh! My darling Calito. We'll be home in a minute.'

It was almost nine-thirty. But, being late June, it was still quite light outside as the Lexus drew up to the front door of the old stone house. There were no lights on, inside, which was some consolation as Weiner didn't feel like company at that very moment. After lying slumped for most of the journey, in the front passenger's seat, he suddenly jumped up, ran indoors, and went straight upstairs.

In his walk-in closet, tucked in an inside breast pocket of one of his suits, he found the package of white powder that he dangerously kept in a pretty obvious place for emergencies. Running into the bathroom, he locked the door, sat down on the toilet, and greedily snorted the contents through a rolled-up twenty-dollar bill.

'Honey! Are you ok?' called Samantha. 'When you are ready, come downstairs and I'll make us some soup.'

'I'm gonna take a shower. I'll be down in a bit,' Weiner replied.

He undressed carefully. The stains were beginning to set, so he concealed his underpants in a plastic bag which he tossed into the garbage bin, making a mental note to take the contents downstairs to the main bins before Freda, the cleaning lady, started poking about. As for the trousers, they could be soaked in the basin and then tumbled dried before heading off to the drycleaners. He'd just hide them away until the morning.

As he stood and let the steaming water wash away the foulness of the last few hours, the cocaine kicked in and he began to feel better. How dare those ungrateful fucks pull a stunt like that, he thought to himself. You want to bite the hand that feeds you? I'll fix you fucking Russians.

Downstairs, in his dressing gown, the soup was good and hot. Dear Samantha, the tireless accommodator of his many moods.

◆ ◆ ◆

Detectives Clarkson and Baines of Toronto's 23 Division had been joined by a third man, Marc-Andre Brisson of the RCMP, the following afternoon, just after 2:30, when their unmarked Ford Taurus arrived at Kingscote Farms.

Samantha Weiner greeted them nervously at the front door of the lavish century farmhouse. 'Gentlemen, come in. I'll tell Calvin that you are here.' She ushered the three through into the main drawing room that looked out from the back of the house into a small tree-lined ravine, with a barn and paddocks in the distance. 'He'll be down in a minute,' she added as she left the room.

Weiner had not slept well. The cocaine had got him revved up and he'd tossed and turned as a thousand negative thoughts had flitted in and out of his head. Then, just as dawn had come up around 5 a.m., he'd finally dozed off. Samantha knew well enough to leave him when he was like this and she had only awakened him with a cup of tea shortly before their visitors had arrived.

Now she found him hurriedly pulling on some jeans and a green golf shirt. 'Put some socks on and comb your hair, darling,' she urged him, flitting around like a mother hen.

Weiner had always been a stubborn man who'd marched to the beat of his own drum once he'd decided that he was infinitely better than his hard-working father. Now he went downstairs with all the arrogant confidence of an immensely rich man in his own domain, fully expecting to blow these irritating cops off with the minimum of fuss. He wasn't going to volunteer anything.

'Good afternoon, gentlemen.' He entered the room with a smile and shook hands with the awaiting policemen, who introduced themselves. 'I'm so sorry to be the cause of dragging you guys all the way out to King City.'

'No worries, sir,' started Tony Clarkson, 'we have all the time in the world and a little trip out into the country, to a beautiful farm like this, well, it breaks the monotony of regular police work, doesn't it, lads,' he continued, smiling and turning to his colleagues.

'Well, what can I do for you?' asked Weiner calmly.

'We have interviewed everyone who was in the paddock at the time of the, er, incident, sir.' Clarkson paused, looking at his notes on a small pad that he'd produced from his jacket pocket. 'And,' he continued, 'we know that you won't remember anything after the shooting as, well, you were out of it.'

Weiner laughed, nervously, as the other two men stared at him.

'I would like to, at this point, bring in Inspector Brisson, here, from the RCMP,' Clarkson continued, 'because I believe that, further to what we have learned from questioning the other witnesses and work that the RCMP have been engaged in, apart from this,' he added, which made Weiner frown, 'he has some questions for you. Inspector,' he deferred to the RCMP man.

'Yes, thank you, Detective.' Brisson opened with a very distinct Québecois accent. 'I only came down from Montreal this morning, Mr. Weiner, after my office at RCMP headquarters learned of the incident at Woodbine racetrack and, er,' he hesitated, 'the people involved.'

Weiner swallowed and tried to not look concerned.

'We 'ave,' Brisson continued 'been...ow do I say eet?' his apparent nervousness accentuating his delivery. 'Been,' he thought for a moment, 'conducting, yes, that is the right word, eh? An enquiry into the financial dealings of certain new citizens to this country, eh?' He looked up.

Weiner smiled. 'And what have you found?' he enquired, not liking where this conversation was going.

'Well, let me put it this way, sir. There has been a lot of money coming into this country and, to cut to the quick of this story, two of the men that we have been watching, eh? Were in the paddock at Woodbine yesterday when, er, Mr. Rogers was assassinated,' and he looked up with an inquisitive frown. 'Do you know these two men?' he continued, placing two eight-by-ten photographs on the table.

Weiner had not been expecting this and his gulp would not have gone unnoticed by the three officers. 'Of course, I do. That's Yuri Bragovski and the other fella, he's Max Jirkhov.' Turning to the detectives, he continued, 'You two gentlemen must know them, they're high rollers about town. Max has a place on the Bridle Path and Yuri is building a monster home in Forest Hill. Great guys!'

'How long have you known these two gentlemen?' continued Brisson. 'And did they know Mr. Rogers, the deceased?'

Weiner interlaced his fingers and cracked his knuckles, leaning back in his chair and looking up at the ceiling, as if wracking his brain. 'Maybe two years?' he paused, 'Could be three. Time flies. Mike and I have, well had, I suppose, a sale each year, up here on the farm and, after we met these guys at the polo, we invited them. It was by invitation only. We knew, after we'd talked to them and heard their story that they had a few bucks,' he laughed. 'Mega bucks!'

'And how did you know that?' asked Brisson.

'Well, you own a $25 million house in the ritziest part of Toronto and show up at the polo in a Bentley, it isn't hard to put two and two together. These guys said they were into property. Developers. I believe that Max is the money behind the new hotel at Bay and Adelaide. You know, the Diamond Tower.'

'So, did these gentlemen purchase any, how would you say it, stock? Is that right? At this, er, sale?'

'Dead right they did,' enthused Weiner, 'and they've done famously. Indeed, they bought into the syndicate that I'm a part manager of, the America's Stable, and not only do they own part of Pravda, who was the favourite for yesterday's Queen's Plate, but they have some very promising two-year-olds down in the States that could be Derby horses next year.'

'Ah, yes, that reminds me,' Brisson continued, 'the America's Stable. That was started by Dr. Hector Delmontez, wasn't it?'

'Yes, Hector and I are partners,' Weiner continued, feeling much more confident about his position and his explanations now horse racing was the topic.

Brisson looked a bit troubled and paused to read his notes. Looking up he asked, 'Have you ever been to South America, sir?'

Weiner was caught off guard and stuttered. 'Well, I, er, actually, I went to a convention in Caracas. Must have been nine or ten years ago.' Brisson noted something, allowing Clarkson to intervene. 'Well, that's just it, sir. Your host on that occasion, Dr. Delmontez, was at the races yesterday. We've interviewed him and we are interested in learning about your syndicate's Toronto-based Russian members and their relationship with Dr. Delmontez.'

'Well,' said Weiner, 'they don't really have a relationship with Hector at all. Mike and I brought them in. They're, as it were, Toronto-based investors. They live here and we, I mean the America's Stable, have horses that they own or part-own, trained here at Woodbine by Danny Johnson. And then we have some other horses with Tim Trebor in the States. He's the top trainer down there. All these horses run under the umbrella of the America's Stable.'

'So, as I understand it, and please correct me if I'm wrong, Dr. Delmontez set up the America's Stable and you run the Canadian contingent. Is that right, sir?'

'Yes, that's right. I do,' he paused. 'And Mike did. We also have some guys in the UK, France, and the Middle East who are part of the America's Stable. But nearly all the horses run in North America – just the very best ones might ship to big races in Dubai or sometimes the UK. You know that Dubai has some very high-class racing, with huge purses?'

'Very interesting,' said Brisson. 'Were Messrs Bragovski and Jirkhov,' he read their names carefully from his notes, 'enjoying, happy with their involvement in the America's Stable?'

'As far as I know. Yes,' said Weiner, not altogether convincingly.

'Why, sir,' Brisson looked at him straight in the face, 'would someone want Mike Rogers dead if everything was going so smoothly?'

'There you've got me, Inspector.' Weiner looked up and smiled, 'Haven't the foggiest. Now, can I get you gentlemen some tea? A nice cuppa for your troubles?'

Sensing that they'd got all they were going to get at that point, Clarkson politely declined. 'So kind. But we've kept you quite long enough, sir. You have been very helpful. Our enquiries will be on-going and you can expect to hear from us, as they progress.'

As Weiner ushered the three men out, he knew what he needed, really badly. Even before his dear wife could debrief him, he was locked away in his bathroom sanctuary, recharging himself.

◆　◆　◆

Hector Delmontez and his wife Patricia spent another comfortable, if unscheduled, night at the Four Seasons Hotel, choosing to order room service rather than chance running into anyone who might want to discuss what they certainly did not want to.

In view of what had happened, the secondary purpose of his visit, namely sorting out Calvin Weiner, would have to wait until another day, as the cops would be watching very closely and any private liaison between two of the main players would have definitely raised additional questions that neither man needed or were prepared to answer.

Phones were easily tapped and mobiles were the first things that law enforcement confiscated when people were taken into custody these days. So it was with great relief that, during the afternoon of his third day in Toronto, he received a call from Detective Clarkson telling him that he was free to leave Canada for the time being: even though he reminded him that his situation was under careful watch and, just because he might be in the USA, he wasn't beyond the long arm of the law.

Only when the El Condor Lear's wheels had lifted off Canadian soil, though, did Hector really relax. Sometimes, he reflected, things can get a little too good. Time to back off.

Since the infamous gathering in Caracas, he had stealthily taken over manipulating North American racing and those who were beholden to him, on pain of ruination for their carnal perversions, drug addictions, or just plain impecunity, now found themselves in an impossible position: knowing they could not do anything to stop the doctor and his horses without precipitating the type of scandal from which they and the sport of horse racing might never recover.

It had been so simple. Flash a bit of cash. Everyone liked conventions in far off, exotic places and he could have invited twice as many influential people, had he wanted to. What he'd ended up with had far exceeded his intended sphere of influence.

Even though many of the leaders of the industry had been preoccupied, he'd managed to get to vulnerable guys in key positions. Weiner had jumped at the opportunity. Realizing that the casino at his flagship racetrack was not going anywhere and the racing base had disintegrated, he needed a new source of income. That he had a personal drug problem had made it that much easier to tie him up in knots that he could never escape.

George Boyce, a casino guy on the board of racing commissioners, had a serious gambling problem. No worries. He'd do anything he was told, including finding out the test procedures of the day, week, or month at virtually every racetrack in the good ol' US-of-A for a steady stipend. Larry Mason, head of the Maryland Racing Commission, was a sorry case: a complete drunk who could not resist the lures of the transvestites at the Anaconda Club. My goodness, Larry was so photogenic in ecstasy. Hector chuckled to himself. As for Geoffrey Gilligan and Patrick Waley-Brown, what beauties they'd turned out to be! Everyone seemed to love a bit of discreet and free perversion, he smiled to himself.

As timing would have it, which turned out perfectly because all the second-eleven guys were much needier than their bosses, some sort of highbrow conference was being held at the same time in Dubai, by Sheikh Bakshish, to which all the top administrators from the UK, France, the US, Australia, and Japan had been invited, so the Magnalls and Beagles had escaped being compromised. Hector smiled when he thought about how that might not have worked so easily as it had for lightweights, like Gilligan and Weiner.

The plan was simple: legitimise dirty money. Hector didn't care where it came from. He just knew that there was a lot coming out of Russia and potentially even more to come from China. First, through his Venezuelan-based company, Condor Servicias, he'd set up his own insurance brokerage house, El Gruppo. Then they'd started shipping South American bloodstock and drugs, hidden on his own charters into the USA. The buyers, in lieu of payment for the drugs, would overpay for Hector's horses. Some of these would do ok. But those that didn't would succumb to illness or accidents and their full inflated value would be compensated for by his own insurance company, El Gruppo, whose position in reputable markets, including Lloyd's of London, would have been set up (per bribes) by Waley-Brown and his friends in high places.

For those seeking to turn their illicit cash into legitimate western currencies, this was a win-win situation. You either traded in bad horses, via Hector, and collected your money per insurance after they had exited, or you purchased drugs of your choice (cocaine, opiods, Carfentanyl, whatever), Hector's main line of business, by making it look like the exchange was for bloodstock. Then you sold the drugs and, if you wanted to, could whack your own horses and realize their full inflated value thanks to El Gruppo coverage and Waley-Brown's corrupt friends in the insurance world, who operated on very lucrative kickbacks on each deal: sometimes up to fifty percent.

El Cordobes had been the perfect foil. He giggled quietly. It had been a double whammy. A coramine-based cocktail, so he thought he was on cloud nine, and the kid Alvarez's machine that had sent him into orbit. It was just a shame that Dr. Mason, obviously so guilt-wracked with what he'd done, had decided to top himself and had sailed off into the sunset. Nice guy, Larry Mason.

But El Matador had set the ball rolling and, now that the America's Stable was up and running, it was the pre-race knowledge of what was being tested for at each racetrack that gave Hector the biggest edge. Not only did the horses of the America's Stable run out of their skins and win many big races, thus further endearing him to the likes of Billy Beagle, whose endorsement he needed to frank his whole operation, but their successes gave them more and more (inflated value) that he could realize through legitimate sales and/or insurance claims.

Hector was playing God. Tim Trebor and the other trainers with horses for the America's Stable could not stop winning and, believe it or not, according to Billy Beagle, their exploits were reviving the reputation of Bluegrass country and Kentucky. Billy had put Hector up for election to the Jockey Club, telling anyone who would listen that Hector was a latter-day Bull Hancock.

As he dozed blissfully at 38,000 feet, Hector figured it was time to coast for a while.

CHAPTER 43

Billy Beagle gazed dreamily out the window. He had everything, so it seemed. But what he'd just been told had left him lost for words.

Across the bay window of his study, Graham Wheater sat on the edge of a wingback chair. The message that he'd just delivered had stunned its recipient and he fidgeted nervously, not sure exactly whether what he'd done was good or bad.

Wheater was forty-five, a tall, willowy 'ah, shucks' type of guy, who'd once been a pitcher in pro-ball: a closer for the Cincinnati Reds. Serious stuff for a local Kentucky boy who'd made the big time. 'The Show,' as they called it and played just down the road for the team that he'd supported as a kid. He was used to tight situations, with a full count, two out and the bases loaded at the bottom of the ninth, with the Reds hanging on grimly to a one-run lead. He loved such adrenalin-fueled moments and, moving on to study law after he'd blown out his valuable arm from one too many one-hundred mile an hour fast balls, he'd found his niche and put his wits to work as a private detective, smoking out guys, as he said, who were speeding.

The thrill was still there, but these days life was a bit quieter and he sure didn't miss the heckling that 'The Thrasher,' as Reds' fans used to call him, got when he blew a save.

The silence was deafening.

'How many people know?' Beagle eventually mumbled softly.

'The whole story? I would say just you and I, and of course T.J., whom you have used to liaise with me.'

Beagle sat, slumped, wringing his hands. 'You mean that that Brisson guy and his people in Venezuela don't know the full extent?'

'Not to my knowledge. The RCMP guys are more concerned about the narcotics and, of course, they are conducting their own investigations into money laundering and the Russian guys.' Wheater paused, then went on. 'Mr. Weiner is a person of interest, though, and I expect someone will put some heat on him soon. But I don't think the Canadian cops are onto the fixing of the race testing. Yet.'

'How about here? The Feds, do they know about Dr. Mason and George Boyce?'

'In so far as they were on the list of people who went to Caracas in 2009, yes, they do. But – and I could be wrong – I don't think they suspect them of anything more than, perhaps, aiding the money laundering. You know, on the surface respectable people. I'm confident that they don't know about the testing business.'

Beagle bit his thumb and frowned. 'When you called me on Derby day, I felt sick. I felt winded and, believe me, I hadn't felt like that since my college days, playing football, when some big ol' linebacker had just sacked the shit out me; just piled me into the turf, and you feel like a bulldozer has run right over the top of you.'

Wheater grimaced. 'I guess we keep our heads down. For the time being, anyway?' he volunteered.

'Yes, yes,' said Beagle. 'Are you sure that Janice Boyce hasn't whispered something to her family, perhaps?'

'Absolutely. She was all shut up like a clam when I went to see her. Couldn't figure out what I might want to know about her George.'

'The guy was a total fuck-up,' fumed Beagle. 'Could not stop gambling. I don't know how he got where he got or who hired him, but he should never have been in the position that he was!'

'I know. I didn't know where to start. You know that Brisson and his people got to some member of that Moreno guy's family. You know, the guy who fell out of the plane in Canada and washed up on a beach? That guy. And this person, I think it might have been his sister or girlfriend told them about how Juan Pablo had told them about some weird stuff that Arko and his boss, Dr. Delmontez – your Hector guy – were up to, and somehow it got back to the convention – wild stuff at the Anaconda Club – and Brisson, through local immigration, got a list of all the people who had attended. Janice can't say anything.'

'Why?'

'Well, our friend George may have been a complete degenerate, when it came to gambling, but he loved his wife and he'd taken out a large life insurance policy in her favour. There was a clause about suicide, but she still got a bundle. Wouldn't have, though, if they'd known what Georgie boy had been up to. So, Janice ain't gonna talk to nobody.'

'Maybe the policy was with El Gruppo?'

'Come to think of it and the fact that it was settled, probably was – like a little pension, for services rendered, eh?' Wheater chuckled.

Beagle was listening, dumbfounded. 'George Boyce was on the list,' continued Wheater, 'and Larry Mason.'

'And my friend Bob Fraser and his lovely wife, who had an unfortunate accident while down there. I bet that fucker Delmontez was involved in some way in that, too.'

'Quite probably. Maybe she smelled a rat? So, could have been the Canadian, Calvin Weiner, and the Brit. Whatisname?'

'Gilligan. Fuck! Fuck! Fuck! All lightweights! They got schooled by a fucking spic!' Beagle was apoplectic.

'Well…' Wheater wasn't quite sure what to say next.

'Thank you, Graham. I knew we could count on you. T.J will take care of your invoices and expenses. We'll think about this and how to deal with it and I would appreciate it if you remain mum when the cops ask you any questions. And they will, in their own good fucking time.'

Billy Beagle ushered Graham Wheater to his old Buick. The last two hours had put a few years on him. As he took a stroll, to get his mind straight, he vowed, 'Hector, my boy, you may think that you've got us by the balls, but we now know your game and you are not going to like our next play. Gotta slow you boys down a little.'

CHAPTER 44

Sheikh Ali had many sides to him and often he'd play little jokes on those fawning before him. He knew what Danvers and Lascelles thought of him: a profligate raghead who'd inherited daddy's money and was playing in his little sandbox. But they weren't shy about feeding at his trough, he smiled to himself. So, now that Ravi Singh had come into his life, he thought he'd have a bit of fun, at their expense, over the Royal Ascot meeting.

Back in Bangalore the boys at Motti-Singh had been fine-tuning their burgeoning toy. As revenues poured in, solicitations for inclusion in the game were what Rahda Sigtia and his team found themselves most preoccupied with.

There was to be another Indian race in the fall, prior to the Melbourne Cup, but Sheikh Ali thought it would be fun to wind up the Brits by dabbling at the Royal Ascot meeting.

'Goodness me,' Rahda had said, when the Sheikh had proposed his idea. 'That would really upset the apple cart. You know, hijacking their game, wouldn't it be?'

'Yes, sir,' gushed Sheikh Ali, 'that's just what I want to do. And, forgive me for saying so, but now that I am very much involved with your splendid endeavour, the sweet part about my involvement is, with all due respect to you guys, that they can complain all they like, but they won't do anything to upset my brother and I. They need us too badly. I love it.'

'Can we not talk to them, again? At least plead our case and give them a friendly prod or heads-up?' Rahda reasoned.

'No. No. They'll twiddle their thumbs and sit on this for an eternity. It must be a surprise. We must shake them up. I would love to be a fly on the wall in the senior steward's office at Portman Square when one of those ex-Army sycophants breaks the news! Ha! Ha! Forgive me, but it will be hilarious, Rahda, my man.'

Nobody spoke to Rahda like that – I'm not your man, he thought – but, thinking about the Sheikh's impertinence, he put himself in the BHA's position and thought, well what can I do about that? Answer: sod all.

'Well, let me talk to Ravi and Kulbir about this. Maybe we can come up with a variation; something not quite so provocative.'

The upshot had been to introduce the next stage of Real Racing a bit sooner than had been planned. The new game was Ghost Riders and the Sheikh was delighted because it would torment the Jockey Club each one of the five days, not just for one race on one day.

'Ghost Riders,' as Ravi explained, 'is an online game, whereby players pay £1 per ticket to enter each day of the five-day Royal Meeting, when ten winners would be drawn, with the first nine allocated one of the top nine jockeys riding at the meet. The first lucky ticket would get the leading rider for the season (up to that point), the second the second, and on down to the ninth. Then the tenth lucky winner drawn would theoretically get the "Joker," who corresponded with all the other jockeys riding that day. The winners are the Ghost Riders, because the riders that each lucky winner has drawn are riding for them.'

'I love it. I love!' cried the Sheikh. 'And what do the winners win?'

'Well, essentially £500,000 every time one of their jockeys wins a race. If they win three, it would be £1.5 million! If the top guys strike out and lesser known jockeys win all six races, for example visiting French or Irish jockeys, the guy who gets the Joker takes the whole pool, which would be £3 million for six races!!! And,' he added dramatically, 'so that those who do not draw a jockey don't lose interest, every ticket has a combination of a runner in each of the six races, with whosever's team records the highest return to a level one pound stake on the tote winning a million pounds!'

'Amazing. I'm going to play,' gushed the Sheikh. 'Oh, do I love this!'

Kept under wraps until the Sunday before the opening day, Tuesday, June 14, Ghost Riders exploded onto the scene via social media and just about every online communications vehicle going. By closing of entries, at midnight on Monday, a total of £125 million tickets had been purchased for the following day's action.

On the Monday morning, a routine disciplinary hearing at the Jockey Club – at which some wretched permit holder from near Bridgenorth in Shropshire was being cautioned about an apparent non-trier in some rock-bottom seller at Ludlow, the previous January – was interrupted by an urgent knock on the door and Major Freddy Ogilvy-Brown poked his bulbous red nose around the door. 'My apologies, sir.'

'What now?' Johnny Cameron, the presiding steward barked. 'Can't you read, man? It says private, do not disturb, on the door!'

'I know, sir. Please accept my most profuse apologies.'

'Get on with it, man!'

'Well, sir, there appears to be a bit of bother.'

'What bother? Can't it wait until we've dealt with Mr. Buckley, here?'

'No, I'm afraid not, sir,' chirped the now puce-faced Ogilvy-Brown. 'It's the Indians, sir.'

'Well, what have they done now? Beaten us at cricket again?' and everyone except Ogilvy-Brown laughed.

'No, sir. A lot more serious than that, sir. They've – how should I put it? – they've, well, actually, they're playing a game at Ascot tomorrow.'

'Really? I thought we were racing tomorrow, not playing cricket,' Cameron joked, to sniggers all around.

'No, no, no, sir. You know they have this thing; Real Racing, they call it. Well, they are, somehow, running a sweepstake-type game, involving jockeys, on tomorrow's races.'

'What do you mean?' exclaimed Cameron, leaping from his chair. 'Mr. Buckley, you're fined £500 pounds. This meeting is over. I don't want to see you again! Now then, Fobby, what's all this nonsense you're on about?'

'I'm afraid it's not nonsense, sir. They're deadly serious.'

'Well, we'll see just how serious these bounders are. Just wait until our solicitors sort them out. Fire a shot across their bumptious bows, eh? That'll fix 'em.'

◆ ◆ ◆

The upshot had been that the Jockey Club's solicitors had been blown off by Tony Palgrave Brown at BCH&H and, to the consternation of those running the so-called Sport of Kings, during its most auspicious week of the year, the Motti-Media corporation donated a cheque for almost £400 million to Unicef, to combat world poverty, at the end of the five-day meeting.

Ghost Riders, if anything, had upstaged the original Real Racing concept. Now everyone knew who Pat Donnelly was, and a whole host of other jockeys most people had never heard of before. On days two and four, the top guys had struck out, leaving two jackpot winners of $3 million: a fisherman in northern Spain, from whence he'd given an interview on his small fishing vessel while catching mackerel in the Bay of Biscay; and a sheep farmer in Western Australia, who boasted about his descendants being convicts transported down under at the beginning of the nineteenth century, and how apropos it was that the family had finally won compensation from the UK, from of all places Royal Ascot and care of Her Majesty the Queen!

Sheikh Ali had had another great royal meeting, visiting the winner's enclosure three times during the five days. But nothing gave him as much pleasure as to see Real Racing and its latest manifestation capture the hearts of fans around the globe, even more so than watching those in charge writhe in embarrassment at their inability to interfere.

CHAPTER 45

When the dust had finally settled at Woodbine, the Queen's Plate was belatedly run two weeks late and duly won most convincingly by Pravda, whose victory set off wild celebrations in the Turf club, where the colt's Russian owners laid waste to the club's supply of vodka.

In the wake of the Rogers business, Hector had decided to lie low in Kentucky and ever since had carefully avoided any contact with Calvin Weiner, who sheepishly was on hand in his freshly dry cleaned clawhammer outfit. Altogether it had been a subdued occasion, monitored carefully by local law enforcement and one or two anonymous observers from the FBI and, unbeknownst to the authorities at Woodbine, Interpol, the USDA, and even their colleagues in the department of Venezuelan narcotics trafficking. Like a Mafia funeral, there were a lot of shifty-looking people, hidden behind reflector sunglasses, watching to see who was there.

Meanwhile, down at Fort Erie, Rocky was rearing to go. His mouth had recovered from the beating it had taken in the Woodbine starting gate and Ronnie and Tom had noticed a much more aggressive horse in his daily training. Indeed, Tom was starting to have trouble holding him, in their steady two-mile gallops.

Reasoning that his negative debut at Woodbine may have left a slight psychological mark and the fact that the surface was all-weather, which he would not be running on again in the future, if his path did take him eventually to the Kentucky Derby, Matt decided that his next start should be at Saratoga.

So, in mid-July, the gooseneck reappeared from down Interstate 90 and Tom and Rocky headed off to join Rikki and the rest of Shenandoah Valley Farms' string, under the tutelage of Basil Foster.

The meeting itself was due to start on July 24 and last until the Monday of Labor Day weekend, in early September. Since Tom had last been there, there had been quite a transformation as the backstretch had filled up with the best horses on the continent.

Basil's team had everything well under control in their little domain. The shedrow had been levelled and new dirt raked in; the wall plaques were mounted on the doors that featured matching webbings, and someone had visited a local garden centre to dress the tranquil little corner up with half a dozen hanging baskets of white geraniums, mixed with blue lobelia.

In the shade of an old oak tree, providing a perfect canopy from the mid-summer heat and humidity, for which Saratoga is famous, Toby had arranged a table and four lawn chairs. Certainly, this operation was not going to be able to use a lack of comfort as a reason for failure on the track.

Vera was installed in her impressive residence on Third Street, just off upper Broadway, and each day would appear, just after the 8:15 a.m. break for harrowing, to watch a set or two train. She would then sit in the shade reading the *Form* and kibitzing with her staff, who would occasionally bring over a horse they might be hosing or grazing, for a pat and a carrot.

Tom rode everything that was going to the track, except on workdays when Joe Magee would come by and, depending on what Matt had decided (back at home base), the two would work their mounts together. Matt trusted Joe and knew that any work he was involved with would not set the clockers' tongues wagging.

On opening day there was a rare five-furlong sprint on the turf, that Matt had spotted when the condition book had come out two weeks before. And this, he decided, looked like a good spot to reintroduce Touch and Go, after a layoff of eighteen months.

Touch and Go was one of Vera's favourite horses, although his style of running was very contrary to Matt's training. Unsold, when he hadn't made his reserve when sent up to the yearling sales at Keeneland, he'd returned home and developed into a veritable speedball who had won his first three races as a two-year-old without ever seeing another horse: so fast was he out of the gate. Unfortunately, as Matt knew only too well, such horses tend to be very hard on themselves. 'Their frames are just not made to go that fast,' he'd said, and consequently Speedy Gonzalez, as the stable had appropriately named him, had sustained a fractured knee.

Many owners would have cut their losses, tapped the joint, injected it with cortisone, and then dropped him into a claimer, for perhaps $50K. And, by now, Speedy would definitely have been dog meat. But Vera loved her little grey rocket and had had the chip removed and taken him home. Now four, his original iron-grey coat was starting to get whiter and he'd put on quite a bit of condition, with huge almost quarter-horse-like hindquarters.

As usual, great patience had been exercised, keeping this little time-bomb from exploding, with hours and hours of steady work. In June Jose had let him run along a bit at Charles Town, where the official work was recorded as a half in 48, and, since arriving at Saratoga, Matt had steadily increased the tempo and distances. Now Tom had a real job holding him and often Basil would accompany them on the pony.

When the entries closed, two days before, there were some quizzical looks in the racing secretary's office, when local agents and pundits noted that the rider of the two-horse in the sixth race, was someone that they'd never heard of before: a Betsy Brewster, claiming the ten-pound bug (apprentice allowance). Indeed, Basil had been visited the next morning by Sal Tuffano, agent for Miguel Munoz, the current leading rider in New York.

Jockeys' agents used to infuriate Matt Pearson during his days at the track and were, according to him, one of the main reasons he'd quit. 'Big loud-mouthed blood-suckers,' he used to say. 'They always use the collective 'we.' Like hey, Matt, we'd like to ride so-and-so. And you'd look at them and say, right, you disgusting 300 pound tub of lard, can you claim the bug?'

Sal Tuffano wasn't quite that bad, but he was bulky in a dishevelled way, with far more chins than he needed, and his tubbiness today wasn't helped by a loud red-and-grey hooped golf shirt that did a poor job disguising his ample contours. Basil had first spotted him leaning his bulk on the rail, by the gap, as he'd gone out on the pony with Tom and Rikki. Sal was sounding off in his harsh New Jersey tones, joking with other trainers and exercise riders, while he chewed on sunflower seeds and spat them out onto the dirt. Now he was hovering at the end of the barn, a bit like a *Far Side* cartoon character. 'Hey. You gotta nice outfit, here,' he barked, spitting more sunflower seeds onto the grass. 'We'd like to ride a few for youse guys.'

Nobody responded. 'Hey. Who's in charge here? Who's the man?' he continued, glancing at his overnight sheet that listed the following day's entries. 'Basil Foster. Are you Basil?' he said to Tom, as he walked by with Rocky.

'No, sir,' Tom replied, 'he's in the feed room, at the end of the barn.'

Tuffano lumbered down the shedrow and Curtis thought to himself, you're lucky Mr. Pearson isn't here, or you'd be out on your ear.

'Hi, there,' said Tuffano, slightly out of breath, to Basil's backside that at that moment was all you could see, as he leaned into a deep feed bin. Basil grunted. 'Sal Tuffano.' The agent continued, 'I represent Miggie Munoz. We're leading rider, right now. Won two stakes at Belmont last weekend.'

Basil straightened up and offered a wrist, as his hand was all covered with wet bran and sweetfeed. 'Basil Foster. What can I do for you?'

'Well, we'd be sure interested in riding for you at this meet. We're pretty busy,' he qualified the statement, 'I'm sure you got some nice horses? Got one in tomorrow, in the sixth. Unbeaten, I see.'

'Yep,' said Basil.

'Ridin' the girl, eh? Gets the weight off, with the bug, I guess.' Tuffano hesitated, 'but, Noo Yawk,' he pronounced it the Jersey way, 'its tough. Got the top riders in the country, here. Maybe the world?' he speculated.

'I know,' said Basil, 'but the boss calls the shots.'

'And who might that be,' Tuffano enquired.

'The owner. Ms. Montagu.' Basil, on instructions, didn't mention Matt, as he continued mixing feeds.

Tuffano looked out to the where a fifty-gallon oil drum, full of water, sat under a tree at the end of the barn, with a propane burner heating its contents. The grooms were tossing corn into the hot water.

'Sure is pretty back here.' But Basil wasn't listening. 'Well, we'll see y'all later. You ever need us to ride work, here's my card,' and he left it on the tack box outside the feed-room, before heeding the call of the coffee truck's horn and its assortment of unhealthy goods.

For Betsy this was a huge honour. She'd had one or two rides at the bush meets in Virginia and won a couple of races at Charles Town, riding a horse for a friend of her dad's. But getting to ride Speedy at Saratoga? When she first got the news from Matt, she'd thought he was playing a joke on her. But no, Vera had thought it was a brilliant idea. Get the weight off and, really, with Speedy's style of running it was just a question of holding on and hoping nobody would catch you: that's where she and Matt had figured the ten pounds could prove decisive.

Going sprint distances, it was generally considered that one pound equalled one fifth of a second, so ten could mean two lengths that, in the blanket finish five-furlong sprints often featured, could be the difference between first and tenth. That they'd drawn the two-hole was most providential.

Betsy flew into Albany on the morning of the race and was picked up by

Basil. She'd not eaten for two days, through excitement and nervousness, but mainly under strict orders from Matt that, if she couldn't make the 108 pounds with saddle and all, it would be the last time he'd indulge her.

Opening day had been looked forward to by Saratoga aficionados for almost eleven months, and when she and Basil arrived at the jocks' room at 11 a.m., more than two hours before the first race, the crowds were already pouring in; many armed with folding chairs and coolers for their picnics under the trees around the paddock.

Right in the middle of this forest, the racing secretary's office and jocks' room was a hive of activity, with jockeys, valets, trainers, agents, punters, and members of the press all excitedly looking forward to the opening of the marquee race meeting of the year.

Betsy felt very lost in the turmoil, as she completed the formalities of being licensed to ride in New York State. She'd brought her own saddle, lent to her by a rider friend at Charles Town. Tipping the scales in her undies at 105 the night before, she reckoned that she could use a bit bigger one than the postage stamp with irons that some riders were forced to use when doing the lightest weights. And Joe Magee had given her a tip about having a bit more to perch on being key when you were riding an equine timebomb like Touch and Go, who would ordinarily explode from the gate like a nuclear missile.

Tom had asked Basil to be allowed to lead Speedy over and it was a good thing that he'd put the lead-shank's chain over his lip, as he was hopping and a bopping as they crossed Union Avenue and headed to the saddling area under the trees behind the grandstand.

Grey horses sweat like all horses, but the evidence is not always so apparent as with chestnuts and bays. And today, even though it was a very hot by the time of the sixth race at 3:30 p.m., Speedy looked cool, albeit revved-up cool.

The turf, being used for the very first time at the meet, was pristine, with not a divot mark, and Betsy noticed, as they circled behind the gate, that the mowers had rolled down a perfect down-grain path from the two-slot, one off the rail.

Vera had made her regular visit to inspect her troops that morning and, having spent the previous night burning the midnight oil while she fastidiously handicapped the race, was up at her favourite table on the third floor terrace, adjacent to the wire, with the Beagles and Lorna Buchanan, up from Tanglewood for the ballet at the Saratoga Performing Arts Centre.

It was a conditions race. And, by virtue of his lengthy absence, Touch and Go had not been too penalised for his three-race unbeaten status. Combining that factor with the unknown bug-rider claiming ten pounds, a girl to boot, and a big step up in class from Laurel, the punters were ignoring them at 20/1.

Vera had e-mailed her Elevator Stable friends to alert them and Reggie had replied that, in a wide-open race with twelve runners, only a fool would try and pick an Exacta. You could run this race ten times, he'd said, and get ten different winners. It's a lottery and depends entirely upon who breaks well and then luck in running, thereafter, as, being such a short distance, there was no room for errors. Play him on the nose. Maybe bet him across the board. Who knows? You might get beat by a 50/1 shot and the place and show would be very rewarding. So, her bet, commissioned by the ever-present Mavis, was $100 across.

Billy Beagle had smiled. 'It's great to see you so excited, Vera,' he'd said.

'My heart is pumping, Billy, dear. You know this is what really gets me going. This race will take less than a minute – probably between 56 and 57 seconds. It's sheer magic! What an adrenalin rush!'

Their chatter was interrupted by the racetrack announcer. 'It is now post time. They're loading.'

Down at the five-eighths pole, not far into the backstretch, Touch and Go loaded without ado and the other seasoned sprinters, mostly sporting gaily coloured blinkers and quite a few matching rundown bandages on all fours, quickly followed suit. There was a bit of shouting, and the eight-horse, getting a bit claustrophobic in the confined space, first tried to sit back and then lunged prematurely at the gate. Then bang, the gate opened, and the bell rang.

Under Betsy, Touch and Go was coiled like a viper, ready to strike. He'd been away from the sports for almost two years and he was ready. Just as hundred metre sprinters have an internal countdown from when they are called to their marks, a good jockey, riding in quarter horse races or over the minimum distance of five furlongs on a thoroughbred, has that instinct to know when to go. Go too soon, you foul out – in the hundred metres, you get one life and then are disqualified if you do it again – in a horse race you crash into the rigid door of the gate and are often recoiling when everyone else, fractions of a second later, are on their way, leaving you in their dust.

Betsy had ridden in sprints at Charles Town, but never on a horse like Touch and Go and she tried to remember what Joe Magee had told her: do not hold onto his mouth, grab a bit of mane, sit into him, and hold on. Let him do it all. And that was what happened.

It was all a blur. Wham! The gate opened, and Speedy exited like a frightened rat up a drain, his powerful hindquarters firing his torso out onto the grass track ahead of him. This was the first time that he'd ever run on turf, but that didn't matter, he was off and away, his low devouring strides gobbling up the track. Betsy never even saw the one-horse and found herself alone on the rail, with what sounded like an amplified version of the Charge of the Light Brigade hot on her heels. Speedy was running on his left-fore lead and sped around the turn.

Up in the stands, the anticipation was fever-pitched, as the tightly packed field of sprinters surged to the top of the stretch. Vera, watching on the little TV monitor attached above the table, had seen the great break that Betsy and Speedy had gotten. Under the table, so the Beagles didn't see, she was snapping her fingers and humming the Cars' famous tune, under her breath: 'Give me what ya got!'

Both Joe and Matt had said to Betsy, 'When he straightens out, he will change onto his right lead. Do not pick up your stick. Sit still, hold him together. If you are still in front at that point, no amount of whipping will do any good and, in all probability, will only get him unbalanced. Just ride him out, hands and heels.'

Up in the box, Billy Beagle had a momentary departure from his usually reserved demeanor and jumped up, as Touch and Go reached the eighth pole with a two-length lead, and shouted wildly, 'Go on girl!' His wife smiled and wondered who was watching and whether he had anything at stake?

On board the tiring Speedy, Betsy was pleading for the wire, as much for herself as her venerable charge who was giving his all. Her leg muscles cramped and ached, her lungs were bursting, the pursuers were closing in a rush. Stay down by the rail, she remembered everyone saying, was the shortest way home. Then, like a sudden sense of smothering, they were upon her and she felt the enormous relief of letting go, as her spent mount galloped out.

She had no idea whether they had held on. Had they won? Maybe second? The horse just outside her had finished like a rocket, going past them in a manner that made them look like they were standing still. But had he got there in time?

Betsy was so shattered that she couldn't pull up her mount until the very end of the backstretch and the outrider, when he reached her, suggested that they should continue on around to the wire, rather than gallop back the other way to unsaddle, as it would be quicker. Gasping and hanging on to Speedy's mane, the combo hobby-horsed back to the gap onto the main track in front of the stands.

'Good on you, girl,' were the four greatest words she'd ever heard, from one of the groundsmen leaning over the inside rail. And, glancing over her left shoulder, she saw number two on the infield board – winner – and burst into tears.

'My goodness me,' said Billy Beagle. 'I didn't know I could get that excited.'

Vera, Mary-Lou, and Lorna were crying, too, and the faithful Mavis produced tissues.

'Forget the price,' said Vera, tearfully, 'you just can't beat that.'

'I'll take a $42-winner anytime,' said Billy. 'Look at the place and show prices: all longshots.'

'You, too!' said his wife, with a smile. 'I thought you never bet?'

Vera's phone rang. It was Matt. Matt, in tears. She couldn't believe the man could get that emotional. Then Reggie, Victor, Colin, and Nils. Her boys. What a day!

CHAPTER 46

Since the incident in the paddock at Woodbine, Calvin Weiner had kept his head down. Mike Rogers, his go-to guy, was gone. Hector, he dared not communicate with and, if the message that had been sent at Woodbine was serious, it was very clear that his new clients, right in his own backyard, were far from happy.

For public consumption, Weiner was vacationing at his cottage in Muskoka. For those in the horse racing world who were familiar with his weaknesses, this wasn't surprising, as they knew that such a retreat was his default position. This was far from being the first time he'd gone AWOL in such circumstances.

At the onset Hector had been a godsend: someone who'd embraced him and elevated his status within the international world of horse racing. Hector had reinforced the bonds between Ontario and Kentucky, per the enthusiastic endorsement of Billy Beagle and the Bluegrass establishment, and, by extension, through the UK set and their powerful Arab owners. The trip to Caracas had confirmed his status as the undoubted leader of the sport in Canada.

However, he was now discovering that this had come at a price. With Mike dead, even he had to admit that his own failings were the reason that he now found himself in such a jam.

How simple it had seemed to ride on the coattails of as charismatic a character as Hector Delmontez, as the good doctor had furnished him with a seemingly endless supply of inviting bloodstock that, along with a few shipments of narcotics here and there, generated much-needed cashflow and the appearance that horse racing in Canada was thriving. But now he was paying the price of this dubious association and, as he slumped in a Muskoka chair on the dock of his exquisite lakefront retreat, looking out aimlessly across the rippling water, he mused that he should get off this train and quickly. But could he?

The trouble was that Hector's business, good or bad, generated the funds for him to keep himself in the fast lane. But now, could or rather would Hector keep up the supply? The punters were becoming too greedy.

Once upon a time, major league crime in Canada had been controlled by various mafia families in Montreal, Hamilton, and the Toronto suburb of Woodbridge. But they had largely kept to themselves; working the usual prostitution, drug-trafficking, and extortion rackets, with a bit of bookmaking, on the side. But the new Russian expats, who had muscled in on the action, were turning out to be a completely different cup of tea.

Weiner remembered that Danvers had warned him about the Russians. Quite candidly, he'd said that horse racing in the UK had been saved by the Arab invasion of the bloodstock market that had started in the late '70s and early '80s. 'We know where we stand with the Sheikhs,' he'd said. 'They may violate human rights back where they come from, and they may not treat their women very well. But, the way we look at it, that's their business and we just have to consider ourselves very fortunate that they have decided to invest so much money in horse racing. If they got upset and took off tomorrow, we'd be in very serious trouble. And, between you and me,' he'd added, 'that whole Al-Bouzouki business – the disqualified St. Leger winner and the mystery plane at Stanstead, with its cargo of unconventional and hitherto unknown stimulants and steroids – could have been very dodgy, had we laid down the law. As it was, we fudged it. They lateralled old Bouzouki who is now, I believe, pensioned off somewhere training camels in the desert, the last time I heard, and everything, after a bit of a hiatus, settled down.'

'Indeed, all things considered, I think that racing in our country is in a pretty healthy state these days, thanks to our Arab friends. We need them and they know that.' Danvers had gone on to explain the dynamic and how invested the various rulers from the Emirates and Saudi were in the UK property market. 'Then, along came the Russians,' and he'd paused.

'Funnily enough,' he had continued, 'Hugo Lascelles and I were laughing about what a London cab driver said to us one night when we'd probably drunk a bit more than we should have. He said something to the effect of: Gentlemen, so nice to have gentlemen in my cab. I have to say that that's not always the case these days, though. At least them Arabs, they was class. Used to go out chasing the ladies, drinking a bit of pop. You know, stuff they shouldn't really have been doing. But they always tipped well. They were gents, even when pissed. Now you have these Russians. Big thugs. No manners. I don't know. They've got pots of money, but no class.'

Weiner had discovered firsthand what Danvers had meant. Sure, when he and Mike had run into Yuri, Maxim, their ladies, and entourage, they'd seemed to be young and carefree, with plenty of moolah. Just what horse racing needed. New blood, as Billy Beagle would have said. But the cabby had been right. As Weiner gazed into the shimmering water, he knew that these bullies were not about to back off.

After two weeks of isolation, Cal Weiner braced himself and returned to the real world. The Saratoga sales were looming: an opportunity to meet with Hector. And his punters had more money burning holes in their pockets.

Mike Rogers had handled the Russians until, it appeared, whatever he'd been doing had been unsatisfactory. So, when Nikolai Balekov called to enquire about transportation and accommodation at the upstate New York spa town, Weiner had his excuses ready. He was driving down early for Jockey Club meetings and would be staying with friends. The best thing to do would be to take their Lear to Albany and arrange for a limo to the Gideon Putnam Hotel, in town, where four suites had been reserved.

Weiner needed time to confer with his controller. On the six-hour drive south-east from Toronto, across the Niagara River into the US at Queenston, and then onto Interstate 90, through the western part of Upstate New York, down past the Finger Lakes to Saratoga, his brain fulminated in silence.

Samantha loved Saratoga, an opportunity to dress up, go shopping, dine in fine restaurants, and luxuriate in a sulphur bath at the famous Roosevelt Baths & Spa. But she'd been left behind. Weiner needed no distractions and, in fact, wasn't staying with friends, as he'd told Nikolai Balekov, but had booked a room at the Sagamore Resort, on Lake George, some twenty miles north of Saratoga.

◆　◆　◆

It was over a month since the tumultuous trip to Toronto and Hector had been doing some reflecting. Saratoga was a major event in the American horse racing calendar and, as the figurehead of arguably its most successful syndicate, he was expected to be front and centre at the sales and on the racetrack managing the America's Stable's interests, which were headed by the very promising two-year-old, Sputnik, trained by Tim Trebor, who had won impressively on his recent debut at Belmont Park.

But after the incident at Woodbine, things needed to be calmed down and managed more discretely.

At the private sales that Weiner and Rogers had held on the former's farm, it had been a straightforward case of laundering hot money into respectable funds, in house. Saratoga was a little more tricky, though, as it was a public sale with far more scrutiny, that Hector knew was now a lot more focused on him than it had been.

Hector, furthermore, knew that his phones were now vulnerable. So, after receiving a brief call from a payphone in Batavia, just off Interstate 90, to one of the few that he still had confidence in, it was arranged that he and Weiner would meet at the Sagamore, where Weiner had suggested that they could take a boat out on the lake and have an uninterrupted chat.

◆　◆　◆

Built in 1883, the Sagamore Resort is set on a private island, on Lake George – accessed by a draw bridge. During July and August, it teems with prosperous New York families, seeking the coolness of its shoreline breezes that present welcome refuge from the mid-summer heat and humidity. As such, it was a perfect place to blend in and nobody paid attention to two men in shorts and T-shirts, topped by ball caps and wraparound sunglasses, when they climbed into a small, clinker-built rowing boat and pushed off into the willow-shrouded channel.

The relationship between the two men had been strictly one-way ever since the fateful convention in Caracas. And, knowing only too well what a termination would mean, Weiner was nervous: rowing quietly, while Hector sat in the stern, facing him, his arms braced behind him against the edge of the craft.

Despite the seriousness of the occasion, Hector looked relaxed. Whereas Weiner, stripped down, looked pallid, with his long and skinny white legs poking out from a pair of dark blue cotton shorts. An accomplished rower from his days at college, he had no difficulty with the oars. It was just what he knew they were going to talk about that made him feel so awkward and had sweat already rolling down the inside of the back of his white T-shirt.

As they drifted away into seclusion, Hector broke the ice. 'I think you know that we must back off a bit,' he hesitated. 'You know, after the business with Mike. We should stop shipments for a while, eh?'

Weiner bit his tongue and swallowed hard. This was what he'd expected. 'I know, the authorities are conducting a pretty thorough investigation. They haven't charged anyone yet, though,' he added, hopefully, though it didn't sound convincing to Hector.

'Yes, but you have to tell your guys that they need to be patient. They have done very nicely. Tell them to just enjoy what they have for a while. They have Pravda and they have this really nice horse Sputnik to watch. He could be a Derby horse and,' he exclaimed, 'they are both legit. These horses will make them money. No need to liquidate them. What these guys need, Cal, is to blend in, look natural, stop the aggression, and start acting like people who are quite comfortable with their status, as bone fide citizens of Canada. Of North America.'

'I know, I know,' Weiner almost bleated. 'I keep telling them that. But they're thugs, Hector. Where they come from, its all about money, power, control, and more and more of it.'

'Well, the important thing, Cal, is that they only know about the fact that we are helping them to move their money to a place where it is respectable. That way, they stand to lose as much, if not more, than us. Make no mistake, they are involved in many other similarly dodgy schemes that are none of our business.' Hector sneezed from the pollen that was raining down on them from some low hanging willow branches, as they nudged up against the bank. 'What they must not know, Cal, is that we are controlling the – how do you call it? – the spit box. If they find out that their good fortune on the racetrack is due to that, they'll step all over us. And, if you think being extorted to provide more narcotics isn't fun, just wait until you have them wanting to fix races, at a whim. Can't happen, or it's all over.'

Weiner absorbed this in silence. He thought about the message that had been directed his way in the paddock and he felt all queasy.

'So,' said Hector, 'no more shipments for at least a year. Let's let this die down. Enjoy your racing and the America's Stable.' He looked at Weiner. 'Comprende?'

Weiner shrugged. It sounded a lot easier than he knew it would be. 'I guess.' He knew that whatever he thought didn't matter. Hector had him by the balls.

'Now, let's return to the hotel. I will leave immediately, as I have a ride back to the Gideon Putnam. We'll see you at the races tomorrow. All smiles, eh Calvin, amigo?'

Weiner docked. And, as Hector disembarked and headed off, jauntily, he felt sick. He hadn't risked bringing any gear with him across the border, so there wasn't even any immediate respite. Dark days ahead.

CHAPTER 47

The first Saturday of the Saratoga meet preceded the following Tuesday and Wednesday evenings' sales, with amongst other important races the Sanford Stakes for two-year-olds over six furlongs; infamous for the one and only time the great Man o' War met with defeat, appropriately at the hands of a horse called Upset.

The America's Stable's Sputnik, off his impressive debut at Belmont Park three weeks earlier, was already being touted as a future champion. Along with the Russian contingent from Toronto, Hector and a host of other prominent members of the Kentucky breeding set were slated to be on hand to observe the budding star.

After the July sales Billy Beagle always took a six-week break from Kentucky and high on his list of priorities, at the start of the Saratoga meet, was the annual Round Table conference at The Reading Room on Union Avenue, where horse racing's regulators and marketers got together to discuss contentious issues and exchange novel ideas regarding reaching broader and younger audiences.

Just as Calvin Weiner had taken a time-out to take stock of his options in the wake of the Mike Rogers affair, Beagle had had his head down, too, since his sobering meeting with Graham Wheater. For him and, for that matter, the general public at large, the integrity of the sport was sacrosanct. What he now knew could never be divulged or leaked, or no one would ever bet on horses again, with any confidence; forget the fact that an organization like PETA would close horse racing down.

So he had decided that a serious shot needed to be fired across the bows of those seeking to undermine post-race testing of blood and urine samples. And, as a forewarning of what he had in mind, the headlines of Friday's *Daily Racing Form* had announced something that had always seemed to be elusive. Namely, that at this year's Round Table the number one issue would be federally regulated testing at one centralized laboratory. No more, the article went on to say, would trainers shipping from state to state be able to take advantage of varying thresholds and local rules. Every racetrack would abide by the same standards, with the same chemists and analysts working together in the same laboratory, with all samples coded and completely anonymous to all but the Jockey Club in New York City.

Beagle knew that Hector Delmontez would have gulped when he read this news. It still might be a pipe dream, as he also knew just how intransigent local Horseman's Benevolent and Protective Associations were, from state to state, as they sought to represent their constituents like rabid unions for whom a right to make a living on the racetrack trumped all manner of chicanery and abuses of animal rights. But he wanted to send a message that would at least make him feel like he was doing something, while he figured out how to deal with the people he now knew were corrupting the sport.

The Reading Room doesn't have great capacity. But, on the morning of Monday, August 1, by the time the conference was called to order, shortly after ten, if you'd fired a shot gun into the room, you'd have taken out the brains trust of world horse racing, so illustrious was the assemblage.

After a short introduction from T.J. Van der Meer, Billy Beagle took the lectern. Decked out in a light cream linen suit, white cotton shirt, and green Keeneland tie with matching pocket hanky, he mopped his brow as he welcomed the crème de la crème of the turf. 'So many friends. I know you haven't really come here to listen to me. Saratoga is its own magnet. So, I'll get on with it.'

After a brief pause, he continued. 'Last month at Keeneland. Here over the next couple of days, and at sales throughout this great country over the next few months, the pride of American bloodstock will be put up for auction. I wish I could say that today we are as proud of our stock as we should be. As we once were.' He paused, drank some water, and looked at his notes. 'Our sport has become truly international over the past few decades, as is confirmed by y'all's presence here today. Yet, sadly, the United States has lagged behind when it comes to restricting the use of performance enhancing drugs and painkillers that have rendered our young horses fragile and unsound,' he looked up from the rostron, 'unable to compete without such assistance on the world stage.'

There were murmurs around the room which, despite powerful airconditioning humming away, had become quite stuffy.

Beagle went on to outline his plan to crack down on the use of illicit drugs in North American horse racing, detailing how there should be one centralized lab with federally approved thresholds. After almost forty minutes he received a standing ovation. But an astute observer would have been able to point out that those applauding were predominantly foreigners and, had the same message been given to a townhall meeting of horseman at any racetrack throughout the continent, the reception would not have been so raptuous.

After representatives of various marketing and IT communications firms had had their ten minutes to make their pitches, the meeting ended and those in attendance repaired for lunch in the adjoining dining room that opened out through a screened porch onto a lawn, where cocktails were being served.

Beagle accepted multiple pats on the back and made a point of introducing Hector as almost a companion in arms in the fight against skulduggery. The wily chameleon in Hector lapped it up, however he may have wondered if he wasn't being sent a not so subtle message.

Everyone was talking about Hector's latest wonder horse, Sputnik, who had bolted home unchallenged in the Sanford Stakes and would now be heading for the seven-furlong Hopeful Stakes on the last weekend of the meet, which was generally considered to be a stepping-stone to stardom.

'Dear Hector, I want to introduce you to Dick Taverner,' gushed Beagle, 'Dick is with the Department of Justice, ex FBI. He's going to be leaving his position as assistant attorney general for the State of Kentucky and will be joining us to co-ordinate this new 'war' on those who would seek to cheat in our great sport.'

All six-foot-five and two-hundred and twenty-five well-toned pounds of Dick Taverner towered over Hector, who grimaced as he spilt a smoke salmon canapé, that he'd been carefully doing a balancing act with, onto his white alligator shoes.

'Pleased to meet ya, Senor,' boomed Taverner.

'Hector is the founder and, er, manager of the America's Stable,' Beagle continued. 'Sputnik is theirs.'

'Mighty impressive,' said Taverner in a clipped assessment. 'Shame the owners didn't make it,' he added, and Hector frowned, as across the room he saw Calvin Weiner catch his eye.

'Yes,' said Beagle, 'that was a shame. What exactly happened?' he enquired, looking at both men.

'Spot of bother with immigration at Albany airport's what I heard,' said Taverner.

'Yes, most unfortunate,' said Hector. 'Immigration held up my Russian friends from Toronto and they missed the race. I think it was just a misunderstanding. I guess, in these rural parts, at small airports, they are not set up to handle such exotic visitors.'

Beagle watched Hector carefully. This man is cool, he thought to himself. But, drip, drip, drip.

'Well, they're here now,' said Cal Weiner, joining the group, as Billy Beagle excused himself to usher his Japanese guests into lunch.

'Cal, this is Mr. Taverner,' Hector introduced Weiner to the towering lawman. 'He is the guy that is going to straighten out horse racing.'

'Well, good luck to you,' said Weiner. 'Easier said than done.'

'The way I look at it,' boomed the big man, 'is there's just too many jurisdictions. Every state's different: different thresholds, different testing systems. Can you imagine the net being at a different height in tennis, in each state? Or the hole in golf being bigger on some courses than others? That would be nonsensical. We're gonna visit every God damn racetrack. Check their testing. Where they're doin' it. Who's doin' it. Who's in charge. Gonna file an assessment and shake things up. As Mr. Beagle says, we're aimin' high, going for a centralized office. We're gonna catch the speeders. None of that blamin' Jimsun weed bullshit or contaminated feed. Know what I mean?'

'Yeah. What do they say? Not everyone who goes to the track is a crook, but all crooks go to the track!' cracked Weiner.

'I like that one,' hooted Taverner 'Ha! Ha! The track's a good place to start, then?'

They went into lunch where Hector and Calvin were more than pleased to see that Dick Taverner was required at a different table to theirs.

◆ ◆ ◆

Nikolai Balekov had seen it all before. Ex-FSB, he was no fool and recognized the b.s. at Albany, right away. No Mike Rogers to grease palms and open doors, and that maggot Weiner had opted out of his responsibilities. They should have known that they were ripe to be turned over, he mused to himself, as he chewed on a nail and looked out over Saratoga racetrack from the America's Stable's box.

Rogers had bitten the hand that had been feeding him. Some said it had, in fact, been Cal Weiner, the dirty little user, but Maxim had cautioned his colleagues: 'Don't fuck with the establishment.' Weiner, for all his faults, was Hector's guy and, for that matter, Beagle's guy, too. He was in with the sport's establishment..

Nikolai examined his now bleeding pinkie and sucked the seeping blood up. Canada had been the perfect backwater. Safe. Secure. On the back of the real estate boom in Vancouver, driven by Hong Kong and Far Eastern money, it had been easy to find a home for his boss's cash. Lots of it now discretely tied up in multi-million-dollar projects in that West Coast haven and the country's biggest city by far, Toronto.

The trouble was that the Canadians were so hospitable and accommodating and it hadn't taken long before the next generation, SOOs Viktor called them, son's of Oligarch's, had been sucked in by the decadence that such wealth inevitably spawns. 'Just how much money do you need?' Nikolai had wondered. 'For heavens sake, you greedy bastards, the money that you have set yourselves up with in this great country was all stolen in the first place. Do you have to parlay these ill-gotten gains into more nefarious activities?'

Nikolai's boss, Dimitri Chatrov, was these days domiciled in Monte Carlo, minding his own business. When he'd got word that Mike Rogers had been eliminated, he'd reminded his man in Canada that they didn't need the attention. 'Can't you guys just enjoy yourselves? Enjoy a great and beautiful country. Enjoy the hockey. Enjoy your fancy cars. Enjoy the women. Enjoy whatever you like. But keep your fucking heads down!'

The punks who'd wiped out Mike Rogers in front of the who's who of Canadian racing were friends of Oleg Chatrov, a remittance man who took his father's money but not advice. These people, Nikki knew, were lowlifes. They'd wanted to impress young Oleg who was, they thought, unhappy that there weren't more dope shipments. Nikki knew that their idyllic situation would blow up in their faces, if they didn't back off. Now, as the bugler called the field for the first race onto the racetrack below, he heard them coming. Drunken Russians at Saratoga not only did not go down well with the locals but made Nikki seethe. Fucking peasants, he thought to himself, as they fell into the box. No manners. Their flashy five-thousand-dollar suits could not disguise them.

Squeezed into the corner by a loud blonde who once upon a time might have charmed him in his pre-FSB days at the KGB, he sucked in his tight waist, within the anonymous black-suited, reflector-sunglass world that he lived in, and grimaced.

At the sales that night the young Russians were again front and centre, while Hector ducked and dived, pandering to them on the one hand, while all the time hoping that Cal Weiner would keep them under control so they would not embarrass their hosts and, above all, Billy Beagle.

Nikki sat at the bar, tucked away in a corner at one end, nursing his Stoly on the rocks. The to-and-fro of the sale and its intracacies intrigued him. But the loudness and brash excesses of his comrades were not doing them any favours, as prices skyrocketed. Young Oleg didn't care. He'd never actually earned an honest dollar in his life. Easy come, easy go. The entitlement irked Nikki.

◆ ◆ ◆

After Touch and Go's triumph, Matt Pearson had granted Betsy leave to stay on in Saratoga for a few extra days to help Tom out with the two yearlings that the farm had consigned, and they'd been partying. Mark and Algy were in town and Tom had encouraged them to court Bog, who had got over the Java Raja embarrassment quite nicely through his association with Lucy Beagle and was enjoying his position as official agent for the America's Stable.

'Don't count on Bog to help you out, in a pinch, though,' Mark had warned Tom. 'But, if you ignore him, he'll think that, after the Java Raja business, you may be hiding something.'

Algy laughed. 'It's a good thing that Mr. Singh has got his mind on other things.'

To the boys' great amusement, CBS signed the $1.4 million ticket for lot 89, a nice but not spectacular colt from Shenandoah Valley Farms, on behalf of his boisterous Russian clients.

Algy, being consummately polite, congratulated Bog and laughed a lot with Mark, when he told him that he'd 'had to have the colt, as he'd exuded class.'

Hector observed all of this, quietly, enjoying Billy Beagle's enthusiasm over the new and much needed money that Cal Weiner and his Canadian – he didn't call them Russian – syndicate members had brought into the sport. Vera, meanwhile, sipped a cold glass of chardonnay with Mary-Lou Beagle and smiled. The colt, unfortunately, would be going to be trained by Tim Trebor, but $1.4 million was a bonus that she was not going to turn her nose up at.

The Sales broke all records. Bog's 'boys,' as Algy, Mark, and Tom now referred to them, signed for four yearlings for a tad under $5 million. Back in Newmarket, Danvers and Lascelles had their calculators out. And, reflecting upon the extraordinary upsurge he'd just witnessed, Billy Beagle pinched himself and smiled, as he luxuriated in a sulphur bath at the Roosevelt Spa.

Maybe Hector could be controlled, he mused. He may be the slimiest man in the sport, but boy could he generate money and that's what made Billy's world go around. Just gotta find a way of neutralizing him, without anyone finding out. That was the $64-dollar challenge: he had to abide by the rules from now on and if he could do that, then past indiscretions could be swept under the rug. But Billy realized, only too well, if anyone apart from Hector had any knowledge whatsoever of the spit box scandal, they'd be a huge threat to blackmail him. In fact, as he lay back in the steamy mud, the uncomfortable realization dawned upon him, they'd have to be eliminated.

◆　◆　◆

Saratoga basked…misty backstretch mornings, brunches on the patios of downtown Broadway, hot dusty afternoons, punctuated by roars from the grandstand at the racetrack, boozy, humid evenings that ran far into the night, as revellers partied like there was no tomorrow.

In Barn 7, on the Oklahoma side of Union Avenue, Rocky was primed. The Woodbine experience was now a distant memory and he'd really taken to his new quarters.

Back at Shenandoah Valley and even at Fort Erie it had been very quiet. But here there was a hustle and a bustle, as close to fifteen hundred horses went through their paces every morning: walking, jogging, galloping, working from the gate.

Rocky stood behind his webbing, watching alertly, his ears pricked, coat slick, muscles rippling. While Betsy had been in town, Matt had sent up instructions to let her work 'The two-year-old,' as he referred to the barn's only member of that age. 'Let's let him run along a bit from the gate and see how he's progressed,' he'd said.

So one morning Tom had accompanied the pair, on the pony, just after the main track had been harrowed at 8:15 a.m. and, as luck would have it, four other two-year-olds of Tim Trebor's were apparently bent on the same mission.

Tom knew that Trebor worked his horses hard and it would be a good test. He also knew that Matt wouldn't want any 'bullets' (best work of the day) on Rocky's work line, so he'd cautioned Betsy to not outwork Team Trebor. Just sit in behind them, and let them post the fast time. He knew the clockers would be paying attention to the leading trainer's representatives and that the other horse, whoever it was, would not be the focus.

Sometimes works don't go according to plan. But this one, from the gate at the three-quarter pole to the wire, had gone perfectly. The bell rang. Team Trebor exited with gusto, the Hispanic exercise riders chirping and whistling as they sent their charges roaring down the backstretch. On the outside, Rocky had obviously learned his painful lesson and popped out smoothly, in their wake. Betsy let him drift over to the rail, to get a bit of dirt in his face, and then picked him up as they'd turned for home, running on very strongly along the rail with the minimum of urging, to finish less than a length back of the fatiguing horses in front of them.

Had she wanted to, she knew that Rocky would have galloped out a lot stronger than her rivals that day, but she knew her orders and when Tom had given her the time recorded for Team Trebor, of 59 and 2 , she hoped she hadn't done too much.

Off that work, Matt had found a perfect spot, going seven furlongs, during the last week of the meet. The feature of the Labor Day weekend was going to be The Hopeful Stakes, over the same distance, with Sputnik the short-priced favourite, and there were several maidens taking their chances for the $250,000 purse and prestigious black type. But Matt felt that there was no point in possibly over-matching his secret weapon so early in his career. While no maiden race at Saratoga is a formality, this spot looked tailor made for Rocky's natural progression.

Again, Trebor had an entry. In fact, two of the horses that had worked from the gate with Rocky and Betsy the week before. And, in a full field of twelve, Rocky drew the five-hole, with the ever-reliable Joe Magee. They were listed in the morning line at 8/1, based upon the promising debut at Woodbine and the DRF byline of 'Behind a Good One in Canada.'

As soon as the form had come out, the Elevator Stable's WhatsApp communication had sprung to life and all members made plans to be in attendance. For Reggie and Nils this wasn't a big deal as they were 'Toga regulars,' as the latter said. 'We seldom miss and, with this being the last week until next July, every race is just pure joy.'

The consensus amongst the experts was, as usual, conflicting. 'Why?' wrote Colin, 'are we going seven furlongs? Last Post gets sprinters. That work from the gate was sharp. Wouldn't three-quarters be a better trip this time?' Reggie was of the same school, ever the pessimist, contributing, 'This ain't Canada. Gonna be a lot tougher in here.' Vera had calmed them down, by saying that Matt knew what he was doing, 'He has a fit horse.' 'I know, I know,' Victor had said, 'but my numbers make him a cinch at six.' To which Vera had cryptically added, 'maybe Matt knows something you don't?'

Just having a runner at Saratoga, though, was the greatest honour and an occasion to dress up and enjoy an afternoon at a racetrack which Reggie had declared was the finest by far in all of North America and a place where he'd had left instructions that his ashes should one day be scattered.

On a perfect sun-drenched early September afternoon when, by the final and eleventh race of the day, a coolish breeze, bringing harbingers of fall, wafted through the trees and out across Reggie's desired final resting place, the first spark of something special was witnessed by those gathered there that day.

Joe Magee had boldly made the call after the Woodbine race, through the blood from his broken nose. 'They won't beat him next time,' and even though these horses were measurably superior, he was proved to be right, because Rocky did not let down his supporters.

Backed down to 7/2, he toyed with the opposition. Sitting just off the pace, like a veteran, when Joe changed his hands and let him ease down inside the leading group at the top of the stretch, as they tired and drifted out, it was all over. Under a hand-ride, with Joe not needing to even show him his stick, Rocky bolted in by six lengths in a time of 1:22 /2 which was faster than Sputnik would take to win the Hopeful two days later.

As ecstatic as the Elevator Stable was, their joy could not match the pride within Tom as he led Rocky back to the barn. 'You're the real thing. The real deal,' he kept saying to himself. 'You're gonna be a champ.'

CHAPTER 48

Post-Saratoga, the thoroughbred circus in North America flowed on to Kentucky for Keeneland and the September sales and ultimately to the Breeders' Cup which was being held at Santa Anita, next to the Sierra Madre Mountains in the Los Angeles suburb of Arcadia.

Buoyed by the prospect of another champion, in his star two-year-old Sputnik, Tim Trebor lapped up the limelight, as his deep-pocketed patrons dueled for the best bloodstock in the world.

Trebor was a slick salesman who knew what made his billionaire clients tick and played them like a well-tuned violin. From his Marlborough Man good looks, omni tan, and rugged six-foot-six frame, sporting his trademark Stetson, he looked the part and charmed all around him with his pitch. Tim found the limelight and being in it, whether outbidding titans of industry in a straight up war of whose wallet was the fattest or being photographed in the winner's circle with winners of the world's most valuable and prestigious races, was addictive. The way he looked at it was: there are only so many top-class horses, so you try and acquire as many as possible, knowing that, while some may disappoint and wither on the vine, others will keep you up there at the top of the lists of races and money won. Always in the headlines.

Some of Tim Trebor's critics despised him for this shameless shotgun approach, calling him Neon. But nobody could deny that his methods worked and he always seemed to have plenty of glamourous and wealthy people around him.

Sputnik had gone on from Saratoga to win the Champagne Stakes at Belmont by a wide margin and was now red-hot favourite for the $1.5 million Breeders' Cup Juvenile over a mile and a sixteenth. On the first night of the Keeneland Sale, Johnny Ward-Clarke, acting on behalf of the America's Stable and ostensibly their powerful Toronto-based contingency of Russians, who were very voluble in the bars afterwards, was the successful bidder for his full-brother, for the eye-popping sum of $3.5 million. Trebor purred about the colt, suggesting he'd be the next star that he would put into orbit. After, of course, Sputnik won next year's Kentucky Derby. And Maxim, Yuri, and young Oleg lapped it up.

Hector modestly accepted pats on the back from people he knew hated his guts and smiled for the cameras. And Billy Beagle invited him into his private office where, over a shot of home reserve Hickory Hill bourbon, he informed him that his election to the Jockey Club would be announced at the upcoming meetings at the Breeders' Cup.

◆　◆　◆

While the Trebor show had rolled on to bigger and better things, Matt Pearson had reeled his stable in when the meet at Saratoga had closed after Labor Day. Now his one and only two-year-old was back home, recharging his very considerable engine.

There was no doubt that the little foal, who had been rescued so dramatically from the fire, was the real thing. He was Bob Fraser's budding legacy.

Now training, in earnest, began.

The Elevator Stable had been great. No interference and Rikki had done them proud, but this was going to be a completely different ball game. For Matt knew that whatever might be said about the Breeders' Cup and, hell, there was an awful lot of money at stake, nothing compared to the pressure and build up to the Kentucky Derby.

During the next six months he was going to get more unwanted advice than he ever needed, not least of all from home. Here he was with the real deal. He and a very few people knew that. But, on the face of things, he had a colt with a dubious sprinter's pedigree that had won just one race. And already Reggie and Victor were making noises about him never staying more than a mile.

Matt knew that Sputnik would be on his home turf at Santa Anita, where Tim Trebor was king, and that on that very fast west coast track, he'd be doubly tough to beat. Besides, he liked it at home and didn't want to go through all the hassle of shipping out there, no matter how much money was on the table. No, he was going to lie low and give his guy a race over the Churchill Downs strip, where he hoped he'd peak the following May, and then head on down to Florida. And, yes. After much deliberation Matt had been persuaded by Vera to reapply for his license.

'Ronnie got him going,' she'd said. 'Basil was down as trainer at Saratoga, even though everyone knows that you were calling the shots. But now I think it is time, Mr. Pearson, for you to re-emerge from the sidelines.'

Matt had spent sleepless nights tossing and turning. If this could be redemption for Tom, he thought, could it also be my ultimate vindication, too? It was in his grasp. He had to take the plunge, as he'd never forgive himself if he let this one slip through his fingers. He owed it to Bob Fraser.

The plan was to test the waters in Kentucky, as Vera felt (or rather knew) that Billy Beagle could pull a few strings. And on a rainy fall day, Matt, Tom, and Rocky headed off to Louisville, a week prior to the Jockey Club Stakes, a $150,000 Grade 3 stakes race for two-year-olds, over a mile and an eighth, just one furlong short of the Derby distance, their ultimate goal.

The Breeders' Cup had gone off with a bang the previous weekend in front of a hundred thousand sun-drenched Californian fans. Sputnik had improved his unbeaten record to four, with a facile wire-to-wire performance in the Juvenile and was now being put away until a West Coast spring campaign, featuring the Santa Anita Derby, would take him to Churchill Downs on the first Saturday of May.

Meanwhile, completely under the thoroughbred radar, Matt passed his trainer's test and satisfied the local Kentucky Racing Commission and stewards that he was a reformed character who posed no further threat to rival horsemen.

When the entries for the Jockey Club Stakes came out, there were a few murmurs throughout racing circles in Maryland. But anyone familiar with Vera Montagu's MO would not have been too surprised, as they knew her game.

It was a small but competitive field of eight, comprised mostly of local horses whose owners felt the Breeders' Cup was a step too far, plus Rocky and a ship-in from New York: not altogether surprisingly from that satellite of the Trebor operation.

Joe Magee shipped in and, in an uneventful race, in which Last Hurrah went off favourite at 6/5, his mount confirmed the progress he was making with a very workmanlike winning effort.

Matt had told Joe to test him a bit. 'Get him up with the leaders, in a good position, going into the first turn, something he'd have to do in the twenty-horse field of the Derby, and then see if he'll settle and conserve something for a stretch run,' he'd said. And, after being briefly checked at the top of the backstretch, he'd levelled off, circled the field and run on well to win by two. Joe reported that he'd galloped out really strongly and could not have been more happy with him: adding that he'd been impressed with his maturity and by the way he'd rallied when checked at such a key point in the race.

In the following day's *Daily Racing Form*, the publication's pedigree expert expressed some doubt about whether he was a serious Derby contender and wondered if, when the chips were down, he'd have the quality and stamina for the Run for the Roses. Vera, Matt, and Tom read the comments with a smile, while Victor, Reggie, Nils, and Colin smelt money and were thinking, sell.

◆ ◆ ◆

Just as the United States' most famous race, the Kentucky Derby, is always run on the first Saturday of May. Down under, Australia's most famous race, the Melbourne Cup, stops a nation for just over three minutes on the first Tuesday of every November.

An iconic handicap, run over just under two miles at Flemington racecourse, with often close to thirty runners, The Cup, as Tommo Thompson had been championing ever since he had been approached by Motti-Media, was 'a natural Real Race.'

After a year's fine-tuning, the IT crew in Bangalore had ironed out the bugs and dramatically increased not only the capacity but security of their product. As a goodwill gesture, it had been jointly agreed between Motti-Media and TAB that the beneficiaries would be the indigenous people of Australia. 'A no-brainer,' Tommo had declared on Channel 9 TV, as the draw for the twenty-seven runners was made on the preceding Friday by the Great White Shark, Greg Norman.

Australians, as a nation, didn't need any more revving up. But, beyond the usual global TV and national radio audience, the new element of a $20 million prize for whoever drew the eventual winner had generated feverish interest from people around the world who, before this running, had never even heard of the Melbourne Cup. Meanwhile, high up in the palatial air-conditioned suite of the Australian Jockey Club, Chubby Magnall contemplated the spectacle with much envy.

Legislating a UK-based Real Race on the Grand National was as logical as all the undoubted objections from bookmakers and anti-monopolies protectors was illogical. As he watched the Real Racing phenomenon blossom, Lord Magnall knew that he could no longer stand pat and watch parasites, as he referred to bookmakers, profiting from his sport while returning next to nothing in the form of betting tax and levies to support prizemoney and the general well-being of British horse racing.

When first confronted by the proposition, the Singh brothers' proposal had been greeted with the minimum of confidence by British horse racing's establishment as the fly-by-night endeavour of a couple of snake-oil salesman. But the Ghost Riders ambush at Ascot had been embarrassing. Frankly put, the Jockey Club could not afford to look a gift horse in the mouth, as, for all the superficial bluster, horse racing in the UK was struggling mightily.

Then the matter had become redundant, with the involvement of Sheikh Ali and the powerful ruling family in Dubai. For Magnall knew that you played by their rules or they'd simply go elsewhere. Like the Ascot affair, though, stealth would have to be employed so that no objections could be mounted or impediments put in the way. This was the beauty of the Internet and current social media, news travelled fast and one didn't need a long lead-in.

As Tommo Thompson had predicted, The Cup set a Real Racing record: $740 million of sales, twenty-seven winners won a million each, for drawing a horse; the ultimate winner, Ballyjamesduff, from Ireland, netted a lucky ticket-holder in France $20 million, with the second and third taking home ten and five, respectively, and the bonus Superfecta (first six in correct order) rewarded twenty-two winners with $1 million each. After the dust had settled and numbers crunchers had done their stuff, factored in costs and the TAB/Motti-Media cut, the Aboriginals received just over $600 million.

As Chubby Magnall dozed in his first-class seat on the Quantas flight from Melbourne to Heathrow, via Dubai, he dreamed of a self-sustainable sport; not having to sell racecourses for housing development and a life out from under the suffocation of bookmakers. He could not wait for the spring meeting at Aintree, where it had been agreed, at a whistle-stop meeting in Dubai with the Sheikhs, that the Grand National would, indeed, be the UK's first official Real Race, with proceeds going to the much beleagured National Health Service.

Were he not already titled, he mused to himself, engineering such a coup would almost certainly have landed him an honour. And he chuckled.

RUN FOR THE ROSES

CHAPTER 49

For the first time in more than five years, Matt Pearson toasted in the new year with a sense of purpose and optimism. His secret weapon was turning three and this was it: his classic year. As he reflected upon the March night in Kentucky almost three years before, and the chain of events that had been triggered by the fire and death of his friend Bob Fraser, he had to concede that so far, touch wood, everything had worked out as well as he and his cousin Vera could have hoped.

Their secret was alive and living up to expectations. It was now up to Matt to steer him to his destiny. Fingers were crossed.

Ordinarily the Shenandoah horses would have spent the winter at home, recharging their batteries for summer campaigns on the racetrack. These were exceptional times, though, with a live Kentucky Derby contender in the barn, and the decision was made to ship six horses down to the Payson Park training centre, about an hour and a half north of Miami, up the Florida Turnpike, near Indiantown – a small citrus-growing settlement of two thousand, twenty miles inland from Stuart, on Florida's Atlantic coast.

Matt Pearson knew Payson Park from ten years previous, when, just out of the Marines, he'd started his training career there. He knew that the deep, forgiving dirt track was a perfect place to leg a horse up for his biggest test and, also, that the isolation amongst the orange groves was good for his soul. He and Tom would rent a trailer between the track and Indiantown and Vera would spend from January to the end of March with her cousin Lois Combes, at her lovely property on the beach at nearby Hobe Sound.

◆ ◆ ◆

Three thousand miles away, on the other side of the continent, Sputnik trained forwardly at Santa Anita. Tim Trebor, never shy with his superlatives, trumpeted the progress that he'd made on his daily blog, TT Racing, and his owners in Kentucky and Toronto started talking about the Triple Crown.

In Kentucky, Hector appreciated that America's Stable was constantly in the headlines, as it was good for business. But, although they should have been enjoying the Sputnik journey, the Toronto brigade were still the source of considerable concern.

After Saratoga, Cal Weiner had supervised another profitable sale of Canadian-bred yearlings that his Russian friends had availed themselves of. But, after Sputnik's win at the Breeders' Cup, winter had set in and the boys were getting bored, with no live racing and no more shipments of dope, now that Hector had shut down the charters into Canada.

Indeed, Weiner was feeling the heat, again. Still unable to communicate with any assurance that his phone and electronic devices weren't being tapped by the RCMP and others, he was getting desperate. The punters needed a renewed supply and he had nowhere to go.

Now a member of the Jockey Club, Hector really didn't need Cal Weiner anymore and certainly not his out-of-control Russian friends. Billy Beagle's new man had cracked down on testing procedures, so that avenue for chicanery was as dead as Larry Mason and George Boyce. And, as he sat in his office, looking out at the early January snow, it occurred to him that the whole Canadian business needed to be wrapped up, pronto.

It was time for Arko to send a little message, while Hector headed south to his Pacific island retreat near San Jose, Costa Rica.

After his stint in Russia, Arko had steered clear of his native Cuba and along the way learnt fluent English, in addition to Russian. Possessing a variety of central American passports and identities, he moved under the radar, courtesy of the Condor umbrella. A mystery man, whose professions matched the task in hand: oil and gas consultant in eastern Europe, produce broker in the USA and Canada. A chameleon of circumstance and ruthless fixer.

Arko had profited greatly, thanks to his boss, Hector Delmontez, and had quietly set himself and his Russian girlfriend, Irma Morovskaya, a one-time Bolshoi ballerina, up in an oceanside villa on the borders of Ecuador and Peru, in an idyllic spot that was about as far from the long arm of the law as anyone could get. He was now fifty-five and some mornings would feel the effects of his often-violent youth in Angola, Siberia, and Chechnya on his brisk runs along the never-ending white Pacific sands. More solid than lithe, these days, he still bench-pressed two-fifty and anyone who valued their forearms steered well clear of arm wrestling with Arkito, if they knew what was good for them, after a few tequilas.

One day soon, he and Irma would retreat to luxuriate in their remote haven. But, for the time being, when Hector called, Arko listened.

In the helter-skelter of central America, both men knew that they had plenty of enemies and only communicated with each other via burner cell phones that they changed every month. Just as nobody knew who was really behind Condor or El Gruppo, so, too, Arko was a bit of an enigma – off the radar.

On that late January afternoon, as the flight from Seattle to Toronto touched down in the gloom, a shiver went through Leonardo Andreas Santos, travelling on a fake Ecuadoran passport, as he looked out at the deep snow. It just looked so uninviting outside, reminding him of his days in Siberia.

He'd travelled from Quito to Mexico City and then changed onto a United Airlines flight directly to Seattle. Senor Santos had attracted no more than perfunctory questions from US immigration and entering Canada from Seattle certainly wasn't going to raise any red flags. He'd be leaving in two days for Boston, he told the Canadian immigration officer who stamped his passport and thereafter, he knew, he would disappear: off the radar once more. In his line of business, planning was of essence. His new persona travelled light, sported a perfect glass eye and was prepared for the task in hand.

Senor Santos checked into the Marriot Hotel on Queen's Quay with a superior waterfront room overlooking Lake Ontario. This Marriott was smaller than others in the chain and had seen better days, but it suited him due to its proximity to his business and subsequent exit from Canada, via the adjacent downtown Billy Bishop airport. No customs or immigration until destination and by then whoever had any questions for him would certainly not have any reason to believe that he was fleeing anything but the cold.

◆　◆　◆

The Toronto business had surprised Hector. Who knew that so much money was so discreetly squirreled away in such a seemingly law-abiding city nestled between the great lakes Huron, Erie, and Ontario? But still waters run deep and Calvin Weiner, through his own greed and unfortunate addiction, had got a little out of his depth when he'd started dallying with the local Russian community.

Back in his pre-Perestroika days, at the Belarus factory in Minsk, the Russians that Arko had met had been hard-nosed communists, simple folk. But the new generation, sent overseas by their Oligarch parents were a completely different bunch. Used to the immense wealth bestowed upon them, they were brash and entitled, building immense and gaudy faux chateaux-style houses, driving muscle cars, and flaunting extravagant and flashy women.

Few bothered these mega-rich invaders in such a backwater. CSIS (the Canadian CIA or MI5) were certainly well aware of who was who, but the money these Russians had brought with them was irresistible. Canada was a safe haven, with trusted big banks and institutions, and its government was stable. Canada was part of North America but not the USA. An important consideration.

Everything had seemed to be going well up until the previous summer's hiccup at the Queen's Plate. Cal Weiner ran horse racing in Ontario as if it was his private fiefdom and his partner in crime, Mike Rogers, had been the perfect salesman when it had come to recruiting investors, be they into narcotics or bloodstock. Then the clients had become greedy. They wanted more regular shipments, more opportunities to launder their money and win races to fuel their insatiably decadent lifestyle, and this greed had seriously blunted the goose with the golden eggs that Hector had decided would not be laying any more until the heat was off.

Weiner had been truly shaken up by the hit on Mike Rogers, but now found himself stuck between a rock and a hard place. He needed money and, after the CART deal had fallen apart due to his mismanagement and squandering of the Ontario government's generous subsidies, he appreciated only too well that horse racing in Canada needed new investment no matter where it came from, and however much he despised the new people he and Mike had unwittingly brought into their backyard.

Hector had been unrelenting when they'd met at Saratoga. But now he'd agreed to send someone up to sort things out and Weiner had been informed that he'd be contacted, regarding the resumption of services. So, there was hope.

Thoroughbred racing at Woodbine had ended in mid-November and those who could afford to make the trip and had stock able to compete at racetracks south of the border had fled to the sunshine of Gulfstream in Miami or The Fairgrounds in New Orleans, leaving the hardy trotters that Weiner so despised to entertain local gamblers. Like comparing Formula One to Nascar or sailing to stink-pots, as he disdainfully referred to motor-powered boats. He had no time for the jugheads.

Mike Rogers was gone. So nobody was left to scheme with, as he'd burnt his boats with all the decent local horseman who felt he'd ignored them over the years and was now pandering to some Johnny-come-lately Russians who had no real interest in horse racing - just making money and flaunting their wealth.

It was a brutally cold and very clear night and Weiner could see the stars as he looked out across Lake Ontario to the lights of Burlington, thirty miles across the bay in the distance, from his thirty-fifth floor condominium at 65 Harbour Square.

He kept the one bedroom, 750-square foot unit for entertaining his mistresses. The latest, a very trim young lady named Shannon, whom he'd met in a bar on Wellington Street two months before, had, by the looks of things, figured him out and, after a passionate few weeks, moved on. She'd said she'd meet him in the usual place at seven, but it was almost eleven. As he nursed a Scotch and rued the fact that he was no longer the playboy of his youth and maybe shouldn't be treating Samantha, at home in King City, this way, his cell phone rang and he was jolted back into reality.

Nobody, well, very few, knew this number. He hesitated, frightened to pick up the pulsing little black rectangle. Unknown caller. 'Hello?' There was a delay.

'Mr. Weiner?' a smooth baritone voice purred.

'Yes, speaking,' Weiner answered nervously.

'Leo Santos. Hector sends his regards. We will meet.'

Weiner gulped. 'Where?'

'Where are you?' the voice continued, without giving away any further details.

'When would you like to meet? I'm...I'm downtown. Actually, right downtown, not far from the lake,' Weiner spluttered.

'That is good. Do you have a car?'

'Yes, yes, of course.'

'You will pick me up in thirty minutes on the northwest corner of Lakeshore and Bathurst. I will be wearing a black coat and a Yankees baseball cap.'

'Yes, I know it. There's a gas station, Esso I think, on the south side. I'll be there...' But the line had gone dead.

Cal Weiner was sweating as he hurriedly put on his winter boots, a Blue Canada Goose down-filled jacket, that his wife Samantha had given him for Christmas, a black cashmere scarf, and a black toque. Don't hurry, he told himself as he scurried down the long hallway to the elevator. On the seventh floor he exited and cut through to the parking lot, where a blast of cold air hit him as he emerged close to his black Mercedes SUV.

It had taken him all of ten minutes. No rush, he reminded himself as the car wound its way down to the ground-level exit onto Queen's Quay and he turned left. Normally a busy part of town, with two lanes of traffic both ways and a streetcar line down the middle, the road was almost deserted. The wind howled and gusted snow, drifting it up against the sidewalk and newspaper boxes, as he waited at a red light at the junction with Bay Street.

He turned right at York and then quickly left onto Lakeshore Boulevard, under the Gardiner Expressway where it was more sheltered. Weiner shivered as he passed a group of homeless people huddling by a small fire under a viaduct, out of the wind. The Lakeshore swung right and elevated as it crossed over lower Spadina Avenue and dropped down to Bathurst. He looked at his watch, it was eleven twenty-five. The light was green, and he crossed to the west side, but there was no one standing on the corner. He pulled over and waited. He was a bit early, he thought, and drove on to the next street on the right, around the block and back. This time, coming down Bathurst, he saw a figure, head down, crossing Lakeshore from the south. As he turned the corner, it was standing there, with the distinctive Yankees emblem. Santos approached and got in.

'Leo?' enquired Weiner.

'Yes. Let's drive,' replied Arko

Weiner headed west, down past the Canadian National Exhibition grounds, onto the waterfront where in July the annual Molson Indy IRL race would be held, along past Ontario Place on the left. Now exposed to Lake Ontario, the wind howled, and the gusts whipped up the snow that had fallen, creating a white fog, off which the car's headlight beams reflected.

They continued in silence, past the Palais Royale. In the distance the lights from the twin towers of Palace Pier flickered. At Colbourne Lodge, Arko said, 'Make a U-turn here, at the lights.'

'Can't do that,' said Weiner anxiously, 'we don't want to attract the attention of the cops, do we?'

Arko remained silent.

'Where do you want to go?'

Arko had taken a run out to where the Humber River entered the lake, about two miles west of his hotel, just before the Palace Pier towers, and had noticed parking lots down by the water. 'Over there, we can park,' he motioned.

'Ok, we'll go up the South Kingsway, turn around, and come back down. They're not all open at this time of year. We'll have to see if there's one that's been plowed.' He turned the Mercedes around in the parking lot of a Mac's Milk, dropped back down onto Lakeshore Boulevard, and turned left, back towards downtown.

'There,' said Arko.

Weiner turned the now snow-covered car into the parking lot on the right, where a plow had made a few passes to enable access.

'This isn't exactly the best spot,' said Weiner. 'There's nobody else here and, as I say, we don't need any attention. Let's turn into Exhibition Place. There'll be cars parked there and we won't stand out.'

'Ok, ok,' said Arko, impatiently.

Eventually the Mercedes halted just behind BMO Field, in the middle of a row of snow-covered vehicles, and Weiner turned off the lights. 'I'll leave the engine running,' he said.

The two men sat in silence. 'I like soft, clean snow,' said Arko, eventually. He'd reverted into his sing-songy Cuban dialect. 'El nieve, we call it, saw plenty of it in Russia. Man, is that a cold country!'

Weiner sat impassively, staring out through the windshield that was rapidly becoming snow-covered. He chewed his right thumb nervously. In the dark, Arko couldn't see, but there was a glisten of sweat over his greyish pallor, highlighted now and again by the passing headlights of cars on Lakeshore Boulevard.

'So,' said Arko, with a sudden emphasis that jolted Weiner from his temporary stupor, 'your Russian friends have been putting the heat on, eh?' He smiled to himself, using that familiar Canadian rejoinder.

'Fucking greedy, that's what they are,' Weiner blurted out. 'Mike was doing a good job. You can't win all the time.' He paused. 'Besides, whatever they might have thought about the losses – I mean, when we unloaded a lemon on them – they were making their cash legit. But, oh no, they wanted the maximum all the time. Hector warned us…'

'Si, Si,' Arko interrupted him, 'El Gruppo is under investigation. What's the guy, Gilligan, eh? He's running scared. Gotta sit tight, let the dust settle. Your guys have got lots going on and the boss says that they may win the Derby this time.'

'I know, I know. I keep telling them that. But they're out of control. Just too much money, fast cars, and have you seen their women? Just crazy. I don't think that Oleg's dad has any idea what's going on.'

Arko laughed. 'They're like his mules. They make the money legit. He don't care. He's on his yacht in Marbella or Monte Carlo.'

'He'll care plenty if his boys carry on the way they have been. Whacking Mike in the paddock on Queen's Plate day shook up some people around here.

Too much attention. Doing what they're doing, you don't need that attention.'

The snow had by now completely covered the windscreen, despite the best efforts of the heater, and Weiner switched on the wiper blades. 'So, what do we do? Hector said you'd have a plan?'

'He does. No more charters to Canada. For a while, anyway, until things settle down.'

Weiner grimaced. 'None? Nothing?' he pleaded.

'Too much heat, comrade.' Arko slipped into his Russian.

'What about the other business? Surely we can keep that pipeline open?'

'Probably. But, there again, the heat is watching.'

'What heat?' Weiner instantly regretted saying that.

'What do you mean? What heat? Are you stupid?' Arko turned to his left. He still had his leather gloves on, and it crossed his mind that he should throttle this miserable little piss-baby beside him, who had caused his boss so much trouble. One snap from those vice-like hands and they wouldn't have to worry about Mr. Canadian Big-Shot anymore. But that would have been clumsy. 'Now you listen to me! You are in operation because of us. You fucked up your little private horse show here in…here in…' he struggled for the right words, 'here in Toronto, and the boss saves your arse. You do what we fucking say! Ok? Ok?'

'Yes, yes, I hear you,' a cowed Weiner replied.

Both men sat in silence.

'I'll talk to the boss and maybe, just maybe, we can put something together for you in a few weeks. We have something going on that I can't tell you about, but we should be able to steer some gear you guys way. If things work out.'

'Weeks? You don't understand. These guys are onto me daily. Samantha, my wife, she's getting calls in the middle of the night. We tried going to the cottage, but they know! They know where we live. I'm concerned!'

Arko thought he detected a tear. 'Here, this'll make you feel better.' And he reached into his quilted jacket and brought out a small plastic bag. 'Compliments of the house. Looks like you could do with a little boost.'

Weiner took the bag greedily. 'You don't mind?'

'Go ahead, I won't watch. Besides, you guys up here are liberalizing everything. Soon this shit will be all over the place. Legal. We'll be outta business, thanks to the government. How do you like that?'

The drugs had got Weiner's attention and he sat up and pulled a small notepad out from the glove compartment and placed it on the central consul, totally consumed in his handiwork. Then he poured three short lines of white powder from the packet onto the smooth surface and produced a short hollow tube from his jacket pocket. He looked over at Arko who appeared to be deep in thought, with his eyes shut, and smiled conspiratorially.

A snorting-cum-sucking sound filled the silence and was followed by a single muffled gasp. It was all too simple. Arko didn't need to look. He picked up the package, replaced it with another full one, and exited into the storm.

CHAPTER 50

Matt Pearson was now official, once more. Some cynics might have said that he'd served his own self-imposed course in anger management, down on the farm. But it had still taken exceptional circumstances, and the emergence of a horse that had truly inspired his latent emotions, to make the big move.

The horse-racing experts and pundits had already decided that the unbeaten champion two-year-old and Breeders' Cup winner Sputnik was a foregone conclusion to win the Kentucky Derby, but nonetheless a few wise heads had noticed the handsome, dark bay Virginia-bred at Saratoga and again, in the last of his three starts, at Churchill Downs, when he'd toyed with his opponents over the very same track where he'd be tilting for the Roses come the first Saturday in May. Matt had laughed when he noticed that Last Hurrah had got a 50/1 quote. 'Better than being just a field horse,' he'd said. But that's the way he liked it: under the radar, no pressure.

The whole hype of the Triple Crown was something Matt had had no time for, believing that too many good horses had been ruined chasing this rainbow before they were ready. 'Why is it,' he opined, 'the same people always seem to show up with a horse and often several on the first Saturday of every May?' But now here he was on a collision course with everything that he'd always eschewed.

Whatever his thoughts were, though, Vera was definitely the captain of this ship. And, as far as he knew, only a handful of people knew the real story, which was fine. Having a Derby horse was different and, no matter how well she managed them, Matt knew that his main problem wouldn't be just getting his charge to the starting gate for the Derby in prime condition, but controlling the increasingly excited owners.

Over the winter the Elevator Stable had speculated wildly. Reggie had been the most sanguine, suggesting that the colt had punched above his weight, with the sprinter's pedigree that he had. While there were always exceptions and he might well train on to be a nice three-year-old, reality suggested that he was 'just a horse' and 'maybe we should cash him in now? You know, people go crazy to have a horse in the Derby. Maybe we can get some mug to give us a million dollars?' he'd said. To which Vera had kicked this idea down the road by responding, 'Let's see how he likes Florida and leave it up to Matt. Maybe you are right - he's just a sprinter. But let's wait and see.'

Victor, Colin, and Nils each had their own theories, but going to the Derby appealed to them. As Victor said, 'We've only been in the business for five minutes, but we have a horse with a legitimate shot. Some people spend a fortune and a lifetime trying to get where we are.'

'Yeah,' Reggie had replied, but before he'd had a chance to expound upon 'never going broke if you take a profit' he'd been voted down. As Colin had pointed out, from his one trip to the Kentucky Derby as a spectator, the build-up to the race and the subsequent month, all the way to New York and the Belmont Stakes, was a surreal experience, and to be a part of it would be priceless. 'There are so many scenarios. They say Trebor's horse – hey, he's got several that on their day could win it all – is a lock and our guy may not get the trip, but we won't know that unless we try. I have complete faith in Matt Pearson. After all,' he pointed out to Reggie, 'wasn't he the only reason you got involved in this caper, in the first place? We've got so little invested, we gotta let him run.'

And that was about that, until agents started phoning. The trouble was, they didn't know how to get in touch with the trainer. Every time one got through to the farm, the staff who had been well-briefed, told them that Ms. Montagu or Mr. Pearson were unavailable or in Florida.

The Florida route to Kentucky was a no-brainer. Trebor would be honing his team on the west coast and a one-two warm-up on the dirt at Gulfstream, using a prep then the Florida Derby in late March, as the stepping stone six weeks out, was exactly what Matt thought his colt would benefit most from. So, shortly after Christmas, the team of six horses had shipped down to Payson Park training centre.

◆ ◆ ◆

The last three years had sped by. Sometimes when he woke in the middle of the night, Tom found himself trying to think back PR, pre-Rocky, as he now referred to that time. What had sustained him since then, mentally as much as financially, per the machinations of his dear aunt, was a horse. It wasn't true compensation for the loss of his parents, but he buoyed himself, in rare moments of sadness, with the knowledge that his father would be right beside him and this was his destiny.

Rocky, like great athletes, had a presence about him. Like a fighter with a chip on his shoulder, his dubious, unbeknownst provenance seemed to make him special. To Tom, anyway. This underdog status seemed to calm everyone around him, because there were no great expectations from those who didn't know the story, and those precious few who did were just happy to be along for the ride.

What Matt liked was that his charge was just treated like any old horse, and while he knew that if they made it to the big show there'd be plenty of inquisitive know-it-alls bugging him, he'd deal with that in his own way at that time.

Toby had everyone, including the normally pensive Matt, in stitches when he had speculated about choice of rider and how Matt would cope with the gormless media and their mindlessly stupid questions at Churchill Downs. 'We gonna have to hide you away, boss,' he'd say, 'when all them media guys come swarmin' round the barn.'

'Maybe we'll do a Billy Turner and direct them to another horse?' said Tom. 'You know how Billy always invented stories about The Slew. Little Hughie they called him. What was it, his exercise rider was Lawlor Yates or something like that? A combination of two people that nobody could figure out.'

'Yeah, and they always wondered why he rode Cruguet,' said Matt.

'Just like they'll wanna know why you ride Joe Magee all the time, boss,' laughed Toby.

'I can see it coming,' said Matt. 'Had that fucking Tuffano guy on the phone, the other day. Don't know how he got my number. Says: We want to ride your horse. I said what horse? You weigh three hundred pounds. Stop bugging me. Just won't go away. Good thing we're up here, not down at Gulfstream, as he'd be round the barn every day, touting his rider.'

'Hey, Tom, are they ready for round two, at Gulfstream?' laughed Toby. 'Lovato got off light at Laurel. Our man's bin in trainin'. No tellin' what he might do to a guy who'd mess with this big hoss.' And he gave Rocky, who was leaning out of his stall munching on his hay net, an affectionate slap on the shoulder.

'Don't you worry about me, man. Me and Joe Magee. We'll show ya!' Matt chuckled.

◆　◆　◆

As the classic contenders stirred themselves in both Europe and North America for their biggest task, focus in the latter featured a series of key races, predominantly in Florida and California.

Matt Pearson had let Last Hurrah down after his last race, back in November at Churchill Downs, but had kept him ticking over sufficiently on the farm that, within two weeks of arriving at Payson Park, he made the worksheet, with a sedate half-mile in fifty-two seconds, over the deep racetrack.

The physical transition from two to three, and relative maturity of a horse that is targeting major tests early in his second year in training, is a very critical time. Last Hurrah wasn't a big horse, standing just over sixteen hands, but he was beautifully conformed and balanced, so there had been no awkwardness in his development and he'd always stepped up when asked to increase the workload. The races as a two-year-old had sharpened him. Speed, according to his listed pedigree, was considered natural but the way he'd run his races, settling and showing a great turn of foot, when asked, augured well for the future, going around two turns, and that last race at Churchill had confirmed that the quality was there.

Matt didn't want to sprint Rocky again. So his prep for the Florida Derby was going to be over a mile and a sixteenth (two turns), sometime in mid-to late-February. He knew that his horse would tell him when. There was no need to burn the track up with bullet workouts. Just steady progress, with Tom in the saddle, pushing 140 pounds.

The Elevators boys had made Matt promise not to ambush them with Rocky's first start back. He laughed at some of the suggestions he'd received from Colin regarding the overall program and maybe a more fashionable rider.

So it was that, despite several intrusive calls from Sal Tuffano about Munoz being the man for Last Hurrah, when the entries came out for the seventh race at Gulfstream on Saturday, February 24, there was the four-horse, Last Hurrah, and Joe Magee.

It was an open allowance race for three-year-olds and, because he'd won a Grade 3 stakes race, Rocky was top weight with 126 pounds, giving weight to the whole field. Matt had decided to stay away from the feature of the day, the Fountain of Youth Stakes, because, although it was a traditional prep for the Florida Derby, it was a much more competitive race. Figuring that a horse's first race, or first race back off a break, took more out of them than subsequent races back-to-back, he felt that this easier spot was a better way to kick off in a manner that would leave plenty of gas, he hoped, in the tank come Derby time.

The *Daily Racing Form* touted Last Hurrah as their best bet of the day at Gulfstream, with the byline 'Time to Show That He's Trained On.' Reggie guffawed into his track Bible as he read this and swatted up on the competition's form.

As it turned out, Rocky had made the expected progress from two to three seamlessly and the outcome was never in doubt, as Joe Magee stalked a quick opening half in forty five and two before letting his charge ease back and around his weakening rivals at the three-eighths pole and drawing off for a facile victory by three lengths, in the good time of one minute forty and two-fifths. Again, the style in which he had settled and put away challengers impressed an increasing army of believers.

◆　◆　◆

Three thousand miles away, Tim Trebor was firing live rounds at Santa Anita, as his powerful stable took three races on the Saturday card, headed by the very impressive wire-to-wire victory in the Malibu Stakes of Sputnik, much to the great satisfaction of a beaming Hector Delmontez and his ever-increasing entourage of glamorous and stylish admirers, the latest of which, Cindy Li-Chen, raised a few eyebrows in Arcadia.

Hector was happy. The America's Stable were front and centre, with the favourite for the Kentucky Derby. His European syndicate members had exciting prospects for the upcoming races at the Dubai World Cup in March. His Canadian headache was over and now the lovely Ms. Li-Chen had surfaced. Business was good and, as a new member of the Jockey Club, his mentor, Billy Beagle, could not have been happier…he thought, anyway.

◆　◆　◆

Arko had done the job masterfully. His swansong, as he referred to it when Hector had recently visited him at his Pacific coast beach house in Ecuador. 'That's it, boss! I'm retired. Not going back to Yankee-land no more.'

As they'd walked along the endless white sands with the breakers crashing on their right, Arko had explained the decision he'd made. 'When I got there, you could see he was desperate. Those Russians had him scared and he was going to be a liability, no matter how we fixed him up. I thought I'd take care of him in the conventional way.' Hector, walking through the surf in just his white Bermuda shorts, listened between the crashes. 'It would have been so easy. But then, when he sounded more concerned about the dope than anything else, I knew. Amazing how that stuff works – Coramine with the coke asphyxiates you. Pronto! Just like that!' And he snapped his fingers. 'Do you remember that kid who used to work on the farm? I forget his name. Well it just gets you. Quicker than cyanide. He didn't even turn to look at me. Never said a word. One gasp, dead.' He made a chopping motion across his throat.

The two men walked on. 'Nice touch, spooking his amigos,' said Hector.

'Yes, I thought you'd like that,' Arko smiled. 'It snowed very heavily that night. Everything got buried. Even if they'd gone out looking for him, they'd have taken days to find him. Besides, he wasn't supposed to be down there, messing with his girlfriend. Naughty boy! When my plane took off from the Island airport at eight the next morning, we flew over the Exhibition grounds. And, when I looked down, it was like a newly iced cake. All those cars just buried. They didn't find him for three days.'

'Yes, so I read,' said Hector. 'Police put it down to an overdose.'

'Same as that Randy kid. I guess they've never come across the cocktail, eh?'

'Best that they didn't,' said Hector with a chuckle.

'Well, knowing what you told me about the Ruskies and that stuff in the paddock at Woodbine, you know "you'll be next" stuff and the heat getting all revved up about their local Russians, the same guys who were threatening our guy, I thought I'd put a word in their controller's ear.'

'You mean old man Chatrov, in Monaco?'

'Ya, him. It was hilarious. I'm in Boston, and I call this number and pretend I'm a Russian. I say Novochoksi here, and there's a silence. Then, in my best Russian gangster accent, you know, from my time over there, I tell Big Daddy that sonny is going to see a lot of heat when the cops find the guy, that his mates threatened, has croaked. The phone went dead, but I guess they got the message, as those kids were outta Toronto within hours. Long before they found amigo, Cal.'

'Yep, Senor Beagle and I went to the funeral. Pretty sad, really. The guy inherits a fortune from his dad, who worked his guts out. And he frittered it all away. And, along the way, fucks everything up by squandering the over $4 billion horse racing got from the slots.' Hector paused. 'It always amazes me the stuff they write about people when they die. The obituaries in the Toronto papers and the *Racing Form* were nonsense. You know, stuff about what he'd done for horse racing. Just fake news, completely false. He was a weak man, hooked on drugs. Pathetic. But he still coulda done something, if he hadn't got involved with those Russian schmucks.'

'Greed does it every time. Lie with dogs and you'll get fleas, eh? And, as you said, boss, using the product always ends badly.'

'Good work Arko. Two or, actually, several birds killed with one stone. They served their purpose, bringing in some money, helping the America's Stable to get launched. Senor Beagle liked that and that whole Jockey Club solidarity that he and Weiner had, you know, the US and Canada. Just like he has with the folks who run racing in the UK. But we couldn't afford to have him on the loose, with what he had on the spit box. No, they aren't going to bother us again.'

'Anytime, boss. Just know that I'm not going back to the States anymore.'

'Well, I might just have one more little job. But we'll bring those cuckoos to the nest. It'll be local. Hasta luego amigo.'

CHAPTER 51

The fox hunting season had been spectacular and Algy Sinclair was enjoying his position as manager of horse racing for Ravi Singh, a title that not only covered his boss's horses, and in particular the ongoing successes of Java Raja, but also now involved acting as liaison for Motti-Media's burgeoning Real Racing interests that had taken off following the partnership with Sheikh Ali Al-Bhakandar.

Now known as Real Racing Global, a new office had been opened in London and there was considerable buzz in the sports and horse racing media about major sweepstakes upcoming during the World Cup meet in Dubai at the end of March and in England in early April, on the Grand National.

Ravi and Kulbir could not believe how many doors Sheikh Ali had magically opened. As Kulbir not so subtly put it, after he'd had a quiet word with Jos Danvers and Hugo Lascelles, 'that it would be in their interests to persuade their stuffy friends at Portman Square to get the shit out of their eyes and wake up to the reality that the Internet has no boundaries.' They seemed to get it, all of a sudden.

There had been a lot of hemming and hawing and dire warnings from superannuated solicitors about the consequences of violating monopolies rules. Whereas two humble Indians had little to bargain with, the Sheikh carried a big stick and he knew just how much not only his minders relied upon him to keep up appearances, but the entire sport of horse racing in the UK relied upon the A-rabs, as they were collectively known, for survival.

Both Java Raja and Prince Ali were targeting major races on the big day in Dubai that, over the past twenty five years or so, had become a major highlight of the international racing calendar: a must-stop for all celebrities and high rollers in what Algy, in private of course, now referred to as 'The sport of Sheikh's.'

As he relaxed with a cappuccino on the balcony of his eighteenth-floor room at the Burj Al Arab hotel, looking out at the Dhows trundling in and out of the busy port of Dubai far below, he smiled wistfully. Not bad for a struggling bloodstock agent, he mused. Thank God for cricket, Uncle Teddy's exposure of Bog, and the latter's extraordinarily pompous behaviour at Keeneland, or he might never have met the amazing Mr. Singh.

It's all about timing, he reasoned, being in the right place at the right time, and it did help a bit to know the right people. From there the domino effect had kicked in and, thanks to the irrepressable Sheikh Ali, here they were, with a couple of live horses and the global sensation that Real Racing had become. How sweet it was.

This moment of contemplative bliss was just then interrupted by the vibration of his mobile phone in his pocket. It was Bog. 'Algy. John here. There is a car coming to take us to the draw for the Real Race, in twenty minutes. I'll see you in the lobby.'

As he hung up, Algy smiled at the emphasis Bog had put upon 'Real Race,' as if it was some sort of fake race or an uninvited guest to the week's festivities. Bog hadn't missed a beat since blowing the Singh account, though, and, if anything, had elevated his bumptiousness. Now engaged to Lucy Beagle, to whom he'd proposed in Hong Kong while attending the races at Shatin back in January, Bog, as was his wont, had unwittingly backed into a client of unimaginable promise. While obliging his fiancé with a visit to a local concert – something as alien to Bog as visiting Lords cricket ground had been three years before – he'd been introduced to the star cellist, the very lovely Cindy Li-Chen. Being the mega schmoozer that he was, he'd very quickly discovered Ms. Li-Chen's love of horses, inviting her to Santa Anita to see his syndicate (a bit of an exaggeration), the America's Stable's Sputnik, win the Malibu Stakes, just the week before. Swept along by Mr. Smooth, here they were in Dubai. An absolute 'must-do,' in Bog's world.

The diminutive Cindy Li-Chen looked stunning in a turquoise figure-hugging sequined bodysuit that made her look like a celestial mermaid, as Bog assisted her into the back of the dark blue Rolls Royce Corniche. This was one punter whom he was going to play very carefully. Danvers and Lascelles might even make him a partner if he could reel her in, he thought.

'Cindy,' he waffled. 'I don't think you've met Algy, have you?'

'Ms. Li-Chen, how charming you look,' beamed Algy.

'We met in Hong Kong,' Bog gushed on. Algy wondered just how well this show of enthusiasm was being taken on board by Lucy Beagle. 'A thorn between two roses, eh Bog?' he said without thinking and had to bite his lip to stop laughing hysterically, as he'd corrected himself, 'Johnny, John, of course,' deeply wanting to ask the delightful Ms. Li-Chen how on earth she'd met this bounder.

'Algy's man, Mr. Ravi Singh, an Indian chap, invented this Real Racing phenomena that we're off to see drawn today,' Bog continued, explaining where they were going to his rapt guest.

'Well, actually, his brother Kulbir did, but that's beside the point, really, as today it's the hottest multimedia sports sweepstake in the world.' Algy corrected him. 'To be fair, it wasn't until Johnny's agency's main man, Sheikh Ali, one of our very generous hosts here in Dubai, came on board that the endeavour took real wings. Ha! Ha!' He laughed at his own joke.

'Yep, hard to believe, but, even though the best horses in the world are competing here in Dubai this week, it is just an ordinary handicap that's generating all the excitement.'

'Fascinating,' said Cindy Li-Chen. 'Back in China, they'd love this.'

'Well, who knows? Maybe that's the next stop?'

'First, we're doing the Grand National,' said Algy. 'That race always struck me as the best one to do. Such a big field. Such a spectacle. Everyone knows about The National, so you don't need to do much promotion.'

The car had by now arrived at Meydan Racecourse which had the appearance, in the dusk of evening, of a glitzy Las Vegas casino shimmering in the desert, gilded by a thousand stars. As Bog had predicted, the draw for the Gulf Handicap turned out to be the main event of the evening, as players around the world who'd tuned in per hundreds of satellite TV connections, learnt whether they'd got lucky and drawn a horse in what promised to be one of the biggest horse racing extravaganzas in history.

At the centre of proceedings were Sheikh Ali and his brother Sultan, hosts for the evening. Tommo Thompson, sporting an electric blue suit and patriotically Aussie-yellow tie was the MC and an A-list of international movie stars complimented a large Bollywood and Indian cricket presence.

To Bog's glee, his guest received five-star treatment and was even asked up onto to the stage to draw a horse that most appropriately was won by a Hong Kong resident who, through the wonders of social media, was very quickly beamed onto a screen where the audience was able to see him celebrating in his Kowloon apartment.

It was like a surreal mid-summer night game show, orchestrated by sheikhs and princes, with the biggest prizes ever played for. That horse racing, a sport that had been spiralling into oblivion in the face of more entertaining competition and poor marketing, was the vehicle for such frenzied excitement over what, for purists, was a nothing burger, was the supremest irony.

CHAPTER 52

Following the Dubai show the circus moved on to Aintree racecourse, just outside Liverpool in north-western England, for the grandaddy of steeplechases. If ever there was a lottery of races, it was this one, with up to forty or more starters taking their very precarious chances over a hazard-filled course of thirty fences and a distance slightly in excess of four miles.

This supreme handicap, with weights ranging from eleven stone ten pounds, (164 pounds) all the way down to ten stone (140 pounds), is definitely a case where luck and a good clear passage through the carnage will always triumph over the logic of superior form.

As Ravi and Sheikh Ali salivated over the enormous pool that this quintessential test would generate, even the former had to pinch himself to appreciate just what he and has brother had started. So enthused was Sheikh Ali that he even instructed his managers to go out and buy a runner, breaking with the tradition of staying away from such a risky sport with such puny returns.

While the British press whipped the public into a frenzy and ridiculed the Jockey Club for not having thought of such an idea, despite the precedent of the Irish Hospital Sweepstakes more fifty years before, the appetite for tickets was further fuelled by the announcement that in addition to the NHS, proceeds would be going towards cancer research and the draw would be made by two members of the British Royal Family.

◆ ◆ ◆

Stateside, Derby fever was fomenting – within racing circles, anyway – even if not at the forefront of sports media.

Tongues were first set wagging by a very lacklustre effort from Sputnik in the Santa Anita Derby. Endeavouring to wire the field, in his usual front-running style, Tim Trebor's colt faded noticeably in the stretch and only hung on grimly by a head from his lesser fancied stablemate, Mayan Warrior, the horse that had won Last Hurrah's first race at Woodbine, ten months before.

After the race, Trebor, in his usual sugarcoated generalizations, suggested that he'd take a blood test and watch to see if his charge ate up and how he bounced out of this uncharacteristically dull performance. Back in the barn, not for public consumption, there was big concern and shrewder observers were hedging their bets.

Meanwhile, across the continent, all was tickety-boo at Payson Park after Rocky had demolished ten opponents in the Florida Derby, stalking a quick early pace and drawing off to win by four, on the bridle. Following in the wake of Sputnik's unimpressive performance, in his Derby prep out west, the name of Last Hurrah had begun trending and places to hide were becoming more difficult to find for Matt Pearson.

The good news was that Payson Park is an hour and a half out into the sticks, north of Miami. But, as a bone fide contender, Last Hurrah could not be hidden away completely until the first Saturday in May and Vera and her co-owners had decisions to make.

Matt had a plan and wanted to stick to it and, in his corner, he had Joe Magee as an ally. The horse, trainer, jockey combination had come out of nowhere and, all of a sudden, there was a host of experts who felt they knew better. This horse is a freak who is punching over his weight. His trainer is a certified nutcase who will choke and make a fatal error in the pressurized cauldron at Churchill Downs. As for his rider? At forty-seven, he's a dinosaur.

Amongst the increasing turmoil and media attention, Vera held a firm line. She and Shenandoah Valley Farms represented the one established element of this ragtag team, and when the Elevator Stable met at Payson Park on April 1, she quickly asserted that there would be one voice: hers.

Matt and Tom, as far as Vera was prepared to admit, were still the only people who knew the real story. When Matt had shown up with the little orphan foal three years before, she'd acted instinctively and had never really given much thought to future consequences, telling herself that they'd jump that fence when or if they got to it.

Now, though, they'd reached that fence and it was vital to play their hand in as low-key a manner as possible. Her Elevator Stable partners, in their blissful ignorance, were enjoying the ride of their lives. She could handle their input and suggestions, however whacky some might be, and keep them away from Matt. But, as the meeting broke up, when Tom told her that he'd had a call from his friend Algy, and would like to talk to her in private, the whole charade took a very different turn.

They met the following day, after training, at the Hobe Sound beach house. Vera was reclining in a chaise longue on the lawn, just where it adjoined the white sand, and the azure blue breakers of the Atlantic could be heard crashing beyond. As always, the dogs greeted Tom with a chorus of excited barks.

'Well, Tom, I bet you never thought we'd come this far?'

Tom picked up Monty, who had been pestering him for his attentions, and sat in an Adirondack chair. 'Quite something, isn't he?'

'The colt, you mean?'

'Of course! But you're right, I never really thought about this. I mean, him being a Derby horse.'

'Why not? He has the pedigree. He doesn't know that there's anything odd about where he is or what he's doing,' said Vera.

'Perhaps that's best. And, you know, with nobody giving him special attention, he's come through.'

'We – well you, actually – have nothing to lose. Per the agreement, he's provided you with an income and if he does win the Derby, that is your father's legacy. It was meant to be, Tom. If not, it will have, at least, been a great ride and the experience of the last three years will, I hope, have helped you to move on.'

'Yep, I don't know what I would have done. When I came down to see you, I was lost and then you gave me hope. Something to live for.'

'Well, enjoy it while it lasts, because so few get to be in a position like yours. Now, tell me what's on your mind?'

'Yesterday I received a call from Algy. You remember that he came to the farm?'

'Yes, indeed. A most charming young man.'

'Well, since then, Algy has done very well for himself. He's now manager for the very wealthy Indian IT guy who owns that very good horse, Java Raja.'

'Oh, yes, the 2000 Guineas winner, bred by your friend in Kentucky?'

'Well, no, that's Mark, he's the breeders' agent.'

'Isn't this Indian guy the guy who started Real Racing?'

'Yeah, that's him – it's a sensation – anyway, Algy called me because he has been asked whether Last Hurrah is for sale.'

Vera was visibly taken aback. Eventually she asked, 'Who wants to buy him?'

'Well, I'm not sure. But Algy's friend, Johnny Ward-Clark, who is with CBS, has a client and he approached Algy because he knows that he knows me.'

'This puts a new spin on things, doesn't it? You haven't discussed this with anyone else, I hope?'

'No, no. I thought you should know first.'

'Well, it's a good thing that this has come through a discreet line of enquiry. We wouldn't want the press speculating, as the next thing we'd have Reggie and the boys getting their calculators out.' Vera stared out to sea. 'Well, I know… you know, what with the pedigree thing. Yes, yes, I'm thinking. Please bear with me. We can't have anyone putting our guy under a magnifying glass at this stage.'

'If you think about it, they'd be getting more than they expect,' said Tom, hoping to be helpful as his aunt's mind spun through the gears of potential disasters associated with the revelation that one of the leading contenders for the upcoming Derby is not what he appears to be. It would be a shocking scandal – fraud, even – and the whole incident with the fire would be reopened and, oh, my God, Matt would be under the gun. Jesus Christ! Billy Beagle would do his nut!

'Phew! We should be celebrating. But this!' Vera hesitated for a moment, 'This has to be handled very carefully.' She paused again, deep in thought. 'Ok. Tell your friend that I speak for the owners and that we will consider an offer. But, tell Algy to keep whatisname – Johnny? – under control. Tell him that he is the only person to have expressed interest so far, therefore, don't stir things up or there could be competition.'

As he drove back to Payson Park, along the seemingly endless, long straight roads through the orange groves, Tom's mind wandered wildly. Bog has a rich Arab who is going to make him financially secure for the rest of his life. This is Dad's gift. Rocky will win the Derby. No, he'll win the Triple Crown. But, if he's been sold, would we have got enough? And – and this troubled him the most – we'd have missed the excitement, a once-in-a-lifetime experience. He could imagine, though, that wily old Reggie would want to cash in. He could just hear him saying, 'Hey, we got lucky, with a sprinter who so far hasn't done nuthin' special. Take the money. You gotta be crazy not to. He runs up the track in the Derby and he's not worth two dead flies and a box of spent matches!'

But what if the buyer wants the colt checked out by his vets and they want to do some DNA checking to make sure, for his future career at stud? What happens then if they discover that he's not what his papers say he is? That would precipitate a disaster that was hard to imagine. People could go to jail. Vera and Matt would be totally discredited, at the least, and warned off the turf for life and the already severely damaged image of horse racing would be tarnished for ever. Billy Beagle would certainly not be able to handle this.

Tom came to his senses suddenly, as a fifty-three-foot semi blasted its horn and he swerved back into his lane. The long, straight road, warm afternoon sun, and his racing mind had put him in another world. Almost permanently.

CHAPTER 53

The Dubai World Cup meet had been a tour de force for Algy and Johnny. Java Raja confirmed his status as the best miler on the planet with another impressive victory and Prince Ali had delighted his owners by adjusting to the dirt and landing the richest race in the world, the $10 million World Cup, and the Real Racing Gulf Handicap had eclipsed even the previous fall's Melbourne Cup takings, with Sheikh Sultan proudly donating a cheque for $450 million to Unicef.

For the high-flying Euro racing crowd, the next stop was the opening of the flat racing seasons in England, Ireland, and France, and for Motti-Media the Grand National on the first Saturday in April promised to be a publicity and fund-raising bonanza.

For the two young bloodstock agents, though, there was additional business to be done. Algy found himself having to draw upon his most diplomatic reserves to curb the sudden and earnest attentions of his sometime friend, but, too often, flighty opportunist, Bog.

Bog was on a roll. While his bosses massaged their main breadwinner, Sheikh Ali, and completely unjustifiably basked in the Real Racing frenzy surrounding the Grand National sweepstake, Bog, who now was completely in charge of North American operations, was hell-bent on bringing in new punters with deep pockets to cement his position with Hector Delmontez and, above all, his future father-in-law, Billy Beagle.

The Russians had gone cold, which was not altogether a bad thing. Now, in their place, he had an even more interesting client on the radar. With Sputnik having sent out alarming distress signals in his final Derby prep, Bog felt that this was the time to play a trump card. So he'd, uncharacteristically, generously offered Algy a ride home from Dubai in Sheikh Ali's Lear jet. This immediately made the latter wonder just what Bog thought he could do for him and the subject of the Kentucky Derby had come up, when he'd mentioned taking Cindy Li-Chen to Santa Anita.

Never being one to let the grass grow under his nifty shoes, Bog had speculated that, with Sputnik rumoured to have problems, Last Hurrah represented a very interesting opportunity for Ms. Li-Chen to break into the sport with a bang.

It was very much an eleventh hour and highly audacious proposition, and it was particularly galling for him to have to approach Algy, because of his close association with the owners, for the inside track on the deal, after the Java Raja fiasco. But he felt that the horse could be bought. He wasn't going to reveal by whom, knowing full well his bosses would sit on the fence and let him burn if it didn't work out. But, he figured, it could be a career-maker.

Enjoying Bog's full and unusually friendly attention, Algy had demurred, explaining it was a real longshot that people with a major contender would sell in such circumstances. And, even if they did entertain an offer, it would have to be for serious money. He'd asked Bog if he was representing the Sheikh, but he'd been coy on the potential buyer. However, he had agreed to sound out Tom Fraser and get back to him.

Not a fan of social media and definitely a person leery of e-mails that left a trail, upon hearing back from Tom that his aunt would entertain an offer on behalf of the Elevator Stable, Algy had suggested a meeting the morning after they'd returned from Dubai, at which Bog had proposed $5 million for Last Hurrah.

'Who is his client?' Vera had first asked, when communicated this offer.

'Wouldn't tell me,' said Algy. 'But I have a feeling, based upon what I heard on the plane back from Dubai, that Bog is grooming a new client. Maybe this young Chinese lady?'

'Who is she?' asked Vera.

'Not much known about her. But I gather her father, who lives in Shanghai, has made a fortune in property development there. Anyway, Cindy, who was educated in Europe, went to the Sorbonne, etcetera, and speaks perfect English and French, is somewhat of a celebrated cellist. Bog met her at a concert that he took his fiancé to.'

'Lucy Beagle?'

'Yes.'

'That makes sense. This Bog guy, what do you call him? Is a slick mover?'

'His name is Johnny Ward-Clark and he works for the CBS agency in Newmarket.'

'Whatever makes him feel that $5 million is a fair price? You have to think about the deal with Victor, Reggie, and the boys and all of the fees and commissions. It wouldn't leave a lot for you, Tom.'

'He says his people at CBS think our horse is light on pedigree.'

'He does, does he. Wise guy, your friend Bog, isn't he?'

'He's not my friend, Aunt Vera, he's Algy's, and he would be the first to say that he's not his mate, as they say over there. Just an associate. They work together in the bloodstock business.'

'Let's keep Matt right out of this at this point and let him concentrate on training his horse. This sort of thing would send him right off the deep end. Besides, I know, although he won't admit it, that he's really enjoying this lark. The prospect of training a Derby winner would give him a lot of internal satisfaction and silence his many critics.'

'Well, I would stipulate that any deal, no matter for how much, would be contingent upon Rocky staying with Matt. I can't imagine sending him to Tim Trebor or whoever the new owners might have in mind. Matt would shoot himself.'

'Yes, you're right. He sure would. I've been thinking about this and, knowing what a practical man your father was, we have to look at it like he would have. This is a colt, he would have said. We sell the colts and this is the best prospect we've ever had. Well, we know that because of who he is. But this is a results-driven industry and even just considering your own future, Tom, the right sale makes sense.'

'So, what have you in mind?'

'How about $5 million for half? On the face of things his pedigree is light, but after you have won the Derby that becomes less important. Tell Algy that you have spoken to me and that I represent the Elevator Stable. And that we would consider $5 million for half, with the horse remaining with Matt and continuing to run in our colours. Let's do any negotiating through Algy. He can represent us.'

Last Hurrah continued training strongly. Matt Pearson started behaving much more professionally and, amazingly, was polite, patient, and courteous with the media, announcing that his colt would train into the Derby at Payson Park and then at Churchill Downs.

The Elevator boys thought they'd died and gone to heaven. 'The build-up. All the dreaming. That's what makes this experience irresistible,' Colin reminded his chums as they greedily gobbled up the increasing coverage in the *Daily Racing Form* and sporting websites that, with the supposed most exciting two minutes in sport on the radar, were finally giving the Sport of Kings a bit of coverage, even if token. Not a word about a sale, though.

◆ ◆ ◆

Meanwhile, all was definitely not well in the favourite's camp and Hector found himself fielding increasingly worried questions from the Russian syndicate members of the America's Stable. Tim Trebor had gone off the boil, by his standards, since just after the Breeders' Cup, with his powerful stable's win-rate hovering around 10%, in stark contrast to the lofty 28% that had just seen him crowned leading trainer in North America for the sixth successive year at the Eclipse Awards. Gone was the swagger and, for someone who lapped up the positive media coverage that his successes had earned him, with frequent hyperbole, his muted explanation for Sputnik's worrying performance in the Santa Anita Derby confirmed many experts' growing opinions that something in general was wrong with all of Trebor's horses, not just the Derby favourite.

Some, off the record of course, even hinted that maybe he didn't have the right juice anymore. Others, drunk on the usual Trebor b.s. pointed out that he had three horses in the race and maybe Mayan Warrior, who had finished second to his more illustrious stable companion, could now be the one?

The America's Stable was still well-stocked with talent. But the Russian element seemed only interested in the best and were not happy about what they were reading about the horse that they thought would win them the Derby. However, in the wake of Calvin Weiner's death, they were at least keeping their heads down, and Hector smiled wryly at Arko's handiwork.

◆ ◆ ◆

In his office at Keeneland, Billy Beagle smiled for very different reasons.

Graham Wheater had done a great job since the Boyce affair. It had been a shame about Cal Weiner, but it did appear that things were returning to normal in Canada. The Russians, for all their boorish behaviour, had been useful: they'd injected cash at a key time. Where it had come from didn't much concern him. They'd made a splash and that was good for business. But now, he'd just heard from his future son-in-law there was a new player in town, one who, he said, would really stir up international interest in this year's Derby, and that reminded him of the call that he'd had from Chubby Magnall of the Jockey Club in England.

Beagle had been at the Dubai World Cup, along with international horse racing's movers and shakers, as a guest of Sheikh Sultan. His host had boasted about the success of the Gulf handicap and how the Real Racing sweepstake had generated such global interest in what had, up until then, been a relatively esoteric event. Now Lord Magnall was on the phone, warning that the Real Racing people – as he referred to Ravi Singh and Motti-Media, forgetting altogether that in fact the most powerful family in all of racing were now their equal partners – were talking about the Kentucky Derby being their next target after the Grand National.

'They can't do that,' had been Billy's initial reaction. 'We have strict laws about Internet gambling in North America. You can't just buy tickets online because your credit card company won't process the purchase!' he'd exclaimed.

'Well, frankly, they don't care,' Magnall had replied. 'In a nutshell: they have a global audience that is anxious for action. If North American racing wants to take its ball and go home, more fool them. You'll be missing out.'

'Well, they haven't even asked us.' Then he thought about the meeting with Ravi and how the NHRA guys had pooh-poohed him and given him the bum's rush. 'Well, Mr. Singh, did make a proposal to us, but our guys didn't like it. Said it would never fly.'

'Well, it has. It is. And it's flying right in your direction,' said Magnall. 'Just a heads-up: they ambushed us at Ascot last year. In fact, they embarrassed us greatly when they presented a huge cheque to charity and their next race is this Saturday's Grand National at Aintree.'

'And you're letting them do this?' Beagle was stunned.

'Billy, Billy. Calm down. There is nothing we can do. Rest assured that the Jockey Club has looked into every possible way to stop this. Our legal experts, who felt so confident about monopolies' restrictions, etcetera, were laughed at by Singh's solicitors. Realizing that we can't beat them, we've joined them. And I suggest you do, too. There are just too many powerful people behind this now, Billy. We need the Arabs. You know how our business is struggling. And here we have an extraordinary phenomenon which has reversed the decline. We now have a new and greater audience than ever before. And the public loves the idea. Horse racing is real racing, Billy. Join the crowd. See you at Aintree.'

CHAPTER 54

Algy had his hands full. The Grand National sweepstake was seemingly the only thing that fans of Real Racing around the world were talking about. As the official spokesman for the Internet's hottest property, he found himself doing endless TV interviews, explaining that the National, as all UK and Irish-based fans of horse racing called it, was the greatest test in all of steeplechasing.

The draw was being held in the London Eye, with a host of celebrities on hand, including England soccer hero, Harry Kane; Tour de France winner, Geraint Thomas; and Algenon Sinclair was front and centre, representing Motti-Media, and the Singh interests.

This was prime time. But, at the same time, Algy was delicately liaising between Johnny Ward-Clark and the Elevator Stable regarding the purchase of the now, in many experts' eyes, favourite for the upcoming Kentucky Derby.

When Bog had a new 'important' client in his sights – except, of course, Algy reminded himself, when it was an insignificant Indian – he was relentless in his pursuit of the deal.

However, the $5 million for half of Last Hurrah was way more than his collegues at CBS had said that the horse was worth, and he didn't like the partnership aspect at all. This should, he felt strongly, be a clear-cut purchase for a new group of Chinese investors, separate from the America's Stable. Hector would then be happy. Danvers and Lascelles would be happy that this consolidated their business between Newmarket and Lexington. And above all, his future father-in-law, the big cheese in Kentucky and, for that matter, North

American racing, would be ecstatic: new money coming into the business, dubious Russians being faded out.

This was a deal that he would make on his own: one that, should Last Hurrah win the Kentucky Derby in less than a month's time, would instantly propel him to the forefront of the bloodstock world. He wanted this badly. But, at the same time, he did not want Algy to dictate the terms or, worse still, know his position and how he felt.

Face meant everything. Algy had got lucky, in his view, pinching Ravi Singh most irritatingly at his expense. He cursed Geoffrey Gilligan. What a pompous fool. Not appreciating or admitting, for a moment, that he and his know-it-all friend, Patrick Waley-Brown, were really soulmates.

When he'd called Algy on his mobile, Algy was about to do an interview for NBC, on the Grand National. He'd said he would call Bog right back. And Bog had chewed his nails and paced up and down in his new London pad, watching the man who stood between him and the respect and great wealth that he knew this deal could bring, charming TV viewers. It was infuriating to be in such a position, at the behest of a guy who didn't know, in his opinion, half what he did and had only got to where he was through family and connections.

Standing on the landing side of Becher's Brook, the most famous of the huge obstacles, Algy, looking the part in an old Barbour jacket and beaten-up trilby, was charming a young lady in a pink ski jacket and long white-leather boots. 'You have your two most exciting minutes in sport, every year at the Kentucky Derby. The Aussies have the Melbourne Cup that they say stops the nation for, what does it take? Just under two miles, so let's say about three and a half minutes. And we have the National, that goes on for over nine minutes over thirty big guys like this one,' he said, looking up to Becher's, towering above him. 'It captures the imagination of a huge audience because it's so wide open. You don't have to know anything, just gaze into a crystal ball, close your eyes, and stick a pin into a list of runners. That's why the Real Racing sweepstake, to use a North American term, is a no-brainer!'

'Awesome, just awesome,' cooed the pink apparition beside Algy, as Bog gnawed on a piece of freshly bitten nail. 'Who do you like?' the young lady continued.

'Well, apart from you, dear! Ooops, shouldn't really have said that, should I. Ha! Ha! I'll get into trouble,' giggled Algy and his interviewer did the same. 'Seriously, your guess is probably as good as mine. That's what makes this a magical race. But, as my Uncle Teddy would say – and he's ridden in this race and is a serious hunting man, so he should know – pick a good jumper, especially one that has completed this course before. Then look at the jockey, as experience counts a lot. So,' and theatrically Algy looked to the heavens, twirled his hand, and stabbed down onto an imagined target, 'iiiiit's Colonel Bogey,' and he launched into his whistling version of Kenneth Alford's famous march.

'Well, there you have it, folks. The Derby and Indy 500 combined with thirty or so crazy English and Irishman. Thrills and spills. Our coverage begins at 10 a.m. Eastern Time.' And Bog turned off the TV.

Moments later his phone rang. 'Sorry, Bog. A lot of excitement, here. Got a job to do.'

'Ok.' Bog was unimpressed, or pretended to be, anyway. 'What's the story?'

'The story is that my people don't want to sell their horse. There is something special about him and because they don't have much money in him, they have nothing to lose by keeping him.'

'Is that what Ms. Montagu says?' asked Bog.

Algy lied. 'She speaks for the syndicate. You know how they met? It's a great story.'

Bog chewed his pen in thought, not wishing to sound too desperate. 'What would make them change their minds? You know as well as I do that this horse could put his foot in a hole, get cast, or sustain any number of injuries and be worth next to nothing in a nanosecond. It's not like we're talking about a very well-bred filly that has residual value in the breeding shed.'

'I know, I know, and,' Algy paused, 'they know this.'

'Well? You haven't answered my question.' There was a silence.

'I'll tell you what Bog, let me speak to Tom. His father was a practical Scot and I know that his Aunt Vera has always had a policy at Shenandoah Valley of selling colts, for the very reasons you have just outlined. Maybe he can reason with the syndicate members? They're rookies, really,' he added. 'Maybe Ms. Montagu can talk some sense into them?'

'Ok. Please get me a decision quickly, as I need to tell my client. If this goes through, there will be a bunch of stuff to do: vetting, insurance, new ownership registration etcetera, and the race is three weeks from next Saturday. So we need to know by this Saturday. That is in three days time.'

'Absolutely,' said Algy, putting the phone down with a smile. He had Bog. This was a lot of fun.

◆　◆　◆

After a lengthy phone discussion with Tom, Vera composed an e-mail to the Elevator Stable, with the subject line 'Strictly Confidential.'

My dear colleagues, please read this e-mail carefully and, by all means, discuss it amongst yourselves. But, for the time being, with nobody else outside our syndicate.

We have been approached by a friend of Tom's, acting on behalf of a foreign client, who is interested in buying Last Hurrah.

Let me confirm that any decision will be decided by a vote between the five of us, per the terms of the lease.

Additionally, I want you to know, because there is a certain degree of urgency, if the sale goes through, Tom and I have had preliminary discussions with the agent involved, as we felt that it would be better to gauge the seriousness of interest before getting you guys involved.

Tom feels that we could get around $10-12 million, but, because the potential buyer's agents are concerned about the relatively light sprinter's pedigree, that figure may be a bit steep. So he has suggested asking $5 million for half, with Matt continuing to train the colt who will run in our colours.

If that is accepted, per the terms of the lease, the existing five syndicate members would share 10% of the sale, over the $50,000 original lease fee that would be returned to you. But I will wave my interest, so that would mean 10% of $4.95 million, divided fours ways, which would work out around $123,750 each for you guys, plus the $12,500 refund from your initial investments.

In the deal with the new owner, our five partner agreement, within the Elevator Stable will stay the same, but with each of us owning an outright 20% share of the 50% that we retain, and Last Hurrah will be owned by The Elevator Stable and Partner

I hope this makes sense?

Your thoughts as soon as possible. And I need hardly say: not a word to anyone.

Vera

With the Kentucky Derby less than a month away, the Elevator boys were gobbling up every minute reference to their star colt in the media. So it wasn't five minutes before Vera's phone started pinging.

As she'd expected, Reggie was a seller. 'How about ten for half?' he'd suggested. Victor wasn't sure what to do until he spoke to Gladys and he instantly became a seller. Colin, on the other hand, was almost indignant. 'Daylight robbery!' was all he wrote. Smiling, Vera wondered if he knew something that he shouldn't? Nils was the last to respond, confessing that he'd turned his phone off for a recital. Always a bit of a romantic, he was in Colin's corner, reasoning that, 'this hasn't cost us anything, and having a serious Derby horse was a once-in-a-lifetime thrill.' He would go along with the popular vote, but felt they should let it ride and keep Rocky.

Two, two. Vera found herself the deciding vote and knew which way she was going. She and Tom didn't even know if the buyer would go for a half share, but her reply was compelling:

> *I agree, in part, with all four of you and my heart definitely says let's keep him. But this is a business and, if we can make a deal for 50%, we'll have the best of both worlds.*
>
> *We don't know who the buyer is. But, if they turn out to be a major player with deep pockets, they may, one day, want to buy us out. And, at that point, we could be in a very strong position if our guy wins the Derby. We will eventually sell him, anyway. So, as the deciding vote, I say net $5 million for 50%. The buyer pays their agent's commission. Rocky stays with Matt and runs in the syndicate's colours.*

When Algy communicated this proposal to Bog, there was a silence. 'You've got to be kidding! If this colt had gone through any sales ring, as a yearling, he'd have hardly attracted a bid. You'd have been lucky to get twenty thousand for him. He's by a nothing burger out of a zero. He has no pedigree.'

'Then why are you so interested in purchasing him?' asked Algy.

There was a gulp on the other end of the line.

'I'll tell you why,' Algy continued, 'because he's a running fool and anyone who has watched him will tell you that he is for real.' He paused. 'Did California Chrome have any pedigree?' he rubbed it in, 'by a little known sire out of a cheap filly the breeders claimed for eight thousand.'

There was more silence. Algy continued, 'These people weren't even thinking about selling before you came along.' He waited. Nothing. 'Dear

Johnny,' Bog cringed at the condescension, 'you know that the favourite, that horse of Hector Delmontez's. Whatisname? The favourite?'

Bog blurted out, 'Sputnik.'

'Yes, you know he's sore. The Santa Anita Derby was a bad race. He was stopping. Those other horses weren't going anywhere. He was stopping, Bog, and I think Hector and Trebor know that he'll be lucky to hit the board in the Derby. I don't know who your client is, but this looks like an insurance move to me. One of Hector's specialities.'

'What do you mean?' said Bog, audibly annoyed.

'Look, maybe, with the spotlight on, Hector wouldn't off a Derby favourite, but when horses cease to be of value to him, he has little use for them. He's in the winning business. The image of the America's Stable is all important. That's what attracts more investors. I wasn't born yesterday, Bog.'

The deflation at the other end of the line was audible. 'Well, what shall I tell my client?'

'The owners love their horse. They think he is going to win the Kentucky Derby and they do not want to sell him. However, if someone comes along with $5 million, net to them, for 50%, with the horse remaining with Matt Pearson as his trainer and running in their colours, you have a deal. That is the bottom line. If you want to put in extra clauses about buying them out after the Derby or if the colt wins the Triple Crown, that is your prerogative.'

Algy hung up the phone. It was time to head to the Grosvenor Hotel in Chester, for Motti-Media's gala pre-Grand National dinner. Ravi and Kulbir Singh were entertaining Lord Magnall, Billy Beagle, and friends.

CHAPTER 55

Saturday, April 4th's *Racing Post* headline heralded 'Real Racing is Here' and detailed how, after the very successful 'Ghost Riders Ambush' at Ascot the previous summer, horse racing's authorities were now working together with Motti-Media of Bangalore, India, to make their beleaguered sport prime-time entertainment again.

On page four, in the international section, a three-paragraph column announced that a fifty per cent interest in leading Kentucky Derby hope, Last Hurrah, had been sold to Chinese owner, Cindy Li-Chen, for an undisclosed amount. Further down the page there was a story headed 'Bloodstock Insurer and Well-Known Agent Found Dead in Caracas, Venezuela,' confirming that the bodies of well-known Newmarket racing official Geoffrey Gilligan and prominent bloodstock insurer, Patrick Waley-Brown, had been discovered dead outside a local nightclub, and that police were investigating suspicious circumstances.

Algy read this news in his hotel room. What the *Racing Post* had not reported was that the following week, upon his return to the United States, Billy Beagle, chairman of Keeneland and the National Horseracing Racing Association, would be making an announcement regarding the upcoming Kentucky Derby. As Chubby Magnall had so persuasively convinced him, 'When you can't beat 'em, you might as well join 'em.'

The announcement in the UK and Ireland had stunned bookmakers. But, as Lord Magnall had said, 'What are they going to do about it? They've been shafting racing for the last seventy-five years, and finally we have a product that they cannot offer their punters. It's just too bad.' He'd added that, really, they should applaud this initiative as it will increase interest in horse racing that would be bound to increase gambling on all fronts. Besides, the cheque that Ravi and Sheikh Ali would be presenting to the NHS after today's race would summarily shut up everyone who had a complaint.

As for the sale of 50% of Last Hurrah, Algy had been the official conduit and confirmed Bog's acceptance of the Elevator Stable's price and terms. When Bog had informed his bosses that the deal was in the offing, they'd been their usual non-committal selves: Your deal, Johnny. Your client. Your call. He knew only too well what that meant. If it comes off, we're with you and it'll look good on CBS. If it fizzles, it was a minor hiccup, nothing to do with us or Sheikh Ali. We march on.

Bog had demurred with Java Raja and lost a client. Now he was taking a chance and putting his neck on the block, but there were just too many upsides. If Last Hurrah wins the Kentucky Derby, he told himself, I look like a genius and my bosses, both in the UK and Hector and Billy in the US, will be delighted. If we strike out, maybe Hector and Tim Trebor will have fixed up Sputnik and him winning the Derby would be good for the America's Stable and keep the Russians on-side. If everything fails – well, that just won't happen, he'd reasoned. So, he'd rolled the dice.

Both Bog and Algy read the bit about Gilligan and Waley-Brown with mixed emotions. Geoffrey had backed Bog, though he didn't know quite why. Maybe it was the birds of a feather stuff, as his colleagues had whispered: two bounders, well matched. But Hector had gone cool on both men and it was probably time to move on. So adios Geoffrey, hasta luego Patrick. At least you weren't around to put me off making the decision on Last Hurrah.

Reading the same stories in his office at Caledonia, on a bright spring morning in Kentucky, Hector smiled. The Real Racing stuff was good for business. That Johnny had reeled in a major Chinese player was even better and now, to round out a perfect trifecta, Arko had cleaned things up. No more loose ends around El Gruppo. Two weak guys, he mused. Waley-Brown and Gilligan were suckers for the ladies. An invitation, with free first class return air-tickets, from the Anaconda Club, and Geoffrey and his pal were off on another bird watching excursion, as they had informed their other halves. Like lambs to the slaughter. Too easy, he thought. A home game for Arko.

◆ ◆ ◆

The Grand National did not disappoint its vast new audience, with an action-packed race full of thrills and spills: four fallers at the very first fence and a total of twenty-seven out of the forty-two horses, who lined up, failed to finish. In the carnage, many of the most fancied runners came to grief and the result was a 50/1 winner, Glockamorah. An eleven-year-old ex-Point-to-Pointer from Ireland who jumped like a stag, dodged every bullet that came his way, and seemed to relish the taxing four miles.

In the winner's enclose an exultant Algy Sinclair confirmed record participation in the Real Racing sweepstake and joked with the press that he'd given American viewers good advice. 'The winner has never fallen in over fifty races! Gotta jump those fences and we have an Irish winner, too, Mr. Eamon O'Malley from Cork. Eamon's the winner of twenty million sterling, for drawing Glockamorah in the sweepstake. How about that?'

Watching high up in the Jockey Club box, Billy Beagle took in the buzz below. In less than a month, he hoped he'd be contemplating a similar scene at Churchill Downs, and realized that when on-course attendance and total betting handle were announced, they would be but a drop in the ocean compared to the benefits to his beloved sport that the injection of Real Racing was about to generate.

At the dinner the previous Thursday, he'd sat between Kulbir Singh and Algy Sinclair, who had convinced him that, with the draw for the Kentucky Derby on the Wednesday, three full days before the big race, for the first time Motti-Media and Real Racing Global were going to try and fly in as many sweepstake winners as possible if they contacted the competition's organizers in time and flights could be arranged. Billy, while thinking that was a great publicity stunt that would give US TV networks plenty of fodder, warned them that, with winners quite likely to come from obscure and not necessarily friendly places, US immigration could be an issue.

'It's been uphill, all the way, as we've dragged horse racing back to the forefront,' Kulbir had laughed. 'We'll find a way.'

Upon his return to Lexington, the first item on the Beagle's agenda was requisitioning four boxes on millionaires' row for Real Racing. When told that every one had been rented to corporate interests, years in advance, Billy was prepared. 'How many boxes do we have for the NHRA, Breeders' Cup, SMTV, and Keeneland? How many has Churchill got set aside for its chums?' He was on a mission.

'Things are going to change around here, starting right now. For too long we've allowed ourselves to be hoodwinked by marketing wiseguys. Sheesh, we've spent millions on stupid slogans, handing out tote bags, and delivering syrupy messages: You win and you're in! What's that supposed to mean? It's all been a sham,' he stormed to his PA, Handley Mortenson. 'I want to meet with those suckers at SMTV. Get 'em in here Wednesday morning!'

'Yes, sir,' blurted a startled Mortenson.

'How long is their contract for?'

'I don't know, sir. I'll find out, sir.'

'You do that, Handley. I'm sick and tired of this b.s. We've been made to look like fools by a bunch of Indians. These guys haven't a clue. Get me Gerald Cleever on the phone. We need to put an end to this. Terminate these useless, overpaid bloodsuckers.'

'Yes, sir.' Mortenson backed quickly out of Billy Beagle's office.

In Kentucky, when the big chief was unhappy, things got done quickly. Wednesday morning by 8:05 a.m. a chastened group of spin doctors and snake-oil salesman from SMTV had been sent packing in the wake of a five-minute torrent of abuse and chastisement from the most powerful man in North American racing.

When Handley Mortenson cautiously poked his head around the corner of his boss's door, some ten minutes later, to enquire if he would like a cup of coffee, Billy Beagle had his head in his hands, seated in his shirt sleeves, tie loosened, behind the massive oak desk in the corner. It was early in the day, but it looked like he'd been ten rounds with a tough opponent.

'Coffee, sir?'

Billy looked up. 'Yes, thank you, Handley. I need a shot of something.'

CHAPTER 56

When the sale had been officially confirmed, apart from Vera, the rest of the Elevator Stable members weren't quite sure how to react. They'd been so preoccupied with Last Hurrah's journey to the Derby that the offer and its suddenness had taken them by surprise. Was it a good deal? Had they sold-out too cheaply? Who was their new partner? So many questions but very few definitive answers.

As always, Reggie was philosophical. 'Think about it,' he argued, 'three years ago we had nothing, no horses, and certainly no Derby contender. Then along comes Rikki, who is a star and makes us far more money than he cost, gives us a whale of a time watching him, and enables us to buy Rocky. I remind you that, at the time, I was against this purchase: a two-year-old with nothing special about him who after two years might turn out to be just that – nothing special. But we played on and got lucky. Yes, very lucky! And for very little money, and look where we are. Now someone is putting a $130 grand into each of our pockets and we still have an interest in a colt who is one of the favourites for the Kentucky Derby. A dream for us all. Frankly, I am ecstatic about this.'

Victor was lost for words. Nothing in every piece of data that he exhaustedly analysed had ever suggested such a scenario.

Colin, who'd become a slave to social media and every minutia related to Last Hurrah since his Florida Derby win, was another who kept pinching himself. This was too good to be true. But, in the middle of the night, he still found himself waking up and wondering, was $5 million for half enough? As a disciple of various well-known publications on the science of breeding and the complex blend of blood required to produce a Derby horse, he was starting to believe conspiracy theories and one in particular, put out by someone in the cyber world of sublime thoroughbred matings, that Last Hurrah was the product of an immaculate formula that was inexplicable to any logical patterns.

Little did he or the author of that crank speculation realize how close to the truth they in fact were.

As for Nils, he was in the nothing-to-lose school. He'd advocated no sale, but money in the bank was nice and now everything that came their way would be gravy. The colt was staying with Matt and he'd be sporting their colours. He, his wife, and a host of chums would make sure that they enjoyed every minute of what promised to be an unforgettable experience.

Amongst all this drama, perhaps the least affected was the horse himself. Quietly training away at Payson Park, under the watchful eye of Matt, Rocky was locked on target. Now it was just a question of keeping him healthy for another two weeks.

He had always been a very athletic horse who got the maximum out of his training, but Matt was acutely aware of having him at his prime too soon. The deep and well-cushioned dirt training track at Payson was a silent ally, as the miles of powerful galloping, while keeping him fit, were most forgiving. Joe Magee had been up from Miami twice to ride work. Just maintenance moves, and the day before shipping to Churchill, the Friday before the following week's big day, they motored a handy three-quarters in a minute and fourteen, galloping out seven furlongs in 1:27 and pulling up a mile just a hair over 1:40. A very solid move on a track that was always at least a few seconds slower than the speed-tuned racetrack that Matt knew lay ahead.

Usually, by late April, most horses had flown north and there would have been no clockers on hand, which would have suited Matt perfectly. But, with a major contender still on the grounds, each visit to the track was hawkishly watched by an ever-increasing band of supporters and media. Nothing went unreported and no matter how Matt tried to poor cold water on the seriousness of what was going on, the pressure was increasing day by day.

Unconventional, as usual, Matt decided that instead of going all the way down to Miami and flying his colt to Louisville, as every other trainer in his position would have done, Rocky would travel by road. There were too many unpredictables about flying, such as mechanical and technical problems with planes that often were delayed and could cause unnecessary waiting on the tarmac, in often blazing-hot weather. So, after the Friday work, Toby's 'big horse' left Payson Park in the cool of the evening, just after the sun had dipped over the horizon

Travelling through the night directly to Churchill Downs, only stopping for fuel and a replenishing of hay nets and water buckets, they covered the nine hundred and eighty miles in just over seventeen hours, pulling into Churchill Downs just before midday Saturday, April 28, one week before the big showdown.

The Churchill Downs that greeted them was a far cry from the dank and gloomy racetrack that Matt, Tom, and Rocky had visited the previous November. Derby week was in full flow and the Spring Meet started that very day.

What, on their last visit, had seemed faded and downtrodden was now all spruced up, with the stark, prison-like breeze-block barns of the backstretch alive with TV crews and media. Even though it was the middle of the day and all training was long over, with the first race still over two hours away, the place was swarming with people: Matt's worst nightmare.

Maybe he should have taken a pass and stayed at home? Basil loved this sort of action, he mused. Dr. Hyatt had come along, saying 'I might never get a chance to see a Derby like this again.' And the good doctor jokingly reminded Matt, 'you and your horse need your own physicians more than ever, at a time like this!'

Having Ralph on hand would help keep Matt sane, Vera knew, and she had booked them and Tom into a Holiday Inn, just around the corner from the track, within walking distance. Derby fans seemed to have taken over every hotel within miles. But one call from Vera to Billy Beagle's office and the immediate intervention of the by the now more than ever-willing Handley Mortenson, had resolved this.

◆　◆　◆

The buzz around the backstretch was the firing of the company that had been scheduled, until Beagle's now infamous outburst in Lexington, to promote and oversee the big event. SMTV had huffed and puffed and their lawyers had issued all manner of threats, but the show was going on. And, in Billy Beagle's opinion, would be run a lot more professionally now that 'these clowns,' as he now called them, having tempered down his rhetoric, 'were out of the way.'

There had been concerns about credentials and that, if the SMTV guys were gone, maybe the system would crash. But the crafty Beagle had anticipated such fallout and got Mortenson to request, strictly for security purposes 'in case we get hacked,' that all existing operations be backed up by Churchill Downs, the NHRA, and the Jockey Club.

The staff at 625 Harrodsburg Road had come in early the previous Wednesday, when they'd heard what was afoot, and T.J. Van der Meer, who always seemed to somehow find humour in horse racing's debacles, had run a $20 winner-takes-all sweepstake on how long the fateful meeting would last. The over-under had been speculated to be five minutes and, in fact, Charmaine Duncan, the front desk receptionist, had scooped the $260 prize when the hapless marketeers had headed for the parking lot in disarray, precisely five minutes and thirteen seconds after their arrival, closest to her prediction of five, fifteen.

Since then angry threats had been issued by lawyers, representing a host of people who felt they had somehow been hard done by. But Beagle was defiant, telling NBC that if they thought their loyalty was to SMTV they were gravely mistaken. 'You drop us,' he'd said, 'and we'll have CBS or ABC in here so fast that your heads will spin. You don't get it, folks. This is Real Racing! We finally have an audience, no thanks to your buddies, and this year we're going to set records.

'Let whoever wants to sue us, sue us. Paying them off, if we have to, after we've received the benefits of doing what we're about to do will seem cheap when the dust settles,' he'd added before slamming down the phone. The third that he was on, after the previous two had succumbed to extreme trauma over the preceding few days.

◆ ◆ ◆

Down in Barn 25, as far away from the racetrack as was possible, Toby and Tom introduced Rocky to his new quarters. Matt kept reminding himself to focus on the horse and not worry about the graffiti on the walls of the barn, chain-link fencing, pervasive weeds, and omnipresent dank smell of pine sol, urine, and some nasty acrid smell that he could not put his finger upon, but had instructed Toby to eliminate.

It had already been decided by Vera, who would stay with the Beagle's on their farm near Paris, that Matt would train Rocky early each day and then make himself available to the press, where he would answer their questions politely. Tom had come up with a great idea that, because Algy had negotiated the sale through CBS with the new owner and would be at Churchill Downs promoting the Derby and its Real Racing sweepstake on behalf of Motti-Media, he could take some of the attention off Matt by distracting the media with Real Racing news. Furthermore, he'd thought that he would get Mark to be on hand to charm Ms. Li-Chin. If nothing else, they could chat about music, he thought, knowing full well that his amiable colleague would lap up this PR opportunity and the congenial company of such a charming young lady.

The week ticked by. Having only one horse to attend to each day and having unlimited staff meant an awful lot of standing around bullshitting. If Matt had had his way, he'd have been back in his hotel room by 8 a.m. for a good breakfast, followed by a nap, some golf, and watching baseball on TV. But, as he was finding out, the Kentucky Derby was different. Unlike the Breeders' Cup, unlike any other horse race, it attracted people who for the remaining fifty-one weeks of the year had no interest whatsoever in horse racing.

For this one week, at the beginning of May each year, Churchill Downs was where it was at. Hoards of media from not only North America, but this year because of the Real Racing sweepstake and a Chinese involvement, from all over the world, descended upon the backstretch to interrogate participants with the dumbest of questions.

Matt had found the occasional intrusion by the local correspondents from the *Daily Racing Form* and *Baltimore Sun* to be irritating on the deserted backstretches at Pimlico and Laurel. But this was something else, and he was extremely grateful that apart from Tom, he had Algy, Mark, and even members of the Elevator Stable, who ordinarily would have been a huge nuisance, to engage the mindless chatter.

Set back in the shadows, twenty-five yards behind a barricade of sawhorses, a raggedy bit of what once had been a lawn, partially hidden behind two large fans that wafted cool air in his direction, the object of all the fuss was fortunately oblivious to the excitement that he was apparently generating.

A large Pinkerton security guard blocked the entrance to the shedrow at the end of the barn and, in front of Rocky's stall, Toby reclined in a canvas director's chair with CHIEF written in bold black letters on its back. Under strict instructions from Matt, Toby, who was on double-pay, was never to let his charge out of his sight. And, when nature called, he was only allowed to leave his sentry-duty, if Tom or the security guard held the fort.

Matt had explained numerous times to the pesky visitors that, if they wanted to see his horse, they would have to be on hand at 6 a.m. when he would be going to the racetrack. Once his training had been completed, he did not want him to be disturbed. No photo ops other than those pictures that you take between 6 a.m. and whenever he returns to the barn for his bath, he'd said, over and over again.

Such unforthcomingness, of course, wasn't what Churchill Downs or the many media outlets had in mind, but fortunately there were others who could not get enough publicity, relishing the occasion to schmooze and drum up, they hoped, new business. Such was the case in Barn 5, right across from the racing secretary's office, in about as central a spot as could be found on the entire backstretch, where Tim Trebor was holding court.

Having won two out of the last three Derbies and again holding a hot hand, with three leading entries, the flamboyant and handsome Trebor was playing to the audience. There wasn't a microphone or camera that he didn't like and, for a high percentage of his fawning audience, focusing on these three horses, about which there seemed to be unlimited anecdotes and information, was much easier than trying to get blood out of a stone at Matt Pearson's barn.

Trebor looked at horse racing from a completely polar opposite to Matt Pearson. Everything about his operation was flashy, from the fresh-looking white paint his crew had splashed on the faded concrete of his temporary barn, to the new sand in the shedrow, shiny wall plaques, webbings, and tack boxes and lavish bedding that flowed right out onto the shedrow, in front of his white-haltered charges. The whole barn buzzed with neatness and excess, with every horse done up in four whites and teams of young ladies in uniformed khaki pants and pale blue T-shirts showing videos and pampering visitors.

Leaning on a sawhorse, the six-foot-five, rugged frame of the blue-jean-clad Trebor sported a white Stetson. He could have been posing as the Marlboro Man and readily would have done so, if that is what it took to bring another punter on board.

Two of Trebor's horses, Sputnik and Mayan Warrior, were owned by America's Stable. And, while their trainer was never shy when it came to self-promotion on such an illustrious occasion, Hector's absence was unusual.

Knowledgeable students of form were aware that Team Trebor had not been firing on all cylinders of late. But this fact escaped many of the neophytes and one time per annum members of the press, so Trebor was quick to deflect anything too direct from hardcore interogators, when it came to explaining his barn's recent poor run of form, to easy to answer stuff, like 'Tell us what makes each of your runners different?' Blah! Blah! Blah! And, when anyone did put him on the spot, he would adroitly defer to Johnny Ward-Clark, saying that this gentleman looks after the owners, I'm sure that he can answer that question.

Certainly, if Last Hurrah had been a bit of a mystery horse to everyone other than serious students of form, when the week had started, the news that an interest in him had been purchased by a young Chinese cellist had stirred curiosity, with fingers eagerly tapping the Google search app on phones, to learn more about Cindy Li-Chen.

CHAPTER 57

Sunday, Monday: Rocky galloped two miles, with Tom in the saddle, after jogging a circuit clockwise first and then standing at the end of the one-mile chute, where a gross of cameras clicked away.

Matt, watching at the gap, with his ever-increasing entourage, bit his lip and stayed mute, mumbling 'You saw him' when asked how he thought his charge had trained. Aboard Rocky, on the track, Tom, unabashed, was front and centre, making the front page of the Louisville papers and featuring in ESPN's Derby doings.

Tuesday, with the track in perfect condition, Joe Magee was in the irons as Rocky emerged into the mist at 6 a.m. on the dot and, per Matt's instructions, jogged a circuit with a lead pony before cantering quietly around to the wire where Joe eased him down to the rail and reached up for a shorter hold. The moment never ceased to excite him. After more than thirty years riding horses, when the lead pony lets you go, the feel of over half a ton of pent-up power welling under him never ceased to excite. He'd ridden in the Derby before, but on no-hopers for dreamers who Matt would have said didn't belong. This year, in the twilight of his career, he finally had a live one.

Joe had worked thousands of horses before. But, like a great tennis player who serves aces for fun, then tenses with nightmares of double faults on match point as he bounces the ball, he was almost there. Just one more last tune-up. Don't mess up now, Joe, he thought.

As Matt watched, holding his stopwatch tightly in his pocket, he knew that this was the culmination of eighteen months of tender care, going all the way back to when they'd put the first tack on the precocious yearling back on the farm. He knew the story and even though a casual observer, oblivious to all the drama, would never have known, he was nervous! He crossed his fingers around the watch.

The plan was to let Rocky get onto his left lead and, once in the backstretch, motor along from the three-quarter pole, picking it up in the stretch and galloping out strongly past the wire. When asked by the clockers how far he was going, Matt had said three-quarters and at the gap Joe had mumbled one circuit, which had everyone baffled and made Joe chuckle.

To everyone's relief, the workout went perfectly and the combo returned to the barn, led by a mightily relieved Matt Pearson. According to his watch, they'd gone in a minute thirteen, and change. Several others who'd put their watches on the dark bay thought it might be a bit quicker. 'Whatever,' as Joe related to Matt, he'd done it in hand, 'when I picked him up and chirped to him at the top of the stretch, he switched leads and took off. He's ready.' He'd winked at Matt, who didn't see because he was already on his cell phone, relaying the good news to Vera.

Back at the barn, the word was that Last Hurrah had worked seven-eighths in a minute and twenty-five. Some clockers had him down for a mile in one thirty-nine and change. One thing was quite clear, nobody in the Last Hurrah camp cared much what it was: the move had gone off just as planned.

As Toby scraped the rinse water off his charge after his bath, the cameras clicked the steamy apparition before them, while Tom held the shank. It was a little before seven and it promised to be another long hot and humid day.

Like the build-up to a prize fight, with combatants trash-talking each other at the weigh-in, horse racing's premier classic is carefully choreographed through the final week, with the draw, on the Wednesday, a huge publicity deal. This year it promised to be even more so, with the Real Racing sweepstake eagerly anticipated.

Billy Beagle had made his decision, though this hadn't stopped lawmakers throughout the US challenging what they considered to be a violation of 'wire fraud' statutes. Per the good old American fondness for litigation, dozens of suits were being filed at different levels and in different courts by groups as disparate as Christians against immoral causes (gambling in this case) and even First Nations and Indian bands, who believed that they alone had the right to rip off vulnerable Americans, when it came to online gambling. There was even a challenge made by the Ontario Casino Corporation, which had made

Billy Beagle smile when he'd taken Tim Tyler's indignant call. The fact was, he'd explained, you can't do anything about this and we have instructed the Twin Spires OTB platform to offer Real Racing as an At-Home feature, thereby making all North American credit card transactions from compatible sources legal, before slamming his fourth phone into extinction.

Ravi and Kulbir, as usual, were keeping their heads down. But an appearance at the breakfast draw was essential, now that there was such a global focus on the race, with TV stations from China interested in Last Hurrah and just about every existing sports network in any location of importance capitalizing on the fan-interaction element in what was being billed as the most exciting sports related game to come along in generations.

In the wake of SMTV's firing, Handley Mortenson had reappropriated six five-star boxes on behalf of Real Racing, for those lucky winners able to attend. With a generous contribution to his Sky's the Limit charity pledged from the final distribution of funds, superstar Lemar Daman was taking a rare day off from the NBA playoffs to make the draw.

As usual, Sheikh Ali was front and centre, as was Bog who was chaperoning his glamourous Chinese client like a limpet-mine on the side of a battle cruiser, much to the apparent irritation of his fiancé.

In their efforts to spice up Derby week, over the years countless marketing gurus had spun the event in multitudes of ways that they felt would increase the demographic, each hoping to reach new audiences and make the dying sport viable again. But the 146th Derby, ironically sans SMTV, was proving to be a sell-out, with security already muttering about the likelihood of excess rowdiness in the in-field being a cause for concern.

As for the breakfast draw, an event that had never before received coverage from national TV, let alone twenty-five stations from around the world, the usually cliché-filled bun fight with the same cast of characters lamely trundling out the same stories each year to an increasingly older and diminishing crowd of insiders, there was not an empty seat for cold scrambled eggs and chewy bagels. And Churchill Downs' popular race-caller, Terry Walker, welcomed the buzzing guests to what he called the draw for 'the greatest race on earth and most exciting two minutes in sport.'

When Walker had finished his spiel, it was Billy Beagle's turn to talk about what he described as new life being breathed into our noble but beleagured sport. 'We have been told,' he droned on, 'that horse racing does not appeal to the young anymore and that, as our fans get older, the media, and particularly TV, can no longer justify coverage for such a small audience. The ratings have been in a steady decline and, quite frankly, folks have found other forms of entertainment to be more enjoyable. But I am here to tell you today, and this is despite a whole bunch of folks trying to sue us right now,' which drew guffaws of laughter, 'yes, the same guys who have been doing such a good job destroying our sport, while charging us most richly, are now trying to submarine us just when there is hope. Can you believe that?' There was laughter all around. 'We are anticipating something special on Saturday, and I want to pass the microphone now to a man who has created what I believe is the single most important new platform for horse racing in my lifetime. I'm not a cyber guy. God help me, I can barely operate my cell phone. So, ladies and gentlemen, I would like to introduce you, without further ado, to Mr. Real Racing, Kulbir Singh. Mr. Singh…'

To rapturous applause, Kulbir Singh rose from his table, beside his smiling brother Ravi, Sheik Ali, and Algy Sinclair. For the occasion, he sported a natty khaki safari suit. 'Thank you,' he began. 'I have to tell you that, as a boring accountant by trade – a numbers man – gambling never appealed to me, nor horse racing.' He turned to his brother. 'When my brother Ravi started buying racehorses, I said to him, Ravi, you are insane, never invest in something that eats and can die!' and the whole room erupted in laughter, with Lemar Daman who was sitting beside Sheikh Ali, leading the hoots.

'But,' Kulbir continued, 'you should never say never, and by resurrecting a successful idea that the Irish had done very well with, over sixty years ago, long before the Internet and social media that today has drawn the world so much closer – until, that is, your president came along!' The room erupted again, with Lemar almost falling off his chair with mirth, as one or two well-known Kentucky hardboot members of the GOP cringed. 'I digress,' Kulbir continued. 'Before the action starts – and let me tell you that having an interactive component, whereby fans have a chance of drawing a horse, really does involve the general public – we will also be featuring Ghost Riders and when our honoured guest, Mr. Daman here, has drawn for the field; he will draw a further ten tickets whose owners will have the leading riders riding for them this Saturday, with $1 million per race that each one wins.' This drew wows and oohs and ahs. 'So now I hand you back to our MC and Mr. Lemar Daman!'

Then like a carnival barker-cum-auctioneer Terry Walker took over. 'Now ladies and gentlemen, I would like to draw your attention to the big screen on which the twenty horses for the 146th running of the Kentucky Derby are listed. In front of me is a bin from which Lemar will draw the name of one horse at a time. As these names are drawn their connections will select the post position of their liking and simultaneously the Real Racing computer, which today is being monitored by KPMG, will randomly select the number of the ticket for this horse that will be assigned to its lucky owner.'

The drums rolled, the crowd buzed, and Lemar reached an enormous hand into the bin that had just stopped spinning. As the world waited with bated breath he read out 'Meteor Man.'

'Meteor Man is trained by Eddie Freeman for Gloria Mandell of San Diego, California,' Terry Walker called out. 'A representative from the West Coast,' he said, turning to see where Meteor Man's connections were sitting, 'the field is yours, guys. Take your pick.'

Several tiers up, a decision was made quickly, and the word came down that Meteor Man would start from the seven-hole. 'Lucky Seven,' enthused Walker. 'And,' he drew it out with the maximum of drama, 'the computer is telling us that the holder of the ticket drawn by the Real Racing computer is a resident of Buenos Aires. That's Argentina, the last time I looked at a map. Holy cow, they're watching us down there, can you believe that?'

At the head table Ravi and Kulbir smiled and Sheikh Ali congratulated Billy for having the smarts to 'join us in making horse racing great again,' to hell with the USA and the president, he said to himself, as the draw continued.

At table five, Vera, Matt, Bog, and his important new client, Cindy Li-Chin, and a full compliment of Elevator boys had to wait until almost half the field had been drawn before Last Hurrah's name emerged from Lemar's grasp.

There had been much discussion during the week about this moment, but Matt and Reggie had brought order to any confusion by announcing that until Rocky's name was drawn there was no point in speculating about something out of your control. They all knew they didn't want the inside and particularly the rail, because of the traffic going into the first turn, and neither did they want to be caught up on the outside, five-wide at that juncture. Deferring to Matt's suggestion that, with a big crowd, some horses could get skittish and become reluctant to load into the gate, meaning that those loaded from the rail out could be left standing for a longish time, it was decided to take the fourteen hole.

Reggie, not having a suspicious bone in his body, would have taken thirteen, but was overruled by a majority. So, it was fourteen and they then learnt that some lucky ticket sold in Edinburgh, Scotland, had drawn their big hope.

In between, a raucous group at the America's Stable, including a bunch of already well-oiled Russians who seemed to have reappeared on the scene after the Weiner wipeout, selected the ten-hole for the favourite, Sputnik, and then subsequently six and seventeen for their two other runners, while an uncharacteristically subdued Trebor looked on. Most notable was the continued absence of Hector Delmontez, called away, apparently, on urgent matters.

Bog was beginning to find the Russian members of the America's Stable an embarrassment at sales and on such occasions. He had loved their money and the limelight that signing big tickets, on their behalf, at sales had brought him. But he now had a much more intriguing and sophisticated client in Ms. Li-Chen. Besides, with his betrothal to Lucy Beagle just around the corner, he could not afford to blot his copy book with any indiscreet behaviour that he knew the Ruskies were all too prone to.

According to the experts, Tim Trebor would land his fourth Derby, but something wasn't quite right. Hector had not been his usual charming and optimistic self. Sure, the barn's form over the past few months had been surprisingly poor, but it was just a sixth sense that Bog had about Hector and his radar warned him that his future father-in-law did not like him at all, despite all the stuff about how he'd injected new life into the industry and what an addition to the Jockey Club he now was.

Sitting between Vera Montagu and Cindy Li-Chen, chameleon Bog felt was politically the right place to be.

At the conclusion of the draw, Lemar was asked to say a few words and make his selection. The big man drew the loudest applause all morning when he took the microphone. 'Thank you for inviting me,' he began, grinning from ear to ear. 'Feels a bit strange being down here in hardboot country,' he joked, to sniggers, 'but, when Ravi Singh and Billy Beagle reached out to offer support from this great cause for my school program for kids, the least I could do is fit this event in. Just happened that my new team, the Lakers, are playing tomorrow night, down the road in Memphis, so here we are!'

'And who do you like?' Terry Walker prompted him.

'Well, I don't know nothing about form,' Lemar replied, 'but sittin' here, talkin' to my new friends, Sheikh Ali and a gentleman called Algy, I got to hear about Last Hurrah and I thought to myself, hey, this deal in L.A. with the Lakers, might just be my Last Hurrah in the NBA. So. What the heck. Last Hurrah, he's my man!'

As the cheers echoed and Lemar beamed, Matt Pearson closed his eyes and thought, Oh, fuck, now we've got every basketball nut in the country on our backs, too!

◆ ◆ ◆

Now the die was cast. Thursday's advance edition of the *Daily Racing Form* for Saturday's Derby headlined with 'Last Hurrah for Lemar' bringing a rapt audience of at least twice as many to Barn 25 to check out the fourteen-horse.

Everyone was looking for a story and the origin of the Elevator Stable spawned numerous columns. When some wiseguy from the *Baltimore Sun* cracked that Louisville, the home of Mohammed Ali, was a good spot for 'Pugilist Pearson,' as he called him, everyone was so obsessed with Victor's account of being shut out in the elevator at Pimlico, plus Cindy Li-Chen discussing her music, that nobody paid any attention to the man leading his horse around the barn, which suited Matt fine.

'An awful lot of money,' said Jay Firestone, the DRF's pedigree analyst, to Ms. Li-Chen, 'for such a light pedigree. Do you think he'll get the mile and a quarter?'

Cindy Li-Chen smiled charmingly, and Bog answered on her behalf. 'He doesn't know that,' which drew laughs. 'It's a great opportunity for Ms. Li-Chen to get involved in our sport. This colt has done everything that has been asked of him. He comes into this race in the peak of condition, thanks to our trainer, and we think that he'll be hard to beat. Whoever beats him wins the race, I say.'

'And who are you, sir?' a voice in the crowd enquired.

'I'm the chap,' Bog continued with growing confidence, 'who put the deal together. You can go to the sales and spend that kinda money on a yearling and wait two years to find out that you've got a lemon. Here,' and he paused, 'I know we're rolling the dice, but it's instant action. We're just lucky that Ms. Montagu and her partners let us have a bit of their pie.' Bog grinned, knowing full well that he'd gone out on a limb. But what the heck. He'd come a long way, he mused to himself, and jumping on this bandwagon, however late, could only improve his chances.

The questions, some so dumb as to be not worthy of answers, kept coming. 'Why Joe Magee? Isn't he past his prime? There are so many other better riders.' On and on it went, but the Elevator Stable, Algenon Sinclair, Johnny Ward-Clark and his engaging new client fended them off and charmed the crowd.

Now it was the eve of the big day. As Matt Pearson was only too aware, there is only one Kentucky Derby in a horse's life. Miss it for any reason and a horse never gets another chance. The field that had now been drawn represented the twenty best three-year-olds ready to put their best foot forward on the first Saturday of May. The ultimate winner might not turn out to be the best of his class, by the end of the season, but he or she would be forever a Kentucky Derby winner and nobody could ever take away that prestigious honour.

As Matt and Ralph fretted in their motel room, the schmoozing, partying, and speculating continued on, as fans from all across the United States homed in on Louisville, and lucky winners in the Real Racing sweepstake suddenly found themselves bound for Churchill Downs, a place that they'd mostly never heard of before Wednesday's fateful draw, all on a first-class, all-expenses paid junket.

For Tom Fraser, the wave that had picked him up some three years and a bit previously and carried him along ahead of his many emotions, was about to break. But he had no time to consider what the outcome might be. Were Rocky to win the Derby, his life would be made. Even if he didn't, the benefits accrued during the last few years, both financial and emotional, had already helped him remake a life that would never be the same again. No point worrying, now, about things that might not happen, Algy had reminded him. Ride this one.

CHAPTER 58

As the sun peeked up over the eastern horizon, just after five on Derby day morning, the dawning promised glorious weather and a fast track.

Matt and Ralph munched on their bagels and sipped their coffees, appreciating that there would be no excuses. Matt chuckled at the news that had greeted them at the stable gate, when they'd arrived in the darkness half an hour before.

'Yep,' he said quietly, 'I guess they finally caught up with him.'

'How long have they been doing it?' said Ralph.

It was still dark in the shedrow, as the two men watched Toby brushing out Last Hurrah's mane and tail in preparation for one last bit of fine-tuning out on the shadowy dirt track.

Before Matt could respond, an anxious voice behind them cried, 'The favourite's scratched! The favourite's scratched! Do you guys know that?' It was a breathless Steve Ashwood of the DRF, who, when awakened by a 4 a.m. call from his editor in New York, somehow had managed to disengage his 350-pound frame from his motel bed and hightail his large arse down to the backstretch.

'Figured,' was all Matt would say.

'What do you mean?' gasped the out-of-breath Ashwood. 'Hey, do you guys have any more of those doughnuts?'

'Help yourself,' said Matt. 'What I meant was, I'm not surprised. He was a sore horse at Saratoga last summer when he won the Hopeful. His shins were really bothering him, but they went on with him. I hear he got a bit of a knee, before the Breeders' Cup, but they went into it. Tapped him, you know, when they should have stopped.' Ashwood was scribbling away frantically as Matt continued. 'He hasn't been the same horse this year. Was stopping badly, in that last race. I'm glad he's not running. Not just because we have one less to beat, but because if, as the favourite, he broke down in the Derby, it would be very bad for the sport. We don't need accidents on one of the few days all year when the nation's TV cameras are all focused on our main race. No sir,' he trailed off.

'But,' mumbled Ashwood, 'but, this is the Derby. Couldn't they do something? You know, get him some help for this one big race?'

'Now ya talking,' said Matt. 'That's just the problem. This place has been far too slack for too long.' He paused. 'You just don't know where you are. One track you can use certain shit, another you can't. On those rock-hard, speed-oriented tracks out west, horses get sore. You look at all the two-year-olds on Bute and Lasix and God knows what that they don't test for. No wonder they don't last. Kentucky should be the toughest place, but it's never been that way. Maybe, finally, they've raised the bar and Mr. Trebor knows he can't get away with what he's been using.'

'You mean he's a juicer?' said the still breathless Ashwood.

'I'm not sayin' nuthin',' said Matt, starting to regret that he'd got into this, 'but you look at what the stats say for Trebor's horses this year: he was close to a twenty-five percent guy last season, now not even ten. I'll leave it at that. Someone somewhere has tightened things up. If you want to still have a job by the end of the day and still be kosher here at Churchill Downs, you'll forget what I just told you and burn those notes. Here we go. Here comes the big horse,' and Matt and Ralph followed Rocky out of the barn.

It was getting lighter and, as 6 a.m. and Last Hurrah's scheduled visit to the track had approached, the mob was regrouping, lenses primed. Like the pied piper, they followed, and Matt wondered just what it was that held their fascination? He'd probably said too much to fat Ash. But the elation of having made it this far, with everything intact, had got to him and finally he was at ease.

Meanwhile, Ashwood scurried off to the kitchen for further sustenance and to report his scoop to his editor. 'So,' the latter replied after his sweaty scribe had poured out the dirt on Tim Trebor, 'you think we should run a story that the Derby favourite has been scratched because his trainer can't use the juice he needs and not that he's running a temperature and didn't eat up, as his connections have put out for public consumption! You're a wise guy, all of sudden, eh?'

'Well, I heard Matt Pearson with my own ears. It's what he thinks,' said a meek voice.

'Yeah? The same guy who got ruled off for decking a rider at Laurel? You're going to put that in, too, by way of qualifying your source, eh? Leave it alone Steve, if we print shit like this the PETA brigade will shut down this sport so fast you'll be bagging groceries at Walmart before you even read about it. Now, go and get us a story about this Chinese dame. Her horse looks like the favourite, now. Get on to it!'

◆ ◆ ◆

On the track, Tom turned Rocky at the gap and they stood motionless, the latter's ears pricked, appearing to drink in the importance of the moment, his breath mingling with the mist, as horse and rider looked across the infield to the famous twin spires, silhouetted against the pink early morning sky.

Then, with the quietest of direction from his right boot, they trotted off in a precise, well-balanced gait, confirming that every sinew and muscle of Rocky's thirteen-hundred-pound frame was perfectly synchronized. Tom was riding full length of his leg, for he knew that he was sitting on a powder keg that could be so easily set off by an errant camera flash or a sudden movement from a thousand onlookers. They'd come so far, falling off at this point and letting the now-favourite loose was uncontemplatable. After completing a circuit, they pulled up at the end of the mile-chute and walked back to the barn.

Rocky was on his toes, wondering why no gallop today, but that is the way Matt wanted him: sharp as a tack when the gate opened in close to twelve hours time, to take up a good position in the cavalry charge to the clubhouse turn. He knew that you couldn't win the race at that point, but you sure could lose it and he wanted his charge to be ready, not caught flat-footed.

Back at the barn the crowd was buzzing, as late arrivals took in the news that the favourite had been scratched and people wanted to know what the trainer thought about Rocky's chances now that he had inherited that mantle. The trouble was that apart from a handful of local beat writers, nobody knew who the trainer actually was, thanks to the artful distractions of Algy, Tom, Bog, and various other members of the Elevator Stable, which brought a smile to Matt, enabling him to hide out in the shadows while others held court.

'Yes,' Bog had announced convincingly, although not really meaning it at all, 'I feel so bad for Tim Trebor and the owners. To have come so close. But don't rule him out yet, as he still has two other horses who belong and could be dangerous,' and, quickly, interrogating the trainer was forgotten, as Algy stepped in to confirm that Last Hurrah was Lemar's selection. With him, he had Florence McDougal, the lucky person who had drawn him in the Real Racing Sweepstake and who had flown in the previous evening from Scotland. Focus was immediately transferred to the diminutive 75-year-old McDougal, in her natty tartan jacket that she said was of her clan, which immediately had everyone Googling Scottish dress and the significance of the colours.

◆　◆　◆

Seventy miles away, Billy Beagle and his house guests were breakfasting at Hickory Hills when a phone call from WBCTV Lexington requested a few words, on air, at 9 a.m. about the day's big race and the fact that the favourite had been scratched at the eleventh hour.

'Make no mistake,' he began, when prompted by the host of the morning sports report, Travis Chambers, 'Getting to the Derby is not easy. These are fragile thoroughbreds, not race cars. I feel so bad for Hector Delmontez and the members of the America's Stable, who've been enjoying such good fortune of late with their horses, and of course Tim Trebor. They must be gutted at this time.'

'Tell us, for those listening who think that all horse racing is fixed,' continued Chambers, 'that this is legit. You know, the favourite being scratched at this point sounds pretty fishy to me?'

'On the contrary,' a clearly irritated Beagle barked, 'you have no idea how conscientious the horsemen who work around these beautiful animals are. I salute Tim Trebor for putting his horse first. They're finely tuned animals. You have to watch their every move because they can't talk to you, you know, tell you they have a gut ache or are not feeling well. You've gotta know them. So any little bitty problem, like not eating up or running a temperature, however slight, is a sign that all is not well. Would you rather that a horse went to the post, the favourite in our most celebrated race, in this instance, that wasn't 100%? Don't you think that the public would be entitled to feel cheated if they bet all their money on a horse that the trainer knew beforehand had a problem?'

Chambers was temporarily flummoxed, out of his depth on a subject that was way beyond his almost nerdish fascination with baseball stats and NFL injuries. 'Well, yes, I hear you, sir,' he stumbled on. 'Well, there you go folks. They call it the most exciting two minutes in sport and you've just heard from horse racing's big cheese that there's no place for sissies or invalids, when they line up to Run for the Roses later today. Yes folks, don't forget to tune in for post time at 6:27 – we'll be right back with a lucky fan who has drawn a horse in today's race and now stands to win maybe $10 million.' The music came up under him as he thanked Billy Beagle for his input, and the station went to a commercial.

Billy Beagle hung up the phone in his office and sat quietly in the wingback chair behind his desk, looking out across the lawns to the foals being let out into their pristine paddocks, and smiled to himself. 'You think you can fix our game, Senor Delmontez? Well think again, pal. We fixed you this time.' He thought about his friend Bob Fraser and his final words. 'We've done the best we can for you, Bob. It's up to the horse now.'

CHAPTER 59

In the barn all was quiet but for the hum of two big fans that Toby had positioned in front of Rocky's stall. Inside, now comfortably bathed and done up in four fluffy white bandages, Rocky snoozed in his deep straw bed.

Some trainers believe in drawing their runners, as they say on the racetrack, by putting a muzzle on them or bedding them on shavings or peat moss, so they can't gorge straw and have full stomachs at race time. Matt preferred to treat every horse differently and, knowing that Rocky was not a bed-hogger and would be happier left alone, he wasn't about to change things now. All that mattered was that he was relaxed and, thanks to the TLC of Toby and distractions of his entourage, the mission had almost been accomplished.

Homing in on Churchill Downs from all sides, twelve of the lucky sweepstake winners were going to be on hand and Algy was busily making sure that their experience was a memorable one: arranging interviews with the press and NBC TV. A full compliment was in town to represent the Elevator Stable, all dressed to the nines and biting their nails, as they could never have imagined.

Joe Magee had eschewed the build up after the draw, for which attendance was virtually mandatory, and now he was in the jock's room, sweating away in the sauna. A ride in the third would give him a chance to see how the track, billed as fast, was riding. He'd then have a nap, while, like the build-up to a major prize-fight, the tension gradually ratcheted up, agonizingly, bit by bit.

Up in the trustees' lounge, Billy Beagle and T.J. Van der Meer welcomed guests and the glitterati of global horse racing. Mint juleps flowed and he went out of his way to console Hector Delmontez and his Russian cortège, doing further interviews, but as was his wont, never volunteering a partisan position: woe betide an inkling as to whose corner he was in. Watching and knowing her husband better than most people gave her credit for, Mary-Lou sat in the background, playing the gracious hostess, knowing that her Billy was happy that today all was on the up-and-up and therefore a few over-the-top kisses, planted on the lips of the lovely Russian beauties on hand, was all in a good cause.

As the clock ticked around at the end of the barn and the roars from the grandstand ebbed and flowed, Team Rocky checked and rechecked tack. Every buckle scrutinized and shone for the umpteenth time. Every inch of leather, from noseband to throat lash and all the way to the end of the reins that Joe Magee would knot in his own patented way, checked, double-checked, and lovingly manicured with saddle soap.

Toby had a new suit, which he would put on at the last-minute before they set off on the walk over that those who've taken part in say is the moment when the shivers start. It was a hot day, but the fans were doing their job and when the announcement was finally made to 'get your horses ready for the 146th Derby,' the butterflies took off.

By now Rocky had figured that it was a race day. But as his experiences of late had been positive, no anxious sweating for him. Unlike many of his rivals on this day, no need to stand in ice or inhale cocktails from nebulizers, to open up air passages, either.

Ralph Hyatt had no need to administer pre-race medication and now it was time for a refreshing bath. Tack on. A final wipe from his adoring groom with a mixture of alcohol and fly spray that only Toby knew the full recipe of… and they were off.

It was a lovely early evening, with the intensity of the humidity just beginning to break as they emerged onto the racetrack and into the sunshine. Matt had said his prayers ever since the Florida Derby, exhorting the good lord for a fine day and fast track, and here it was. Never one for the schmoozing, up in the boxes of the grandstand, he walked behind his charge, led by Toby and flanked on his right by Tom. They were the favourite, but you could not have told that from the low-key and quiet demeanour surrounding number 14.

Up in the stands, Victor and Gladys Todd admired their pride and joy through binoculars, as the procession made its way towards them, before descending to the gathering mayhem in the paddock.

Vera had decided to watch in the Jockey Club box that had a private elevator. 'Just in case we need to head down to the in-field, to have our photo taken,' she'd said with a wink. Despite Matt's pleas to stay out of the way, nobody else was going to miss the action and with the Elevator Stable now including Cindy Li-Chin and the ever-present Bog, there was quite a crowd assembled in front of the stall where the 14-horse was designated to be saddled.

Now down to nineteen horses, it was still a far bigger field than the usual Churchill maximum of twelve, and the paddock was teeming with people that Matt Pearson felt did not belong. But he knew that all he had to do was concentrate on saddling his horse with the minimum of fuss. Even though he was challenged by a security guard who, because he'd been so obscure for the previous seven days, didn't know who he was, he managed to keep his cool.

Rocky, meanwhile, had not turned a hair. In passing to saddle his two runners, Tim Trebor, the consummate smoothy who was today sporting a black suit with matching Stetson and black bolo tie, à la Johnny Cash, complimented Matt on how well his charge looked.

There was nothing that hadn't been discussed a thousand times and agonized over in a lifetime of dreams that Matt and Joe could say as the veteran Irishman hopped lightly into the saddle. As they walked out under the stands and Tom heard the strains of 'My Old Kentucky Home,' a tear came to his eye and he looked down, lest the fearless Rocky, by his side, caught him in his moment.

It was a long way from the pastures at Tanglewood, that lazy August day with the bees buzzing, almost three years before, when they had first met one another, and little Rocky had hid shyly under the belly of his enormous Clydesdale step-mom. If only he knew. If only everyone knew, he mused, as Toby handed Rocky to the outrider.

At the draw Kulbir Singh had mentioned that the preliminary count, when entries for the Real Racing sweepstake had closed, looked like exceeding that of the previous month's Grand National of $680 million and every lucky ticketholder who'd drawn a horse would be winning $1 million, with the ultimate winner to receive $20 million, the second $10 million, and third $5 million, with close to $600 million projected for charity.

Up in the boxes on the fifth floor, twelve of the lucky winners who had been interviewed on TV, along with the remaining eight via Skype connection and affiliated TV stations around the world where they lived, waited tantalizingly. (Sputnik had been drawn to run. So, even though he was now a scratch and would not be taking part, the lucky person who'd drawn him had still won $1 million.)

As the field paraded below them, Billy Beagle uncharacteristically hugged Ravi Singh and Sheikh Ali. 'It's alive!' he proclaimed, almost like Dr. Frankenstein regarding his monster. 'It's alive! Can't you feel it? You guys have found the silver bullet!' His ear-to-ear smile said it all: the Kentucky Derby had recaptured the nation and way, way beyond.

Sitting beside Mary-Lou Beagle, Vera thought about what Bob Fraser would have made of this: a story born out of tragedy but resurrected to this magic moment. A tale of redemption that was meant to be, she hoped.

A few boxes over, Vera could see Hector Delmontez and his clients with Johnny Ward-Clark, Cindy Li-Chen, and Lucy Beagle. All innocents to what was happening. Just in front of her were her equally unwitting partners, the boys of the Elevator Stable, who had transformed sadness and made the journey over the past three years so delightful. As the last few horses loaded, Billy Beagle sat down beside her and winked.

Vera thought she detected a tear.

At the rail below, Matt, Tom, Ralph, and Toby had staked out their position with a view of the start away to the left of them, at the top of the stretch. Tom looked up at the infield tote board to see that Rocky, the 14-horse, was the 5/2 favourite. As he glanced at Matt, he could see that his eyes were closed. Maybe in a moment of prayer, he mused.

Then they were away! The crowd roared and the nineteen thoroughbreds thundered towards them. So great was the din that it drowned out the commentator's voice, as the field sped past. A chestnut with red and white colours was on the lead, with a myriad of silks fanned out across the track in his wake. Tom thought Rocky looked to be in a good position, about tenth, three off the rail and about a dozen lengths off the lead.

Rocky had broken perfectly and, perched above his eager mount, Joe Magee sat quietly amongst the charge to the clubhouse turn. Not a marquee name, by any stretch of the imagination, he'd been touched by the words of encouragement from his fellow riders. Not a stylist, never a hotdogger, they nonetheless respected the quiet Irishman's poise. They knew what it meant for him.

Now, all around him things were happening fast. So many jostling for position. So many startled and running so freely. Split decisions made in an instant. He knew that this moment might never come again. It was now or never.

The field vanished around the clubhouse turn and those at ground level, whose view was blocked by the immense infield crowd, tents, and billboards transferred their gaze to the infield screens. 'Northern King continues to lead,' the commentator droned, 'they've gone a half in forty-five and three. Then it's Meteor Man, Mayan Warrior, and a gap back to Cajun Clown, with the favourite, Last Hurrah, saving ground on the rail.'

At the mention of Rocky's name, Tom's heart jumped and Toby let out a yell. 'Go on Rocky! You can do it!'

Joe had had an uninterrupted passage through the first turn and, reaching up to discard the top of four sets of goggles, he had eased Rocky down onto the rail. Ahead were maybe half a dozen and he could see their riders starting to work on them. Beneath him, Rocky was flowing. He hadn't asked him a question.

The most exciting two minutes in sport, they say. Yet just a few seconds was all it took to dash hopes to smithereens, and Joe smiled grimly through the dirt in his gum-shield. He could hear the cracks of whips behind him. They weren't going anywhere. And those ahead were in his sights.

As the field came back into view and turned for home, an enormous roar greeted the race caller's pronouncement of 'And down the stretch they come.'

Through a sea of waving arms, Tom could just make out Mayan Warrior, Rocky's old adversary, taking up the running. But he was tiring and drifting off the rail as his desperate rider hammered him right-handedly in vain.

The field was closing. Four horses, fighting for the lead, fanned out across the track, giving their all. And then he saw him. On the rail. The gold cap. The unmistakable pumping style of Joe's arms. It was Rocky. His baby. Rocky drawing clear.

At the top of the stretch, the horse in front of him had drifted out and Joe had sent Rocky through the hole. With under a quarter of a mile to run, it was now or never. And, with a full head of steam, the combination burst through along the rail and hit the front. Ahead lay a narrow open path to immortality, flanked by roars that he would never forget.

They weren't going to be caught then. A momentary glance over his right shoulder and he had driven for the wire. He would watch this moment a thousand times on TV reruns, over and over again, but never could he have ever imagined in all his dreams that feeling.

Toby ran out onto the track. Tom hugged Matt. They knew.

Upstairs the Elevator boys had gone completely mental. The cheering had started up at about the three eighths pole, when Joe had reached up and asked his mount, and had degenerated into demented screaming, as he'd answered the bell at that critical moment in the final round of his ultimate test.

Billy Beagle picked Vera up right out of her chair and hugged her with unabashed joy. Reggie Halpern conceded a tear below his panama's brim. Not much moved the old curmudgeon in his twilight years, but there was a lump in this throat at that moment when he'd uttered a bellow well familiar to his fellow New York afficionados, as he'd removed the ubiquitous soggy Puerto Rican cigar from the corner of his mouth, as the favourite had gone clear of the field at the eighth pole: 'It's over! It's over! This race is history!'

Victor and Gladys danced a jig, with the former hugging everyone within range, much to many of the staid hardboot audience's very evident surprise. Colin pointed to the time recorded on the infield board. 'Two minutes flat! Only the great Secretariat has run faster!' he let everyone in earshot know, whether they were interested or not. 'And by five!' Nils chimed in.

Down on the track, Tom hugged Rocky, planting kisses upon his dirt-covered nose, as Joe Magee beamed from up top and the garland of red roses was placed over his mount's withers.

A winning favourite always draws extra cheers, but there was something very special about the adulation that day. As Toby led the winner around in front of the packed grandstands, awaiting the arrival of his happy owners in the winner's enclosure, he speculated that Lemar had anointed Rocky as his choice. So people were happy.

This Derby, too, now had the additional aspect of a multi-million dollar sweepstake winner, with a live presentation of the cheque in front of a global TV audience, as a somewhat overwhelmed and slightly embarrassed Florence McDougal joined Vera, Cindy-Li Chen, Bog, the Elevator Boys, and a rapidly growing fan club in that famous infield enclosure which has welcomed Derby winners for almost a hundred and fifty years.

Governor Chance made a brief speech and presented the trophy to Vera, in her wheelchair, on behalf of the Elevator Stable and Ms. Li-Chen. Joe Magee rallied his veteran bones for a Frankie Dettori-style leap from the saddle and the party began.

For the deliriously happy owners this meant multiple interviews, photos, and a trip up to the hospitality suites on the fifth floor for copious toasts. Meanwhile, Matt Pearson, who'd been completely lost in the scrum, had composed himself and was walking his hero back to the test barn and his own little low-key celebrations. It would sink in, once he got back to Shenandoah and he and Ripken looked out through the early morning mist one day, what they'd achieved. Then a thousand internal demons would have been exorcized and he'd know that sometimes the good guys really do get a break. The obsession had yielded the Holy Grail. He had, and he knew this more than anyone, stepped into the breach and not only saved a future Derby-winner but also nurtured and steered him to his supreme destiny.

Up in the Turf Club, Billy Beagle announced a record on track Derby day handle of $225 million and joked that horse racing was now another domain of Lemar. The big man would be plying his trade in New York that evening but, Billy continued, he'd be smiling when he learned of the percentage that his school's program was getting from the new record Real Racing sweepstake. 'Today,' he gushed, 'our great sport has awakened. For too long horse racing has been considered to be elitist and esoteric. Dare I say it, fixed, in the eyes of many. But I am here to tell you that sports fans, across the world,' and he flung open his arms, 'were watching Churchill Downs this evening, morning, night. All over the world, in all their time zones, people were watching. They had an interest. It was more than just some privileged folks picking up a big cheque, thanks to Motti-Media, Ravi Singh, and his brother, Kulbir, and the folks in Bangalore who ingeniously made this work. Not just via their computer skills, which I can't even begin to understand, but also in the way that they have convinced everyone that this is not only a fair contest but a truly benevolent one for worthy causes far beyond the sport of horse racing itself.' The raucous cheers of the alcohol-fueled audience erupted. And once again Last Hurrah and Mrs. McDougal were toasted.

◆ ◆ ◆

Tom was shattered. What a day! Rocky had made his last appearance for a barrage of flash-photographers seeking one more snap of the day's hero peering out over his rose clad webbing and was now guzzling his well-earned feed.

Empty bottles of champagne and beer littered the shedrow rail. Matt and Ralph had long retreated to the air-conditioned bar of their hotel. So it was just the two Ts, Tom and Toby, and the by now familiar Pinkerton security guard.

He'd walk the two blocks to the hotel. Close to 10 p.m., the sun was just dipping behind the iconic twin spires of the Grandstand to his right, as he walked along beside the racetrack where less than four hours before his dream had come true.

Now there was silence. A smell of charred meat and the hint of grey smoke from dying barbecues wafting on the gentle breeze from the infield, as he strolled along, jacket over his shoulder, tie long gone, the two top buttons of his shirt open.

'I guess he's going home?' a familiar voice called out in the dusk. Tom looked around.

'Up here, in the tower.'

Tom swivelled and could see a silhouette against the sky, standing in the patrol judge's tower at the half-mile pole. 'Who's there?'

'Billy Beagle, Tom. Up here. It's been quite a day. Sometimes I come here on an evening like this, after a long day. It's very peaceful. A great place to reflect upon things.'

Below, Tom bit his lip and looked up to the shape outlined against the golden horizon. 'You were there!'

Leaning on the rail, looking across the iconic racetrack at the setting sun, Beagle didn't turn. But, after a pause, did his best to explain. 'In a time of crisis, to whom do you turn? He was desperate, Tom, with the stuff going on at Caledonia.'

'But why have you not done anything about Hector Delmontez? Why have you promoted and encouraged him? He was the cause of everything.' Tom had had a few drinks and wasn't backing off.

Temporarily lost for words, Beagle turned and looked down at Tom. 'Life is a funny thing, Tom – I'm just trying to think of a good analogy – it's a bit like an elaborate game of snakes and ladders, in a way. You must have played that as a kid? You know, you try to get on the ladders and avoid stepping on the snakes. In life some people are good at both. While they slither around the snakes, often directing them towards other people, their rivals, and killing them off at opportune moments, they also see ladders coming before others and not only don't miss them, but make the best of them: more than the ordinary guy who may do things the way he thinks they're supposed to be done, but falls through the cracks.' Billy looked down at Tom. 'Hector is one of those sorts of guys. I'm not condoning what he does, one bit. But what could I do, being party to two deaths and then,' he paused, 'and then covering up around the colt?' he trailed off.

Tom stood speechless. 'It's all about winning, Tom. Surviving.' Billy Beagle continued, 'Look at the Brits, their racing is what it is today because of the Arab investment. Do you think Jos Danvers cares where his clients got their money? Did they do anything when one of them got caught red-handed by customs with a planeload of drugs for his horses, stuff so obscure, so powerful that I doubt even Hector would have known what it was? These Russian and Chinese guys who are buying up our country, do you think the authorities prosecute all of them? It's just the way life is, Tom.' He paused. 'And it looks like you've got another one of those people I was talking about, in your new partner, the young Chinese girl, eh? Johnny, my son-in-law to be, tells me her people are buying Caledonia and, if they can buy you guys out, would like to stand Last Hurrah there. She may be a very talented musician, but everyone knows where the money is coming from. Her people made a smart move. In fact, a lot smarter than any of them know.'

'Yep. Like Bog.'

'Who?'

'Oh, just a guy I know.'

The two men stood in silence. 'Well, we'll see y'all at the wedding, won't we?'

'You bet, Mr. Beagle. I'm escorting Ms. Li-Chen. Wouldn't miss it!'

'There you go!'

THE END

An excerpt from the sequel to
LAST HURRAH…

SETTLING THE SCORE

*Tom Fraser, now married to Cindy Li-Chen and the master of Caledonia,
splits his time between Lexington, Kentucky and Paris, France.*

However much she loved her horses, the cultural wilderness that Cindy Fraser
had found Kentucky to be was not a place that she wanted her little Genevieve
to grow up in.

So, not long after their daughter's fifth birthday, the Frasers had purchased
a property near Fontainebleau, just south of Paris, where young Genevieve
attended the local Lycée, studied music under her mother's enthusiastic tutelage,
rode ponies, and immersed herself in the civility of the French countryside.

Life was good for the Frasers and particularly so for their talisman, Last
Hurrah. Now a ten-year-old, the Derby-winner was the leading sire in both
North America and Europe, commanding a stud fee of three hundred thousand
dollars. Indeed, hardly a week went by without a son or daughter of the great
horse registering a victory in a major race, on some racetrack somewhere
around the world.

Cindy loved the fashion and élégante couture of Paris and the stylishness of
the ladies at Longchamp, now and again stealing a glance at the Moulin that had
featured in so many of Toulouse-Lautrec's paintings…a magical background
to the famous artist's colourful impressionism. Here, she had horses…but so
much more in so many ways.

Today Tom was taking Cindy to an exclusive riding club that his smart friends had suggested the family might enjoy. Hidden away in the discreet arrondisement of Saint-Germain-en-Laye, it was one of those uniquely French establishments that you could drive right past, if you did not know to enter the large double wooden doors between two Plane trees or see the small brass-plated sign, Club Hippique.

The doors opened into a neat, cobbled courtyard, with cascades of Wisteria almost obscuring the shuttered windows that looked down upon about half a dozen sleek, high-end motor cars. It was mid-morning and, from nearby, the metallic sound of a local church clock chimed eleven times, scattering a covey of warbling doves.

Nobody appeared to be around. So they proceeded down a sun-lit walkway and entered the relative cool and murkiness of a large indoor arena. Somewhere, from up above, a voice barked in French and three horses startled them as they pranced by: their stylish cavalières attired in slender stretch-jodhpurs, shiny black riding boots, navy blue jackets, and matching velvet caps as they carved figure-eights at a perfect sitting trot, with backs ramrod straight, hands posed, lips pursed, and eyes far away. The only sound a muffled thud of hooves over the peaty surface and the squeaking of seasoned leather.

'Pretty sight, eh?' The voice was hauntingly familiar.

'Up here.' Tom craned his neck. Like a recurring bad nightmare, there was Hector. The man never aged.

'Bienvenidas, Tom...or bienvenue, as they say over here...come on up. Of course you know Johnny Ward-Beagle...and I want to introduce you to our host, Andre de Bourbon.' Hector motioned to the new arrivals. 'Andre, this is Tom and Cindy Fraser, from Kentucky. You will have heard of Last Hurrah, of course?'

'Enchanté...mais bien sur.' A lithe man in jeans, a pink polo shirt and tan suede loafers, above which Tom could observe sockless and dark hairy legs stretching upwards, waved down at them. 'You are most welcome,' he continued in a fluent but charmingly accented tone, sweeping back a mop of well-groomed, prematurely greying hair from a craggy visage that Tom assessed put him in his mid-forties.

'Like a bad penny, ha!' joked Johnny. 'Keep showing up...in all the right places, eh?'

'What does he mean by that?' Cindy whispered to Tom, as they mounted the stairs at the back of the viewing stand.

'Oh...that. That's just Bog being English. Its just an expression that they have. You know, he's winding me up. Typical of him...and Hector, for that matter, to be schmoozing with a French nobleman.'

'Darling, I keep telling you...you can't call him Bog anymore! You know, now that he's Ward-Beagle, not Clarke. Can't you grow up?'

Tom smiled. 'They've got plenty of phonies over here, too. This Bourbon guy and the 'de' part.'

'Didn't Hector just say that he was some kind of Prince?'

'Ha!' said Tom...'Princes, Comptes, Ducs, they come a dime a dozen over here. They lost. Or, rather, let go of these titles, conveniently, if they managed to keep their heads, back in the revolution. But, now that the dust has settled, the 'de' part is just a reminder that they come from nobility. Back in the States, they make fun of such pretentiousness by putting stickers on the bumpers of their beat-up old cars that say 'My other car is a Bentley!' You'll meet plenty of bogus aristocrats over here.'

'Hello guys! What do they say about birds of a feather?' Tom stole Bog's march.

This visit was impressive, as Andre de-whatever introduced his guests to the staff and bevy of trim riders who seemed to be always buzzing around him. A superb lunch was produced on a terrace overlooking a boxwood maze. And, as Cindy dozed on the way home, dreaming about riding through the forests of Chantilly and along the beaches at Deauville, that their charming host had regaled her of, Tom was deep in thought, wondering...what on Earth are these guys up to now?

◆ ◆ ◆

To learn more about the author, Robin Dawson,
and his background in International horse racing, visit his website:
www.robindawson.com

Lightning Source UK Ltd.
Milton Keynes UK
UKHW040434131220
374938UK00014B/875/J